TRAFFICS AND DISCOVERIES

Rudyard Joseph Kipling was born in Bombay in 1865. His father, John Lockwood Kipling, was the author of ... ... ast and Man in India and his m... ... ... dy Burne-Jones. In 1871 K... ... d spent five unhappy year... ... ... perience he later drew o... ... years he spent at the Unit... ... ... children, are depicted in S... ... the character of Beetle is something of a self... It was during his time at the college that he began writing poetry and *Schoolboy Lyrics* was published privately in 1881. In the following year he started work as a journalist in India, and while there, produced a body of work, stories, sketches and poems – notably *Plain Tales from the Hills* (1888) – which made him an instant literary celebrity when he returned to England in 1889. *Barrack Room Ballads* (1892) contains some of his most popular pieces, including 'Mandalay', 'Gunga Din' and 'Danny Deever'. In this collection Kipling experimented with form and dialect, notably the cockney accent of the soldier poems, but the influence of hymns, music-hall songs, ballads and public poetry can be found throughout his verse.

In 1892 he married an American, Caroline Balestier, and from 1892 to 1896 they lived in Vermont, where Kipling wrote *The Jungle Book*, published in 1894. In 1901 came *Kim* and in 1902 the *Just So Stories*. Tales of every kind – including historical and science fiction – continued to flow from his pen, but *Kim* is generally thought to be his greatest long work, putting him high among the chroniclers of British expansion.

From 1902 Kipling made his home in Sussex, but he continued to travel widely and caught his first glimpse of warfare in South Africa, where he wrote some excellent reportage on the Boer War. However, many of the views he expressed were rejected by anti-imperialists who accused him of jingoism and love of violence. Though rich and successful, he never again enjoyed the literary esteem of his early years. With the onset of the Great

War, his work became a great deal more sombre. The stories he subsequently wrote, *A Diversity of Creatures* (1917), *Debits and Credits* (1926) and *Limits and Renewals* (1932) are now thought by many to contain some of his finest writing. The death of his only son in 1915 also contributed to a new inwardness of vision.

Kipling refused to accept the role of Poet Laureate and other civil honours, but he was the first English writer to be awarded the Nobel Prize, in 1907. He died in 1936 and his autobiographical fragment *Something of Myself* was published the following year.

Hermione Lee is a Reader in English Literature at York University. She reviews for the *Independent on Sunday* and for the *New Republic*. Her books include *The Novels of Virginia Woolf* (1977), *Elizabeth Bowen: An Estimation* (1981), *Philip Roth* (1982), *Stevie Smith: A Selection* (1983), *The Mulberry Tree: Writings of Elizabeth Bowen* (1986), *Willa Cather: A Life Saved Up* (1989), an edition of Willa Cather's stories (1989) and two selections of stories by women writers, *The Secret Self* (1985, reissued 1991).

RUDYARD KIPLING

TRAFFICS
AND DISCOVERIES

EDITED
WITH AN INTRODUCTION AND NOTES
BY HERMIONE LEE

PENGUIN BOOKS

PENGUIN BOOKS

Published by the Penguin Group
Penguin Books Ltd, 27 Wrights Lane, London W8 5TZ, England
Penguin Books USA Inc., 375 Hudson Street, New York, New York 10014, USA
Penguin Books Australia Ltd, Ringwood, Victoria, Australia
Penguin Books Canada Ltd, 10 Alcorn Avenue, Toronto, Ontario, Canada M4V 3B2
Penguin Books (NZ) Ltd, 182–190 Wairau Road, Auckland 10, New Zealand

Penguin Books Ltd, Registered Offices: Harmondsworth, Middlesex, England

First published 1904
Published in Penguin Classics 1987
Reprinted in Penguin Books 1992
1 3 5 7 9 10 8 6 4 2

Introduction and notes copyright © Hermione Lee, 1987
All rights reserved

Printed in England by Clays Ltd, St Ives plc
Typeset in Lasercomp Ehrhardt

Contents

Introduction   7
Further Reading   30
Note on the Text   31

TRAFFICS AND DISCOVERIES

From the Masjid-al-Aqsa of Sayyid Ahmed (Wahabi)   35
The Captive   36

Poseidon's Law   59
The Bonds of Discipline   61

The Runners   85
A Sahibs' War   87

The Wet Litany   105
'Their Lawful Occasions'   107

The King's Task   143
The Comprehension of Private Copper   144

The Necessitarian   155
Steam Tactics   156

Kaspar's Song in 'Varda'   180
'Wireless'   181

Song of the Old Guard   200
The Army of a Dream   202

The Return of the Children   242
'They'   243

From Lyden's 'Irenius'   266

Mrs Bathurst   268

'Our Fathers Also'   286

Below the Mill Dam   287

Notes   304

Introduction

In the hot summer of 1913 (almost ten years after *Traffics and Discoveries*), Kipling was watching army manoeuvres 'round Frensham Ponds at Aldershot' with his friend from Cape Town days, the journalist H. A. Gwynne. He describes the scene in his autobiography:

Many of the officers had been juniors in the Boer War, known to Gwynne, one of the guests, and some to me. When the sham fight was developing, the day turned blue-hazy, the sky lowered, and the heat struck like the Karroo, as one scuttled among the heaths, listening to the uncontrolled clang of the musketry fire. It came over me that anything might be afoot in such weather, pom-poms for instance, half heard on a flank, or the glint of a helio through a cloud-drift. In short I conceived the whole pressure of our dead of the Boer War flickering and re-forming as the horizon flickered in the heat; the galloping feet of a single horse, and a voice once well-known that passed chanting ribaldry along the flank of a crack battalion. ('But Winnie is one of the lost – poor dear!' was that song, if any remember it or its Singer in 1900–1901.) In an interval, while we lay on the grass, I told Gwynne what was in my head; and some officers also listened. The finale was to be manoeuvres abandoned and a hurried calling-off of all arms by badly frightened Commandants – the men themselves sweating with terror though they knew not why.[1]

In the end, he did not turn his 'conception' into a story: it came to seem 'more and more fantastic and absurd, unnecessary and hysterical'. By the time war broke out he felt it would have 'done no good', and would have laid him open to approaches from the 'psychical experiences' types. He gives it as an example of a 'close shave', of being told by his 'Personal Daemon' when *not* to make use of an experience.

But this ghost of an unwritten ghost-story is a telling one, and it powerfully evokes the strange tensions in *Traffics and*

Discoveries. In its fantasy of British soldiers, rehearsing for war in 'safe' sunny England, suddenly haunted by a Boer 'army of a dream', there's an echo of the General's voice in 'The Captive', calling the Boer War 'a first-class dress-parade for Armageddon'. The imaginary army of ghosts stands for a real haunting: in Kipling's view, the lesson of the Boer War was to shape twentieth-century England and its disappearing Empire. Those ghosts are there too at the end of his most practical, public, official story, 'The Army of a Dream', showing their old wounds from Sanna's Post 'against the darkness that had swallowed up the battalions behind us'. The eerie metamorphosis of the Home Counties into the veldt can be read as a historical truth: these two landscapes are indeed interdependent. Aldershot and the Karroo are not so remote; what happens in one affects the other. It is as much a reflection of Kipling's politics as of his life between 1901 and 1904 that the stories in *Traffics and Discoveries* move between Sussex and Bloemfontein, between the English Channel and the naval port at Simonstown. For 'what should they know of England who only England know?'[2] Kipling has nothing but scorn for the 'little Englanders' who think 'her Empire still is the Strand and Holborn Hill',[3] for obnoxious liberal politicians with, as he obnoxiously puts it, their 'tupenny-hapenny politics – the wisdom of the four-mile cab radius and the self-control of women'.[4] In his 'Tommy's' words, back from the Boer War to 'awful old England', 'there's somethin' gone small with the lot'.[5]

The unwritten ghost-story provides an image for Kipling's twentieth-century politics. But what is even more striking about it is that it troubled him so much, enough for him not to write it, so 'fantastic and absurd, unnecessary and hysterical' did he find it. The anxious emphases suggest that he is as disturbed by his self-conjured ghosts as the haunted narrators of, say, 'The House Surgeon', or 'A Madonna of the Trenches'. It is a revealing example of that doubleness which makes Kipling's work so hard to manage or to categorize. Here is the famous laureate of Empire, champion of the ordinary soldier, close observer of England's defences, chairman of the Rottingdean Rifle Range, enthusiast for the Boy Scout movement and advocate of national conscription, lounging at ease in the grass with his distinguished right-wing friend, the editor of the *Morning Post*, and with army officers whom he remembers from his first-hand experience of the Boer War. He is the expert public patriot, the V.I.P. in the know. The narrative glints with inside information, like that 'glint of a helio through a cloud-drift', or the swankily telling detail about the rude song of the time. The tone is soldierly, confident and confidential (to any who remember), manly-among-men, as in 'juniors' and 'crack battalion'. But what is imagined is intensely strange and alarming: the phrase 'flickering and re-forming as the horizon flickered in the heat' moves us uneasily on to the plane of mirage and hallucination, and makes the narrator, for all his public-spirited comradeliness, seem alone 'in his head'.

The split is in character, and noticeable everywhere in his writing, but perhaps most of all in *Traffics and Discoveries*. From a distance of eighty years the book seems remote from contemporary sensibilities. 'There is always something alien about Kipling, as of a visitor from another planet,' Eliot said in 1941.[6] And this becomes more and more the case, as the end of Empire, the world wars, the harrowing and reorganization of Europe, nuclear weapons, the wars over Vietnam and the Falklands – all the traumas of our century – make Kipling seem distant, irrelevant, and, often, disagreeable. Easy enough, now, to call him 'horrible old Kipling',[7] to mark him down, as Robert Buchanan did in 1899, as the voice of all that is 'most retrograde and savage' in 'Hooligan Imperialism',[8] to describe him as 'the bard of the banjo [marching] ahead of the throng, shouting his songs of the barrack-room, telling his tales of the camp-fire and the jungle, proclaiming the worship of the great god Jingo'.[9]

The temptation is especially great with a volume of stories so dedicated to the training and action of 'men, not children or servants, tempered and taught to the end'.[10] *Traffics and Discoveries* is in love with tactics and manoeuvres, disciplines and outfits, loyalties and defences, men's works and men's pranks. Motor-cars and the Navy are its idol. There is a passion for expertise, for the technicalities of new inventions: guns, cars, ships, the electric telegraph, the cinematograph. The keynote of the volume is supposed to be 'The Army of a Dream' (which, as Philip Mason says, anyone else 'would have put in an article in *The Times*',[11]) a vision of England manned for war by a permanent, trained, volunteer citizens' army, where 'every man's capacity for command must be tested to the utmost', and where 'we're all in the game'. Being 'in the game' is of the essence: the 'I' of these stories is a privileged observer, avid for in-talk and know-how, beside himself with thigh-slapping glee at Petty Officer Pyecroft's idiosyncratic sea-talk and maverick manoeuvrings, as much an *aficionado* of naval ways as Hemingway of the bullfight or Surtees of the hunt. This is what C. S. Lewis calls 'the slave of the Inner Ring'.[12] It is the Kipling of *A Fleet in Being: Notes of Two Trips with the Channel Squadron* (1898), of articles in *The Times* and speeches to the Anglo-African Writers Club about the position of the British in South Africa, of a *Daily Mail* fund-raising poem for 'Tommy' in South Africa ('The Absent-Minded Beggar', set to music by Sir Arthur Sullivan), of letters to *The Complete Motorist* about the joys of the Locomobile or to the *Navy League Journal* arguing for a standing army. The argument was to be reiterated in *The New Army in Training* (1915), with its 'join-now' peroration: 'What will be the position in years to come of the young man who has deliberately elected to out-caste himself from this all-embracing brotherhood?' 'The contemporary *bien pensant*', as John Bayley sardonically puts it, might well be repelled by this 'insistence on the disciplines of the pack, their condemnations and retributions'.[13]

But there is more to these stories than brotherhood and boyscoutery. Certainly Kipling's idea of Empire, here as ever, takes the form of 'the day's work' well done. Men must know their jobs, be fit to obey or command, sense that they work interdependently even when, like the mower in Robert Frost's poem, they may appear to be working alone. For an example of the work ethic at its most ludicrously utilitarian, take the remark about Sir James Hawkins, head of the Famine Relief operation in 'William the Conqueror': 'Things were going well with his world. Three of his more grossly incompetent men had died, and their places had been filled by their betters.'[14] Inefficiency makes you expendable, casts you outside the charmed circle where men in the know are getting on with the job, and don't need to have the assumptions behind the work explained. A sentimental passage in *A Fleet in Being* (headed 'Things One Takes For Granted') makes this ideal, with all its bullying, pious group chauvinism, very clear indeed:

We had a common tradition, one thousand years old, of the things one takes for granted. A warrant officer said something, and the groups melted quietly about some job or other. That same caste of man – that same type of voice – was speaking in the commissariat in Burma; in barracks in Rangoon; under double awnings in the Persian Gulf; on the Rock at Gibraltar – wherever else you please – and the same instant obedience, I knew, would follow on that voice. And a foreigner would never have understood – will never understand! But I understood, as you would have understood had you been there.[15]

We read this belief in the unique British talent for government, efficiency and discipline as characteristically late Victorian. Kipling shared it with Rider Haggard and Joseph Chamberlain and Cecil Rhodes, who held 'us' to be 'the best people in the world . . . with the highest ideals of decency and justice and liberty and peace, and the more of the world we inhabit, the better it is for humanity'.[16] Even Conrad, with his utterly different tragic sense of the hollowness and greed underlying nineteenth-century capitalist colonialism, shared Kipling's conviction that the 'real work' was being done where there was red on the map.[17] This professional, administrative idea of Empire imagined the 'Pax Britannica', in Jan Morris's phrase, as 'a great surgical clamp, an elaborate device of joints and fittings which, adjusted properly in its straps and trolleys, kept any dislocated limb stoutly on the mend'.[18]

But for all that *Traffics and Discoveries* noisily endorses this vision, its imperialism is neither smug nor orthodox. Though frequently misread as such (Orwell, for example, complains that it is 'strange and even disgusting' for a writer to 'identify

himself with the ruling power and not with the opposition'[19]),
Kipling is not a sabre-rattling glorifier or missionary of Empire.
He is extremely uneasy with, and critical of, unquestioned
traditions, ruling-class hierarchies, and complacent establish-
ments. His most famous poem, 'Recessional', written for the
Queen's Diamond Jubilee in 1897 at the height of British
Imperialist pride, is a warning reminder of responsibilities, not
a celebration of glory, and speaks prophetically, in the old *ubi
sunt* tradition, of the passing of temporal power:

> The tumult and the shouting dies;
> The Captains and the Kings depart.

Events after 1897 all confirmed Kipling's warning. The Boer
War created a profound disillusionment with the 'old guard's'
administration and defence of Empire; Kipling's writings about
it are all 'more admonitory than laudatory'.[20] But even setting
aside, for the moment, Kipling's anger and uncertainty over
what the war revealed and led to, his attitude to authority and
brotherhood is an ambivalent one. Part of what makes him
interesting rather than simply repellent is his admiration for
irregulars, adventurers, mavericks. Admittedly this takes a
somewhat tedious form in the malapropist Pyecroft, with his
rib-nudging advice to 'buy an 'am an' see life' rather than stay
with the official fleet and the big guns. But Pyecroft, and his
young lone-ranger captain, and Kurban Sahib fighting his
personal campaign in 'A Sahibs' War', belong with Stalky and
Kim, 'good bad boys', pirates on the side of the angels, craftily
testing the limits of authority for its own good. Of course the
established methods – as in 'The Bonds of Discipline' – have to
be professionally immaculate before they can be subverted. But
it is the tactics of subversion which most enthral Kipling. His
authorities, like the unfortunate policeman in 'Steam Tactics',
are often the butts, and the charmed circle is outside the establishment.

And there is a more profound, more intriguing split in the
volume between brotherhood and isolation. Angus Wilson
reads Kipling as a neurotic, torn by the incompatible need 'to

seek group association that would assuage his anxious search for himself'.[21] The paradox is a frequent one in late-nineteenth-century literature, which is full of splits between daylight and night-time selves,[22] public society and private nightmare, ethics and anarchy: Henry James's terrifying stories 'The Jolly Corner' and 'The Beast in the Jungle', Wilde's 'The Portrait of Dorian Gray', Stevenson's 'Dr Jekyll and Mr Hyde' and Conrad's 'Heart of Darkness' are the outstanding examples. For all his robust muscularity, Kipling belongs here too. Edmund Wilson finds, more than ever in the stories of this period, 'a lunatic head' thrusting 'out of a window of the well-bricked façade'.[23]

But the 'otherness' in Kipling is not simply split off from the safe, loud, public voice: it inhabits it. Pyecroft is the jauntiest, most externalized, least profound of all Kipling's hero-narrators and South Africa is the setting for some of his most bellicose stories, but it is Pyecroft in South Africa who tells, without understanding it, the alarming and mysterious story of Vickery and Mrs Bathurst, in which the feeling of infinite aloneness and estrangement – in Freud's terms the 'unheimlich' – belies Pyecroft's homely, confidential narrative manner. The new Marconi installations add to Kipling's childlike admiration for the Royal Navy, which sets the high-spirited tone for 'Their Lawful Occasions' and 'The Bonds of Discipline'. But the same fascination with wireless also sparks off a strange, dreamlike story in which the narrator sees the spirit of Keats transmitted into the soul of a love-lorn tubercular chemist. The motor-car is the instrument of some of Kipling's noisiest wheezes and japes – the sort where the narrator and his friends (though possibly not the reader) end up rolling on the ground with mirth, ceasing not 'till we had arrived at the extremity of exhaustion'.[24] But the car also takes the narrator deeper and deeper into England until he reaches the secret house in 'They', where he is allowed to find what he has lost:

> Ridiculous the waste sad time
> Stretching before and after.[25]

'They' derives its intensely and atypically personal tone from the death of Kipling's seven-year-old daughter Josephine. The tragedy happened in New York in 1899, when he was himself very ill, and it marked the end of the Kiplings' American period, which had already gone sour in Vermont with a stupid, shameful court-case against Kipling's feckless brother-in-law. Edmund Wilson attributes to Kipling's disenchantment with American democracy the turning-point in his imaginative career. From this time, Wilson says, he acquired 'a generalized hatred of those nations, groups and tendencies . . . which stand toward the dominating authority in the relationship of challengers or victims'.[26] This is an overly hostile judgement on the later work, I think, which doesn't (for example) allow for the fact that *Kim* was written in the late 1890s. But it is certainly true that after leaving America Kipling solidified his patriotic and nationalistic feelings.

These partly attached themselves to the Navy, which had welcomed Kipling on board as a distinguished visitor for manoeuvres and speed trials with the Channel Fleet in 1897 and 1898, and partly to Sussex, which he was exploring by motor-car – first in an erratic steam-powered Locomobile, then in a Lanchester. The 'chief end', for him, of this pioneering form of transport, was 'the discovery of England'.[27] He and his wife spent the summers of 1900 and 1901 looking for houses: they wanted to get away from Rottingdean, where they had lived since 1897, with its memories of Josephine and its tourists from Brighton staring over the wall at the Great Man. The move to Bateman's in 1902 confirmed Kipling as a Sussex squire and a historian of England. *Puck of Pook's Hill*, in which his two other children, John and Elsie, were played by Dan and Una, and Old England spoke out of every tree and stream of 'the Weald and the Marsh and the Down countrie', was the next book to be published after *Traffics and Discoveries*.

These elements were all fed into the stories of the period, but the most powerful influence was, of course, the Boer War, which began only a few months after the Kiplings left America. Kipling's first visit to South Africa had been in 1891, but his deeper connections with it began in the winter of 1897–8, when he met Milner and Rhodes and visited the township of Bulawayo in Rhodes's new province. In October 1900, soon after the war started, the Kiplings went back to Cape Town. That winter, Kipling visited military hospitals, gave his services (at the invitation of the Commander-in-Chief, Lord Roberts) to an army newspaper, *The Friend*, at Bloemfontein, and witnessed an inconclusive battle at Karree Siding and the flight of British troops from their defeat at Sanna's Post. The following winter the Kiplings were given a house at Cape Town by Cecil Rhodes, next door to his own Groote Schuur. They spent every winter at The Woolsack until 1908, by which time South Africa had become intolerable to them.

The Boer War, in its effects on the British Empire, is Kipling's war: no other English writer has ever said so much, so influentially, about a national event. Kipling's war poems and speeches spoke for, and to, a deep swathe of British feeling. His influence travelled, too: it has been suggested that the American government's refusal to accede to pro-Boer propaganda and intervene against the British was largely due to Kipling's transatlantic popularity.[28]

The war was a head-on clash. On one side, Kruger's extremist quest for Boer supremacy, with his apartheid policy against the 'Uitlanders' (foreigners, mostly British) who had settled in the Transvaal during the gold rush of the 1880s, his appeals for help to the Kaiser, his importing of arms from Europe and his subverting of British loyalty among the Cape Dutch, was a profound threat to the Empire. On the other side was the intransigent British Conservative insistence, embodied in High Commissioner Sir Alfred Milner and Prime Minister Joseph Chamberlain, on the absolute desirability of British paramountcy in South Africa. Rayne Kruger, a South African writer, sums up the conflict:

The Boer War was fought because each half of the white community in the Transvaal wanted to dominate. Hostilities broke out upon expiry of a Boer ultimatum which narrowly preceded one already prepared by the British.

The Boers said the war was for liberty. The British said it was for equality. The majority of the inhabitants, who were not white at all, gained neither liberty nor equality.

The war was fought with great incompetence by either side. For a number of reasons unconnected with nationality this is inevitable in every war. Men have never yet devised a more wasteful method of settling their differences.[29]

Kipling, however, had no doubts about the justice of the Conservative position, as his speech of 1898 made clear:

> The Boers of the Transvaal consider themselves our masters and our bosses . . . we have allowed them to put back the clock throughout the whole of South Africa and to make a festering sore . . . [if] . . . they rise and cause trouble . . . then would be the time to scoop them out.[30]

He had no time for the Liberal opposition (as voiced by Campbell-Bannerman in the House and newspapers such as the *Manchester Guardian*), which was shouted down at the start by vociferous war-fever (and much singing of 'The Absent-Minded Beggar'), but which gained ground during the war. At one extreme the 'pro-Boers' argued that the war was a conspiracy of international financiers and Jews trying to keep its interests (and its cheap labour) in South Africa; at the other, that the Boers had been harassed into issuing an ultimatum by an aggressive British policy which intended all along to annex the Boer republics, the Transvaal and the Orange Free State. Kipling thought that 'liberal "principle" ends . . . in blood-shed'[31] and, though his bellicosity is disagreeable, he was not stupid, or wrong, about the Krugerite ambitions:

> They want to sweep the English into the sea, to lick their own nigger and to govern South Africa with a gun instead of a ballot box. It is only the little Englanders in London who say that the Transvaal is merely fighting for its independence; but out here both sides realize it is a question of which race is to run the country.[32]

The Jameson Raid of 1895, a botched attempt to overthrow Kruger's regime which made war inevitable, was masterminded by two of Kipling's greatest friends and heroes, Dr Jameson (whose character inspired 'If —''s prescription for true manhood) and Cecil Rhodes, whose dream of South Africa as one of 'five nations' – 'Mother Britain' and her sister colonies, South Africa, Canada, Australia and New Zealand, which would be independent but part of the British Empire – became Kipling's. Like Rhodes, Kipling thought the British had a duty, and a right, to govern the Afrikaners and to penetrate further and further into the continent. When peace was proclaimed in May 1902, and Kipling's redoubtable pacifist aunt, Georgiana Burne-Jones, hung a placard out of her Rottingdean window reading 'We have killed and taken possession', Kipling protected her from the fury of the villagers, but was far from endorsing her protest. In the ensuing years he watched with horror as the Boers began to take back South Africa, with Milner withdrawn from the 'reconstruction' in 1905, Jameson losing his majority as premier of the Cape Colony in 1907, and the Liberals bringing in the South African Act in 1909, which set up a Union of South Africa under General Botha, and in which, it would come to be seen, 'the British government washed their hands of responsibility for the political rights of Africans, Asians and coloured people'.[33] Kipling was not much concerned with such rights – his attitude to the non-whites of South Africa is probably best summed up by 'Sambo' the Ethiopian's acceptance of his lot ('"Oh, plain black's best for a niggcr"') in 'How the Leopard got his Spots' (*Just So Stories*, 1902). This imperceptiveness sets his South African work miles apart from his Indian stories. But he did see, bitterly, what the British had left behind them: 'We put them in a position to uphold and expand their primitive lust for racial domination, and thanked God we were "rid of a knave".'[34]

Kipling's reaction to the Imperial crisis was not simply anti-Boer. As the war progressed, in fact, he developed an admiration for the fighting Afrikaners, sentimentally expressed by his 'Tommy' ('I've known a lot o' men behave a dam' sight worse than Piet', etc.). His hostility, as his essay of March 1900, 'The Sin of Witchcraft', and all his South African stories show, was directed at the traitors – 'neutrals' who secretly supported the Boers, foreigners (like the repentant American in 'The Captive') who sold their services to the wrong side, the slippery Boers who put out white flags and then ambushed you (as in 'A Sahibs' War'), the renegades in sympathy with the 'rebs', like Private Copper's shifty prisoner.

But the treachery was also inside the 'mother hive'. Kipling's greatest scorn, as in the breezily unfeeling ending of 'The Comprehension of Private Copper', was for the whingeing Liberals who saw fit to complain about Kitchener's scorched earth and concentration camps policy, and, still more, for the privileged, entrenched 'old guard' who had – as in the Crimean War – turned out an incompetent and ill-prepared army. When the war began Kipling proposed an ironic toast to Kruger as 'the Empire-builder' who had 'taught the British Empire its responsibilities . . . and turned the loafer of the London Streets into a man'.[35] As it progressed, it became apparent that the 'dress-parade for Armageddon' was not going smoothly. The British had lamentably underestimated the Boers, and the early defeats in the war, culminating in the 'Black Week' at the end of 1899, came as a great shock. Wherever Kipling wrote about it – in *The Friend*, in letters home, in his autobiography – it is apparent that 'his confidence was sapped [by] the spectacle of this mighty Empire struggling desperately to defeat a handful of Boer farmers':[36]

The Boers hit us just as hard and just as often as they knew how; and we advanced against 'em as if they were street-rioters that we didn't want to hurt. They spied on us at their leisure, and when they wanted a rest they handed up any old gun and said they'd be loyal subjects. Then they went to their homes and rested for a week or two; and then they went on the warpath again with a new coat and a full stomach.[37]

Faced with this sort of humiliating trickery, it was even more irritating, in Kipling's view, that the native Indian army could not be roped in to finish off the Boers – since it had been early on decided that this was a 'sahibs' war'.

But the sahibs seemed to have gone soft. Kipling's famous poems of the time deride the Empire as given up to the adulation of 'the flannelled fools at the wicket or the muddied oafs at the goals', needing to be taught 'no end of a lesson'. What was needed was a ruthless cleaning out of old stock (as in 'Below the Mill Dam'), and a nation prepared:

> . . . each man born in the Island entered at youth to the game –
> As it were almost cricket, not to be mastered in haste,
> But after trial and labour, by temperance, living chaste.[38]

The tone makes for some rousing verse statements to the nation, but it is a dangerous one for fiction. 'The Army of a Dream' suffers from it most, with its chronically jocular, clubby informants and its adulatory narrator ('I rejoice to the marrow of my bones thus to be borne along on billows of surging music among magnificent men'), drinking in the technical proficiency and good morale of a system in which, if you don't join up, you rank with 'lunatics, women, and minors'. The abusive irony of 'Song of the Old Guard' and 'Below the Mill Dam' is preferable. There's an attractive spitefulness to the characterization of the Grey Cat and the Black Rat, Tory parasites lazily clinging on to their entrenched privileges. And the Mill Wheel's pastiche Domesday-book dead-letter meanderings, set against the busy, forward-pushing bossiness of the utilitarian Waters, makes an energetic counterpoint. Mechanical parts learning to pull together are anthropomorphized more interestingly in 'The Ship That Found Herself', but the smug Mill Wheel, slow to realize that it is being used for electricity, not flour, is enjoyably pompous: 'I am engaged in the trituration of farinaceous substances whose ultimate destination it would be a breach of the trust reposed in me to reveal.' Angus Wilson complains that the new forces which clear out this 'dark, decaying corner' are 'lifeless' and 'unfelt'.[39] I find the story's ending not so much lifeless as brutal. Like the Bee Master's smoking out, in a later story, of the 'mother hive', which has been infiltrated with 'oddities' and parasites by a waxmoth, the mill-owner blasts his corner of Old England with an 'intolerable white light'. No room for 'oddities' or dark corners – or spoilt female felines – in the new mechanically functioning nation: everyone must fall in and be a man.

The Boer War stories, with their Punch cartoon, speech-maker's vehemence, direct this brutality, very unpleasantly, at racial degeneracy. Private 'Tommy Atkins' Copper's encounter with a sneering enemy, who reminds him at once of a half-caste in Umballa and an English squire, is meant to equate treachery to the mother country with racial impurity. C. A. Bodelson suggests that the renegade's anomalous racial characteristics are used to show that the 'Uitlanders' were being racially debased and morally degraded by their enforced subservience to the Boers and, at the same time, that the Boers in the Transvaal were aping the manners of the Master Race.[40] It is an indirect and awkward way of making a political point. What strikes us now is not so much the 'message', as comprehended by Private Copper, about the dangers of Boer supremacy, but the dubious relish with which Kipling projects the racial impurity of the renegade, who, unlike the solid, loyal Tommy, goes all to pieces when captured (''E screams like a woman!'). The narrator gloats over this in the same way as he dwells on the 'tainted stock' of the treacherous Boer family in 'A Sahibs' War' – the idiot boy, the fat woman, the man with a wart. Kipling's imagination takes ruthless short-cuts here in order to impose his view of events. Too many of the characters in these stories have the 'right' opinions coming out of their mouths like bubbles: the Kentuckian in 'The Captive' who accuses his compatriot Zigler of 'going back on the White Man' all over the world by selling his gun to the Boers – 'you'll fetch up fighting for Niggers, as the North did'; the joker of D Company, Private Copper's mate, who makes short work of liberal outrage at the concentration camps; the loyal Sikh narrator of 'A Sahibs' War', who is made to comment on the waste of horse power, the valour of the colonial troops, and the ineffectuality of the British campaign. This story, though, is rescued by its powerful sense of place. Kipling's experience at Karree Siding, with the pom-poms echoing through 'the enormous pale landscape',[41] pays off impressively here.

Upon this we rode across the valley of stones, and men fired at us from the nullah behind the house, and from the hill behind the nullah, as well as from the roof of the house – so many shots that it sounded like a drumming in the hills.

It is a suitable setting for a ghost in battle. 'A Sahibs' War' is much the best of the war stories. The Sikh's bitter lament for his master is feelingly heard; and the Sahib's ghost comes vividly out of the great dark empty landscape, imposing its futile legacy of 'civilized' white behaviour.

Pyecroft's jollity appears to be in contrast to the war stories, but this is misleading. He is no Falstaff, and his stories do not embrace the riches of human life as Kipling seems to have wanted them to. Pyecroft is bulked out with lingo, and so strenuously set up by the narrator's efforts to persuade us of his immensity ('If it takes me two years, I'll try') that he seems to have no private nature, no personal 'self' at all. The farces in which he stars have a mechanical quality: they are exercises in seeing how far a crafty technical plot (of travestying the daily running of a naval cruiser, or sabotaging the manoeuvres of the Fleet) can be taken. And the harsh malevolence of the South African stories finds its way even into 'the Urns of Mirth'. M. de C.'s Gallic discomfiture (which preceded Kipling's later love-affair with France)[42] and the punishing of the police-officer – an inferior class of man – in 'Steam Tactics' are pursued with Stalkyish relentlessness. There is some pleasure to be had from the stories as period pieces: 'Steam Tactics' is excitedly taken up with motoring as a form of dare-devil pioneering, and the sea-stories do absorb us into the feel of the pre-First World War Navy, with what Kipling calls 'profligate abundance of detail'.[43] The best moments are when this passion for thick physical specificity gets out of hand and turns the mechanical into something more organic, with a weird life of its own. So, in 'Their Lawful Occasions', the frantic account of night-time seasickness on board the torpedo boat almost anthropomorphizes the hostile machinery, and the daunting bulk of the great ships looming up out of the fog is felt as 'an iron world palpitating with life'. The big car's euphoric devouring of the English countryside in 'Steam Tactics' is good too: by the time the passengers end up in an outdoor tropical zoo in the middle of Sussex, the car itself has come to seem like a greedy exotic animal.

In 'Mrs Bathurst', Pyecroft is much subdued by what he has

to tell; his jargon seems less redundant, more functional (since it continually reminds us of the safe world of service, habit and camaraderie from which Vickery has cut loose), and his knowingness is undermined. Pyecroft understands that there is more to any story than can be judged by 'seein' and hearin''. In this, Kipling's most mysterious narrative, everyone sees and hears a separate part, and tries to read what they see. This extends from the narrator's encompassing interest, to the momentary 'reading' of minor characters like the cox who tries to diagnose his captain's facial expression, or the inspector of railways in the Zambesi who sees the two 'tramps' when they are still alive. But these several readings do not quite add up (much to the annoyance of some commentators[44]); the elaborately narrated evidence, which appears to be steadily accumulating towards an explanation, is collapsed into uncertain obscurity. Guesses have been made: that Mrs Bathurst, in love with Vickery, has followed him to England and discovered he has a pregnant wife and a daughter; that she has killed herself and so is dead (like his 'lawful' wife, who has died in childbirth) when he sees her on the screen in Cape Town; that it is her ghost who joins him at his moment of death; that Vickery has plotted but failed to murder his 'lawful' wife; that Vickery, as the song heard by the narrators, 'The Honeysuckle and the Bee', implies, is not a murderer but a bigamist; that Mrs Bathurst is alive when he sees her on the screen and that she succeeds in finding him in Africa and dying with him; or that the other tramp, whom everybody in the story assumes to be a man, is a random companion for Vickery's last wanderings, placed there only to show that Vickery stood up to attract the lightning.[45] The last grotesque piece of evidence, Vickery's set of false teeth, which might have closed the story with a 'click', is not produced after all, but left hidden in Hooper's waistcoat pocket.

The uncertainty of the story makes an alluring contrast to most of the rest of *Traffics and Discoveries*. 'Mrs Bathurst' undermines the assertive, vigorous, masculine language of Kipling and his narrators. It looks at the start as if it is to be the story of men at work in the far reaches of the Empire; a railway story, this time, not a ship or car yarn. It begins and ends in a railway siding, and its two crucial scenes are of the platform at Paddington station where the Great Western from Plymouth has just pulled in, and a railway line in Southern Rhodesia. The railway invokes, though, not technical mastery and imperial advance, but – as John Bayley says – the sense of 'human isolation' and the 'vast indifference of the world'.[46] As usual in Kipling, the four men talking refer to 'other stories' than Vickery's. These are all stories, from all over the Empire, of misfits and failures, escapees and madmen; stories of the casualties of the system, told in the aftermath of the Boer War, in a damaged brake-van, with the Cape south-east wind outside blowing up the sand on a shore 'locked in' by 'a circle of dry hills'. Boy Niven's practical joke, ruefully recalled by Pritchard and Pyecroft, sets 'seven or eight able-bodied seamen and marines' going round and round in pointless circles, on a 'dirty little outlyin' un-inhabited island', looking for a home and a territory that don't exist. Later, one of these men dies of fever, another goes native, a third jumps ship in the South Seas. Vickery's de-sertion reminds Hooper of other absconders, men who find their way up to Lake Nyasa, where no questions are asked. The seamen exchange stories of women they've known and forgotten 'all over the world'; Pyecroft remembers the madmen he's come across in the service; Hooper's coda to the story speaks of the 'heaps of tramps' the railway men have seen up in Rhodesia since the end of the war. The margins of the story are thus littered with flotsam and jetsam, those who have cut loose from the brotherhood so crucial to the other stories, and who must wander the face of the earth with-out belonging anywhere. Vickery is the main subject, but any of these peripheral stories of estrangement might have been as strange. 'Home and Friends', the title of the 'biograph' show, only accentuates the unhomeliness of the story. The only home we see is Mrs Bathurst's pub in Auckland, with its consistency, its memory of the past, and its domestic warmth (niece Ada and the hair-ribbons), which Pritchard relies on finding just as it was, after five years' absence.

When Mrs Bathurst leaves it in her search for Vickery she becomes a homeless ghost, wandering through time and space.

The discontinuity of the narrative, which is passed from teller to teller like a parcel no one quite wants to open, seems to set Vickery and Mrs Bathurst outside the course of natural time (in which, in due course, Mrs Bathurst would have remarried and Vickery would have drawn his pension and gone home). This is intensified by our not knowing how long Mrs Bathurst has been looking for Vickery, or whether she ever found him, or how long it is since he has seen her, or even whether she is still alive when he recognizes her on the screen. I think this uncertainty is essential for the sense of an awful unnatural destiny. The flickering, repeated sight of Mrs Bathurst as a ghost in the machine, coming up to the camera and 'melting out of the picture', which has to be watched over and over again by the obsessed Vickery, is an image for the mechanical, unnatural process which takes over both the protagonists. Vickery, it has been remarked,[47] is hardly characterized at all, except by his frantic, repetitious, mechanical reactions to the film, and by his ill-fitting teeth, clicking 'like a Marconi ticker'. But this is surely a brilliant strategy. All we see of him, and all that is left of him, is that mechanically clicking dislocated part: something that imitates, but is not, nature, like the film – or like a ghost. Vickery's face when he sees Mrs Bathurst looks to Pyecroft like a pickled foetus (too strong a detail, this, for the magazine readers of the story). When lightning strikes, he and his mysterious watching 'mate' are turned from natural bodies into fossilized carbon figures. Some awful stroke of fate – an obsessional adulterous or bigamous love which neither can solve or escape – has struck and 'locked' these figures into a state outside nature, which is at once fixed and endlessly itinerant, repetitious and insoluble. Even if the story is not 'solved', morally and imaginatively its images of mechanical repetition, of guilt and haunting, and of the outcasts of Empire, do cohere: like the nomadic escapees from service to the country (which Kipling regards as 'natural'), Vickery and Mrs Bathurst have cut loose from a natural personal life – home, bed, faith, family, laws – and are 'doom'd for a certain term to walk the night'.

'Mrs Bathurst' makes its effects through omission and indirection. If it feels in this respect like a story by Henry James – 'The Figure in the Carpet' or 'The Real Thing' – then 'Wireless' feels much more like a story by Poe. It too contains an unsolved mystery, but this is packed round with commentary and explanation, not left to float loose in the mind. The story is brilliantly ingenious and atmospheric, one of Kipling's most dazzling pieces of craftiness and craftsmanship, but its emotions are thin: the chemist's pathetic love is merely a technical device, the narrator's amazement is calculated to arouse the reader's.

'Wireless' tricks us into accepting a bizarre idea which no writer but Kipling – except, possibly, Poe, who loved galvanism and telepathy and colourful atmospherics – would have found manageable or appealing. An electrician in the back room of his uncle's chemist shop in a South Coast town, on a bitterly cold January night, has rigged up a Marconi installation (still in its very early days) and is waiting to receive a wireless signal from Poole. In the shop, the chemist's assistant, a consumptive in love with a blowsy girl called Fanny Brand, is given a drink concocted by the narrator from the shop's medicines, and falls into a kind of trance, in which he unconsciously transcribes lines from poems by Keats (whom he has never read), 'The Eve of St Agnes' and 'Ode to a Nightingale'. Meanwhile: '"There's something coming through from somewhere; but it isn't Poole,"' says the electrician. The narrator, who has come to see the Marconi experiment, instead watches Mr Shaynor's phenomenal 'induction' of Keats, with terror and awe. At the end of the story, Shaynor rouses from his trance, having just failed to reproduce word-for-word the three most 'magical' lines from 'Ode to a Nightingale', and the electrician says he has been picking up signals between two ships in the Channel (the Navy had only just begun to use Marconi), whose transmitters are working but whose 'receivers are out of order'.

There are some resemblances to an earlier story, 'The Finest Story in the World', where the narrator discovers that a bank clerk with literary pretensions is the reincarnation of a Viking and a Greek galley slave who 'speak' through him (with Longfellow's poetry acting as the catalyst). But 'Wireless' is not, exactly, the story of a reincarnation or a haunting. We are not so much meant to think that the spirit of Keats, a ghost in the machine, is coming from outer space through the Hertzian waves into the coherer, and thence into his inferior incarnation, Mr Shaynor; rather, that the unique conditions (meticulously established) have made possible an astounding *parallel* between electrical induction and poetic inspiration, where 'Shaynor is the receiver that is not rightly tuned'.[48]

The story involves a paradox which is felt in the very manner of the telling, at once so busily decoding and so helplessly baffled, retiring at last exhausted in the face of what it has tried to tell. As always in Kipling, there is a passion for the secrets of a craft – in this case of three crafts. First the narrator expresses his enthusiasm for Mr Cashell the chemist's 'zealous' craftsmanship; he is evidently allured himself by the 'romance of drugs', and in the course of the story makes free of the apothecary's shop, like a sorcerer's apprentice 'not knowing what djinns I should evoke'. His second induction is into the craft of wireless, explained to him by young Mr Cashell in terms which make the process very clear (Kipling's pride in having mastered it is evident) but which dwell respectfully on its magic and mystery: '"I never get over the strangeness of it when I work on a sending-machine – waves going into space, you know."' The third craft is writing. Kipling had a theory about inspiration. He told Rider Haggard that 'We are only telephone wires'[49] and in his autobiography he talks of being 'possessed' by his inspiration: 'When your Daemon is in charge, do not try to think consciously. Drift, wait, and obey.'[50] But the same paradoxical confluence of the involuntary and the crafted applies most of all here. What the Daemon sends has to be worked at and worked at, as the narrator tells us in his knowing footnotes to Shaynor's unconscious transcriptions: '"That's it . . . That's how it's blocked out. Go on! Ink it in, man. Ink it in!"' Craft and inspiration are played against each other like science and imagination. It looks as if 'Wireless' is going to be a story in praise of technology. But the narrator is distracted from his passionate interest in a new scientific discovery by the much stranger and more magical activity of the human mind.

Though the technical manoeuvrings of the story are intriguing, 'Wireless' is above all a bravura display of atmospheric and allusive writing. It is full of Keatsian effects: 'The Eve of St Agnes' runs through it like all the fluid, mobile elements which come into the story: coloured water, the east wind, the heated drink, blood, incense, the sound of the sea, scent, electricity. The Keatsian chemist's shop is a sensation; as Randall Jarrell says, 'One feels after reading this: well, no one ever again will have to describe a drugstore.'[51]

Keats's anxiety about his own poetry was always that it would be too feminine, luxurious and sentimental, too 'smokeable', as he said of 'The Eve of St Agnes'.[52] Shaynor, too, a crude version of Keats, is feminized, unmanly: sick, daydreaming, self-deludingly in love. In his trance his eyes go blank, 'as wide and lustreless as those of a dead hare'. Mrs Bathurst was memorable for the 'blindish way she had o' lookin''. In 'They', the secret world of the children is guarded by a blind woman. These are the three 'feminine' stories of the volume, all of which undermine the world of bonded masculine activity. That blindness attaches to them all suggests Kipling's double feeling about being unmanned. It is perilous and terrifying. (His own sight was very poor, his childhood near-blindness is horrifyingly recalled in 'Baa, Baa, Black Sheep', and he strikes his hero blind in *The Light that Failed*.) But it can also be illuminating and consolatory, an alternative, interiorized form of vision.

All three stories are repetitious: protagonists and witnesses have to go through a recurring cycle of actions. Vickery's mechanical 're-viewing' of Mrs Bathurst is an unnatural nightmare of repetition, which has replaced the natural cycle of a domestic life. In 'Wireless', the induced charge of inspiration recurs like repeated waves of electricity, but because the human mind is not a machine the message it transmits is variable. In 'They', the process of repetition is ritualistic and seasonal. The narrator makes three car journeys, in spring, summer and autumn, 'from the other side of the county', to the 'House Beautiful' with its blind woman, its butler and its elusive children. He travels through a richly detailed pastoral landscape to the romantically idealized Elizabethan house, which is defended against the outside world by the 'crumpled hills that interlaced so jealously around it', the 'veil' of woods that conceals it, the deeply descending grass ride, the yew horsemen with their levelled spears, the semicircular screening walls.

On each journey, as in a fairytale, the narrator penetrates more deeply. On the first visit he is lost, 'clean out of my known marks', an uncomprehending 'trespasser'. On the second visit he becomes involved in local action, fetching help for a sick village child. On the third and last visit he is accepted as a 'regular' by the locals, and he enters the house. With the woman, he explores deep into its passages, as though penetrating the 'mysterious heart' of the convex mirror on the wall. Their pursuit of the ever-disappearing children ('In the failing light a door creaked cautiously . . . quick feet through a room beyond') is like Browning's 'Love in a Life':

> But 'tis twilight, you see, – with such suites to explore,
> Such closets to search, such alcoves to importune!

The woman sings a verse from a poem by Elizabeth Barrett Browning, told by a sick woman remembering the 'lost bower' of her childhood, which prefigured all her later losses. So the house and its secret, which the narrator is only allowed to understand at the end of his third and last visit, seems to stand for the hidden centre, easily lost, of an innocent, pastoral, feudal Old England, which the narrator pictures as 'the shut island of the North', in need of defending, with 'all the ships of the world bellowing at our perilous gates'. The blind woman and the narrator have a private understanding (they love the children, they both have the gift of seeing emotions as 'colours') which sets them apart from the foreign adult world of 'brutality'.

The story overcomes its almost irresistible tendency to sentimentalize the house and its inhabitants by making the outside world impinge. The villagers come under the influence of the house: they know what goes on there, and accept the feudal tradition. Even the shifty newfangled tenant at the end is driven out by the blind woman's authority and by his fear. But the narrator's car takes him out of and back into the modern world – usefully, since this may save a sick child.[53] His rapid journey with the doctor to find a nurse (who is taken out of *her* protected sanctuary in order to be of use) is crowded with 'cross-sections of remote and incomprehensible lives through which we raced at right angles', a transverse, speeded-up journey in modern time, cutting across the route to the house, which leads out of time.

The quest to the house anticipates Eliot's *Four Quartets*, which deliberately echoes 'They', not only in the 'Burnt Norton' scene of the children's voices in the garden, but in the idea of a journey undertaken to find what you do not know you are seeking:

> In order to possess what you do not possess
> You must go by the way of dispossession
>
> . . .
>
> And the end of all our exploring
> Will be to arrive where we started
> And know the place for the first time.

The narrator of 'They', however, is not allowed to stay in 'the place'. Kipling obscures the reasons for this (they presumably have to do with his distrust of trafficking with the psychic and the supernatural), but they bear on the deepest, most central idea in his work. 'They' is a very different story from the bellicose South African tales, the naval yarns, the affirmations of militarism, the male pranks, which fill up most of *Traffics and Discoveries*. But those other stories are all dominated by the desire to belong to a group, to be accepted, inside, in the know. The narrator discovers an alternative secret society in 'They': spiritual, feminine, magic, innocent. He learns its private codes, just as he learns about naval manoeuvres or wireless telegraphy. But he cannot belong to it, because, for all Kipling's strenuous efforts to convince us and himself otherwise, he is an outsider, and recognizes solitariness as our condition.

University of York Hermione Lee
1986

Further Reading

Amis, Kingsley, *Rudyard Kipling and his World*, Thames & Hudson, 1975.

Bayley, John, 'The Puzzles of Kipling', *The Uses of Division*, Chatto & Windus, 1976.

Birkenhead, Lord, *Rudyard Kipling*, Weidenfeld & Nicolson, 1978.

Bodelson, C. A., *Aspects of Kipling's Art*, Manchester University Press, 1964.

Carrington, Charles, *Rudyard Kipling*, Macmillan, 1955.

Eliot, T. S., Introduction to *A Choice of Kipling's Verse*, Faber and Faber, 1941.

Gilbert, Elliott (ed.), *Kipling and the Critics*, Peter Owen, 1966.

Green, R. L. (ed.), *Kipling – The Critical Heritage*, Routledge & Kegan Paul, 1971.

Gross, John (ed.), *Rudyard Kipling: The man, his work and his world*, Weidenfeld & Nicolson, 1972.

Jarrell, Randall, *Kipling, Auden & Co.*, Carcanet Press, 1981.

Mason, Philip, *Kipling: The Glass, the Shadow and the Fire*, Jonathan Cape, 1975.

Montefiore, Janet, 'Day and Night in Kipling', *Essays in Criticism*, vol. XXVII, no. 4.

Rutherford, Andrew (ed.), *Kipling's Mind and Art*, Oliver & Boyd, 1964.

Tompkins, J. M. S., *The Art of Rudyard Kipling*, Methuen, 1959.

Wilson, Angus, *The Strange Ride of Rudyard Kipling*, Secker & Warburg, 1977.

Note on the Text

Traffics and Discoveries, consisting of eleven stories and eleven poems, was published in 1904 by Macmillan & Co. in the Uniform Edition, and in America by Doubleday, Page & Co. All the stories had previously appeared in magazines, and six had been published in separate editions. Subsequent collected editions included the Pocket Edition (1908), and the post-humous Sussex Edition (1937–9). This text is that of the Uniform Edition of 1904.

TRAFFICS AND DISCOVERIES

❧ The Captive ❧

From the Masjid-al-Aqsa
of Sayyid Ahmed (Wahabi)

Not with an outcry to Allah nor any complaining.
He answered his name at the muster and stood to the chaining.
When the twin anklets were nipped on the leg-bars that held
                               them,
He brotherly greeted the armourers stopping to weld them.
Ere the sad dust of the marshalled feet of the chain-gang
                         swallowed him,
Observing him nobly at ease, I alighted and followed him.
Thus we had speech by the way, but not touching his sorrow –
Rather his red Yesterday and his regal Tomorrow,
Wherein he statelily moved to the clink of his chains
                         unregarded,
Nowise abashed but contented to drink of the potion awarded.
Saluting aloofly his Fate, he made swift with his story;
And the words of his mouth were as slaves spreading carpets
                         of glory
Embroidered with names of the Djinns – a miraculous
                         weaving –
But the cool and perspicuous eye overbore unbelieving.
So I submitted myself to the limits of rapture –
Bound by this man we had bound, amid captives his capture –
Till he returned me to earth and the visions departed;
But on him be the Peace and the Blessing: for he was
                         great-hearted!

The Captive

He that believeth shall not make haste.

Isaiah

The guard-boat lay across the mouth of the bathing-pool, her crew idly spanking the water with the flat of their oars. A red-coated militiaman, rifle in hand, sat at the bows, and a petty officer at the stern. Between the snow-white cutter and the flat-topped, honey-coloured rocks on the beach the green water was troubled with shrimp-pink prisoners-of-war bathing. Behind their orderly tin camp and the electric-light poles rose those stone-dotted spurs that throw heat on Simonstown. Beneath them the little *Barracouta* nodded to the big *Gibraltar*, and the old *Penelope*, that in ten years has been bachelors' club, natural history museum, kindergarten, and prison, rooted and dug at her fixed moorings. Far out, a three-funnelled Atlantic trans-port with turtle bow and stern waddled in from the deep sea.

Said the sentry, assured of the visitor's good faith, 'Talk to 'em? You can, to any that speak English. You'll find a lot that do.'

Here and there earnest groups gathered round ministers of the Dutch Reformed Church, who doubtless preached con-ciliation, but the majority preferred their bath. The God who Looks after Small Things had caused the visitor that day to receive two weeks' delayed mails in one from a casual postman, and the whole heavy bundle of newspapers, tied with a strap, he dangled as bait. At the edge of the beach, cross-legged, undressed to his sky-blue army shirt, sat a lean, ginger-haired man, on guard over a dozen heaps of clothing. His eyes followed the incoming Atlantic boat.

'Excuse me, Mister,' he said, without turning (and the speech betrayed his nationality), 'would you mind keeping away from these garments? I've been elected janitor – on the Dutch vote.'

The visitor moved over against the barbed-wire fence and sat down to his mail. At the rustle of the newspaper-wrappers, the ginger-coloured man turned quickly, the hunger of a press-ridden people in his close-set iron-grey eyes.

'Have you any use for papers?' said the visitor.

'Have I any use?' A quick, curved forefinger was already snicking off the outer covers. 'Why, that's the New York postmark! Give me the ads. at the back of *Harper's* and *M'Clure's* and I'm in touch with God's Country again! Did you know how I was aching for papers?'

The visitor told the tale of the casual postman.

'Providential!' said the ginger-coloured man, keen as a terrier on his task; 'both in time and matter. Yes! ... The *Scientific American* yet once more! Oh, it's good! it's good!' His voice broke as he pressed his hawk-like nose against the heavily-inked patent-specifications at the end. 'Can I keep it? I thank you – I thank you! Why – why – well – well! The *American Tyler* of all things created! Do you subscribe to that?'

'I'm on the free list,' said the visitor, nodding.

He extended his blue-tanned hand with that air of Oriental spaciousness which distinguishes the native-born American, and met the visitor's grasp expertly. 'I can only say that you have treated me like a Brother (yes, I'll take every last one you can spare), and if ever –' He plucked at the bosom of his shirt. 'Psha! I forgot I'd no card on me; but my name's Zigler – Laughton O. Zigler. An American? If Ohio's still in the Union, I am, Sir. But I'm no extreme States'-rights man. I've used all of my native country and a few others as I have found occasion, and now I am the captive of your bow and spear. I'm not kicking at that. I am not a coerced alien, nor a naturalized Texas mule-tender, nor an adventurer on the instalment plan. *I* don't tag after our Consul when he comes around, expecting the American Eagle to lift me out o' this by the slack of my pants. No, Sir! If a Britisher went into Indian Territory and shot up his surroundings with a Colt automatic (not that *she's* any sort of weapon, but I take her for an illustration), he'd be strung up quicker'n a snowflake 'ud melt in hell. No ambassador of yours 'ud save him. I'm my neck ahead on this game, anyway. That's how I regard the proposition.

'Have I gone gunning against the British? To a certain extent. I presume you never heard tell of the Laughton-Zigler automatic two-inch field-gun, with self-feeding hopper, single oil-cylinder recoil, and ball-bearing gear throughout? Or Laughtite, the new explosive? Absolutely uniform in effect, and one-ninth the bulk of any present effete charge – flake, cannonite, cordite, troisdorf, cellulose, cocoa, cord, or prism – I don't care what it is. Laughtite's immense; so's the Zigler automatic. It's me. It's fifteen years of me. You are not a gun-sharp? I am sorry. I could have surprised you. Apart from my gun, my tale don't amount to much of anything. I thank you, but I don't use any tobacco you'd be likely to carry . . . Bull Durham? *Bull Durham!* I take it all back – every last word. Bull Durham – here! If ever you strike Akron, Ohio, when this fool-war's over, remember you've Laughton O. Zigler in your vest pocket. Including the city of Akron. We've a little club there . . . Hell! What's the sense of talking Akron with no pants?

'My gun? . . . For two cents I'd have shipped her to our Filipeens. 'Came mighty near it too; but from what I'd read in the papers, you can't trust Aguinaldo's crowd on scientific matters. Why don't I offer it to our army? Well, you've an effete aristocracy running yours, and we've a crowd of politicians. The results are practically identical. I am not taking any U.S. Army in mine.

'I went to Amsterdam with her – to this Dutch junta that supposes it's bossing the war. I wasn't brought up to love the British for one thing, and for another I knew that if she got in her fine work (my gun) I'd stand more chance of receiving an unbiassed report from a crowd o' dam-fool British officers than from a hatful of politicians' nephews doing duty as com-missaries and ordnance sharps. As I said, I put the brown man out of the question. That's the way *I* regarded the proposition.

'The Dutch in Holland don't amount to a row of pins. Maybe I misjudge 'em. Maybe they've been swindled too often by self-seeking adventurers to know a enthusiast when they see him. Anyway, they're slower than the Wrath o' God. But on delusions – as to their winning out next Thursday week at 9 a.m. – they are – if I may say so – quite British.

'I'll tell you a curious thing, too. I fought 'em for ten days before I could get the financial side of my game fixed to my liking. I knew they didn't believe in the Zigler, but they'd no call to be crazy-mean. I fixed it – free passage and freight for me and the gun to Delagoa Bay, and beyond by steam and rail. Then I went aboard to see her crated, and there I struck my fellow-passengers – all deadheads, same as me. Well, Sir, I turned in my tracks where I stood and besieged the ticket-office, and I said, "Look at here, Van Dunk. I'm paying for my passage and her room in the hold – every square and cubic foot." 'Guess he knocked down the fare to himself; but I paid. I paid. I wasn't going to deadhead along o' *that* crowd of Pentecostal sweepings. 'Twould have hoodooed my gun for all time. That was the way I regarded the proposition. No, Sir, they were not pretty company.

'When we struck Pretoria I had a hell-and-a-half of a time trying to interest the Dutch vote in my gun an' her potentialities. The bottom was out of things rather much just about that time. Kruger was praying some and stealing some, and the Hollander lot was singing, "If you haven't any money you needn't come round." Nobody was spending his dough on anything except tickets to Europe. We were both grossly neglected. When I think how I used to give performances in the public streets with dummy cartridges, filling the hopper and turning the handle till the sweat dropped off me, I blush, Sir. I've made her do her stunts before Kaffirs – naked sons of Ham – in Commissioner Street, trying to get a holt somewhere.

'Did I talk? I despise exaggeration – 'tain't American or scientific – but as true as I'm sitting here like a blue-ended baboon in a kloof, Teddy Roosevelt's Western tour was a maiden's sigh compared to my advertising work.

''Long in the spring I was rescued by a commandant called Van Zyl – a big, fleshy man with a lame leg. Take away his hair and his gun and he'd make a first-class Schenectady bar-keep. He found me and the Zigler on the veldt (Pretoria wasn't

wholesome at that time), and he annexed me in a somnam-
bulistic sort o' way. He was dead against the war from the start,
but, being a Dutchman, he fought a sight better than the rest
of that "God and the Mauser" outfit. Adrian Van Zyl. Slept a
heap in the daytime – and didn't love niggers. I liked him. I was
the only foreigner in his commando. The rest was Georgia
Crackers and Pennsylvania Dutch – with a dash o' Philadelphia
lawyer. I could tell you things about them would surprise you.
Religion for one thing; women for another; but I don't know as
their notions o' geography weren't the craziest. 'Guess that
must be some sort of automatic compensation. There wasn't one
blamed ant-hill in their district they didn't know *and* use; but
the world was flat, they said, and England was a day's trek
from Cape Town.

'They could fight in their own way, and don't you forget it.
But I guess you will not. They fought to kill, and, by what I
could make out, the British fought to be killed. So both parties
were accommodated.

'I am the captive of your bow and spear, Sir. The position
has its obligations – on both sides. You could not be offensive
or partisan to me. I cannot, for the same reason, be offensive to
you. Therefore I will not give you my opinions on the conduct
of your war.

'Anyway, I didn't take the field as an offensive partisan, but
as an inventor. It was a condition and not a theory that con-
fronted me. (Yes, Sir, I'm a Democrat by conviction, and that
was one of the best things Grover Cleveland ever got off.)

'After three months' trek, old man Van Zyl had his commando in good shape and refitted off the British, and he
reckoned he'd wait on a British General of his acquaintance
that did business on a circuit between Stompiesneuk, Jackhalputs, Vrelegen, and Odendaalstroom, year in and year out.
He was a fixture in that section.

'"He's a damn good man," says Van Zyl. "He's a friend of
mine. He sent in a fine doctor when I was wounded and our
Hollander doc. wanted to cut my leg off. Ya, I'll guess we'll
stay with him." Up to date, me and my Zigler had lived in
innocuous desuetude owing to little odds and ends riding out of

gear. How in thunder was I to know there wasn't the ghost of
any road in the country? But raw hide's cheap and lastin'. I
guess I'll make my next gun a thousand pounds heavier,
though.

'Well, Sir, we struck the General on his beat – Vrelegen it
was – and our crowd opened with the usual compliments at two
thousand yards. Van Zyl shook himself into his greasy old
saddle and says, "Now we shall be quite happy, Mr Zigler. No
more trekking. Joost twelve miles a day till the apricots are
ripe."

'Then we hitched on to his outposts, and vedettes, and
cossack-picquets, or whatever they was called, and we wandered
around the veldt arm in arm like brothers.

'The way we worked lodge was this way. The General, he
had his breakfast at 8.45 a.m. to the tick. He might have been a
Long Island commuter. At 8.42 a.m. I'd go down to the Thirty-
fourth Street ferry to meet him – I mean I'd see the Zigler into
position at two thousand (I began at three thousand, but that
was cold and distant) – and blow him off to two full hoppers –
eighteen rounds – just as they were bringing in his coffee. If
his crowd was busy celebrating the anniversary of Waterloo or
the last royal kid's birthday, they'd open on me with two guns
(I'll tell you about them later on), but if they were disengaged
they'd all stand to their horses and pile on the ironmongery,
and washers, and typewriters, and five weeks' grub, and in half
an hour they'd sail out after me and the rest of Van Zyl's boys;
lying down and firing till 11.45 a.m. or maybe high noon. Then
we'd go from labour to refreshment, resooming at 2 p.m. and
battling till tea-time. Tuesday and Friday was the General's
moving days. He'd trek ahead ten or twelve miles, and we'd
loaf around his flankers and exercise the ponies a piece. Sometimes he'd get hung up in a drift – stalled crossin' a crick – and
we'd make playful snatches at his wagons. First time that
happened I turned the Zigler loose with high hopes, Sir; but
the old man was well posted on rearguards with a gun to 'em,
and I had to haul her out with three mules instead o' six. I was
pretty mad. I wasn't looking for any experts back of the Royal
British Artillery. Otherwise, the game was mostly even. He'd

lay out three or four of our commando, and we'd gather in four
or five of his once a week or thereon. One time, I remember,
'long towards dusk we saw 'em burying five of their boys. They
stood pretty thick around the graves. We wasn't more than
fifteen hundred yards off, but old Van Zyl wouldn't fire. He
just took off his hat at the proper time. He said if you stretched
a man at his prayers you'd have to hump his bad luck before
the Throne as well as your own. I am inclined to agree with
him. So we browsed along week in and week out. A war-sharp
might have judged it sort of docile, but for an inventor needing
practice one day and peace the next for checking his theories, it
suited Laughton O. Zigler.

'And friendly? Friendly was no word for it. We was brothers
in arms.

'Why, I knew those two guns of the Royal British Artillery as
well as I used to know the old Fifth Avenoo stages. *They* might
have been brothers too.

'They'd jolt into action, and wiggle around and skid and spit
and cough and prize 'emselves back again during our hours of
bloody battle till I could have wept, Sir, at the spectacle of
modern white men chained up to these old hand-power, back-
number, flint-and-steel reaping machines. One of 'em – I called
her Baldy – she'd a long white scar all along her barrel – I'd
made sure of twenty times. I knew her crew by sight, but she'd
come switching and teturing out of the dust of my shells like –
like a hen from under a buggy – and she'd dip into a gully, and
next thing I'd know 'ud be her old nose peeking over the ridge
sniffin' for us. Her runnin' mate had two grey mules in the
lead, and a natural wood wheel re-painted, and a whole raft of
rope-ends trailin' around. 'J'ever see Tom Reed with his vest
off, steerin' Congress through a heat-wave? I've been to
Washington often – too often – filin' my patents. I called her
Tom Reed. We three 'ud play pussy-wants-a-corner all round
the outposts on off-days – cross-lots through the sage and
along the mezas till we was short-circuited by cañons. Oh, it
was great fun for me and Baldy and Tom Reed! I don't know
as we didn't neglect the legitimate interests of our respective
commanders sometimes for this ball-play. I know *I* did.

''Long towards the fall the Royal British Artillery grew shy – hung back in their breeching sort of – and their shooting was way – way off. I observed they wasn't taking any chances, not though I acted kitten almost underneath 'em.

'I mentioned it to Van Zyl, because it struck me I had about knocked their Royal British moral endways.

'"No," says he, rocking as usual on his pony. "My Captain Mankeltow he is sick. That is all."

'"So's your Captain Mankeltow's guns," I said. "But I'm going to make 'em a heap sicker before he gets well."

'"No," says Van Zyl. "He has had the enteric a little. Now he is better, and he was let out from hospital at Jackhalputs. Ah, that Mankeltow! He always makes me laugh so. I told him – long back – at Colesberg, I had a little home for him at Nooitgedacht. But he would not come – no! He has been sick, and I am sorry."

'"How d'you know that?" I says.

'"Why, only today he sends back his love by Johanna Van der Merwe, that goes to their doctor for her sick baby's eyes. He sends his love, that Mankeltow, and he tells her tell me he has a little garden of roses all ready for me in the Dutch Indies – Umballa. He is very funny, my Captain Mankeltow."

'The Dutch and the English ought to fraternize, Sir. They've the same notions of humour, to my thinking.'

'"When he gets well," says Van Zyl, "you look out, Mr Americaan. He comes back to his guns next Tuesday. Then they shoot better."

'I wasn't so well acquainted with the Royal British Artillery as old man Van Zyl. I knew this Captain Mankeltow by sight, of course, and, considering what sort of a man with the hoe he was, I thought he'd done right well against my Zigler. But nothing epoch-making.

'Next morning at the usual hour I waited on the General, and old Van Zyl come along with some of the boys. Van Zyl didn't hang around the Zigler much as a rule, but this was his luck that day.

'He was peeking through his glasses at the camp, and I was helping pepper the General's sow-belly – just as usual – when

43

he turns to me quick and says, "Almighty! How all these Englishmen are liars! You cannot trust one," he says. "Captain Mankeltow tells our Johanna he comes not back till Tuesday, and today is Friday, and there he is! Almighty! The English are all Chamberlains!"

'If the old man hadn't stopped to make political speeches he'd have had his supper in a laager that night, I guess. I was busy attending to Tom Reed at two thousand when Baldy got in her fine work on me. I saw one sheet of white flame wrapped round the hopper, and in the middle of it there was one o' my mules straight on end. Nothing out of the way in a mule on end, but this mule hadn't any head. I remember it struck me as incongruous at the time, and when I'd ciphered it out I was doing the Santos-Dumont act without any balloon and my motor out of gear. Then I got to thinking about Santos-Dumont and how much better my new way was. Then I thought about Professor Langley and the Smithsonian, and wishing I hadn't lied so extravagantly in some of my specifications at Washington. Then I quit thinking for quite a while, and when I resumed my train of thought I was nude, Sir, in a very stale stretcher, and my mouth was full of fine dirt all flavoured with Laughtite.

'I coughed up that dirt.

' "Hullo!" says a man walking beside me. "You've spoke almost in time. Have a drink?"

'I don't use rum as a rule, but I did then, because I needed it.

' "What hit us?" I said.

' "Me," he said. "I got you fair on the hopper as you pulled out of that donga; but I'm sorry to say every last round in the hopper's exploded and your gun's in a shocking state. I'm real sorry," he says. "I admire your gun, Sir."

' "Are you Captain Mankeltow?" I says.

' "Yes," he says. "I presoom you're Mister Zigler. Your commanding officer told me about you."

' "Have you gathered in old man Van Zyl?" I said.

' "Commandant Van Zyl," he says very stiff, "was most unfortunately wounded, but I am glad to say it's not serious.

We hope he'll be able to dine with us tonight; and I feel sure," he says, "the General would be delighted to see you too, though he didn't expect," he says, "and no one else either, by Jove!" he says, and blushed like the British do when they're embarrassed.

'I saw him slide an Episcopalian Prayer-book up his sleeve, and when I looked over the edge of the stretcher there was half-a-dozen enlisted men − privates − had just quit digging and was standing to attention by their spades. I guess he was right on the General not expecting me to dinner; but it was all of a piece with their sloppy British way of doing business. Any God's quantity of fuss and flubdub to bury a man, and not an ounce of forehandedness in the whole outfit to find out whether he was rightly dead. And I am a Congregationalist anyway!

'Well, Sir, that was my introduction to the British Army. I'd write a book about it if anyone would believe me. This Captain Mankeltow, Royal British Artillery, turned the doctor on me (I could write another book about *him*) and fixed me up with a suit of his own clothes, and fed me canned beef and biscuits, and give me a cigar − a Henry Clay and a whisky-and-sparklet. He was a white man.

'"Ye-es, by Jove," he said, dragging out his words like a twist of molasses, "we've all admired your gun and the way you've worked it. Some of us betted you was a British deserter. I won a sovereign on that from a yeoman. And, by the way," he says, "you've disappointed me groom pretty bad."

'"Where does your groom come in?" I said.

'"Oh, he was the yeoman. He's a dam poor groom," says my captain, "but he's a way-up barrister when he's at home. He's been running around the camp with his tongue out, waiting for the chance of defending you at the court-martial."

'"What court-martial?" I says.

'"On you as a deserter from the Artillery. You'd have had a good run for your money. Anyway, you'd never have been hung after the way you worked your gun. Deserter ten times over," he says, "I'd have stuck out for shooting you like a gentleman."

'Well, Sir, right there it struck me at the pit of my stomach − sort of sickish, sweetish feeling − that my position needed regularizing pretty bad. I ought to have been a naturalized burgher of a year's standing; but Ohio's my State, and I wouldn't have gone back on her for a desertful of Dutchmen. That and my enthoosiasm as an inventor had led me to the existing crisis; but I couldn't expect this Captain Mankeltow to regard the proposition that way. There I sat, the rankest breed of unreconstructed American citizen, caught red-handed squirting hell at the British Army for months on end. I tell *you*, Sir, I wished I was in Cincinnatah that summer evening. I'd have compromised on Brooklyn.

'"What d'you do about aliens?" I said, and the dirt I'd coughed up seemed all back of my tongue again.

'"Oh," says he, "we don't do much of anything. They're about all the society we get. I'm a bit of a pro-Boer myself," he says, "but between you and me the average Boer ain't over and above intellectual. You're the first American we've met up with, but of course you're a burgher."

'It was what I ought to have been if I'd had the sense of a common tick, but the way he drawled it out made me mad.

'"Of course I am not," I says. "Would *you* be a naturalized Boer?"

'"I'm fighting against 'em," he says, lighting a cigarette, "but it's a matter of opinion."

'"Well," I says, "you can hold any blame opinion you choose, but I'm a white man, and my present intention is to die in that colour."

'He laughed one of those big, thick-ended, British laughs that don't lead anywhere, and whacked up some sort of compliment about America that made me mad all through.

'I am the captive of your bow and spear, Sir, but I do not understand the alleged British joke. It is depressing.

'I was introdooced to five or six officers that evening, and every blame one of 'em grinned and asked me why I wasn't in the Filipeens suppressing our war! And that was British humour! They all had to get it off their chests before they'd talk sense. But they was sound on the Zigler. They had all admired her. I made out a fairy-story of me being wearied of the war, and having pushed the gun at them these last three months in the hope they'd capture it and let me go home. That tickled 'em to death. They made me say it three times over, and laughed like kids each time. But half the British *are* kids; specially the older men. My Captain Mankeltow was less of it than the others. He talked about the Zigler like a lover, Sir, and I drew him diagrams of the hopper-feed and recoil-cylinder in his note-book. He asked the one British question I was waiting for, "Hadn't I made my working-parts too light?" The British think weight's strength.

'At last – I'd been shy of opening the subject before – at last I said, "Gentlemen, you are the unprejudiced tribunal I've been hunting after. I guess you ain't interested in any other gun-factory, and politics don't weigh with you. How did it feel your end of the game? What's my gun done, anyway?"

'"I hate to disappoint you," says Captain Mankeltow, "because I know how you feel as an inventor." I wasn't feeling like an inventor just then. I felt friendly, but the British haven't more tact than you can pick up with a knife out of a plate of soup.

'"The honest truth," he says, "is that you've wounded about ten of us one way and another, killed two battery horses and four mules, and – oh, yes," he said, "you've bagged five Kaffirs. But, buck up," he says, "we've all had mighty close calls" – shaves, he called 'em, I remember. "Look at my pants."

'They was repaired right across the seat with Minneapolis flour-bagging. I could see the stencil.

'"I ain't bluffing," he says. "Get the hospital returns, Doc."

'The doctor gets 'em and reads 'em out under the proper dates. That doctor alone was worth the price of admission.

'I was pleased right through that I hadn't killed any of these cheerful kids; but none the less I couldn't help thinking that a few more Kaffirs would have served me just as well for advertising purposes as white men. No, Sir. Anywhichway you regard the proposition, twenty-one casualties after months of close friendship like ours was – paltry.

'They gave me taffy about the gun – the British use taffy where we use sugar. It's cheaper, and gets there just the same.

They sat around and proved to me that my gun was too good, too uniform – shot as close as a Männlicher rifle.

'Says one kid chewing a bit of grass: "I counted eight of your shells, Sir, burst in a radius of ten feet. All of 'em would have gone through one waggon-tilt. It was beautiful," he says. "It was too good."

'I shouldn't wonder if the boys were right. My Laughtite is too mathematically uniform in propelling power. Yes; she was too good for this refractory fool of a country. The training-gear was broke, too, and we had to swivel her around by the trail. But I'll build my next Zigler fifteen hundred pounds heavier. Might work in a gasoline motor under the axles. I must think that up.

'"Well, gentlemen," I said, "I'd hate to have been the death of any of you; and if a prisoner can deed away his property, I'd love to present the Captain here with what he's seen fit to leave of my Zigler."

'"Thanks awf'ly," says my Captain. "I'd like her very much. She'd look fine in the mess at Woolwich. That is, if you don't mind, Mr Zigler."

'"Go right ahead," I says. "I've come out of all the mess I've any use for; but she'll do to spread the light among the Royal British Artillery."

'I tell you, Sir, there's not much of anything the matter with the Royal British Artillery. They're brainy men languishing under an effete system which, when you take good holt of it, is England – just all England. 'Times I'd feel I was talking with real live citizens, and times I'd feel I'd struck the Beef-eaters in the Tower.

'How? Well, this way. I was telling my Captain Mankeltow what Van Zyl had said about the British being all Chamberlains when the old man saw him back from hospital four days ahead of time.

'"Oh, dam it all!" he says, as serious as the Supreme Court. "It's too bad," he says. "Johanna must have misunderstood me, or else I've got the wrong Dutch word for these blarsted days of the week. I told Johanna I'd be out on Friday. The woman's a fool. Oah, da-am it all!" he says. "I wouldn't have sold old Van Zyl a pup like that," he says. "I'll hunt him up and apologize."

The Captive

'He must have fixed it all right, for when we sailed over to the General's dinner my Captain had Van Zyl about half-full of sherry and bitters, as happy as a clam. The boys all called him Adrian, and treated him like their prodigal father. He'd been hit on the collar-bone by a wad of shrapnel, and his arm was tied up.

'But the General was the peach. I presume you're acquainted with the average run of British generals, but this was my first. I sat on his left hand, and he talked like – like the *Ladies' Home Journal*. 'J'ever read that paper? It's refined, Sir – and innocuous, and full of nickel-plated sentiments guaranteed to improve the mind. He was it. He began by a Lydia Pinkham heart-to-heart talk about my health, and hoped the boys had done me well, and that I was enjoying my stay in their midst. Then he thanked me for the interesting and valuable lessons that I'd given his crowd – specially in the matter of placing artillery and rearguard attacks. He'd wipe his long thin moustache between drinks – lime-juice and water he used – and blat off into a long "a-aah", and ladle out more taffy for me or old man Van Zyl on his right. I told him how I'd had my first Pisgah-sight of the principles of the Zigler when I was a fourth-class postmaster on a star-route in Arkansas. I told him how I'd worked it up by instalments when I was machinist in Waterbury, where the dollar-watches come from. He had one on his wrist then. I told him how I'd met Zalinski (he'd never heard of Zalinski!) when I was an extra clerk in the Naval Construction Bureau at Washington. I told him how my uncle, who was a truck-farmer in Noo Jersey (he loaned money on mortgage too, for ten acres ain't enough now in Noo Jersey), how he'd willed me a quarter of a million dollars, because I was the only one of our kin that called him down when he used to come home with a hard-cider jag on him and heave ox-bows at his nieces. I told him how I'd turned in every red cent on the Zigler, and I told him the whole circus of my coming out with her, and so on, and so following; and every forty seconds he'd wipe his moustache and blat, "How interesting. Really, now? How interesting."

'It was like being in an old English book, Sir. Like *Bracebridge Hall*. But an American wrote *that*! I kept peeking around for the Boar's Head and the Rosemary and Magna Charta and the Cricket on the Hearth, and the rest of the outfit. Then Van Zyl whirled in. He was no ways jagged, but thawed – thawed, Sir, and among friends. They began discussing previous scraps all along the old man's beat – about sixty of 'em – as well as side-shows with other generals and columns. Van Zyl told 'im of a big beat he'd worked on a column a week or so before I'd joined him. He demonstrated his strategy with forks on the table.

'"There!" said the General, when he'd finished. "That proves my contention to the hilt. Maybe I'm a bit of a pro-Boer, but I stick to it," he says, "that under proper officers, with due regard to his race prejudices, the Boer 'ud make the finest mounted infantry in the Empire. Adrian," he says, "you're simply squandered on a cattle-run. You ought to be at the Staff College with De Wet."

'"You catch De Wet and I come to your Staff College – eh," says Adrian, laughing. "But you are so slow, Generaal. Why are you so slow? For a month," he says, "you do so well and strong that we say we shall hands-up and come back to our farms. Then you send to England and make us a present of two – three – six hundred young men, with rifles and wagons and rum and tobacco, and such a great lot of cartridges, that our young men put up their tails and start all over again. If you hold an ox by the horn and hit him by the bottom he runs round and round. He never goes anywhere. So, too, this war goes round and round. You know that, Generaal!"

'"Quite right, Adrian," says the General; "but you must believe your Bible."

'"Hooh!" says Adrian, and reaches for the whisky. I've never known a Dutchman a professing Atheist, but some few have been rather active Agnostics since the British sat down in Pretoria. Old man Van Zyl – he told me – had soured on religion after Bloemfontein surrendered. He was a Free Stater for one thing.

'"He that believeth," says the General, "shall not make haste. That's in Isaiah. We believe we're going to win, and so we don't make haste. As far as I'm concerned I'd like this war to

50

last another five years. We'd have an army then. It's just this way, Mr Zigler," he says, "our people are brim-full of patriotism, but they've been born and brought up between houses, and England ain't big enough to train 'em – not if you expect to preserve."

'"Preserve what?" I says. "England?"

'"No. The game," he says; "and that reminds me, gentlemen, we haven't drunk the King and Fox-hunting."

'So they drank the King and Fox-hunting. I drank the King because there's something about Edward that tickles me (he's so blame British); but I rather stood out on the Fox-hunting. I've ridden wolves in the cattle-country, and needed a drink pretty bad afterwards, but it never struck me as I ought to drink about it – he-red-it-arily.

'"No, as I was saying, Mr Zigler," he goes on, "we have to train our men in the field to shoot and ride. I allow six months for it; but many column-commanders – not that I ought to say a word against 'em, for they're the best fellows that ever stepped, and most of 'em are my dearest friends – seem to think that if they have men and horses and guns they can take tea with the Boers. It's generally the other way about, ain't it, Mr Zigler?"

'"To some extent, Sir," I said.

'"I'm *so* glad you agree with me," he says. "My command here I regard as a training depot, and you, if I may say so, have been one of my most efficient instructors. I mature my men slowly but thoroughly. First I put 'em in a town which is liable to be attacked by night, where they can attend riding-school in the day. Then I use 'em with a convoy, and last I put 'em into a column. It takes time," he says, "but I flatter myself that any men who have worked under me are at least grounded in the rudiments of their profession. Adrian," he says, "was there anything wrong with the men who upset Van Besters' apple-cart last month when he was trying to cross the line to join Piper with those horses he'd stole from Gabbitas?"

'"No, Generaal," says Van Zyl. "Your men got the horses back and eleven dead; and Van Besters, he ran to Delarey in his shirt. They was very good, those men. They shoot hard."

51

'"*So* pleased to hear you say so. I laid 'em down at the beginning of this century – a 1900 vintage. *You* remember 'em, Mankeltow?" he says. "The Central Middlesex Buncho Busters – clerks and floor-walkers mostly," and he wiped his moustache. "It was just the same with the Liverpool Buckjumpers, but they were stevedores. Let's see – they were a last-century draft, weren't they? They did well after nine months. *You* know 'em, Van Zyl? You didn't get much change out of 'em at Pootfontein?"

'"No," says Van Zyl. "At Pootfontein I lost my son Andries."

'"I beg your pardon, Commandant," says the General; and the rest of the crowd sort of cooed over Adrian.

'"Excoose," says Adrian. "It was all right. They were good men those, but it is just what I say. Some are so dam good we want to hands-up, and some are so dam bad, we say, 'Take the Vierkleur into Cape Town.' It is not upright of you, Generaal. It is not upright of you at all. I do not think you ever wish this war to finish."

'"It's a first-class dress-parade for Armageddon," says the General. "With luck, we ought to run half a million men through the mill. Why, we might even be able to give our Native Army a look in. Oh, not here, of course, Adrian, but down in the Colony – say a camp-of-exercise at Worcester. You mustn't be prejudiced, Adrian. I've commanded a district in India, and I give you my word the native troops are splendid men."

'"Oh, I should not mind them at Worcester," says Adrian. "I would sell you forage for them at Worcester – yes, and Paarl and Stellenbosch; but Almighty!" he says, "must I stay with Cronje till you have taught half a million of these stupid boys to ride? I shall be an old man."

'Well, Sir, then and there they began arguing whether St Helena would suit Adrian's health as well as some other places they knew about, and fixing up letters of introduction to Dukes and Lords of their acquaintance, so's Van Zyl should be well looked after. We own a fair-sized block of real estate – America does – but it made me sickish to hear this crowd fluttering

round the Atlas (oh yes, they had an Atlas), and choosing stray
continents for Adrian to drink his coffee in. The old man
allowed he didn't want to roost with Cronje, because one of
Cronje's kin had jumped one of his farms after Paardeberg. I
forget the rights of the case, but it was interesting. They decided
on a place called Umballa in India, because there was a first-
class doctor there.

'So Adrian was fixed to drink the King and Fox-hunting,
and study up the Native Army in India (I'd like to see 'em
myself), till the British General had taught the male white
citizens of Great Britain how to ride. Don't misunderstand me,
Sir. I loved that General. After ten minutes I loved him, and I
wanted to laugh at him; but at the same time, sitting there and
hearing him talk about the centuries, I tell you, Sir, it scared
me. It scared me cold! He admitted everything – he acknowledged the corn before you spoke – he was more pleased to hear
that his men had been used to wipe the veldt with than I was
when I knocked out Tom Reed's two lead-horses – and he sat
back and blew smoke through his nose and matured his men
like cigars and – he talked of the everlastin' centuries!

'I went to bed nearer nervous prostration than I'd come in a
long time. Next morning me and Captain Mankeltow fixed up
what his shrapnel had left of my Zigler for transport to the
railroad. She went in on her own wheels, and I stencilled her
"Royal Artillery Mess, Woolwich", on the muzzle, and he said
he'd be grateful if I'd take charge of her to Cape Town, and
hand her over to a man in the Ordnance there. "How are you
fixed financially? You'll need some money on the way home,"
he says at last.

'"For one thing, Cap," I said, "I'm not a poor man, and for
another I'm not going home. I am the captive of your bow and
spear. I decline to resign office."

'"Skittles!" he says (that was a great word of his), "you'll
take parole, and go back to America and invent another Zigler,
a trifle heavier in the working-parts – I would. We've got more
prisoners than we know what to do with as it is," he says.
"You'll only be an additional expense to me as a taxpayer.
Think of Schedule D," he says, "and take parole."

'"I don't know anything about your tariffs," I said, "but when I get to Cape Town I write home for money, and I turn in every cent my board'll cost your country to any ten-century-old department that's been ordained to take it since William the Conqueror came along."

'"But, confound you for a thick-headed mule," he says, "this war ain't any more than just started! Do you mean to tell me you're going to play prisoner till it's over?"

'"That's about the size of it," I says, "if an Englishman and an American could ever understand each other."

'"But, in Heaven's Holy Name, why?" he says, sitting down of a heap on an ant-hill.

'"Well, Cap," I says, "I don't pretend to follow your ways of thought, and I can't see why you abuse your position to persecute a poor prisoner o' war on *his*!"

'"My dear fellow," he began, throwing up his hands and blushing, "I'll apologize."

'"But if you insist," I says, "there are just one and a half things in this world I can't do. The odd half don't matter here; but taking parole, and going home, and being interviewed by the boys, and giving lectures on my single-handed campaign against the hereditary enemies of my beloved country happens to be the one. We'll let it go at that, Cap."

'"But it'll bore you to death," he says. The British are a heap more afraid of what they call being bored than of dying, I've noticed.

'"I'll survive," I says, "I ain't British. I can think," I says.

'"By God," he says, coming up to me, and extending the right hand of fellowship, "you ought to be English, Zigler!"

'It's no good getting mad at a compliment like that. The English all do it. They're a crazy breed. When they don't know you they freeze up tighter'n the St Lawrence. When they *do*, they go out like an ice-jam in April. Up till we prisoners left – four days – my Captain Mankeltow told me pretty much all about himself there was; his mother and sisters, and his bad brother that was a trooper in some Colonial corps, and how his father didn't get on with him, and – well, everything, as I've said. They're undomesticated, the British, compared with us. They talk about their own family affairs as if they belonged to someone else. 'Tain't as if they hadn't any shame, but it sounds like it. I guess they talk out loud what we think, and we talk out loud what they think.

'I liked my Captain Mankeltow. I liked him as well as any man I'd ever struck. He was white. He gave me his silver drinking-flask, and I gave him the formula of my Laughtite. That's a hundred and fifty thousand dollars in his vest-pocket, on the lowest count, if he has the knowledge to use it. No, I didn't tell him the money-value. He was English. He'd send his valet to find out.

'Well, me and Adrian and a crowd of dam Dutchmen was sent down the road to Cape Town in first-class carriages under escort. (What did I think of your enlisted men? They are largely different from ours, Sir: very largely.) As I was saying, we slid down south, with Adrian looking out of the car-window and crying. Dutchmen cry mighty easy for a breed that fights as they do; but I never understood how a Dutchman could curse till we crossed into the Orange Free State Colony, and he lifted up his hand and cursed Steyn for a solid ten minutes. Then we got into the Colony, and the rebs – ministers mostly and schoolmasters – came round the cars with fruit and sympathy and texts. Van Zyl talked to 'em in Dutch, and one man, a big red-bearded minister, at Beaufort West, I remember, he jest wilted on the platform.

'"Keep your prayers for yourself," says Van Zyl, throwing back a bunch of grapes. "You'll need 'em, and you'll need the fruit too, when the war comes down here. *You* done it," he says. "You and your picayune Church that's deader than Cronje's dead horses! What sort of God have you been unloading on us, you black *aas vogels*? The British came, and we beat 'em," he says, "and you sat still and prayed. The British beat us, and you sat still," he says. "You told us to hang on, and we hung on, and our farms was burned, and you sat still – you and your God. See here," he says, "I shot my Bible full of bullets after Bloemfontein went, and you and God didn't say anything. Take it and pray over it before we Federals help the British to knock hell out of you rebels."

'Then I hauled him back into the car. I judged he'd had a fit. But life's curious – and sudden – and mixed. I hadn't any more use for a reb than Van Zyl, and I knew something of the lies they'd fed us up with from the Colony for a year and more. I told the minister to pull his freight out of that, and went on with my lunch, when another man come along and shook hands with Van Zyl. He'd known him at close range in the Kimberley siege and before. Van Zyl was well seen by his neighbours, I judge. As soon as this other man opened his mouth I said, "You're Kentucky, ain't you?" "I am," he says; "and what may you be?" I told him right off, for I was pleased to hear good United States in any man's mouth; but he whipped his hands behind him and said, "I'm not knowing any man that fights for a Tammany Dutchman. But I presoom you've been well paid, you dam gun-runnin' Yank."

'Well, Sir, I wasn't looking for that, and it near knocked me over, while old man Van Zyl started in to explain.

'"Don't you waste your breath, Mister Van Zyl," the man says. "I know this breed. The South's full of 'em." Then he whirls round on me and says, "Look at here, you Yank. A little think like a King's neither here nor there, but what *you've* done," he says, "is to go back on the White Man in six places at once – two hemispheres and four continents – America, England, Canada, Australia, New Zealand, and South Africa. Don't open your head," he says. "You know right well if you'd been caught at this game in our country you'd have been jiggling in the bight of a lariat before you could reach for your naturalization papers. Go on and prosper," he says, "and you'll fetch up by fighting for niggers, as the North did." And he threw me half-a-crown – English money.

'Sir, I do not regard the proposition in that light, but I guess I must have been somewhat shook by the explosion. They told me at Cape Town one rib was driven in on to my lungs. I am not adducing this as an excuse, but the cold God's truth of the matter is – the money on the floor did it ... I give up and cried. Put my head down and cried.

'I dream about this still sometimes. He didn't know the circumstances, but I dream about it. And it's Hell!

56

'How do you regard the proposition – as a Brother? If you'd invented your own gun, and spent fifty-seven thousand dollars on her – and had paid your own expenses from the word "go"? An American citizen has a right to choose his own side in an unpleasantness, and Van Zyl wasn't any Krugerite . . . and I'd risked my hide at my own expense. I got that man's address from Van Zyl; he was a mining man at Kimberley, and I wrote him the facts. But he never answered. Guess he thought I lied . . . Damned Southern rebel!

'Oh, say. Did I tell you my Captain gave me a letter to an English Lord in Cape Town, and he fixed things so's I could lie up a piece in his house? I was pretty sick, and threw up some blood from where the rib had gouged into the lung – here. This Lord was a crank on guns, and he took charge of the Zigler. He had his knife into the British system as much as any American. He said he wanted revolution, and not reform, in your army. He said the British soldier had failed in every point except courage. He said England needed a Monroe Doctrine worse than America – a new doctrine, barring out all the Continent, and strictly devoting herself to developing her own Colonies. He said he'd abolish half the Foreign Office, and take all the old hereditary families clean out of it, because, he said, they was expressly trained to fool around with continental diplomats, and to despise the Colonies. His own family wasn't more than six hundred years old. He was a very brainy man, and a good citizen. We talked politics and inventions together when my lung let up on me.

'Did he know my General? Yes. He knew 'em all. Called 'em Teddie and Gussie and Willie. They was all of the very best, and all his dearest friends; but he told me confidentially they was none of 'em fit to command a column in the field. He said they were too fond of advertising. Generals don't seem very different from actors or doctors or – yes, Sir – inventors.

'He fixed things for me lovelily at Simonstown. Had the biggest sort of pull – even for a Lord. At first they treated me as a harmless lunatic; but after a while I got 'em to let me keep some of their books. If I was left alone in the world with the British system of book-keeping, I'd reconstruct the whole British Empire – beginning with the Army. Yes, I'm one of their most trusted accountants, and I'm paid for it. As much as a dollar a day. I keep that. I've earned it, and I deduct it from the cost of my board. When the war's over I'm going to pay up the balance to the British Government. Yes, Sir, that's how I regard the proposition.

'Adrian? Oh, he left for Umballa four months back. He told me he was going to apply to join the National Scouts if the war didn't end in a year. 'Tisn't in nature for one Dutchman to shoot another, but if Adrian ever meets up with Steyn there'll be an exception to the rule. Ye-es, when the war's over it'll take some of the British Army to protect Steyn from his fellow-patriots. But the war won't be over yet a while. He that believeth don't hurry, as Isaiah says. The ministers and the school-teachers and the rebs 'll have a war all to themselves long after the north is quiet.

'I'm pleased with this country – it's big. Not so many folk on the ground as in America. There's a boom coming sure. I've talked it over with Adrian, and I guess I shall buy a farm somewhere near Bloemfontein and start in cattle-raising. It's big and peaceful – a ten-thousand-acre farm. I could go on inventing there, too. I'll sell my Zigler, I guess. I'll offer the patent rights to the British Government; and if they do the "reelly-now-how-interesting" act over her, I'll turn her over to Captain Mankeltow and his friend the Lord. They'll pretty quick find some Gussie, or Teddie, or Algie who can get her accepted in the proper quarters. I'm beginning to know my English.

'And now I'll go in swimming, and read the papers after lunch. I haven't had such a good time since Willie died.'

He pulled the blue shirt over his head as the bathers returned to their piles of clothing, and, speaking through the folds, added:

'But if you want to realize your assets, you should lease the whole proposition to America for ninety-nine years.'

❴ The Bonds of Discipline ❵

Poseidon's Law

When the robust and brass-bound man commissioned first for
sea
His fragile raft, Poseidon laughed, and, 'Mariner,' said he,
'Behold, a Law immutable I lay on thee and thine,
That never shall ye act or tell a falsehood at my shrine.

'Let Zeus adjudge your landward kin, whose votive meal and
salt
At easy-cheated altars win oblivion for the fault,
But ye the unhoodwinked waves shall test – the immediate
gulfs condemn –
Unless ye owe the Fates a jest, be slow to jest with them.

'Ye shall not clear by Greekly speech, nor cozen from your path
The twinkling shoal, the leeward beach, and Hadria's
white-lipped wrath;
Nor tempt with painted cloth for wood my fraud-avenging
hosts;
Nor make at all or all make good your bulwarks and your
boasts.

'Now and henceforward serve unshod through wet and wakeful
shifts,
A present and oppressive God, but take, to aid, my gifts –
The wide and windward-opened eye, the large and lavish hand,
The soul that cannot tell a lie – except upon the land!'

In dromond and in catafract – wet, wakeful, windward-eyed –
He kept Poseidon's Law intact (his ship and freight beside),
But, once discharged the dromond's hold, the bireme beached
once more,
Splendaciously mendacious rolled the brass-bound man ashore.

. . .

The thranite now and thalamite are pressures low and high,
And where three hundred blades bit white the twin-propellers
ply;
The God that hailed, the keel that sailed, are changed beyond
recall,
But the robust and brass-bound man he is not changed at all!

From Punt returned, from Phormio's Fleet, from Javan and
Gadire,
He strongly occupies the seat about the tavern fire,
And, moist with much Falernian or smoked Massilian juice,
Revenges there the brass-bound man his long-enforced truce!

The Bonds of Discipline

As literature, it is beneath contempt. It concerns the endurance,
armament, turning-circle, and inner gear of every ship in the
British Navy – the whole embellished with profile plates. The
Teuton approaches the matter with pagan thoroughness; the
Muscovite runs him close; but the Gaul, ever an artist, breaks
enclosure to study the morale, at the present day, of the British
sailorman.

In this, I conceive, he is from time to time aided by the
zealous amateur, though I find very little in his dispositions to
show that he relies on that amateur's hard-won information.
There exists – unlike some other publication, it is not bound in
lead boards – a work by one 'M. de C.', based on the absolutely
unadorned performances of one of our well-known *Acolyte*
type of cruisers. It contains nothing that did not happen. It
covers a period of two days; runs to twenty-seven pages of large
type exclusive of appendices; and carries as many exclamation
points as the average Dumas novel.

I read it with care, from the adorably finished prologue – it
is the disgrace of our Navy that we cannot produce a commissioned officer capable of writing one page of lyric prose –
to the eloquent, the joyful, the impassioned end; and my first
notion was that I had been cheated. In this sort of book-
collecting you will see how entirely the bibliophile lies at the
mercy of his agent.

'M. de C.', I read, opened his campaign by stowing away in
one of her boats what time H.M.S. *Archimandrite* lay off
Funchal. 'M. de C.' was, always on behalf of his country, a
Madeira Portuguese fleeing from the conscription. They discovered him eighty miles at sea and bade him assist the cook.
So far this seemed fairly reasonable. Next day, thanks to his
histrionic power and his ingratiating address, he was promoted
to the rank of 'supernumerary captain's servant' – a 'post

which,' I give his words, 'I flatter myself, was created for me alone, and furnished me with opportunities unequalled for a task in which one word malapropos would have been my destruction.'

From this point onward, earth and water between them held no marvels like to those 'M. de C.' had 'envisaged' – if I translate him correctly. It became clear to me that 'M. de C.' was either a pyramidal liar, or . . .

I was not acquainted with any officer, seaman, or marine in the *Archimandrite*; but instinct told me I could not go far wrong if I took a third-class ticket to Plymouth.

I gathered information on the way from a leading stoker, two seaman-gunners, and an odd hand in a torpedo factory. They courteously set my feet on the right path, and that led me through the alleys of Devonport to a public-house not fifty yards from the water. We drank with the proprietor, a huge, yellowish man called Tom Wessels; and when my guides had departed, I asked if he could produce any warrant or petty officer of the *Archimandrite*.

'The *Bedlamite*, d'you mean – 'er last commission, when they all went crazy?'

'Shouldn't wonder,' I replied. 'Fetch me a sample and I'll see.'

'You'll excuse me, o' course, but – what d'you want 'im *for*?'

'I want to make him drunk. I want to make you drunk – if you like. I want to make him drunk here.'

'Spoke very 'andsome. I'll do what I can.' He went out towards the water that lapped at the foot of the street. I gathered from the pot-boy that he was a person of influence beyond Admirals.

In a few minutes I heard the noise of an advancing crowd, and the voice of Mr Wessels.

' 'E only wants to make you drunk at 'is expense. Dessay 'e'll stand you all a drink. Come up an' look at 'im. 'E don't bite.'

A square man, with remarkable eyes, entered at the head of six large bluejackets. Behind them gathered a contingent of hopeful free-drinkers.

''E's the only one I could get. Transferred to the *Postulant* six months back. I found 'im quite accidental.' Mr Wessels beamed.

'I'm in charge o' the cutter. Our wardroom is dinin' on the beach *en masse*. They won't be home till mornin',' said the square man with the remarkable eyes.

'Are you an *Archimandrite*?' I demanded.

'That's me. I was, as you might say.'

'Hold on. I'm a *Archimandrite*.' A Red Marine with moist eyes tried to climb on the table. 'Was you lookin' for a *Bedlamite*? I've – I've been invalided, an' what with that, an' visitin' my family 'ome at Lewes, per'aps I've come late. 'Ave I?'

'You've 'ad all that's good for you,' said Tom Wessels, as the Red Marine sat cross-legged on the floor.

'There are those 'oo haven't 'ad a thing yet!' cried a voice by the door.

'I will take this *Archimandrite*,' I said, 'and this Marine. Will you please give the boat's crew a drink now, and another in half an hour if – if Mr –'

'Pyecroft,' said the square man. 'Emanuel Pyecroft, second-class petty-officer.'

'– Mr Pyecroft doesn't object?'

'He don't. Clear out. Goldin', you picket the hill by yourself, throwin' out a skirmishin'-line in ample time to let me know when Number One's comin' down from his vittles.'

The crowd dissolved. We passed into the quiet of the inner bar, the Red Marine zealously leading the way.

'And what do you drink, Mr Pyecroft?' I said.

'Only water. Warm water, with a little whisky an' sugar an' per'aps a lemon.'

'Mine's beer,' said the Marine. 'It always was.'

'Look 'ere, Glass. You take an' go to sleep. The picket'll be comin' for you in a little time, an' per'aps you'll 'ave slep' it off by then. What's your ship, now?' said Mr Wessels.

'The Ship o' State – most important?' said the Red Marine magnificently, and shut his eyes.

'That's right,' said Mr Pyecroft. 'He's safest where he is. An' now – here's santy to us all! – what d'you want o' me?'

'I want to read you something.'

'Tracts again!' said the Marine, never opening his eyes. 'Well.
I'm game . . . A little more 'ead to it, miss, please.'

'He thinks 'e's drinkin' – lucky beggar!' said Mr Pyecroft.
'I'm agreeable to be read to. 'Twon't alter my convictions. I
may as well tell you beforehand I'm a Plymouth Brother.'

He composed his face with the air of one in the dentist's
chair, and I began at the third page of 'M. de C.'.

'"*At the moment of asphyxiation, for I had hidden myself under
the boat's cover, I heard footsteps upon the superstructure and
coughed with empress*" – coughed loudly, Mr Pyecroft. "*By
this time I judged the vessel to be sufficiently far from land. A
number of sailors extricated me amid language appropriate to
their national brutality. I responded that I named myself Antonio, and that I sought to save myself from the Portuguese
conscription.*"

'Ho!' said Mr Pyecroft, and the fashion of his countenance
changed. Then pensively: 'Ther beggar! What might you have
in your hand there?'

'It's the story of Antonio – a stowaway in the *Archimandrite*'s
cutter. A French spy when he's at home, I fancy. What do *you*
know about it?'

'An' I thought it was tracts! An' yet some'ow I didn't.' Mr
Pyecroft nodded his head wonderingly. 'Our old man was quite
right – so was 'Op – so was I. Ere, Glass!' He kicked the
Marine. 'Here's our Antonio 'as written a impromptu book! He
was a spy all right.'

The Red Marine turned slightly, speaking with the awful
precision of the half-drunk. ''As 'e got anythin' in about my
'orrible death an' execution? Ex*c*use me, but if I open my eyes,
I shan't be well. That's where I'm different from *all* other
men. Ahem!'

'What about Glass's execution?' demanded Pyecroft.

'The book's in French,' I replied.

'Then it's no good to me.'

'Precisely. Now I want you to tell your story just as it
happened. I'll check it by this book. Take a cigar. I know about
his being dragged out of the cutter. What I want to know is

what was the meaning of all the other things, because they're unusual.'

'They were,' said Mr Pyecroft with emphasis. 'Lookin' back on it as I set here more an' more I see what an 'ighly unusual affair it was. But it happened. It transpired in the *Archimandrite* – the ship you can trust . . . Antonio! Ther beggar!'

'Take your time, Mr Pyecroft.'

In a few moments we came to it thus –

'The old man was displeased. I don't deny he was quite a little displeased. With the mail-boats trottin' into Madeira every twenty minutes, he didn't see why a lop-eared Portugee had to take liberties with a man-o'-war's first cutter. Any'ow, we couldn't turn ship round for him. We drew him out and took him to our Number One. "Drown 'im," 'e says. "Drown 'im before 'e dirties my fine new decks." But our owner was tender-hearted. "Take him to the galley," 'e says. "Boil 'im! Skin 'im! Cook 'im! Cut 'is bloomin' hair! Take 'is bloomin' number! We'll have him executed at Ascension."

'Retallick, our chief cook, an' a Carth'lic, was the on'y one any way near grateful; bein' short-'anded in the galley. He annexes the blighter by the left ear an' right foot an' sets him to work peelin' potatoes. So then, this Antonio that was avoidin' the conscription –'

'*Sub*scription, you pink-eyed matlow!' said the Marine, with the face of a stone Buddha, and whimpered sadly: 'Pye don't see any fun in it at all.'

'*Con*scription – come to his illegitimate sphere in Her Majesty's Navy, an' it was just then that Old 'Op, our Yeoman of Signals, an' a fastidious joker, made remarks to me about 'is hands.

'"Those 'ands," says 'Op, "properly considered, never done a day's honest labour in their life. Tell me those hands belong to a blighted Portugee manual labourist, and I won't call you a liar, but I'll say you an' the Admiralty are pretty much unique in your statements." 'Op was always a fastidious joker – in his language as much as anything else. He pursued 'is investigations with the eye of an 'awk outside the galley. He knew better than to advance line-head against Retallick, so he attacked *ong eshlong*,

speakin' his remarks as much as possible into the breech of the
starboard four point seven, an' 'ummin' to 'imself. Our chief
cook 'ated 'ummin'. "What's the matter of your bowels?" he
says at last, fistin' out the mess-pork agitated like.

'"Don't mind me," says 'Op. "I'm only a mildewed buntin'-
tosser," 'e says: "but speakin' for my mess, I do hope," 'e says,
"you ain't goin' to boil your Portugee friend's boots along o'
that pork you're smellin' so gay!"

'"Boots! Boots! Boots!" says Retallick, an' he run round
like a earwig in a alder-stalk. "Boots in the galley," 'e says.
"Cook's mate, cast out an' abolish this cutter-cuddlin' abori-
gine's boots!"'

'They was hove overboard in quick time, an' that was what
'Op was lyin' to for. As subsequently transpired.

'"Fine Arab arch to that cutter-cuddler's hinstep," he says to
me. "Run your eye over it, Pye," 'e says. "Nails all present an'
correct," 'e says. "Bunion on the little toe, too," 'e says; "which
comes from wearin' a tight boot. What do *you* think?"

'"Dook in trouble, per'aps," I says. "He ain't got the hang
of spud-skinnin'." No more he 'ad. 'E was simply cannibalizin'
'em.

'"I want to know what 'e 'as got the 'ang of," says 'Op,
obstructed-like. "Watch 'im," 'e says. "These shoulders were
foreign-drilled somewhere."

'When it comes to "Down 'ammicks!" which is our naval
way o' goin' to bye-bye, I took particular trouble over Antonio,
'oo had 'is 'ammick 'ove at 'im with general instructions to sling
it an' be sugared. In the ensuin' melly I pioneered him to the
after-'atch, which is a orifice communicatin' with the after-flat
an' similar suites of apartments. He havin' navigated at three-
fifths power immejit ahead o' me, *I* wasn't goin' to volunteer
any assistance, nor he didn't need it.

'"Mong Jew!" says 'e, sniffin' round. An' twice more,
"Mong Jew!" – which is pure French. Then he slings 'is
'ammick, nips in, an' coils down. "Not bad for a Portugee
conscript," I says to myself, casts off the tow, abandons him,
and reports to 'Op.

'About three minutes later I'm over'auled by our sub-lootenant, navigatin' under forced draught, with his bearin's 'eated. 'E had the temerity to say I'd instructed our Antonio to sling his carcass in the alleyway, an' 'e was peevish about it. O' course, I prevaricated like 'ell. You get to do that in the service. Nevertheless, to oblige Mr Ducane, I went an' readjusted Antonio. You may not 'ave ascertained that there are two ways o' comin' out of an 'ammick when it's cut down. Antonio came out t'other way – slidin' 'andsome to his feet. That showed me two things. First, 'e had been in an 'ammick before, an' next, he hadn't been asleep. Then I reproached 'im for goin' to bed where 'e'd been told to go, instead o' standin' by till someone gave him entirely contradictory orders. Which is the essence o' naval discipline.

'In the middle o' this argument the Gunner protrudes his ram-bow from 'is cabin, an' brings it all to an 'urried conclusion with some remarks suitable to 'is piebald warrant-rank. Navigatin' thence under easy steam, an' leavin' Antonio to re-sling his little foreign self, my large flat foot comes in detonatin' contact with a small objec' on the deck. Not 'altin' for the obstacle, nor changin' step, I shuffles it along under the ball of the big toe to the foot o' the hatchway, when, lightly stoopin', I catch it in my right hand and continue my evolutions in rapid time till I eventuates under 'Op's lee.

'It was a small moroccer-bound pocket-book, full of indelible pencil writin' – in French, for I could plainly discern the *doodeladays*, which is about as far as my education runs.

'"Op fists it open and peruses. 'E'd known an 'arf-caste Frenchwoman pretty intricate before he was married; when he was trained man in a stinkin' gunboat up the Saigon River. He understood a lot o' French – domestic brands chiefly – the kind that isn't in print.

'"Pye," he says to me, "you're a tattician o' no mean value. I am a trifle shady about the precise bearin' an' import' o' this beggar's private log here," 'e says, "but it's evidently a case for the owner. You'll 'ave your share o' the credit," 'e says.

'"Nay, nay, Pauline," I says. "You don't catch Emanuel Pyecroft mine-droppin' under any post-captain's bows," I says, "in search of honour," I says. "I've been there oft."

'"Well, if you must, you must," 'e says, takin' me up quick. "But I'll speak a good word for you, Pye."

'"You'll shut your mouth, 'Op," I says, "or you an' me'll part brass-rags. The owner has his duties, an' I have mine. We will keep station," I says, "nor seek to deviate."

'"Deviate to blazes!" says 'Op. "I'm goin' to deviate to the owner's comfortable cabin direct." So he deviated.'

Mr Pyecroft leaned forward and dealt the Marine a large-pattern Navy kick. ''Ere, Glass! You was sentry when 'Op went to the old man – the first time, with Antonio's washin'-book. Tell us what transpired. You're sober. You don't know how sober you are!'

The Marine cautiously raised his head a few inches. As Mr Pyecroft said, he was sober – after some R.M.L.I. fashion of his own devising. ''Op bounds in like a startled anteloper, carryin' 'is signal-slate at the ready. The old man was settin' down to 'is bountiful platter – not like you an' me, without anythin' more in sight for an 'ole night an' 'arf a day. Talkin' about food –'

'No! No! No!' cried Pyecroft, kicking again. 'What about 'Op?' I thought the Marine's ribs would have snapped, but he merely hiccupped.

'Oh, 'im! 'E 'ad it written all down on 'is little slate – I think – an' 'e shoves it under the old man's nose. "Shut the door," says 'Op. "For 'Eavin's sake shut the cabin door!" Then the old man must ha' said somethin' 'bout irons. "I'll put 'em on, Sir, in your very presence," says 'Op, "only 'ear my prayer," or – words to that 'fect . . . It was jus' the same with me when I called our Sergeant a bladder-bellied, lard-'eaded, perspirin' pension-cheater. They on'y put on the charge-sheet "words to that effect". Spoiled the 'ole 'fect.'

''Op! 'Op! 'Op! What about 'Op?' thundered Pyecroft.

''Op? Oh, shame thing. Words t' that 'fect. Door shut. Nushin' more transhpired till 'Op comes out – nose exshtreme angle plungin' fire – or words 'that effect. Proud's parrot. "Oh, you prou' old parrot," I says.'

Mr Glass seemed to slumber again.

'Lord! How a little moisture disintegrates, don't it? When we had ship's theatricals off Vigo, Glass 'ere played Dick Deadeye

to the moral, though of course the lower deck wasn't pleased to
see a leather-neck interpretin' a strictly maritime part, as you
might say. It's only his repartees, which 'e can't contain, that
conquers him. Shall I resume my narrative?'

Another drink was brought on this hint, and Mr Pyecroft
resumed.

'The essence o' strategy bein' forethought, the essence o'
tattics is surprise. Per'aps you didn't know that? My forethought 'avin' secured the initial advantage in attack, it remained
for the old man to ladle out the surprise-packets. 'Eavens!
What surprises! That night he dines with the wardroom, bein'
of the kind – I've told you as we were a 'appy ship? – that likes
it, and the wardroom liked it too. This ain't common in the
service. They had up the new Madeira – awful undisciplined
stuff which gives you a cordite mouth next morning. They told
the mess-men to navigate towards the extreme an' remote
'orizon, an' they abrogated the sentry about fifteen paces out of
earshot. Then they had in the Gunner, the Bo'sun, an' the
Carpenter, an' stood them large round drinks. It all come out
later – wardroom joints bein' lower-deck hash, as the sayin' is –
that our Number One stuck to it that 'e couldn't trust the ship
for the job. The old man swore 'e could, 'avin' commanded 'er
over two years. He was right. There wasn't a ship, I don't care
in what fleet, could come near the *Archimandrites* when we give
our mind to a thing. We held the cruiser big-gun records, the
sailing-cutter (fancy-rig) championship, an' the challenge-cup
row round the fleet. We 'ad the best nigger minstrels, the best
football an' cricket teams, an' the best squee-jee band of anything that ever pushed in front of a brace o' screws. An' *yet* our
Number One mistrusted us! 'E said we'd be a floatin' hell in a
week, an' it 'ud take the rest o' the commission to stop our way.
They was arguin' it in the wardroom when the bridge reports a
light three points off the port bow. We overtakes her, switches
on our search-light, an' she discloses herself as a collier o' no
mean reputation, makin' about seven knots on 'er lawful occasions – to the Cape most like.

'Then the owner – so we 'eard in good time – broke the
boom, springin' all mines together at close interval.

'"Look 'ere, my jokers," 'e says (I'm givin' the grist of 'is arguments, remember), "Number One says we can't enlighten this cutter-cuddlin' Gaulish lootenant on the manners an' customs o' the Navy without makin' the ship a market-garden. There's a lot in that," 'e says, "specially if we kept it up lavish, till we reached Ascension. But," 'e says, "the appearance o' this strange sail has put a totally new aspect on the game. We can run to just about one day's amusement for our friend, or else what's the good o' discipline? An' then we can turn 'im over to our presumably short-'anded fellow-subject in the small-coal line out yonder. He'll be pleased," says the old man, "an' so will Antonio. M'rover," he says to Number One, "I'll lay you a dozen o' liquorice an' ink" – it must ha' been that new tawny port – "that I've got a ship I can trust – for one day," 'e says. "Wherefore," he says, "will you have the extreme goodness to reduce speed as requisite for keepin' a proper distance behind this providential tramp till further orders?" Now, that's what I call tattics.

'The other manoeuvres developed next day, strictly in accordance with the plans as laid down in the wardroom, where they sat long an' steady. 'Op whispers to me that Antonio was a Number One spy when 'e was in commission, and a French lootenant when 'e was paid off, so I navigated at three 'undred and ninety-six revolutions to the galley, never 'avin' kicked a lootenant up to date. I may as well say that I did not manoeuvre against 'im as a Frenchman, because I like Frenchmen, but stric'ly on 'is rank an' ratin' in 'is own navy. I inquired after 'is health from Retallick.

'"Don't ask me," 'e says, sneerin' be'ind his silver spectacles. "'E's promoted to be captain's second supernumerary servant, to be dressed and addressed as such. If 'e does 'is dooties same as he skinned the spuds, *I* ain't for changin' with the old man."

'In the balmy dawnin' it was given out, all among the 'oly-stones, by our sub-lootenant, who was a three-way-discharge devil, that all orders after eight bells was to be executed in inverse ration to the cube o' the velocity. "The reg'lar routine," he says, 'was arrogated for reasons o' state an' policy, an' any flat-foot who presumed to exhibit surprise, annoyance, or amusement, would be slightly but firmly reproached." Then the Gunner mops up a heathenish large detail for some hanky-panky in the magazines, an' led 'em off along with our Gunnery Jack, which is to say, our Gunnery Lootenant.

'That put us on the *viva voce* – particularly when we understood how the owner was navigatin' abroad in his sword-belt trustin' us like brothers. We shifts into the dress o' the day, an' we musters, *an'* we prays *ong reggle*, an' we carries on anticipatory to bafflin' Antonio.

'Then our Sergeant of Marines come to me wringin' his 'ands an' weepin'. 'E'd been talkin' to the sub-lootenant, an' it looked like as if his upper-works were collapsin'.

'"I want a guarantee," 'e says, wringin' 'is 'ands like this. "*I* 'aven't 'ad sunstroke slave-dhowin' in Tajurrah Bay, an' been compelled to live on quinine an' chlorodyne ever since. *I* don't get the horrors off two glasses o' brown sherry."

'"What 'ave you got now?" I says.

'"*I* ain't an officer," 'e says. "*My* sword won't be handed back to me at the end o' the court-martial on account o' my little weaknesses, an' no stain on my character. I'm only a pore beggar of a Red Marine with eighteen years' service, an' why for," says he, wringin' 'is hands like this all the time, "must I chuck away my pension, sub-lootenant or no sub-lootenant? Look at 'em," he says, "only look at 'em. Marines fallin' in for small-arm drill!"

'The leather-necks was layin' aft at the double, an' a more insanitary set of accidents I never wish to behold. Most of 'em was in their shirts. They had their trousers on, of course – rolled up nearly to the knee, but what I mean is belts over shirts. Three or four 'ad *our* caps, an' them that had drawn helmets wore their chin-straps like Portugee earrings. Oh, yes; an' three of 'em 'ad only one boot! I knew what our bafflin' tattics was goin' to be, but even I was mildly surprised when this gay fantasia of Brazee drummers halted under the poop, because of an 'ammick in charge of our Navigator, an' a small but 'ighly efficient landin'-party.

'"'Ard astern both screws!" says the Navigator. "Room for the captain's 'ammick!" The captain's servant – Cockburn 'is name was – had one end, an' our newly promoted Antonio, in a blue slop rig, 'ad the other. They slung it from the muzzle of the port poop quick-firer thort-ships to a stanchion. Then the old man flickered up, smokin' a cigarette, an' brought 'is stern to an anchor slow an' oriental.

'"What a blessin' it is, Mr Ducane," 'e says to our sub-lootenant, "to be out o' sight o' the 'ole pack o' blighted admirals! What's an admiral after all?" 'e says. "Why, 'e's only a post-captain with the pip, Mr Ducane. The drill will now proceed. What O! Antonio, *descendez* an' get me a split."

'When Antonio came back with the whisky-an'-soda, he was told off to swing the 'ammick in slow time, an' that massacritin' small-arm party went on with their oratorio. The Sergeant had been kindly excused from participatin', an' he was jumpin' round on the poop-ladder, stretchin' 'is leather neck to see the disgustin' exhibition an' cluckin' like a ash-hoist. A lot of us went on the fore-an'-aft bridge an' watched 'em like "Listen to the Band in the Park". All these evolutions, I may as well tell you, are highly unusual in the Navy. After ten minutes o' muckin' about, Glass 'ere   pity 'e's so drunk! – says that 'e'd had enough exercise for 'is simple needs an' he wants to go 'ome. Mr Ducane catches him a sanakatowzer of a smite over the 'ead with the flat of his sword. Down comes Glass's rifle with language to correspond, and he fiddles with the bolt. Up jumps Maclean – 'oo was a Gosport 'ighlander – an' lands on Glass's neck, thus bringin' him to the deck, fully extended.

'The old man makes a great show o' wakin' up from sweet slumbers. "Mistah Ducane," he says, "what is this painful interregnum?" or words to that effect. Ducane takes one step to the front, an' salutes: "Only 'nother case of attempted assassination, Sir," he says.

'"Is that all?" says the old man, while Maclean sits on Glass's collar button. "Take him away," 'e says; "he knows the penalty."'

'Ah! I suppose that is the "invincible *morgue* Britannic in the presence of brutally provoked mutiny,"' I muttered, as I turned over the pages of M. de C.

'So, Glass, 'e was led off kickin' an' squealin', an' hove down the ladder into 'is Sergeant's volupshus arms. 'E run Glass forward, an' was all for puttin' 'im in irons as a maniac.

'"You refill your waterjacket and cool off!" says Glass, sittin' down rather winded. "The trouble with you is you haven't any imagination."

'"Haven't I? I've got the remnants of a little poor authority though," 'e says, lookin' pretty vicious.

'"You 'ave?" says Glass. "Then for pity's sake 'ave some proper feelin' too. I'm goin' to be shot this evenin'. You'll take charge o' the firin'-party."

'"Some'ow or other, that made the Sergeant froth at the mouth. 'E 'ad no more play to his intellects than a spit-kid. 'E just took everything as it come. Well, that was about all, I think . . . Unless you'd care to have me resume my narrative.'

We resumed on the old terms, but with rather less hot water. The marine on the floor breathed evenly, and Mr Pyecroft nodded.

'I may have omitted to inform you that our Number One took a general row round the situation while the small-arm party was at work, an' o' course he supplied the outlines; but the details we coloured in by ourselves. These were our tattics to baffle Antonio. It occurs to the Carpenter to 'ave the steam-cutter down for repairs. 'E gets 'is cheero-party together, an' down she comes. You've never seen a steam-cutter let down on the deck, 'ave you? It's not usual, an' she takes a lot o' humourin'. Thus we 'ave the starboard side completely blocked an' the general traffic tricklin' over'ead along the fore-an'-aft bridge. Then Chips gets into her an' begins balin' out a mess o' small reckonin's on the deck. Simultaneous there come up three o' those dirty engine-room objects which we call "tiffies", an' a stoker or two with orders to repair her steamin'-gadgets. *They* get into her an' bale out another young Christmas-treeful of small reckonin's – brass mostly. Simultaneous it hits the Pusser that 'e'd better serve out mess pork for the poor matlow. These things half shifted Retallick, our chief cook, off 'is bed-plate. Yes, you might say they broke 'im wide open. 'E wasn't at all used to 'em.

'Number One tells off five or six prime, able-bodied seamen-gunners to the pork barrels. You never see pork fisted out of its receptacle, 'ave you? Simultaneous, it hits the Gunner that now's the day an' now's the hour for a non-continuous class in Maxim instruction. So they all give way together, and the general effect was *non plus ultra*. There was the cutter's innards spread out like a Fratton pawnbroker's shop; there was the "tiffies" hammerin' in the stern of 'er, an' *they* ain't antiseptic; there was the Maxim-class in light skirmishin' order among the pork, an' forrard the blacksmith had 'is forge in full blast, makin' 'orse-shoes, I suppose. Well, that accounts for the starboard side. The on'y warrant officer 'oo hadn't a look in so far was the Bosun. So 'e stated, all out of 'is own 'ead, that Chips's reserve o' wood an' timber, which Chips 'ad stole at our last refit, needed restowin'. It was on the port booms – a young an' healthy forest of it, for Charley Peace wasn't to be named 'longside 'o Chips for burglary.

'"All right," says our Number One. "You can 'ave the whole port watch if you like. Hell's Hell," 'e says, "an' when there study to improve."

'Jarvis was our Bosun's name. He hunted up the 'ole of the port watch by hand, as you might say, callin' 'em by name loud an' lovin', which is not precisely Navy makee-pigeon. They 'ad that timber-loft off the booms, an' they dragged it up and down like so many sweatin' little beavers. But Jarvis was jealous o' Chips an' went round the starboard side to envy at him.

'"Tain't enough," 'e says, when he had climbed back. "Chips 'as got his bazaar lookin' like a coal-hulk in a cyclone. We must adop' more drastic measures." Off 'e goes to Number One and communicates with 'im. Number One got the old man's leave, on account of our goin' so slow (we were keepin' be'ind the tramp), to fit the ship with a full set of patent supernumerary sails. Four trysails – yes, you might call 'em trysails – was our Admiralty allowance in the un'eard-of event of a cruiser breakin' down, but we had our awnin's as well. They was all extricated from the various flats an' 'oles where they was stored, an' at the end o' two hours' hard work Number One 'e made out eleven sails o' different sorts and sizes. I don't know what exact nature of sail you'd call 'em – pyjama-stun'sles with a touch of Sarah's shimmy, per'aps — but the riggin' of 'em an' all the supernumerary details, as you might say, bein' carried on through an' over an' between the cutter an' the forge an' the pork an' cleanin' guns, an' the Maxim class an' the Bosun's calaboose *and* the paintwork, was sublime. There's no other word for it. Sub-lime!

'The old man keeps swimmin' up an' down through it all with the faithful Antonio at 'is side, fetchin' him numerous splits. 'E had eight that mornin', an' when Antonio was detached to get 'is spy-glass, or his gloves, or his lily-white 'andkerchief, the old man would waste 'em down a ventilator. Antonio must ha' learned a lot about our Navy thirst.'

'He did.'

'Ah! Would you kindly mind turnin' to the precise page indicated an' givin' me a *résumé* of 'is tattics?' said Mr Pyecroft, drinking deeply. 'I'd like to know 'ow it looked from 'is side o' the deck.'

'How will this do?' I said. '"*Once clear of the land, like Voltaire's Habakkuk —*"'

'One o' their new commerce-destroyers, I suppose,' Mr Pyecroft interjected.

'"*— each man seemed veritably capable of all — to do according to his will. The boats, dismantled and forlorn, are lowered upon the planking. One cries 'Aid me!' flourishing at the same time the weapons of his business. A dozen launch themselves upon him in the orgasm of zeal misdirected. He beats them off with the howlings of dogs. He has lost a hammer. This ferocious outcry signifies that only. Eight men seek the utensil, colliding on the way with some many others which, seated in the stern of the boat, tear up and scatter upon the planking the ironwork which impedes their brutal efforts. Elsewhere, one detaches from on high wood, canvas, iron bolts, coal-dust — what do I know?*"'

'That's where 'e's comin' the bloomin' *onjenew*. 'E knows a lot, reely.'

'"*They descend thundering upon the planking, and the spectacle cannot reproduce itself. In my capacity of valet to the captain, whom I have well and beautifully plied with drink since the rising of the sun (behold me also, Ganymede!), I pass throughout observing, it may be not a little. They ask orders. There is none to*

*give them. One sits upon the edge of the vessel and chants inter-
minably the lugubrious 'Roule Britannia' – to endure how long?"'*

'That was me! On'y 'twas "A Life on the Ocean Wave" –
which I hate more than any stinkin' tune I know, havin' dragged
too many nasty little guns to it. Yes, Number One told me off
to that for ten minutes; an' I ain't musical, you might say."

'"*Then come marines, half-dressed, seeking vainly through this
'tohu-bohu'*"' (that's one of his names for the *Archimandrite*, Mr
Pyecroft) "*for a place whence they shall not be dislodged. The
captain, heavy with drink, rolls himself from his hammock. He
would have his people fire the Maxims. They demand which
Maxim. That to him is equal. The breech-lock indispensable is not
there. They demand it of one who opens a barrel of pork, for this
Navy feeds at all hours. He refers them to the cook, yesterday my
master –*"'

'Yes, an' Retallick nearly had a fit. What a truthful an'
observin' little Antonio we 'ave!'

'"*It is discovered in the hands of a boy who says, and they do
not rebuke him, that he has found it by hazard.*" I'm afraid I
haven't translated quite correctly, Mr Pyecroft, but I've done
my best.'

'Why, it's beautiful – you ought to be a Frenchman – you
ought. You don't want anything o' *me*. You've got it all there.'

'Yes, but I like your side of it. For instance. Here's a little
thing I can't quite see the end of. Listen! "*Of this domain which
Britannia rules by sufferance, my gross captain knew nothing, and
his Navigator, if possible, less. From the bestial recriminations and
the indeterminate chaos of the grand deck, I ascended – always
with a whisky-and-soda in my hands – to a scene truly grotesque.
Behold, my captain in plain sea, at issue with his Navigator! A
crisis of nerves due to the enormous quantity of alcohol which he
had swallowed up to then, has filled for him the ocean with dangers,
imaginary and fantastic. Incapable of judgment, menaced by the
phantasms of his brain inflamed, he envisages islands perhaps of the
Hesperides, beneath his keel – vigias innumerable.*" I don't know
what a vigia is, Mr Pyecroft. "*He creates shoals sad and far-
reaching of the mid-Atlantic!*" What was that, now?'

'Oh, I see! That come after dinner, when our Navigator

threw 'is cap down an' danced on it. Danby was quartermaster. They 'ad a tea-party on the bridge. It was the old man's contribution. Does he say anything about the leadsmen?'

'Is this it? *"Overborne by his superior's causeless suspicion, the Navigator took off the badges of his rank and cast them at the feet of my captain and sobbed. A disgusting and maudlin reconciliation followed. The argument renewed itself, each grasping the wheel, crapulous"* (that means drunk, I think, Mr Pyecroft), *"shouting. It appeared that my captain would chenaler"* (I don't know what that means, Mr Pyecroft) *"to the Cape. At the end, he placed a sailor with the sound"* (that's the lead, I think) *"in his hand, garnished with suet."* Was it garnished with suet?'

'He put two leadsmen in the chains, o' course! He didn't know that there mightn't be shoals there, 'e said. Morgan went an' armed his lead, to enter into the spirit o' the thing. They 'eaved it for twenty minutes, but there wasn't any suet – only tallow, o' course.'

'*"Garnished with suet at two thousand metres of profundity. Decidedly the Britannic Navy is well guarded."* Well, that's all right, Mr Pyecroft. Would you mind telling me anything else of interest that happened?'

'There was a good deal, one way an' another. I'd like to know what this Antonio thought of our sails.'

'He merely says that *"the engines having broken down, an officer extemporized a mournful and useless parody of sails"*. Oh, yes! he says that some of them looked like *"bonnets in a needlecase"*, I think.'

'Bonnets in a needlecase! They were stun'sles. That shows the beggar's no sailor. That trick was really the one thing we did. Pho! I thought he was a sailorman, an' 'e hasn't sense enough to see what extemporizin' eleven good an' drawin' sails out o' four trys'les an' a few awnin's means. 'E must have been drunk!'

'Never mind, Mr Pyecroft. I want to hear about your target-practice, and the execution.'

'Oh! We had a special target-practice that afternoon all for Antonio. As I told my crew – me bein' captain of the port-bow quick-firer, though I'm a torpedo man now – it just showed

how you can work your gun under any discomforts. A shell –
twenty six-inch shells – burstin' inboard couldn't 'ave begun to
make the varicose collection o' tit-bits which we had spilled on
our deck. It was a lather – a rich, creamy lather!

'We took it very easy – that gun-practice. We did it in a
complimentary "Jenny-'ave-another-cup-o'-tea" style, an' the
crews was strictly ordered not to rupture 'emselves with unnecessary exertion. This isn't our custom in the Navy when
we're *in puris naturalibus*, as you might say. But we wasn't so
then. We was impromptu. An' Antonio was busy fetchin' splits
for the old man and the old man was wastin' 'em down the
ventilators. There must 'ave been four inches in the bilges, I
should think – wardroom whisky-an'-soda.

'Then I thought I might as well bear a hand as look pretty.
So I let my *bundoop* go at fifteen 'undred – sightin' very
particular. There was a sort of 'appy little belch like – no more,
I give you my word – an' the shell trundled out maybe fifty
feet an' dropped into the deep Atlantic.

'"Government powder, Sir!" sings out our Gunnery Jack to
the bridge, laughin' horrid sarcastic; an' then, of course, we all
laughs, which we are not encouraged to do *in puris naturalibus*.
Then, of course, I saw what our Gunnery Jack 'ad been after
with his subcutaneous details in the magazines all the mornin'
watch. He had redooced the charges to a minimum, as you
might say. But it made me feel a trifle faint an' sickish not-
withstandin', this spit-in-the-eye business. Every time such
transpired, our Gunnery Lootenant would say somethin' sarcastic about Government stores, an' the old man fair howled.
'Op was on the bridge with 'im, an' 'e told me – 'cause he's a
free-knowledge-ist an' reads character – that Antonio's face
was sweatin' with pure joy. 'Op wanted to kick him. Does
Antonio say anything about that?'

'Not about the kicking, but he is great on the gun-practice,
Mr Pyecroft. He has put all the results into a sort of appendix –
a table of shots. He says that the figures will speak more elo-
quently than words.'

'What? Nothin' about the way the crews flinched an' hopped?
Nothin' about the little shells rumblin' out o' the guns so casual?'

'There are a few pages of notes, but they only bear out what you say. He says that these things always happen as soon as one of our ships is out of sight of land. Oh, yes! I've forgotten. He says, "*From the conversation of my captain with his inferiors I gathered that no small proportion of the expense of these nominally efficient cartridges finds itself in his pockets. So much, indeed, was signified by an officer on the deck below, who cried in a high voice: 'I hope, Sir, you are making something out of it. It is rather monotonous.' This insult, so flagrant, albeit well merited, was received with a smile of drunken bonhommy*" – that's cheerfulness, Mr Pyecroft. Your glass is empty.'

'Resumin' afresh,' said Mr Pyecroft, after a well-watered interval, 'I may as well say that the target-practice occupied us two hours, and then we had to dig out after the tramp. Then we half an' three-quarters cleaned up the decks an' mucked about as requisite, haulin' down the patent awnin' stun'sles which Number One 'ad made. The old man was a shade doubtful of his course, 'cause I 'eard him say to Number One, "You were right. A week o' this would turn the ship into a Hayti bean-feast. But," he says pathetic, "haven't they backed the band noble?"

'"Oh! it's a picnic for them," says Number One. "But when do we get rid o' this whisky-peddlin' blighter o' yours, Sir?"

'"That's a cheerful way to speak of a *Vis*count," says the old man. "'E's the bluest blood o' France when he's at home."

'"Which is the precise landfall I wish 'im to make," says Number One. "It'll take all 'ands and the Captain of the Head to clean up after 'im."

'"They won't grudge it," says the old man. "Just as soon as it's dusk we'll overhaul our tramp friend an' waft him over."

'Then a sno – midshipman – Moorshed was 'is name – came up an' says somethin' in a low voice. It fetches the old man.

'"You'll oblige me," 'e says, "by takin' the wardroom poultry for *that*. I've ear-marked every fowl we've shipped at Madeira, so there can't be any possible mistake. M'rover," 'e says, "tell 'em if they spill one drop of blood on the deck," he says, "they'll not be extenuated, but hung."

'Mr Moorshed goes forward, lookin' unusual 'appy, even for

79

him. The Marines was enjoyin' a committee-meetin' in their own flat.

'After that, it fell dark, with just a little streaky, oily light on the sea – an' anythin' more chronic than the *Archimandrite* I'd trouble you to behold. She looked like a fancy bazaar and a auction-room – yes, she almost looked like a passenger-steamer. We'd picked up our tramp, an' was about four mile be'ind 'er. I noticed the wardroom as a class, you might say, was manoeuvrin' *en masse*, an' then come the order to cock-bill the yards. We hadn't any yards except a couple o' signallin' sticks, but we cock-billed 'em. I hadn't seen that sight, not since thirteen years in the West Indies, when a post-captain died o' yellow jack. It means a sign o' mournin', the yards bein' canted opposite ways, to look drunk an' disorderly. They do.

'"An' what might our last giddy-go-round signify?" I asks of 'Op.

'"Good 'Evins!" 'e says. "Are you in the habit o' permittin' leather-necks to assassinate lootenants every morning at drill without immejitly 'avin' 'em shot on the foc'sle in the horrid crawly-crawly twilight?"'

'"Yes," I murmured over my dear book, "*the infinitely lugubrious crepuscule. A spectacle of barbarity unparalleled – hideous – cold-blooded, and yet touched with appalling grandeur.*"'

'Ho! Was that the way Antonio looked at it? That shows he 'ad feelin's. To resoom. Without anyone givin' us orders to that effect, we began to creep about an' whisper. Things got stiller and stiller, till they was as still as – mushrooms! Then the bugler let off the "Dead March" from the upper bridge. He done it to cover the remarks of a cock-bird bein' killed forrard, but it came out paralysin' in its *tout ensemble*. You never heard the "Dead March" on a bugle? Then the pipes went twitterin' for both watches to attend public execution, an' we came up like so many ghosts, the 'ole ship's company. Why, Mucky 'Arcourt, one o' our boys, was that took in he give tongue like a beagle-pup, an' was properly kicked down the ladder for so doin'. Well, there we lay – engines stopped, rollin' to the swell, all dark, yards cock-billed, an' that merry tune yowlin' from the upper bridge. We fell in on the foc'sle, leavin' a large open space by the capstan, where our sail-maker was sittin' sewin' broken firebars into the foot of an old 'ammick. 'E looked like a corpse, an' Mucky had another fit o' hysterics, an' you could 'ear us breathin' 'ard. It beat anythin' in the theatrical line that even us *Archimandrites* had done – an' we was the ship you could trust. Then came the doctor an' lit a red lamp which he used for his photographic muckin's, an' chocked it on the capstan. That was finally gashly!

'Then come twelve Marines guardin' Glass 'ere. You wouldn't think to see 'im what a gratooitous an' aboundin' terror he was that evenin'. 'E was in a white shirt 'e'd stole from Cockburn, an' his regulation trousers, bare-footed. 'E'd pipe-clayed 'is 'ands an' face an' feet an' as much of his chest as the openin' of his shirt showed. 'E marched under escort with a firm an' undeviatin' step to the capstan, an' came to attention. The old man, reinforced by an extra strong split – his seventeenth, an' 'e didn't throw *that* down the ventilator – come up on the bridge an' stood like a image. 'Op, 'oo was with 'im, says that 'e heard Antonio's teeth singin', not chatterin' – singin' like funnel-stays in a typhoon. Yes, a moanin' aeolian harp, 'Op said.

'"When you are ready, Sir, drop your 'andkerchief," Number One whispers.

'"Good Lord!" says the old man, with a jump. "Eh! What? What a sight! What a sight!" an' he stood drinkin' it in, I suppose, for quite two minutes.

'Glass never says a word. 'E shoved aside an 'andkerchief which the sub-lootenant proffered 'im to bind 'is eyes with – quiet an' collected; an' if we 'adn't been feelin' so very much as we did feel, his gestures would 'ave brought down the 'ouse.'

'I can't open my eyes, or I'll be sick,' said the Marine with appalling clearness. 'I'm pretty far gone – I know it – but there wasn't anyone could 'ave beaten Edwardo Glass, R.M.L.I., that time. Why, I scared myself nearly into the 'orrors. Go on, Pye. Glass is in support – as ever.'

'Then the old man drops 'is 'andkerchief, an' the firin' party fires like one man. Glass drops forward, twitchin' an' 'eavin' horrid natural, into the shotted 'ammick all spread out before

81

'im, and the firin' party closes in to guard the remains of the deceased while Sails is stitchin' it up. An' when they lifted that 'ammick it was one wringin' mess o' blood! They on'y expended one wardroom cock-bird, too. Did you know poultry bled that extravagant? *I* never did.

'The old man – so 'Op told me – stayed on the bridge, brought up on a dead centre. Number One was similarly, though lesser, impressed, but o' course 'is duty was to think of 'is fine white decks an' the blood. "Arf a mo', Sir," he says, when the old man was for leavin'. "We have to wait for the burial, which I am informed takes place immejit."

'"It's beyond me," says the owner. "There was general instructions for an execution, but I never knew I had such a dependable push of mountebanks aboard," he says. "I'm all cold up my back, still."

'The Marines carried the corpse below. Then the bugle give us some more "Dead March". Then we 'eard a splash from a bow six-pounder port, an' the bugle struck up a cheerful tune. The whole lower deck was complimentin' Glass, 'oo took it very meek. 'E *is* a good actor, for all 'e's a leather-neck.

'"Now," said the old man, "we must turn over Antonio. He's in what I have 'eard called one perspirin' funk."

'Of course, I'm tellin' it slow, but it all 'appened much quicker. We run down our trampo – without o' course informin' Antonio of 'is 'appy destiny – an' inquired of 'er if she had any use for a free and gratis stowaway. Oh, yes! she said she'd be highly grateful, but she seemed a shade puzzled at our generosity, as you might put it, an' we lay by till she lowered a boat. Then Antonio – who was un'appy, distinctly un'appy – was politely requested to navigate elsewhere, which I don't think he looked for. 'Op was deputed to convey the information, an' 'Op got in one sixteen-inch kick which 'oisted 'im all up the ladder. 'Op ain't really vindictive, an' 'e's fond of the French, especially the women, but his chances o' kicking lootenants was like the cartridge – reduced to a minimum.

'The boat 'adn't more than shoved off before a change, as you might say, came o'er the spirit of our dream. The old man says, like Elphinstone an' Bruce in the Portsmouth election when I was a boy: "Gentlemen," he says, "for gentlemen you have shown yourselves to be – from the bottom of my heart I thank you. The status an' position of our late lamented shipmate made it obligato," 'e says, "to take certain steps not strictly included in the regulations. An' nobly," says 'e, "have you assisted me. Now," 'e says, "you hold the false and felonious reputation of bein' the smartest ship in the Service. Pigsties," 'e says, "is plane trigonometry alongside our present disgustin' state. Efface the effects of this indecent orgy," he says. "Jump, you lop-eared, flat-footed, butter-backed Amalekites! Dig out, you briny-eyed beggars!"

'Do captains talk like that in the Navy, Mr Pyecroft?' I asked.

'I've told you once I only give the grist of his arguments. The Bosun's mate translates it to the lower deck, as you may put it, and the lower deck springs smartly to attention. It took us half the night 'fore we got 'er anyway ship-shape; but by sunrise she was beautiful as ever, an' we resoomed. I've thought it over a lot since; yes, an' I've thought a lot of Antonio trimmin' coal in that tramp's bunkers. 'E must 'ave been highly surprised. Wasn't he?'

'He was, Mr Pyecroft,' I responded. 'But now we're talkin' of it, weren't you all a little surprised?'

'It come as a pleasant relief to the regular routine,' said Mr Pyecroft. 'We appreciated it as an easy way o' workin' for your country. But – the old man was right – a week o' similar manoeuvres would 'ave knocked our moral double-bottoms bung out. Now, couldn't you oblige with Antonio's account of Glass's execution?'

I obliged for nearly ten minutes. It was at best but a feeble rendering of M. de C.'s magnificent prose, through which the soul of the poet, the eye of the mariner, and the heart of the patriot bore magnificent accord. His account of his descent from the side of the *infamous vessel consecrated to blood* in the *vast and gathering dusk of the trembling ocean* could only be matched by his description of the dishonoured hammock sinking unnoticed through the depths, while, above, the bugler played music *of an indefinable brutality*.

'By the way, what did the bugler play after Glass's funeral?'
I asked.

'Him? Oh! 'e played "The Strict Q.T.". It's a very old song.
We 'ad it in Fratton nearly fifteen years back,' said Mr Pyecroft
sleepily.

I stirred the sugar dregs in my glass. Suddenly entered armed
men, wet and discourteous, Tom Wessels smiling nervously in
the background.

'Where is that – minutely particularized person – Glass?'
said the sergeant of the picket.

''Ere!' The marine rose to the strictest of attentions. 'An' it's
no good smellin' of my breath, because I'm strictly an' ruinously
sober.'

'Oh! An' what may you have been doin' with yourself?'

'Listenin' to tracts. You can look! I've 'ad the evenin' of my
little life. Lead on to the *Cornucopia*'s midmost dunjing-cell.
There's a crowd of brass-'atted blighters there which will say
I've been absent without leaf. Never mind. I forgive 'em before'and. *The* evenin' of my life, an' please don't forget it.'
Then in a tone of most ingratiating apology to me: 'I soaked it
all in be'ind my shut eyes. 'Im' – he jerked a contemptuous
thumb towards Mr Pyecroft – ''e's a flat-foot, a indigo-blue
matlow. 'E never saw the fun from first to last. A mournful
beggar – most depressin'.' Private Glass departed, leaning
heavily on the escort's arm.

Mr Pyecroft wrinkled his brows in thought – the profound
and far-reaching meditation that follows five glasses of hot
whisky-and-water.

'Well, I don't see anything comical – greatly – except here
an' there. Specially about those redooced charges in the guns.
Do *you* see anything funny in it?'

There was that in his eye which warned me the night was too
wet for argument.

'No, Mr Pyecroft, I don't,' I replied. 'It was a beautiful tale,
and I thank you very much.'

{ A Sahibs' War }

The Runners

News!
What is the word that they tell now – now – now!
The little drums beating in the bazaars?
 They beat (among the buyers and the sellers)
  'Nimrud – ah Nimrud!
  God sends a gnat against Nimrud!'
Watchers, O Watchers a thousand!

News!
At the edge of the crops – now – now – where the well-wheels
          are halted,
One prepares to loose the bullocks and one scrapes his hoe,
 They beat (among the sowers and the reapers)
  'Nimrud – ah Nimrud!
  God prepares an ill day for Nimrud!'
Watchers, O Watchers ten thousand.

News!
By the fires of the camps – now – now – where the travellers
          meet,
Where the camels come in and the horses: their men conferring,
 They beat (among the packmen and the drivers)
  'Nimrud – ah Nimrud!
  Thus it befell last noon to Nimrud!'
Watchers, O Watchers an hundred thousand!

News!
Under the shadow of the border-peels – now – now – now!
In the rocks of the passes where the expectant shoe their horses,
 They beat (among the rifles and the riders)

85

    'Nimrud – ah Nimrud!
    Shall we go up against Nimrud?'
Watchers, O Watchers a thousand thousand!

       News!
Bring out the heaps of grain – open the account-books again!
Drive forward the well-bullocks against the taxable harvest!
Eat and lie under the tree, – pitch the police-guarded
                         fair-grounds, O dancers!
Hide away the rifles and let down the ladders from the
                           watch-towers!

    They beat (among all the peoples)
    'Now – now – now!
    God has reserved the Sword for Nimrud!
    God has given Victory to Nimrud!
    Let us abide under Nimrud!'
O Well-disposed and Heedful, an hundred thousand
                           thousand!

A Sahibs' War

Pass? Pass? Pass? I have one pass already, allowing me to go by the *rêl* from Kroonstadt to Eshtellenbosch, where the horses are, where I am to be paid off, and whence I return to India. I am a – trooper of the Gurgaon Rissala (cavalry regiment), the One Hundred and Forty-first Punjab Cavalry. Do not herd me with these black Kaffirs. I am a Sikh – a trooper of the State. The Lieutenant-Sahib does not understand my talk? Is there *any* Sahib on this train who will interpret for a trooper of the Gurgaon Rissala going about his business in this devil's devising of a country, where there is no flour, no oil, no spice, no red pepper, and no respect paid to a Sikh? Is there no help? ... God be thanked, here is such a Sahib! Protector of the Poor! Heaven-born! Tell the young Lieutenant-Sahib that my name is Umr Singh; I am – I was servant to Kurban Sahib, now dead; and I have a pass to go to Eshtellenbosch, where the horses are. Do not let him herd me with these black Kaffirs! ... Yes, I will sit by this truck till the Heaven-born has explained the matter to the young Lieutenant-Sahib who does not understand our tongue.

What orders? The young Lieutenant-Sahib will not detain me? Good! I go down to Eshtellenbosch by the next *terain*? Good! I go with the Heaven-born? Good! Then for this day I am the Heaven-born's servant. Will the Heaven-born bring the honour of his presence to a seat? Here is an empty truck; I will spread my blanket over one corner thus – for the sun is hot, though not so hot as our Punjab in May. I will prop it up thus, and I will arrange this hay thus, so the Presence can sit at ease till God sends us a *terain* for Eshtellenbosch ...

The Presence knows the Punjab? Lahore? Amritzar? Attaree, belike? My village is north over the fields three miles from Attaree, near the big white house which was copied from a

certain place of the Great Queen's by – by – I have forgotten
the name. Can the Presence recall it? Sirdar Dyal Singh Attareewalla! Yes, that is the very man; but how does the Presence
know? Born and bred in Hind, was he? O-o-oh! This is quite a
different matter. The Sahib's nurse was a Surtee woman from
the Bombay side? That was a pity. She should have been an up-
country wench; for those make stout nurses. There is no land
like the Punjab. There are no people like the Sikhs. Umr Singh
is my name, yes. An old man? Yes. A trooper only after all
these years? Ye-es. Look at my uniform, if the Sahib doubts.
Nay – nay; the Sahib looks too closely. All marks of rank were
picked off it long ago, but – but it is true – mine is not a
common cloth such as troopers use for their coats, and – the
Sahib has sharp eyes – that black mark is such a mark as a silver
chain leaves when long worn on the breast. The Sahib says that
troopers do not wear silver chains? No-o. Troopers do not wear
the Arder of Beritish India? No. The Sahib should have been
in the Police of the Punjab. I am not a trooper, but I have been
a Sahib's servant for nearly a year – bearer, butler, sweeper, any
and all three. The Sahib says that Sikhs do not take menial
service? True; but it was for Kurban Sahib – my Kurban Sahib
– dead these three months!

Young – of a reddish face – with blue eyes, and he lilted a little
on his feet when he was pleased, and cracked his finger-joints.
So did his father before him, who was Deputy-Commissioner of
Jullundur in my father's time when I rode with the Gurgaon
Rissala. *My* father? Jwala Singh. A Sikh of Sikhs – he fought
against the English at Sobraon and carried the mark to his
death. So we were knit as it were by a blood-tie, I and my
Kurban Sahib. Yes, I was a trooper first – nay, I had risen to a
Lance-Duffadar, I remember – and my father gave me a dun
stallion of his own breeding on that day; and *he* was a little
baba, sitting upon a wall by the parade-ground with his ayah –
all in white, Sahib – laughing at the end of our drill. And his
father and mine talked together, and mine beckoned to me, and
I dismounted, and the baba put his hand into mine – eighteen –
twenty-five – twenty-seven years gone now – Kurban Sahib –

my Kurban Sahib! Oh, we were great friends after that! He cut
his teeth on my sword-hilt, as the saying is. He called me Big
Umr Singh – Buwwa Umwa Singh, for he could not speak
plain. He stood only this high, Sahib, from the bottom of this
truck, but he knew all our troopers by name – every one ...
And he went to England, and he became a young man, and
back he came, lilting a little in his walk, and cracking his finger-
joints – back to his own regiment and to me. He had not
forgotten either our speech or our customs. He was a Sikh at
heart, Sahib. He was rich, open-handed, just, a friend of poor
troopers, keen-eyed, jestful, and careless. *I* could tell tales about
him in his first years. There was very little he hid from *me*. I
was his Umr Singh, and when we were alone he called me
Father, and I called him Son. Yes, that was how we spoke. We
spoke freely together on everything – about war, and women,
and money, and advancement, and such all.

We spoke about this war, too, long before it came. There
were many box-wallas, pedlars, with Pathans a few, in this
country, notably at the city of Yunasbagh (Johannesburg), and
they sent news in every week how the Sahibs lay without
weapons under the heel of the Boer-log; and how big guns were
hauled up and down the streets to keep Sahibs in order; and
how a Sahib called Eger Sahib (Edgar?) was killed for a jest by
the Boer-log. The Sahib knows how we of Hind hear all that
passes over the earth? There was not a gun cocked in Yunasbagh
that the echo did not come into Hind in a month. The Sahibs
are very clever, but they forget their own cleverness has created
the *dak* (the post), and that for an anna or two all things
become known. We of Hind listened and heard and wondered;
and when it was a sure thing, as reported by the pedlars and the
vegetable-sellers, that the Sahibs of Yunasbagh lay in bondage
to the Boer-log, certain among us asked questions and waited
for signs. Others of us mistook the meaning of those signs.
Wherefore, Sahib, came the long war in the Tirah! This Kurban
Sahib knew, and we talked together. He said, 'There is no
haste. Presently we shall fight, and we shall fight for all Hind
in that country round Yunasbagh.' Here he spoke truth. Does
the Sahib not agree? Quite so. It is for Hind that the Sahibs

are fighting this war. Ye cannot in one place rule and in another bear service. Either ye must everywhere rule or everywhere obey. God does not make the nations ringstraked. True – true – true!

So did matters ripen – a step at a time. It was nothing to me, except I think – and the Sahib sees this, too? – that it is foolish to make an army and break their hearts in idleness. Why have they not sent for the men of the Tochi – the men of the Tirah – the men of Buner? Folly, a thousand times. *We* could have done it all so gently – so gently.

Then, upon a day, Kurban Sahib sent for me and said, 'Ho, Dada, I am sick, and the doctor gives me a certificate for many months.' And he winked, and I said, 'I will get leave and nurse thee, Child. Shall I bring my uniform?' He said, 'Yes, and a sword for a sick man to lean on. We go to Bombay, and thence by sea to the country of the Hubshis' (niggers). Mark his cleverness! He was first of all our men among the native regiments to get leave for sickness and to come here. Now they will not let our officers go away, sick or well, except they sign a bond not to take part in this war-game upon the road. But *he* was clever. There was no whisper of war when he took his sick-leave. I came also? Assuredly. I went to my Colonel, and sitting in the chair (I am – I was – of that rank for which a chair is placed when we speak with the Colonel) I said, 'My child goes sick. Give me leave, for I am old and sick also.'

And the Colonel, making the word double between English and our tongue, said, 'Yes, thou art truly *Sikh*'; and he called me an old devil – jestingly, as one soldier may jest with another; and he said Kurban Sahib was a liar as to his health (that was true, too), and at long last he stood up and shook my hand, and bade me go and bring my Sahib safe again. My Sahib back again – aie me!

So I went to Bombay with Kurban Sahib, but there, at sight of the Black Water, Wajib Ali, his bearer, checked, and said that his mother was dead. Then I said to Kurban Sahib, 'What is one Mussulman pig more or less? Give me the keys of the trunks, and I will lay out the white shirts for dinner.' Then I beat Wajib Ali at the back of Watson's Hotel, and that night I prepared Kurban Sahib's razors. I say, Sahib, that I, a Sikh of the Khalsa, an unshorn man, prepared the razors. But I did not put on my uniform while I did it. On the other hand, Kurban Sahib took for me, upon the steamer, a room in all respects like to his own, and would have given me a servant. We spoke of many things on the way to this country; and Kurban Sahib told me what he perceived would be the conduct of the war. He said, 'They have taken men afoot to fight men ahorse, and they will foolishly show mercy to these Boer-log because it is believed that they are white.' He said, 'There is but one fault in this war, and that is that the Government have not employed *us*, but have made it altogether a Sahibs' war. Very many men will thus be killed, and no vengeance will be taken.' True talk – true talk! It fell as Kurban Sahib foretold.

And we came to this country, even to Cape Town over yonder, and Kurban Sahib said, 'Bear the baggage to the big dak-bungalow, and I will look for employment fit for a sick man.' I put on the uniform of my rank and went to the big dak-bungalow, called Maun Nihâl Seyn,* and I caused the heavy baggage to be bestowed in that dark lower place – is it known to the Sahib? – which was already full of swords and baggage for officers. It is fuller now – dead men's kit all! I was careful to secure a receipt for all three pieces. I have it in my belt. They must go back to the Punjab.

Anon came Kurban Sahib, lilting a little in his step, which sign I knew, and he said, 'We are born in a fortunate hour. We go to Eshtellenbosch to oversee the despatch of horses.' Remember, Kurban Sahib was squadron-leader of the Gurgaon Rissala, and *I* was Umr Singh. So I said, speaking as we do – we did – when none was near, 'Thou art a groom and I am a grass-cutter, but is this any promotion, Child?' At this he laughed, saying, 'It is the way to better things. Have patience, Father.' (Aye, he called me father when none were by.) 'This war ends not tomorrow nor the next day. I have seen the new Sahibs,' he said, 'and they are fathers of owls – all – all – all!'

So we went to Eshtellenbosch, where the horses are; Kurban

* Mount Nelson?

Sahib doing the service of servants in that business. And the whole business was managed without forethought by new Sahibs from God knows where, who had never seen a tent pitched or a peg driven. They were full of zeal, but empty of all knowledge. Then came, little by little from Hind, those Pathans – they are just like those vultures up there, Sahib – they always follow slaughter. And there came to Eshtellenbosch some Sikhs – Muzbees, though – and some Madras monkey-men. They came with horses. Puttiala sent horses. Jhind and Nabha sent horses. All the nations of the Khalsa sent horses. All the ends of the earth sent horses. God knows what the army did with them, unless they ate them raw. They used horses as a courtesan uses oil: with both hands. These horses needed many men. Kurban Sahib appointed me to the command (what a command for me!) of certain woolly ones – *Hubshis* – whose touch and shadow are pollution. They were enormous eaters; sleeping on their bellies; laughing without cause; wholly like animals. Some were called Fingoes, and some, I think, Red Kaffirs, but they were all Kaffirs – filth unspeakable. I taught them to water and feed, and sweep and rub down. Yes, I oversaw the work of sweepers – a *jemadar* of *mehtars* (headman of a refuse-gang) was I, and Kurban Sahib little better, for five months. Evil months! The war went as Kurban Sahib had said. Our new men were slain and no vengeance was taken. It was a war of fools armed with the weapons of magicians. Guns that slew at half a day's march, and men who, being new, walked blind into high grass and were driven off like cattle by the Boer-log! As to the city of Eshtellenbosch, I am not a Sahib – only a Sikh. I would have quartered one troop only of the Gurgaon Rissala in that city – one little troop – and I would have schooled that city till its men learned to kiss the shadow of a Government horse upon the ground. There are many *mullahs* (priests) in Eshtellenbosch. They preached the Jehad against us. This is true – all the camp knew it. And most of the houses were thatched! A war of fools indeed!

At the end of five months my Kurban Sahib, who had grown lean, said, 'The reward has come. We go up towards the front with horses tomorrow, and, once away, I shall be too sick to return. Make ready the baggage.' Thus we got away, with some Kaffirs in charge of new horses for a certain new regiment that had come in a ship. The second day by *terain*, when we were watering at a desolate place without any sort of a bazaar to it, slipped out from the horse-boxes one Sikandar Khan, that had been a *jemadar* of *saises* (head-groom) at Eshtellenbosch, and was by service a trooper in a Border regiment. Kurban Sahib gave him big abuse for his desertion; but the Pathan put up his hands as excusing himself, and Kurban Sahib relented and added him to our service. So there were three of us – Kurban Sahib, I, and Sikandar Khan – Sahib, Sikh, and *Sag* (dog). But the man said truly, 'We be far from our homes and both servants of the Raj. Make truce till we see the Indus again.' I have eaten from the same dish as Sikandar Khan – beef, too, for aught I know! He said, on the night he stole some swine's flesh in a tin from a mess-tent, that in his Book, the Koran, it is written that whoso engages in a holy war is freed from ceremonial obligations. Wah! He had no more religion than the sword-point picks up of sugar and water at baptism. He stole himself a horse at a place where there lay a new and very raw regiment. I also procured myself a grey gelding there. They let their horses stray too much, those new regiments.

Some shameless regiments would indeed have made away with *our* horses on the road! They exhibited indents and requisitions for horses, and once or twice would have uncoupled the trucks; but Kurban Sahib was wise, and I am not altogether a fool. There is not much honesty at the front. Notably, there was one congregation of hard-bitten horse-thieves; tall, light Sahibs, who spoke through their noses for the most part, and upon all occasions they said, 'Oah Hell!' which, in our tongue, signifies *Jehannum ko jao*. They bore each man a vine-leaf upon their uniforms, and they rode like Rajputs. Nay, they rode like Sikhs. They rode like the Ustrelyahs! The Ustrelyahs, whom we met later, also spoke through their noses not little, and they were tall, dark men, with grey, clear eyes, heavily eyelashed like camel's eyes – very proper men – a new brand of Sahib to me. They said on all occasions, 'No fee-ah,' which in our tongue means *Durro mut* ('Do not be afraid'), so we called them the

Durro Muts. Dark, tall men, most excellent horsemen, hot and angry, waging war *as* war, and drinking tea as a sandhill drinks water. Thieves? A little, Sahib. Sikandar Khan swore to me – and he comes of a horse-stealing clan for ten generations – he swore a Pathan was a babe beside a *Durro Mut* in regard to horse-lifting. The *Durro Muts* cannot walk on their feet at all. They are like hens on the high road. Therefore they must have horses. Very proper men, with a just lust for the war. Aah – 'No fee-ah,' say the *Durro Muts*. *They* saw the worth of Kurban Sahib. *They* did not ask him to sweep stables. They would by no means let him go. He did substitute for one of their troop-leaders who had a fever, one long day in a country full of little hills – like the mouth of the Khaibar; and when they returned in the evening, the *Durro Muts* said, 'Wallah! This is a man. Steal him!' So they stole my Kurban Sahib as they would have stolen anything else that they needed, and they sent a sick officer back to Eshtellenbosch in his place. Thus Kurban Sahib came to his own again, and I was his bearer, and Sikandar Khan was his cook. The law was strict that this was a Sahibs' war, but there was no order that a bearer and a cook should not ride with their Sahib – and we had naught to wear but our uniforms. We rode up and down this accursed country, where there is no bazaar, no pulse, no flour, no oil, no spice, no red pepper, no firewood; nothing but raw corn and a little cattle. There were no great battles as I saw it, but a plenty of gun-firing. When we were many, the Boer-log came out with coffee to greet us, and to show us *purwanas* (permits) from foolish English Generals who had gone that way before, certifying they were peaceful and well disposed. When we were few, they hid behind stones and shot us. Now the order was that they were Sahibs, and this was a Sahibs' war. Good! But, as I understand it, when a Sahib goes to war, he puts on the cloth of war, and only those who wear that cloth may take part in the war. Good! That also I understand. But these people were as they were in Burma, or as the Afridis are. They shot at their pleasure, and when pressed hid the gun and exhibited *purwanas*, or lay in a house and said they were farmers. Even such farmers as cut up the Madras troops at Hlinedatalone in Burma! Even such farmers as slew Cavagnari Sahib and the Guides at Kabul! We schooled *those* men, to be sure — fifteen, aye, twenty of a morning pushed off the verandah in front of the Bala Hissar. I looked that the Jung-i-lat Sahib (the Commander-in-Chief) would have remembered the old days; but — no. All the people shot at us everywhere, and he issued proclamations saying that he did not fight the people, but a certain army, which army, in truth, was all the Boer-log, who, between them, did not wear enough of uniform to make a loin-cloth. A fool's war from first to last; for it is manifest that he who fights should be hung if he fights with a gun in one hand and a *purwana* in the other, as did all these people. Yet we, when they had had their bellyful for the time, received them with honour, and gave them permits, and refreshed them and fed their wives and their babes, and severely punished our soldiers who took their fowls. So the work was to be done not once with a few dead, but thrice and four times over. I talked much with Kurban Sahib on this, and he said, 'It is a Sahibs' war. That is the order'; and one night, when Sikandar Khan would have lain out beyond the pickets with his knife and shown them how it is worked on the Border, he hit Sikandar Khan between the eyes and came near to breaking in his head. Then Sikandar Khan, a bandage over his eyes, so that he looked like a sick camel, talked to him half one march, and he was more bewildered than I, and vowed he would return to Eshtellenbosch. But privately to me Kurban Sahib said we should have loosed the Sikhs and the Gurkhas on these people till they came in with their foreheads in the dust. For the war was not of that sort which they comprehended.

They shot us? Assuredly they shot us from houses adorned with a white flag; but when they came to know our custom, their widows sent word by Kaffir runners, and presently there was not quite so much firing. *No fee-ah!* All the Boer-log with whom we dealt had *purwanas* signed by mad Generals attesting that they were well disposed to the State. They had also rifles not a few, and cartridges, which they hid in the roof. The women wept very greatly when we burned such houses, but they did not approach too near after the flames had taken hold of the thatch, for fear of the bursting cartridges. The women of the Boer-log are very clever. They are more clever than the men. The Boer-log are clever? Never, never no! It is the Sahibs who are fools. For their own honour's sake the Sahibs must say that the Boer-log are clever; but it is the Sahibs' wonderful folly that has made the Boer-log. The Sahibs should have sent *us* into the game.

But the *Durro Muts* did well. They dealt faithfully with all that country thereabouts – not in any way as we of Hind should have dealt, but they were not altogether fools. One night when we lay on the top of a ridge in the cold, I saw far away a light in a house that appeared for the sixth part of an hour and was obscured. Anon it appeared again thrice for the twelfth part of an hour. I showed this to Kurban Sahib, for it was a house that had been spared – the people having many permits and swearing fidelity at our stirrup-leathers. I said to Kurban Sahib, 'Send half a troop, Child, and finish that house. They signal to their brethren.' And he laughed where he lay and said, 'If I listened to my bearer Umr Singh, there would not be left ten houses in all this land.' I said, 'What need to leave one? This is as it was in Burma. They are farmers today and fighters tomorrow. Let us deal justly with them.' He laughed and curled himself up in his blanket, and I watched the far light in the house till day. I have been on the Border in eight wars, not counting Burma. The first Afghan War; the second Afghan War; two Mahsud Waziri wars (that is four); two Black Mountain wars, if I remember right; the Malakand and Tirah. I do not count Burma, or some small things. *I* know when house signals to house!

I pushed Sikandar Khan with my foot, and he saw it too. He said, 'One of the Boer-log who brought pumpkins for the mess, which I fried last night, lives in yonder house.' I said, 'How dost thou know?' He said, 'Because he rode out of the camp another way, but I marked how his horse fought with him at the turn of the road; and before the light fell I stole out of the camp for evening prayer with Kurban Sahib's glasses, and from a little hill I saw the pied horse of that pumpkin-seller hurrying to that house.' I said naught, but took Kurban Sahib's glasses from his greasy hands and cleaned them with a silk handkerchief and returned them to their case. Sikandar

Khan told me that he had been the first man in the Zenab valley to use glasses – whereby he finished two blood-feuds cleanly in the course of three months' leave. But he was otherwise a liar.

That day Kurban Sahib, with some ten troopers, was sent on to spy the land for our camp. The *Durro Muts* moved slowly at that time. They were weighted with grain and forage and carts, and they greatly wished to leave these all in some town and go on light to other business which pressed. So Kurban Sahib sought a short cut for them, a little off the line of march. We were twelve miles before the main body, and we came to a house under a high bushed hill, with a nullah, which they call a donga, behind it, and an old sangar of piled stones, which they call a kraal, before it. Two thorn bushes grew on either side of the door, like babul bushes, covered with a golden-coloured bloom, and the roof was all of thatch. Before the house was a valley of stones that rose to another bush-covered hill. There was an old man in the verandah – an old man with a white beard and a wart upon the left side of his neck; and a fat woman with the eyes of a swine and the jowl of a swine; and a tall young man deprived of understanding. His head was hairless, no larger than an orange, and the pits of his nostrils were eaten away by a disease. He laughed and slavered and he sported sportively before Kurban Sahib. The man brought coffee and the woman showed us *purwanas* from three General-Sahibs, certifying that they were people of peace and goodwill. Here are the *purwanas*, Sahib. Does the Sahib know the Generals who signed them?

They swore the land was empty of Boer-log. They held up their hands and swore it. That was about the time of the evening meal. I stood near the verandah with Sikandar Khan, who was nosing like a jackal on a lost scent. At last he took my arm and said, 'See yonder! There is the sun on the window of the house that signalled last night. This house can see that house from here,' and he looked at the hill behind him all hairy with bushes, and sucked in his breath. Then the idiot with the shrivelled head danced by me and threw back that head, and regarded the roof and laughed like a hyena, and the fat woman talked loudly, as it were, to cover some noise. After this I passed to the back of the house on pretence to get water for tea, and I saw fresh horse-dung on the ground, and that the ground was cut with the new marks of hoofs; and there had dropped in the dirt one cartridge. Then Kurban Sahib called to me in our tongue, saying, 'Is this a good place to make tea?' and I replied, knowing what he meant, 'There are over many cooks in the cook-house. Mount and go, Child.' Then I returned, and he said, smiling to the woman, 'Prepare food, and when we have loosened our girths we will come in and eat'; but to his men he said in a whisper, 'Ride away!' No. He did not cover the old man or the fat woman with his rifle. That was not his custom. Some fool of the *Durro Muts*, being hungry, raised his voice to dispute the order to flee, and before we were in our saddles many shots came from the roof – from rifles thrust through the thatch. Upon this we rode across the valley of stones, and men fired at us from the nullah behind the house, and from the hill behind the nullah, as well as from the roof of the house – so many shots that it sounded like a drumming in the hills. Then Sikandar Khan, riding low, said, 'This play is not for us alone, but for the rest of the *Durro Muts*,' and I said, 'Be quiet. Keep place!' for his place was behind me, and I rode behind Kurban Sahib. But these new bullets will pass through five men a-row! We were not hit – not one of us – and we reached the hill of rocks and scattered among the stones, and Kurban Sahib turned in his saddle and said, 'Look at the old man!' He stood in the verandah firing swiftly with a gun, the woman beside him and the idiot also – both with guns. Kurban Sahib laughed, and I caught him by the wrist, but – his fate was written at that hour. The bullet passed under his arm-pit and struck him in the liver, and I pulled him backward between two great rocks a-tilt – Kurban Sahib, my Kurban Sahib! From the nullah behind the house and from the hills came our Boer-log in number more than a hundred, and Sikandar Khan said, '*Now* we see the meaning of last night's signal. Give me the rifle.' He took Kurban Sahib's rifle – in this war of fools only the doctors carry swords – and lay belly-flat to the work, but Kurban Sahib turned where he lay and said, 'Be still. It is a Sahibs' war,' and

Kurban Sahib put up his hand – thus; and then his eyes rolled on me, and I gave him water that he might pass the more quickly. And at the drinking his Spirit received permission . . .

Thus went our fight, Sahib. We *Durro Muts* were on a ridge working from the north to the south, where lay our main body, and the Boer-log lay in a valley working from east to west. There were more than a hundred, and our men were ten, but they held the Boer-log in the valley while they swiftly passed along the ridge to the south. I saw three Boers drop in the open. Then they all hid again and fired heavily at the rocks that hid our men; but our men were clever and did not show, but moved away and away, always south; and the noise of the battle withdrew itself southward, where we could hear the sound of big guns. So it fell stark dark, and Sikandar Khan found a deep old jackal's earth amid rocks, into which we slid the body of Kurban Sahib upright. Sikandar Khan took his glasses, and I took his handkerchief and some letters and a certain thing which I knew hung round his neck, and Sikandar Khan is witness that I wrapped them all in the handkerchief. Then we took an oath together, and lay still and mourned for Kurban Sahib. Sikandar Khan wept till daybreak – even he, a Pathan, a Mohammedan! All that night we heard firing to the southward, and when the dawn broke the valley was full of Boer-log in carts and on horses. They gathered by the house, as we could see through Kurban Sahib's glasses, and the old man, who, I take it, was a priest, blessed them, and preached the holy war, waving his arm; and the fat woman brought coffee, and the idiot capered among them and kissed their horses. Presently they went away in haste; they went over the hills and were not; and a black slave came out and washed the door-sills with bright water. Sikandar Khan saw through the glasses that the stain was blood, and he laughed, saying, 'Wounded men lie there. We shall yet get vengeance.'

About noon we saw a thin, high smoke to the southward, such a smoke as a burning house will make in sunshine, and Sikandar Khan, who knows how to take a bearing across a hill, said, 'At last we have burned the house of the pumpkin-seller whence they signalled.' And I said, 'What need now that they

have slain my child? Let me mourn.' It was a high smoke, and
the old man, as I saw, came out into the verandah to behold it,
and shook his clenched hands at it. So we lay till the twilight,
foodless and without water, for we had vowed a vow neither to
eat nor to drink till we had accomplished the matter. I had a
little opium left, of which I gave Sikandar Khan the half,
because he loved Kurban Sahib. When it was full dark we
sharpened our sabres upon a certain softish rock which, mixed
with water, sharpens steel well, and we took off our boots and
we went down to the house and looked through the windows
very softly. The old man sat reading in a book, and the woman
sat by the hearth; and the idiot lay on the floor with his head
against her knee, and he counted his fingers and laughed, and
she laughed again. So I knew they were mother and son, and I
laughed, too, for I had suspected this when I claimed her life
and her body from Sikandar Khan, in our discussion of the
spoil. Then we entered with bare swords . . . Indeed, these
Boer-log do not understand the steel, for the old man ran
towards a rifle in the corner; but Sikandar Khan prevented him
with a blow of the flat across the hands, and he sat down and
held up his hands, and I put my fingers on my lips to signify
they should be silent. But the woman cried, and one stirred in
an inner room, and a door opened, and a man, bound about the
head with rags, stood stupidly fumbling with a gun. His whole
head fell inside the door, and none followed him. It was a very
pretty stroke – for a Pathan. Then they were silent, staring at
the head upon the floor, and I said to Sikandar Khan, 'Fetch
ropes! Not even for Kurban Sahib's sake will I defile my sword.'
So he went to seek and returned with three long leather ones,
and said, 'Four wounded lie within, and doubtless each has a
permit from a General,' and he stretched the ropes and laughed.
Then I bound the old man's hands behind his back, and un-
willingly – for he laughed in my face, and would have fingered
my beard – the idiot's. At this the woman with the swine's eyes
and the jowl of a swine ran forward, and Sikandar Khan said,
'Shall I strike or bind? She was thy property on the division.'
And I said, 'Refrain! I have made a chain to hold her. Open the
door.' I pushed out the two across the verandah into the darker

shade of the thorn-trees, and she followed upon her knees and
lay along the ground, and pawed at my boots and howled. Then
Sikandar Khan bore out the lamp, saying that he was a butler
and would light the table, and I looked for a branch that would
bear fruit. But the woman hindered me not a little with her
screechings and plungings, and spoke fast in her tongue, and I
replied in my tongue, 'I am childless tonight because of thy
perfidy, and *my* child was praised among men and loved among
women. He would have begotten men – not animals. Thou hast
more years to live than I, but my grief is the greater.'

I stooped to make sure the noose upon the idiot's neck, and
flung the end over the branch, and Sikandar Khan held up the
lamp that she might well see. Then appeared suddenly, a little
beyond the light of the lamp, the spirit of Kurban Sahib. One
hand he held to his side, even where the bullet had struck him,
and the other he put forward thus, and said, 'No. It is a Sahibs'
war.' And I said, 'Wait a while, Child, and thou shalt sleep.'
But he came nearer, riding, as it were, upon my eyes, and said,
'No. It is a Sahibs' war.' And Sikandar Khan said, 'Is it too
heavy?' and set down the lamp and came to me; and as he
turned to tally on the rope, the spirit of Kurban Sahib stood up
within arm's reach of us, and his face was very angry, and a third
time he said, 'No. It is a Sahibs' war.' And a little wind blew
out the lamp, and I heard Sikandar Khan's teeth chatter in his
head.

So we stayed side by side, the ropes in our hand, a very long
while, for we could not shape any words. Then I heard Sikandar
Khan open his water-bottle and drink; and when his mouth was
slaked he passed to me and said, 'We are absolved from our
vow.' So I drank, and together we waited for the dawn in that
place where we stood – the ropes in our hand. A little after
third cockcrow we heard the feet of horses and gun-wheels
very far off, and so soon as the light came a shell burst on the
threshold of the house, and the roof of the verandah that was
thatched fell in and blazed before the windows. And I said,
'What of the wounded Boer-log within?' And Sikandar Khan
said, 'We have heard the order. It is a Sahibs' war. Stand still.'
Then came a second shell – good line, but short – and scattered

dust upon us where we stood; and then came ten of the little quick shells from the gun that speaks like a stammerer – yes, pom-pom the Sahibs call it – and the face of the house folded down like the nose and the chin of an old man mumbling, and the forefront of the house lay down. Then Sikandar Khan said, 'If it be the fate of the wounded to die in the fire, *I* shall not prevent it.' And he passed to the back of the house and presently came back, and four wounded Boer-log came after him, of whom two could not walk upright. And I said, 'What hast thou done?' And he said, 'I have neither spoken to them nor laid hand on them. They follow in hope of mercy.' And I said, 'It is a Sahibs' war. Let them wait the Sahibs' mercy.' So they lay still, the four men and the idiot, and the fat woman under the thorn-tree, and the house burned furiously. Then began the known sound of cartouches in the roof – one or two at first; then a trill, and last of all one loud noise and the thatch blew here and there, and the captives would have crawled aside on account of the heat that was withering the thorn-trees, and on account of wood and bricks flying at random. But I said, 'Abide! Abide! Ye be Sahibs, and this is a Sahibs' war, O Sahibs. There is no order that ye should depart from this war.' They did not understand my words. Yet they abode and they lived.

Presently rode down five troopers of Kurban Sahib's command, and one I knew spoke my tongue, having sailed to Calcutta often with horses. So I told him all my tale, using bazaar-talk, such as his kidney of Sahib would understand; and at the end I said, 'An order has reached us here from the dead that this is a Sahibs' war. I take the soul of my Kurban Sahib to witness that I give over to the justice of the Sahibs these Sahibs who have made me childless.' Then I gave him the ropes and fell down senseless, my heart being very full, but my belly was empty, except for the little opium.

They put me into a cart with one of their wounded, and after a while I understood that they had fought against the Boer-log for two days and two nights. It was all the one big trap, Sahib, of which we, with Kurban Sahib, saw no more than the outer edge. They were very angry, the *Durro Muts* – very angry indeed. I have never seen Sahibs so angry. They buried my

Kurban Sahib with the rites of his faith upon the top of the ridge overlooking the house, and I said the proper prayers of the faith, and Sikandar Khan prayed in his fashion and stole five signalling-candles, which have each three wicks, and lighted the grave as if it had been the grave of a saint on a Friday. He wept very bitterly all that night, and I wept with him, and he took hold of my feet and besought me to give him a remembrance from Kurban Sahib. So I divided equally with him one of Kurban Sahib's handkerchiefs – not the silk ones, for those were given him by a certain woman; and I also gave him a button from a coat, and a little steel ring of no value that Kurban Sahib used for his keys, and he kissed them and put them into his bosom. The rest I have here in that little bundle, and I must get the baggage from the hotel in Cape Town – some four shirts we sent to be washed, for which we could not wait when we went up-country – and I must give them all to my Colonel-Sahib at Sialkote in the Punjab. For my child is dead – my baba is dead! . . .

I would have come away before; there was no need to stay, the child being dead; but we were far from the rail, and the *Durro Muts* were as brothers to me, and I had come to look upon Sikandar Khan as in some sort a friend, and he got me a horse and I rode up and down with them; but the life had departed. God knows what they called me – orderly, *chaprassi* (messenger), cook, sweeper, I did not know nor care. But once I had pleasure. We came back in a month after wide circles to that very valley. I knew it every stone, and I went up to the grave, and a clever Sahib of the *Durro Muts* (we left a troop there for a week to school those people with *purwanas*) had cut an inscription upon a great rock; and they interpreted it to me, and it was a jest such as Kurban Sahib himself would have loved. Oh! I have the inscription well copied here. Read it aloud, Sahib, and I will explain the jests. There are two very good ones. Begin, Sahib:

In Memory of
WALTER DECIES CORBYN
Late Captain 141st Punjab Cavalry

Traffics and Discoveries

The Gurgaon Rissala, that is. Go on, Sahib.

> Treacherously shot near this place by
> The connivance of the late
> HENDRIK DIRK UYS
> A Minister of God
> Who thrice took the oath of neutrality
> And Piet his son,
> This little work

Aha! This is the first jest. The Sahib should see this little work!

> Was accomplished in partial
> And inadequate recognition of their loss
> By some men who loved him
>
> ———
>
> *Si monumentum requiris circumspice*

That is the second jest. It signifies that those who would desire to behold a proper memorial to Kurban Sahib must look out at the house. And, Sahib, the house is not there, nor the well, nor the big tank which they call dams, nor the little fruit-trees, nor the cattle. There is nothing at all, Sahib, except the two trees withered by the fire. The rest is like the desert here – or my hand – or my heart. Empty, Sahib – all empty!

The Wet Litany

When the water's countenance
Blurrs 'twixt glance and second glance;
When that tattered smokes forerun
Ashen 'neath a silvered sun;
When the curtain of the haze
Shuts upon our helpless ways –
    Hear the Channel Fleet at sea;
    Libera nos Domine!

When the engines' bated pulse
Scarcely thrills the nosing hulls;
When the wash along the side
Sounds, a sudden, magnified;
When the intolerable blast
Marks each blindfold minute passed.

When the fog-buoy's squattering flight
Guides us through the haggard night;
When the warning bugle blows;
When the lettered doorways close;
When our brittle townships press,
Impotent, on emptiness.

When the unseen leadsmen lean
Questioning a deep unseen;
When their lessened count they tell
To a bridge invisible;
When the hid and perilous
Cliffs return our cry to us.

Traffics and Discoveries

When the treble thickness spread
Swallows up our next-ahead;
When her siren's frightened whine
Shows her sheering out of line;
When, her passage undiscerned,
We must turn where she has turned —
    Hear the Channel Fleet at sea;
    Libera nos Domine!

'Their Lawful Occasions'

... And a security for such as pass on the seas upon their lawful occasions.

Navy Prayer

Part I

Disregarding the inventions of the Marine Captain, whose other name is Gubbins, let a plain statement suffice.

H.M.S. *Caryatid* went to Portland to join Blue Fleet for manoeuvres. I travelled overland from London by way of Portsmouth, where I fell among friends. When I reached Portland, H.M.S. *Caryatid*, whose guest I was to have been, had, with Blue Fleet, already sailed for some secret rendezvous off the west coast of Ireland, and Portland breakwater was filled with Red Fleet, my official enemies and joyous acquaintances, who received me with unstinted hospitality. For example, Lieutenant-Commander A. L. Hignett, in charge of three destroyers, *Wraith*, *Stiletto*, and *Kobbold*, due to depart at 6 p.m. that evening, offered me a berth on his thirty-knot flagship, but I preferred my comforts, and so accepted sleeping-room in H.M.S. *Pedantic* (15,000 tons), leader of the second line. After dining aboard her I took boat to Weymouth to get my kit aboard, as the battleships would go to war at midnight. In transferring my allegiance from Blue to Red Fleet, whatever the Marine Captain may say, I did no wrong. I truly intended to return to the *Pedantic* and help to fight Blue Fleet. All I needed was a new toothbrush, which I bought from a chemist in a side street at 9.15 p.m. As I turned to go, one entered seeking alleviation of a gum-boil. He was dressed in a checked ulster, a black silk hat three sizes too small, cord-breeches, boots, and pure brass spurs. These he managed painfully, stepping like a prisoner fresh from leg-irons. As he adjusted the pepper-plaster to the gum the light fell on his face, and I recognized Mr Emanuel Pyecroft, a late second-class petty officer of H.M.S. *Archimandrite*, an unforgettable man, met a year before under Tom Wessels' roof in Plymouth. It occurred to me that when a petty officer takes to spurs he may conceivably meditate desertion. For that reason I, though a taxpayer, made no sign. Indeed, it was Mr Pyecroft, following me out of the shop, who said hollowly: 'What might you be doing here?'

'I'm going on manoeuvres in the *Pedantic*,' I replied.

'Ho!' said Mr Pyecroft. 'An' what manner o' manoeuvres d'you expect to see in a blighted cathedral like the *Pedantic*? *I* know 'er. I knew her in Malta, when the *Vulcan* was her permanent tender. Manoeuvres! You won't see more than "Man an' arm watertight doors!" in your little woollen undervest.'

'I'm sorry for that.'

'Why?' He lurched heavily as his spurs caught and twanged like tuning-forks. 'War's declared at midnight. *Pedantics* be sugared! Buy an 'am an' see life!'

For a moment I fancied Mr Pyecroft, a fugitive from justice, purposed that we two should embrace a Robin Hood career in the uplands of Dorset. The spurs troubled me, and I made bold to say as much. 'Them!' he said, coming to an intricate halt. 'They're part of the *prima facie* evidence. But as for me – let me carry your bag – I'm second in command, leadin'-hand, cook, steward, an' lavatory man, with a few incidentals for sixpence a day extra, on No. 267 torpedo-boat.'

'They wear spurs there?'

'Well,' said Mr Pyecroft, 'seein' that Two Six Seven belongs to Blue Fleet, which left the day before yesterday, disguises are imperative. It transpired thus. The Right Honourable Lord Gawd Almighty Admiral Master Frankie Frobisher, K.C.B., commandin' Blue Fleet, can't be bothered with one tin-torpedo-boat more or less; and what with lyin' in the Reserve four years, an' what with the new kind o' tiffy which cleans dynamos with brick-dust and oil (Blast these spurs! They won't render!), Two Six Seven's steam-gadgets was paralytic. Our Mr Moorshed

done his painstakin' best – it's his first command of a war-
canoe, matoor age nineteen (down that alley-way, please!) but
be that as it may, His Holiness Frankie is aware of us crabbin'
ourselves round the breakwater at five knots, an' steerin' *pari
passu*, as the French say. (Up this alley-way, please!) If he'd
given Mr Hinchcliffe, our chief engineer, a little time, it would
never have transpired, for what Hinch can't drive he can coax;
but the new port bein' a trifle cloudy, an' 'is joints tinglin' after
a post-captain dinner, Frankie come on the upper bridge seekin'
for a sacrifice. We, offerin' a broadside target, got it. He told
us what 'is grandmamma, 'oo was a lady an' went to sea in
stick-and-string bateaus, had told him about steam. He throwed
in his own prayers for the 'ealth an' safety of all steam-packets
an' their officers. Then he give us several distinct orders. The
first few – I kept tally – was all about going to Hell; the next
many was about not evolutin' in his company, when there; an'
the last all was simply repeatin' the motions in quick time.
Knowin' Frankie's groovin' to be badly eroded by age and lack
of attention, I didn't much panic; but our Mr Moorshed, 'e
took it a little to heart. Me an' Mr Hinchcliffe consoled 'im as
well as service conditions permits of, an' we had a *résumé*-
supper at the back o' the camber – secluded *an*' lugubrious!
Then one thing leadin' up to another, an' our orders, except
about anchorin' where he's booked for, leavin' us a clear 'orizon,
Number Two Six Seven is now – mind the edge of the wharf –
here!'

By mysterious doublings he had brought me out on to the
edge of a narrow strip of water crowded with coastwise shipping
that runs far up into Weymouth town. A large foreign timber-
brig lay at my feet, and under the round of her stern cowered,
close to the wharf-edge, a slate-coloured, unkempt, two-fun-
nelled craft of a type – but I am no expert – between the first-
class torpedo-boat and the full-blooded destroyer. From her
archaic torpedo-tubes at the stern, and quick-firers forward
and amidships, she must have dated from the early 'nineties.
Hammerings and clinkings, with spurts of steam and fumes of
hot oil, arose from her inside, and a figure in a striped jersey
squatted on the engine-room gratings.

'She ain't much of a war-canoe, but you'll see more life in 'er than on an whole squadron of bleedin' *Pedantics*.'

'But she's laid up here – and Blue Fleet have gone,' I protested.

'Pre-cisely. Only, in his comprehensive orders Frankie didn't put us out of action. Thus we're a non-neglectable fightin' factor which you mightn't think from this elevation; *an'* m'rover, Red Fleet don't know we're 'ere. Most of us' – he glanced proudly at his boots – 'didn't run to spurs, but we're disguised pretty devious, as you might say. Morgan, our signalizer, when last seen, was a Dawlish bathing-machine proprietor. Hinchcliffe was naturally a German waiter, and me you behold as a squire of low degree; while yonder Levantine dragoman on the hatch is our Mr Moorshed. He was the second cutter's snotty – *my* snotty – on the *Archimandrite* –two years – Cape Station. Likewise on the West Coast, mangrove-swampin', an' gettin' the cutter stove in on small an' unlikely bars, an' manufacturin' lies to correspond. What I don't know about Mr Moorshed is precisely the same gauge as what Mr Moorshed don't know about me – half a millimetre, as you might say. He comes into awful opulence of his own when 'e's of age; an' judgin' from what passed between us when Frankie cursed 'im, I don't think 'e cares whether he's broke tomorrow or – the day after. Are you beginnin' to follow our tattics? They'll be worth followin'. Or *are* you goin' back to your nice little cabin on the *Pedantic* – which I lay they've just dismounted the third engineer out of – to eat four fat meals per diem, an' smoke in the casement?'

The figure in the jersey lifted its head and mumbled.

'Yes, Sir,' was Mr Pyecroft's answer. 'I 'ave ascertained that *Stiletto*, *Wraith*, and *Kobbold* left at 6 p.m. with the first division o' Red Fleet's cruisers except *Devolution* and *Cryptic*, which are delayed by engine-room defects.' Then to me: 'Won't you go aboard? Mr Moorshed 'ud like someone to talk to. You buy an 'am an' see life.'

At this he vanished; and the Demon of Pure Irresponsibility bade me lower myself from the edge of the wharf to the tea-tray plates of No. 267.

'What d'you want?' said the striped jersey.

'I want to join Blue Fleet if I can,' I replied. 'I've been left behind by – an accident.'

'Well?'

'Mr Pyecroft told me to buy a ham and see life. About how big a ham do you need?'

'I don't want any ham, thank you. That's the way up the wharf. *Good*-night.'

'Good-night!' I retraced my steps, wandered in the dark till I found a shop, and there purchased, of sardines, canned tongue, lobster, and salmon, not less than half a hundredweight. A belated sausage-shop supplied me with a partially cut ham of pantomime tonnage. These things I, sweating, bore out to the edge of the wharf and set down in the shadow of a crane. It was a clear, dark summer night, and from time to time I laughed happily to myself. The adventure was preordained on the face of it. Pyecroft alone, spurred or barefoot, would have drawn me very far from the paths of circumspection. His advice to buy a ham and see life clinched it. Presently Mr Pyecroft – I heard spurs clink – passed me. Then the jersey voice said: 'What the mischief's that?'

"'Asn't the visitor come aboard, Sir? 'E told me he'd purposely abandoned the *Pedantic* for the pleasure of the trip with us. Told me he was official correspondent for the *Times*; an' I know he's littcry by the way 'e tries to talk Navy-talk. Haven't you seen 'im, Sir?'

Slowly and dispassionately the answer drawled long on the night; 'Pye, you are without exception the biggest liar in the Service!'

'Then what am I to do with the bag, Sir? It's marked with his name.' There was a pause till Mr Moorshed said 'Oh!' in a tone which the listener might construe precisely as he pleased.

'*He* was the maniac who wanted to buy a ham and see life – was he? If he goes back to the *Pedantic* –'

'Pre-cisely, Sir. Gives us all away, Sir.'

'Then what possessed *you* to give it away to him, you owl?'

'I've got his bag. If 'e gives anything away, he'll have to go naked.'

At this point I thought it best to rattle my tins and step out of the shadow of the crane.

'I've bought the ham,' I called sweetly. 'Have you still any objection to my seeing life, Mr Moorshed?'

'All right, if you're insured. Won't you come down?'

I descended; Pyecroft, by a silent flank movement, possessing himself of all the provisions, which he bore to some hole forward.

'Have you known Mr Pyecroft long?' said my host.

'Met him once, a year ago, at Devonport. What do you think of him?'

'What do *you* think of him?'

'I've left the *Pedantic* – her boat will be waiting for me at ten o'clock, too – simply because I happened to meet him,' I replied.

'That's all right. If you'll come down below, we may get some grub.'

We descended a naked steel ladder to a steel-beamed tunnel, perhaps twelve feet long by six high. Leather-topped lockers ran along either side; a swinging table, with tray and lamp above, occupied the centre. Other furniture there was none.

'You can't shave here, of course. We don't wash, and, as a rule, we eat with our fingers when we're at sea. D'you mind?'

Mr Moorshed, black-haired, black-browed, sallow-complexioned, looked me over from head to foot and grinned. He was not handsome in any way, but his smile drew the heart. 'You didn't happen to hear what Frankie told me from the flagship, did you? His last instructions, and I've logged 'em here in shorthand, were' – he opened a neat pocket-book – '"*Get out of this and conduct your own damned manoeuvres in your own damned tinker fashion! You're a disgrace to the Service, and your boat's offal.*"'

'Awful?' I said.

'No – offal – tripes – swipes – ullage.' Mr Pyecroft entered, in the costume of his calling, with the ham and an assortment of tin dishes, which he dealt out like cards.

'I shall take these as my orders,' said Mr Moorshed. 'I'm chucking the Service at the end of the year, so it doesn't matter.'

We cut into the ham under the ill-trimmed lamp, washed it down with whisky, and then smoked. From the foreside of the bulkhead came an uninterrupted hammering and clinking, and now and then a hiss of steam.

'That's Mr Hinchcliffe,' said Pyecroft. 'He's what is called a first-class engine-room artificer. If you hand 'im a drum of oil an' leave 'im alone, he can coax a stolen bicycle to do type-writin'.'

Very leisurely, at the end of his first pipe, Mr Moorshed drew out a folded map, cut from a newspaper, of the area of manoeuvres, with the rules that regulate these wonderful things, below.

'Well, I suppose I know as much as an average stick-and-string admiral,' he said, yawning. 'Is our petticoat ready yet, Mr Pyecroft?'

As a preparation for naval manoeuvres these councils seemed inadequate. I followed up the ladder into the gloom cast by the wharf edge and the big lumber-ship's side. As my eyes stretched to the darkness I saw that No. 267 had miraculously sprouted an extra pair of funnels – soft, for they gave as I touched them.

'More *prima facie* evidence. You runs a rope fore an' aft, an' you erects perpendick-u-arly two canvas tubes, which you distends with cane hoops, thus 'avin' as many funnels as a destroyer. At the word o' command, up they go like a pair of concertinas, an' consequently collapses equally 'andy when requisite. Comin' aft we shall doubtless overtake the Dawlish bathin'-machine proprietor fittin' on her bustle.'

Mr Pyecroft whispered this in my ear as Moorshed moved toward a group at the stern.

'None of us who ain't built that way can be destroyers, but we can look as near it as we can. Let me explain to you, Sir, that the stern of a Thornycroft boat, which we are *not*, comes out in a pretty bulge, totally different from the Yarrow mark, which again we are not. But, on the other 'and, *Dirk, Stiletto, Goblin, Ghoul, Djinn,* and *A-frite* – Red Fleet dee-stroyers with 'oom we hope to consort later on terms o' perfect equality – *are* Thornycrofts, an' carry that Grecian bend which we are now

adjustin' to our *arrière-pensée* – as the French would put it – by
means of painted canvas an' iron rods bent as requisite. Between
you an' me an' Frankie, we are the *Gnome*, now in the Fleet
Reserve at Pompey – Portsmouth, I should say.'

'The first sea will carry it all away,' said Moorshed, leaning
gloomily outboard, 'but it will do for the present.'

'We've a lot of *prima facie* evidence about us,' Mr Pyecroft
went on. 'A first-class torpedo-boat sits lower in the water than
a destroyer. Hence we artificially raise our sides with a black
canvas wash-streak to represent extra freeboard; *at* the same
time paddlin' out the cover of the forward three-pounder like
as if it was a twelve-pounder, an' variously fakin' up the bows
of 'er. As you might say, we've took thought an' added a cubic
to our stature. It's our len'th that sugars us. A 'undred an' forty
feet, which is our len'th, into two 'undred and ten, which is
about the *Gnome*'s, leaves seventy feet over, which we haven't
got.'

'Is this all your own notion, Mr Pyecroft?' I asked.

'In spots, you might say – yes; though we all contributed to
make up deficiencies. But Mr Moorshed, not much carin' for
further Navy after what Frankie said, certainly threw himself
into the part with avidity.'

'What the dickens are we going to do?'

'Speaking as a seaman gunner, I should say we'd wait till the
sights came on, an' then fire. Speakin' as a torpedo-coxswain,
L.T.O., T.I., M.D., etc., I presume we fall in – Number One
in rear of the tube, etc., secure tube to ball or diaphragm, clear
away securin'-bar, release safety-pin from lockin'-levers, an'
pray Heaven to look down on us. As second in command o' 267,
I say wait an' see!'

'What's happened? We're off,' I said. The timber-ship had
slid away from us.

'We are. Stern first, an' broadside on! If we don't hit anything too hard, we'll do.'

'Come on the bridge,' said Mr Moorshed. I saw no bridge,
but fell over some sort of conning-tower forward, near which
was a wheel. For the next few minutes I was more occupied
with cursing my own folly than with the science of navigation.

Therefore I cannot say how we got out of Weymouth Harbour, nor why it was necessary to turn sharp to the left and wallow in what appeared to be surf.

'Excuse me,' said Mr Pyecroft behind us, '*I* don't mind rammin' a bathin'-machine; but if only *one* of them week-end Weymouth blighters has thrown his empty baccy-tin into the sea here, we'll rip our plates open on it; 267 isn't the *Archimandrite*'s old cutter.'

'I am hugging the shore,' was the answer.

'There's no actual 'arm in huggin', but it can come expensive if pursooed.'

'Right O!' said Moorshed, putting down the wheel, and as we left those scant waters I felt 267 move more freely.

A thin cough ran up the speaking-tube.

'Well, what is it, Mr Hinchcliffe?' said Moorshed.

'I merely wished to report that she is still continuin' to go, Sir.'

'Right O! Can we whack her up to fifteen, d'you think?'

'I'll try, Sir; but we'd prefer to have the engine-room hatch open − at first, Sir.'

Whacked up then she was, and for half an hour we careered largely through the night, turning at last with a suddenness that slung us across the narrow deck.

'This,' said Mr Pyecroft, who received me on his chest as a large rock receives a shadow, 'represents the *Gnome* arrivin' cautious from the direction o' Portsmouth, with Admiralty orders.'

He pointed through the darkness ahead, and after much staring my eyes opened to a dozen destroyers, in two lines, some few hundred yards away.

'Those are the Red Fleet, destroyer flotilla, which is too frail to panic about among the full-blooded cruisers inside Portland breakwater, and several millimetres too excited over the approachin' war to keep a look-out inshore. Hence our tattics!'

We wailed through our siren − a long, malignant, hyena-like howl − and a voice hailed us as we went astern tumultuously.

'The *Gnome* − Carteret-Jones − from Portsmouth, with orders −mm − mm − *Stiletto*,' Moorshed answered through the megaphone in a high, whining voice, rather like a chaplain's.

'*Who?*' was the answer.

'Carter – et – Jones.'

'Oh Lord!'

There was pause; a voice cried to some friend, 'It's Podgie, adrift on the high seas in charge of a whole dee-stroyer!'

Another voice echoed, 'Podgie!' and from its note I gathered that Mr Carteret-Jones had a reputation, but not for independent command.

'Who's your sub?' said the first speaker, a shadow on the bridge of the *Dirk*.

'A gunner at present, Sir. The *Stiletto* – broken down – turns over to us.'

'When did the *Stiletto* break down?'

'Off the Start, Sir; two hours after – after she left here this evening, I believe! My orders are to report to you for the manoeuvre signal-codes, and join Commander Hignett's flotilla, which is in attendance on *Stiletto*.'

A smothered chuckle greeted this last. Moorshed's voice was high and uneasy. Said Pyecroft, with a sigh: 'The amount o' trouble me an' my bright spurs 'ad fishin' out that information from torpedo-coxswains and similar blighters in pubs, all this afternoon, you would never believe.'

'But has the *Stiletto* broken down?' I asked weakly.

'How else are we to get Red Fleet's private signal-code? Anyway, if she 'asn't now, she will before manoeuvres are ended. It's only executin' in anticipation.'

'Go astern and send your coxswain aboard for orders, Mr Jones.' Water carries sound well, but I do not know whether we were intended to hear the next sentence: 'They must have given him *one* intelligent keeper.'

'That's me,' said Mr Pyecroft, as a black and coal-stained dinghy – I did not foresee how well I should come to know her – was flung overside by three men. 'Havin' bought an 'am, we will now see life.' He stepped into the boat and was away.

'I say, Podgie!' – the speaker was in the last of the line of destroyers, as we thumped astern – 'aren't you lonely out there?'

'Oh, don't rag me!' said Moorshed. 'Do you suppose I'll have to manoeuvre with your flo-tilla?'

'No, Podgie! I'm pretty sure our commander will see you sifting cinders in Tophet before you come with our flo-tilla.'

'Thank you! She steers rather wild at high speeds.'

Two men laughed together.

'By the way, who is Mr Carteret-Jones when he's at home?' I whispered.

'I was with him in the *Britannia*. I didn't like him much, but I'm grateful to him now. I must tell him so some day.'

'They seemed to know him hereabouts.'

'He rammed the *Caryatid* twice with her own steam-pinnace.'

Presently, moved by long strokes, Mr Pyecroft returned, skimming across the dark. The dinghy swung up behind him, even as his heel spurned it.

'Commander Fasset's compliments to Mr L. Carteret-Jones, and the sooner he digs out in pursuance of Admiralty orders as received at Portsmouth, the better pleased Commander Fasset will be. But there's a lot more –'

'Whack her up, Mr Hinchcliffe! Come on to the bridge. We can settle it as we go. Well?'

Mr Pyecroft drew an important breath, and slid off his cap.

'Day an' night private signals of Red Fleet *com*plete, Sir!' He handed a little paper to Moorshed. 'You see, Sir, the trouble was, that Mr Carteret-Jones bein', so to say, a little new to his duties, 'ad forgot to give 'is gunner his Admiralty orders in writin', but, as I told Commander Fasset, Mr Jones had been repeatin' 'em to me, nervous-like, most of the way from Portsmouth, so I knew 'em by heart – an' better. The Commander, recognizin' in me a man of agility, cautioned me to be a father an' mother to Mr Carteret-Jones.'

'Didn't he know you?' I asked, thinking for the moment that there could be no duplicates of Emanuel Pyecroft in the Navy.

'What's a torpedo-gunner more or less to a full lootenant commandin' six thirty-knot destroyers for the first time? 'E seemed to cherish the 'ope that 'e might use the *Gnome* for 'is own 'orrible purposes; but what I told him about Mr Jones's

sad lack o' nerve comin' from Pompey, an' going dead slow on
account of the dark, short-circuited *that* connection. "M'rover,"
I says to him, "our orders is explicit; *Stiletto*'s reported broke
down somewhere off the Start, an' we've been tryin' to coil
down a new stiff wire hawser all the evenin', so it looks like
towin' 'er back, don't it?" I says. That more than ever jams his
turrets, an' makes him keen to get rid of us. 'E even hinted that
Mr Carteret-Jones passin' hawsers an' assistin' the impotent in
a sea-way might come pretty expensive on the taxpayer. I agreed
in a disciplined way. I ain't proud. Gawd knows I ain't proud!
But when I'm really diggin' out in the fancy line, I sometimes
think that me in a copper punt, single-'anded, 'ud beat a cutter-
full of De Rougemongs in a row round the fleet.'

At this point I reclined without shame on Mr Pyecroft's
bosom, supported by his quivering arm.

'Well?' said Moorshed, scowling into the darkness, as 267's
bows snapped at the shore seas of the broader Channel, and we
swayed together.

'"You'd better go on," says Commander Fasset, "an' do
what you're told to do. I don't envy Hignett if he has to dry-
nurse the *Gnome*'s commander. But what d'you want with
signals?" 'e says. "It's criminal lunacy to trust Mr Jones with
anything that steams."

'"May I make an observation, Sir?" I says. "Suppose," I
says, "you was torpedo-gunner on the *Gnome*, an' Mr Carteret-
Jones was your commandin' officer, an' you had your reputation
as a second in command for the first time," I says, well knowin'
it was his first command of a flotilla, "what 'ud you do, Sir?"
That gouged 'is unprotected ends open – clear back to the
citadel.'

'What did he say?' Moorshed jerked over his shoulder.

'If you were Mr Carteret-Jones, it might be disrespect for
me to repeat it, Sir.'

'Go ahead,' I heard the boy chuckle.

'"Do?" 'e says. "I'd rub the young blighter's nose into it till
I made a perishin' man of him, or a perspirin' pillow-case," 'e
says, "which," he adds, "is forty per cent more than he is at
present."

'Whilst he's gettin' the private signals – they're rather particular ones – I went forrard to see the *Dirk*'s gunner about borrowin' a holdin'-down bolt for our twelve-pounder. My open ears, while I was rovin' over his packet, got the followin' authentic particulars.' I heard his voice change and his feet shifted. 'There's been a last council o' war of destroyer-captains at the flagship, an' a lot o' things 'as come out. To begin with, *Cryptic* and *Devolution*, Captain Panke and Captain Malan –'

'*Cryptic* and *Devolution*, first-class cruisers,' said Mr Moorshed dreamily. 'Go on, Pyecroft.'

'– bein' delayed by minor defects in engine-room, did *not*, as we know, accompany Red Fleet's first division of scouting cruisers, whose rendezvous is unknown, but presumed to be somewhere off the Lizard. *Cryptic* an' *Devolution* left at 9.30 p.m. still reportin' copious minor defects in engine-room. Admiral's final instructions was they was to put into Torbay, an' mend themselves there. If they can do it in twenty-four hours, they're to come on and join the battle squadron at the first rendezvous, down Channel somewhere. (I couldn't get that, Sir.) If they can't, he'll think about sendin' them some destroyers for escort. But his present intention is to go 'ammer and tongs down Channel, usin' 'is destroyers for all they're worth, an' thus keepin' Blue Fleet too busy off the Irish coast to sniff into any eshtuaries.'

'But if those cruisers are crocks, why does the Admiral let 'em out of Weymouth at all?' I asked.

'The taxpayer,' said Mr Moorshed.

'An' newspapers,' added Mr Pyecroft. 'In Torbay they'll look as they was muckin' about for strategical purposes – hammerin' like blazes in the engine-room all the weary day, an' the skipper droppin' questions down the engine-room hatch every two or three minutes. *I've* been there. Now, Sir?' I saw the white of his eye turn broad on Mr Moorshed.

The boy dropped his chin over the speaking-tube.

'Mr Hinchcliffe, what's her extreme economical radius?'

'Three hundred and forty knots, down to swept bunkers.'

'Can do,' said Moorshed. 'By the way, have her revolutions any bearing on her speed, Mr Hinchcliffe?'

'None that I can make out yet, Sir.'

'Then slow to eight knots. We'll jog down to forty-nine, forty-five, or four about, and three east. That puts us say forty miles from Torbay by nine o'clock tomorrow morning. We'll have to muck about till dusk before we run in and try our luck with the cruisers.'

'Yes, Sir. Their picket boats will be panickin' round them all night. It's considered good for the young gentlemen.'

'Hallo! War's declared! They're off!' said Moorshed.

He swung 267's head round to get a better view. A few miles to our right the low horizon was spangled with small balls of fire, while nearer ran a procession of tiny cigar ends.

'Red hot! Set 'em alight,' said Mr Pyecroft. 'That's the second destroyer flotilla diggin' out for Commander Fasset's reputation.'

The smaller lights disappeared; the glare of the destroyers' funnels dwindled even as we watched.

'They're going down Channel with lights out, thus showin' their zeal an' drivin' all watch-officers crazy. Now, if you'll excuse me, I think I'll get you your pyjamas, an' you'll turn in,' said Pyecroft.

He piloted me to the steel tunnel, where the ham still swung majestically over the swaying table, and dragged out trousers and a coat with a monk's hood, all hewn from one hairy inch-thick board.

'If you fall over in these you'll be drowned. They're lammies. I'll chock you off with a pillow; but sleepin' in a torpedo-boat's what you might call an acquired habit.'

I coiled down on an iron-hard horse-hair pillow next the quivering steel wall to acquire that habit. The sea, sliding over 267's skin, worried me with importunate, half-caught confidences. It drummed tackily to gather my attention, coughed, spat, cleared its throat, and, on the eve of that portentous communication, retired up stage as a multitude whispering. Anon, I caught the tramp of armies afoot, the hum of crowded cities awaiting the event, the single sob of a woman, and dry roaring of wild beasts. A dropped shovel clanging on the stokehold floor was, naturally enough, the unbarring of arena gates; our sucking uplift across the crest of some little swell, nothing less than the haling forth of new worlds; our half-turning descent into the hollow of its mate, the abysmal plunge of God-forgotten planets. Through all these phenomena and more – though I ran with wild horses over illimitable plains of rustling grass; though I crouched belly-flat under appalling fires of musketry; though I was Livingstone, painless and in-curious in the grip of his lion – my shut eyes saw the lamp swinging in its gimbals, the irregularly gliding patch of light on the steel ladder, and every elastic shadow in the corners of the frail angle-irons; while my body strove to accommodate itself to the infernal vibration of the machine. At the last I rolled limply on the floor, and woke to real life with a bruised nose and a great call to go on deck at once.

'It's all right,' said a voice in my booming ears. 'Morgan and Laughton are worse than you!'

I was gripping a rail. Mr Pyecroft pointed with his foot to two bundles beside a torpedo-tube, which at Weymouth had been a signaller and a most able seaman. 'She'd do better in a bigger sea,' said Mr Pyecroft. 'This lop is what fetches it up.'

The sky behind us whitened as I laboured, and the first dawn drove down the Channel, tipping the wave-tops with a chill glare. To me that round wind which runs before the true day has ever been fortunate and of good omen. It cleared the trouble from my body, and set my soul dancing to 267's heel and toe across the northerly set of the waves – such waves as I had often watched contemptuously from the deck of a ten-thousand-ton liner. They shouldered our little hull sideways and passed, scalloped, and splayed out, toward the coast, carrying our white wake in loops along their hollow backs. In succession we looked down a lead-grey cutting of water for half a clear mile, were flung up on its ridge, beheld the Channel traffic – full-sailed to that fair breeze – all about us, and swung slantwise, light as a bladder, elastic as a basket, into the next furrow. Then the sun found us, struck the wet grey bows to living, leaping opal, the colourless deep to hard sapphire, the many sails to pearl, and the little steam-plume of our escape to an inconstant rainbow.

'A fair day and a fair wind for all, thank God!' said Emanuel Pyecroft, throwing back the cowl-like hood of his blanket coat. His face was pitted with coal-dust and grime, pallid for lack of sleep; but his eyes shone like a gull's.

'I told you you'd see life. Think o' the *Pedantic* now. Think o' her Number One chasin' the mobilized gobbies round the lower deck flats. Think o' the pore little snotties now bein' washed, fed, and taught, an' the yeoman o' signals with a pink eye wakin' bright 'an brisk to another perishin' day of five-flag hoists. Whereas *we* shall caulk an' smoke cigarettes, same as the Spanish destroyers did for three weeks after war was declared.' He dropped into the wardroom singing:

> If you're going to marry me, marry me, Bill,
> It's no use muckin' about!

The man at the wheel, uniformed in what had once been a Tam-o'-shanter, a pair of very worn R.M.L.I. trousers rolled up to the knee, and a black sweater, was smoking a cigarette. Moorshed, in a grey Balaclava and a brown mackintosh with a flapping cape, hauled at our supplementary funnel guys, and a thing like a waiter from a Soho restaurant sat at the head of the engine-room ladder exhorting the unseen below. The following wind beat down our smoke and covered all things with an inch-thick layer of stokers, so that eyelids, teeth, and feet gritted in their motions. I began to see that my previous experiences among battleships and cruisers had been altogether beside the mark.

Part II

> The wind went down with the sunset –
> The fog came up with the tide,
> When the Witch of the North took an Egg-shell (*bis*)
> With a little Blue Devil inside.
> 'Sink,' she said, 'or swim,' she said,
> 'It's all you will get from me.
> And that is the finish of him!' she said,
> And the Egg-shell went to sea.

'Their Lawful Occasions'

The wind got up with the morning,
 And the fog blew off with the rain,
When the Witch of the North saw the Egg-shell
 And the little Blue Devil again.
'Did you swim?' she said. 'Did you sink?' she said,
 And the little Blue Devil replied:
'For myself I swam, but I think,' he said,
 'There's somebody sinking outside.'

But for the small detail that I was a passenger and a civilian, and might not alter her course, torpedo-boat No. 267 was mine to me all that priceless day. Moorshed, after breakfast – frizzled ham and a devil that Pyecroft made out of sardines, anchovies, and French mustard smashed together with a spanner – showed me his few and simple navigating tools, and took an observation. Morgan, the signaller, let me hold the chamois leathers while he cleaned the searchlight (we seemed to be better equipped with electricity than most of our class), that lived under a bulbous umbrella-cover amidships. Then Pyecroft and Morgan, standing easy, talked together of the King's Service as reformers and revolutionists, so notably, that were I not engaged on this tale I would, for its conclusion, substitute theirs.

I would speak of Hinchcliffe – Henry Salt Hinchcliffe, first-class engine-room artificer, and genius in his line, who was prouder of having taken part in the Hat Crusade in his youth than of all his daring, his skill, and his nickel-steel nerve. I consorted with him for an hour in the packed and dancing engine-room, when Moorshed suggested 'whacking her up' to eighteen knots, to see if she would stand it. The floor was ankle-deep in a creamy batter of oil and water; each moving part flicking more oil in zoetrope-circles, and the gauges invisible for their dizzy chattering on the chattering steel bulkhead. Leading stoker Grant, said to be a bigamist, an ox-eyed man smothered in hair, took me to the stokehold and planted me between a searing white furnace and some hell-hot iron plate for fifteen minutes, while I listened to the drone of fans and the worry of the sea without, striving to wrench all that palpitating firepot wide open.

Then I came on deck and watched Moorshed – revolving in

his orbit from the canvas bustle and torpedo-tubes aft, by way of engine-room, conning-tower, and wheel, to the doll's house of a foc'sle – learned in experience withheld from me, moved by laws beyond my knowledge, authoritative, entirely adequate, and yet, in heart, a child at his play. *I* could not take ten steps along the crowded deck but I collided with some body or thing; but he and his satellites swung, passed, and returned on their vocations with the freedom and spaciousness of the well-poised stars.

Even now I can at will recall every tone and gesture, with each dissolving picture inboard or overside – Hinchcliffe's white arm buried to the shoulder in a hornet's nest of spinning machinery; Moorshed's halt and jerk to windward as he looked across the water; Pyecroft's back bent over the Berthon collapsible boat, while he drilled three men in expanding it swiftly; the outflung white water at the foot of a homeward-bound Chinaman not a hundred yards away, and her shadow-slashed, rope-purfled sails bulging sideways like insolent cheeks; the ribbed and pitted coal-dust on our decks, all iridescent under the sun; the first filmy haze that paled the shadows of our funnels about lunch-time; the gradual die-down and dulling over of the short, cheery seas; the sea that changed to a swell; the swell that crumbled up and ran allwhither oilily; the triumphant, almost audible roll inward of wandering fog-walls that had been stalking us for two hours, and – welt upon welt, chill as the grave – the drive of the interminable main fog of the Atlantic. We slowed to little more than steerage-way and lay listening. Presently a hand-bellows foghorn jarred like a corncrake, and there rattled out of the mist a big ship literally above us. We could count the rivets in her plates as we scrooped by, and the little drops of dew gathered below them.

'Wonder why they're always barks – always steel – always four-masted – an' never less than two thousand tons. But they are,' said Pyecroft. He was out on the turtle-backed bows of her; Moorshed was at the wheel, and another man worked the whistle.

'This fog is the best thing could ha' happened to us,' said Moorshed. 'It gives us our chance to run in on the quiet ... Hal-lo!'

A cracked bell rang. Clean and sharp (beautifully grained, too), a bowsprit surged over our starboard bow, the bobstay confidentially hooking itself into our forward rail.

I saw Pyecroft's arm fly up; heard at the same moment the severing of the tense rope, the working of the wheel, Moorshed's voice down the tube saying, 'Astern a little, please, Mr Hinchcliffe!' and Pyecroft's cry, 'Trawler with her gear down! Look out for our propeller, Sir, or we'll be wrapped up in the rope.'

267 surged quickly under my feet, as the pressure of the downward-bearing bobstay was removed. Half-a-dozen men of the foc'sle had already thrown out fenders, and stood by to bear off a just visible bulwark.

Still going astern, we touched slowly, broadside on, to a suggestive crunching of fenders, and I looked into the deck of a Brixham trawler, her crew struck dumb.

'Any luck?' said Moorshed politely.

'Not till we met yeou,' was the answer. 'The Lard he saved us from they big ships to be spitted by the little wan. Where be'e gwine tu with our fine new bobstay?'

'Yah! You've had time to splice it by now,' said Pyecroft with contempt.

'Aie; but we'm all crushed to port like aigs. You was runnin' twenty-seven knots, us reckoned it. Didn't us, Albert?'

'Liker twenty-nine, an' niver no whistle.'

'Yes, we always do that. Do you want a tow to Brixham?' said Moorshed.

A great silence fell upon those wet men of the sea.

We lifted a little toward their side, but our silent, quick-breathing crew, braced and strained outboard, bore us off as though we had been a mere picket-boat.

'What for?' said a puzzled voice.

'For love; for nothing. You'll be abed in Brixham by midnight.'

'Yiss; but trawl's down.'

'No hurry. I'll pass you a line and go ahead. Sing out when you're ready.' A rope smacked on their deck with the word; they made it fast; we slid forward, and in ten seconds saw nothing save a few feet of the wire rope running into fog over our stern; but we heard the noise of debate.

'Catch a Brixham trawler letting go of a free tow in a fog,' said Moorshed, listening.

'But what in the world do you want him for?' I asked.

'Oh, he'll come in handy later.'

'Was that your first collision?'

'Yes.' I shook hands with him in silence, and our tow hailed us.

'Aie! yeou little man-o'-war!' The voice rose muffled and wailing. 'After us've upped trawl, us'll be glad of a tow. Leave line just slack abaout as 'tis now, and kip a good fine look-out be'ind 'ee.'

'There's an accommodatin' blighter for you!' said Pyecroft. 'Where does he expect we'll be, with these currents evolutin' like sailormen at the Agricultural Hall?'

I left the bridge to watch the wire-rope at the stern as it drew out and smacked down upon the water. By what instinct or guidance 267 kept it from fouling her languidly flapping propeller, I cannot tell. The fog now thickened and thinned in streaks that bothered the eyes like the glare of intermittent flash-lamps; by turns granting us the vision of a sick sun that leered and fled, or burying all a thousand fathom deep in gulfs of vapours. At no time could we see the trawler though we heard the click of her windlass, the jar of her trawl-beam, and the very flap of the fish on her deck. Forward was Pyecroft with the lead; on the bridge Moorshed pawed a Channel chart; aft sat I, listening to the whole of the British Mercantile Marine (never a keel less) returning to England, and watching the fog-dew run round the bight of the tow back to its mother-fog.

'Aie! yeou little man-o'-war! We'm done with trawl. You can take us home if you know the road.'

'Right O!' said Moorshed. 'We'll give the fishmonger a run for his money. Whack her up, Mr Hinchcliffe.'

The next few hours completed my education. I saw that I ought to be afraid, but more clearly (this was when a liner hooted down the back of my neck) that any fear which would begin to do justice to the situation would, if yielded to, incapacitate me for the rest of my days. A shadow of spread sails, deeper than the darkening twilight, brooding over us like the wings of Azrael (Pyecroft said she was a Swede), and miraculously withdrawn, persuaded me that there was a working chance that I should reach the beach – any beach – alive, if not dry; and (this was when an economical tramp laved our portrail with her condenser water) were I so spared, I vowed I would tell my tale worthily.

Thus we floated in space as souls drift through raw time. Night added herself to the fog, and I laid hold on my limbs jealously, lest they, too, should melt in the general dissolution.

'Where's that prevaricatin' fishmonger?' said Pyecroft, turning a lantern on a scant yard of the gleaming wire-rope that pointed like a stick to my left. 'He's doin' some fancy steerin' on his own. No wonder Mr Hinchcliffe is blasphemious. The tow's sheered off to starboard, Sir. He'll fair pull the stern out of us.'

Moorshed, invisible, cursed through the megaphone into invisibility.

'Aie! yeou little man-o'-war!' The voice butted through the fog with the monotonous insistence of a strayed sheep's. 'We don't all like the road you'm takin'. 'Tis no road to Brixham. You'll be buckled up under Prawle Point by'mbye.'

'Do you pretend to know where you are?' the megaphone roared.

'Iss, I reckon; but there's no pretence to me!'

'O Peter!' said Pyecroft. 'Let's hang him at 'is own gaff.'

I could not see what followed, but Moorshed said: 'Take another man with you. If you lose the tow, you're done. I'll slow her down.'

I heard the dinghy splash overboard ere I could cry 'Murder!' Heard the rasp of a boat-hook along the wire-rope, and then, as it had been in my ear, Pyecroft's enormous and jubilant bellow astern: 'Why, he's here! Right atop of us! The blighter 'as pouched half the tow, like a shark!' A long pause filled with soft Devonian bleatings. Then Pyecroft, *solo arpeggio*: 'Rum? Rum? Rum? Is that all? Come an' try it, uncle.'

I lifted my face to where once God's sky had been, and

besought The Trues I might not die inarticulate, amid these half-worked miracles, but live at least till my fellow-mortals could be made one-millionth as happy as I was happy. I prayed and I waited, and we went slow – slow as the processes of evolution – till the boat-hook rasped again.

'He's not what you might call a scientific navigator,' said Pyecroft, still in the dinghy, but rising like a fairy from a pantomime trap. 'The lead's what 'e goes by mostly; rum is what he's come for; an' Brixham is 'is 'ome. Lay on, Macduff!'

A white-whiskered man in a frock-coat – as I live by bread, a frock-coat! – sea-boots, and a comforter, crawled over the torpedo-tube into Moorshed's grip and vanished forward.

'’E'll probably 'old three gallon (look sharp with that dinghy!); but 'is nephew, left in charge of the *Agatha*, wants two bottles command-allowance. You're a taxpayer, Sir. Do you think that excessive?'

'Lead there! Lead!' rang out from forward.

'Didn't I say 'e wouldn' understand compass deviations? Watch him close. It'll be worth it!'

As I neared the bridge I heard the stranger say: 'Let me zmell un!' and to his nose was the lead presented by a trained man of the King's Navy.

'I'll tell 'ee where to goo, if yeou'll tell your donkey-man what to du. I'm no hand wi' steam.' On these lines we proceeded miraculously, and, under Moorshed's orders – I was the fisherman's Ganymede, even as 'M. de C.' had served the captain – I found both rum and curaçoa in a locker, and mixed them equal bulk in an enamelled iron cup.

'Now we'm just abeam o' where we should be,' he said at last, 'an' here we'll lay till she lifts. I'd take 'e in for another bottle – and wan for my nevvy; but I reckon yeou'rn shart-allowanced for rum. That's nivver no Navy rum yeou'm give me. Knowed 'ee by the smack tu un. Anchor now!'

I was between Pyecroft and Moorshed on the bridge, and heard them spring to vibrating attention at my side. A man with a lead a few feet to port caught the panic through my body, and checked like a wild boar at gaze, for not far away an unmistakable ship's bell was ringing. It ceased, and another began.

'Them!' said Pyecroft. 'Anchored!'

'More!' said our pilot, passing me the cup, and I filled it. The trawler astern clattered vehemently on her bell. Pyecroft with a jerk of his arm threw loose the forward three-pounder. The bar of the back-sight was heavily blobbed with dew; the foresight was invisible.

'No – they wouldn't have their picket-boats out in this weather, though they ought to.' He returned the barrel to its crotch slowly.

'Be yeou gwine to anchor?' said Macduff, smacking his lips, 'or be yeou gwine straight on to Livermead Beach?'

'Tell him what we're driving at. Get it into his head somehow,' said Moorshed; and Pyecroft, snatching the cup from me, enfolded the old man with an arm and a mist of wonderful words.

'And if you pull it off,' said Moorshed at the last, 'I'll give you a fiver.'

'Lard! What's fivers to me, young man? My nevvy, he likes 'em; but I do cherish more on fine drink than filthy lucre any day o' God's good weeks. Leave goo my arm, yeou common sailorman! I tall 'ee, gentlemen, I bain't the ram-faccd, ruddle-nosed old fule yeou reckon I be. Before the mast I've fared in my time; fisherman I've been since I seed the unsense of sea-dangerin'. Baccy and spirits – yiss, an' cigars too, I've run a plenty. I'm no blind harse or boy to be coaxed with your forty-mile free towin' and rum atop of all. There's none more sober to Brix'am this tide, I don't care who 'tis – than me. *I* know – *I* know. Yander'm two great King's ships. Yeou'm wishful to sink, burn, and destroy they while us kips 'em busy sellin' fish. No need tall me so twanty taime over. Us'll find they ships! Us'll find 'em, if us has to break our fine new bowsprit so close as Crump's bull's horn!'

'Good egg!' quoth Moorshed, and brought his hand down on the wide shoulders with the smack of a beaver's tail.

'Us'll go look for they by hand. Us'll give they something to play upon; an' do 'ee deal with them faithfully, an' may the Lard have mercy on your sowls! Amen. Put I in dinghy again.'

The fog was as dense as ever – we moved in the very womb of night – but I cannot recall that I took the faintest note of it as the dinghy, guided by the tow-rope, disappeared toward the *Agatha*, Pyecroft rowing. The bell began again on the starboard bow.

'We're pretty near,' said Moorshed, slowing down. 'Out with the Berthon. (*We'll* sell 'em fish, too.) And if anyone rows Navy-stroke, I'll break his jaw with the tiller. Mr Hinchcliffe' (this down the tube), 'you'll stay here in charge with Gregory and Shergold and the engine-room staff. Morgan stays, too, for signalling purposes.' A deep groan broke from Morgan's chest, but he said nothing. 'If the fog thins and you're seen by anyone, keep 'em quiet with the signals. I can't think of the precise lie just now, but *you* can, Morgan.'

'Yes, Sir.'

'Suppose their torpedo-nets are down?' I whispered, shivering with excitement.

'If they've been repairing minor defects all day, they won't have anyone to spare from the engine-room, and "Out nets!" is a job for the whole ship's company. I expect they've trusted to the fog – like us. Well, Pyecroft?'

That great soul had blown up on to the bridge like a feather. ''Ad to see the first o' the rum into the *Agathites*, Sir. They was a bit jealous o' their commandin' officer comin' 'ome so richly lacquered, and at first the *conversazione* languished, as you might say. But they sprang to attention ere I left. Six sharp strokes on the bells, if any of 'em are sober enough to keep tally, will be the signal that our consort 'as cast off her tow an' is manoeuvrin' on 'er own.'

'Right O! Take Laughton with you in the dinghy. Put that Berthon over quietly there! Are you all right, Mr Hinchcliffe?'

I stood back to avoid the rush of half-a-dozen shadows dropping into the Berthon boat. A hand caught me by the slack of my garments, moved me in generous arcs through the night, and I rested on the bottom of the dinghy.

'I want you for *prima facie* evidence, in case the vaccination don't take,' said Pyecroft in my ear. 'Push off, Alf!'

The last bell-ringing was high overhead. It was followed by

six little tinkles from the *Agatha*, the roar of her falling anchor, the clash of pans, and loose shouting.

'Where be gwine tu? Port your 'ellum. Aie! you mud-dredger in the fairway, goo astern! Out boats! She'll sink us!'

A clear-cut Navy voice drawled from the clouds: 'Quiet! you gardeners there. This is the *Cryptic* at anchor.'

'Thank you for the range,' said Pyecroft, and paddled gingerly. 'Feel well out in front of you, Alf. Remember your fat fist is our only Marconi installation.'

The voices resumed:

'Bournemouth steamer he says she be.'

'Then where be Brixham Harbor?'

'Damme, I'm a taxpayer tu. They've no right to cruise about this way. I'll have the laa on 'ee if anything carries away.'

Then the man-of-war:

'Short on your anchor! Heave short, you howling maniacs! You'll get yourselves smashed in a minute if you drift.'

The air was full of these and other voices as the dinghy, checking, swung. I passed one hand down Laughton's stretched arm and felt an iron gooseneck and a foot or two of a backward-sloping torpedo-net boom. The other hand I laid on broad, cold iron – even the flank of H.M.S. *Cryptic*, which is twelve thousand tons.

I heard a scrubby, raspy sound, as though Pyecroft had chosen that hour to shave, and I smelled paint. 'Drop aft a bit, Alf; we'll put a stencil under the stern six-inch casemates.'

Boom by boom Laughton slid the dinghy along the towering curved wall. Once, twice, and again we stopped, and the keen scrubbing sound was renewed.

'Umpires are 'ard-'earted blighters, but this ought to convince 'em . . . Captain Panke's stern-walk is now above our defenceless 'eads. Repeat the evolution up the starboard side, Alf.'

I was only conscious that we moved around an iron world palpitating with life. Though my knowledge was all by touch – as, for example, when Pyecroft led my surrendered hand to the base of some bulging sponson, or when my palm closed on the knife-edge of the stem and patted it timidly – yet I felt lonely and unprotected as the enormous, helpless ship was withdrawn, and we drifted away into the void where voices sang:

'Tom Pearce, Tom Pearce, lend me thy grey mare,
 All along, out along, down along lea!
 I want for to go to Widdicombe Fair
 With Bill Brewer, Sam Sewer, Peter Gurney, Harry Hawke,
 Old Uncle Tom Cobley an' all!'

'That's old Sinbad an' 'is little lot from the *Agatha*! Give way, Alf! *You* might sing somethin', too.'

'I'm no burnin' Patti. Ain't there noise enough for you, Pye?'

'Yes, but it's only amateurs. Give me the tones of 'earth and 'ome. Ha! List to the blighter on the 'orizon sayin' his prayers, Navy-fashion. 'Eaven 'elp me argue that way when I'm a warrant-officer!'

We headed with little lapping strokes toward what seemed to be a fair-sized riot.

'An' I've 'eard the *Devolution* called a happy ship, too,' said Pyecroft. 'Just shows 'ow a man's misled by prejudice. She's peevish – that's what she is – nasty-peevish. Prob'ly all because the *Agathites* are scratching 'er paint. Well, rub along, Alf. I've got the lymph!'

A voice, which Mr Pyecroft assured me belonged to a chief carpenter, was speaking through an aperture (starboard bow twelve-pounder on the lower deck). He did not wish to purchase any fish, even at grossly reduced rates. Nobody wished to buy any fish. This ship was the *Devolution* at anchor, and desired no communication with shore boats.

'Mark how the Navy 'olds its own. He's sober. The *Agathites* are not, as you might say, an' yet they can't live with 'im. It's the discipline that does it. 'Ark to the bald an' unconvincin' watch-officer chimin' in. I wonder where Mr Moorshed has got to?'

We drifted down the *Devolution*'s side, as we had drifted down her sister's; and we dealt with her in that dense gloom as we had dealt with her sister.

'Whai! 'Tis a man-o'-war, after all! I can see the captain's whisker all gilt at the edges! We took 'ee for the Bournemouth steamer. Three cheers for the real man-o'-war!'

That cry came from under the *Devolution*'s stern. Pyecroft held something in his teeth, for I heard him mumble, 'Our Mister Moorshed!'

Said a boy's voice above us, just as we dodged a jet of hot water from some valve: 'I don't half like that cheer. If I'd been the old man I'd ha' turned loose the quick-firers at the first go-off. Aren't they rowing Navy-stroke, yonder?'

'True,' said Pyecroft, listening to retreating oars. 'It's time to go 'ome when snotties begin to think. The fog's thinnin', too.'

I felt a chill breath on my forehead, and saw a few feet of the steel stand out darker than the darkness, disappear – it was then the dinghy shot away from it – and emerge once more.

'Hallo! what boat's that?' said the voice suspiciously.

'Why, I do believe it's a real man-o'-war, after all,' said Pyecroft, and kicked Laughton.

'What's that for?' Laughton was no dramatist.

'Answer in character, you blighter! Say somethin' opposite.'

'What boat's *thatt*?' The hail was repeated.

'What do yee say-ay?' Pyecroft bellowed, and, under his breath to me: 'Give us a hand.'

'It's called the *Marietta* – F. J. Stokes – Torquay,' I began, quaveringly. 'At least that's the name on the name-board. I've been dining – on a yacht.'

'I see.' The voice shook a little, and my way opened before me with disgraceful ease.

'Yesh. Dining private yacht. *Eshmesheralda*. I belong to Torquay Yacht Club. *Are* you member Torquay Yacht Club?'

'You'd better go to bed, Sir. Good-night.' We slid into the rapidly thinning fog.

'Dig out, Alf. Put your *nix mangiare* back into it. The fog's peelin' off like a petticoat. Where's Two Six Seven?'

'I can't see her,' I replied, 'but there's a light low down ahead.'

'The *Agatha*!' They rowed desperately through the uneasy dispersal of the fog for ten minutes and ducked round the trawler's bow.

'Well, Emanuel means "God with us" – so far.' Pyecroft wiped his brow, laid a hand on the low rail, and as he boosted me up to the trawler, I saw Moorshed's face, white as pearl in the thinning dark.

'Was it all right?' said he, over the bulwarks.

'Vaccination ain't in it. She's took beautiful. But where's 267, Sir?' Pyecroft replied.

'Gone. We came here as the fog lifted. I gave the *Devolution* four. Was that you behind us?'

'Yes, sir; but I only got in three on the *Devolution*. I gave the *Cryptic* nine, though. They're what you might call more or less vaccinated.'

He lifted me inboard, where Moorshed and six pirates lay around the *Agatha*'s hatch. There was a hint of daylight in the cool air.

'Where is the old man?' I asked.

'Still selling 'em fish, I suppose. He's a darling! But I wish I could get this filthy paint off my hands. Hallo! What the deuce is the *Cryptic* signalling?'

A pale masthead light winked through the last of the fog. It was answered by a white pencil to the southward.

'Destroyer signallin' with searchlight.' Pyecroft leaped on the stern-rail. 'The first part is private signals. Ah! now she's Morsing against the fog. "P–O–S–T – yes, postpone" – "D–E–P- (go on!) departure – till – further – orders – which – will – be com (he's dropped the other m) unicated – verbally. End." He swung round. '*Cryptic* is now answering: "Ready – proceed – immediately. What – news – promised – destroyer – flotilla?"'

'Hallo!' said Moorshed. 'Well, never mind. They'll come too late.'

'Whew! That's some 'igh-born suckling on the destroyer. Destroyer signals: "Care not. All will be known later." What merry beehive's broken loose now?'

'What odds! We've done our little job.'

'Why – why – it's Two Six Seven!'

Here Pyecroft dropped from the rail among the fishy nets and shook the *Agatha* with heavings. Moorshed cast aside his cigarette, looked over the stern, and fell into his subordinate's arms. I heard the guggle of engines, the rattle of a little anchor going over not a hundred yards away, a cough, and Morgan's subdued hail . . . So far as I remember, it was Laughton whom I hugged; but the men who hugged me most were Pyecroft and Moorshed, adrift among the fishy nets.

There was no semblance of discipline in our flight over the *Agatha*'s side, nor, indeed, were ordinary precautions taken for the common safety, because (I was in the Berthon) they held that patent boat open by hand for the most part. We regained our own craft, cackling like wild geese, and crowded round Moorshed and Hinchcliffe. Behind us the *Agatha*'s boat, returning from her fish-selling cruise, yelled: 'Have 'ee done the trick? Have 'ee done the trick?' and we could only shout hoarsely over the stern, guaranteeing them rum by the hold-full.

'Fog got patchy here at 12.27,' said Henry Salt Hinchcliffe, growing clearer every instant in the dawn. 'Went down to Brixham Harbour to keep out of the road. Heard whistles to the south and went to look. I had her up to sixteen good. Morgan kept on shedding private Red Fleet signals out of the signal-book, as the fog cleared, till we was answered by three destroyers. Morgan signalled 'em by searchlight: "Alter course to South Seventeen East, so as not to lose time." They came round quick. We kept well away – on their port beam – and Morgan gave 'em their orders.' He looked at Morgan and coughed.

'The signalman, acting as second in command,' said Morgan, swelling, 'then informed destroyer flotilla that *Cryptic* and *Devolution* had made good defects, and, in obedience to Admiral's supplementary orders (I was afraid they might suspect that, but they didn't), had proceeded at seven knots at 11.23 p.m. to rendezvous near Channel Islands, seven miles N.N.W. the Casquet light. (I've rendezvoused there myself, Sir.) Destroyer flotilla would therefore follow cruisers and catch up with them on their course. Destroyer flotilla then dug out on course indicated, all funnels sparking briskly.'

'Who were the destroyers?'

'*Wraith*, *Kobbold*, *Stiletto*, Lieutenant-Commander A. L.

Hignett, acting under Admiral's orders to escort cruisers received off the Dodman at 7 p.m. They'd come slow on account of fog.'

'Then who were you?'

'We were the *Afrite*, port-engine broke down, put in to Torbay, and there instructed by *Cryptic*, previous to her departure with *Devolution*, to inform Commander Hignett of change of plans. Lieutenant-Commander Hignett signalled that our meeting was quite providential. After this we returned to pick up our commanding officer, and being interrogated by *Cryptic*, marked time signalling as requisite, which you may have seen. The *Agatha* representing the last known rallying-point – or, as I should say, pivot-ship of the evolution – it was decided to repair to the *Agatha* at conclusion of manoeuvre.'

We breathed deeply, all of us, but no one spoke a word till Moorshed said: 'Is there such a thing as one fine big drink aboard this one fine big battleship?'

'Can do, sir,' said Pyecroft, and got it. Beginning with Mr Moorshed and ending with myself, junior to the third first-class stoker, we drank, and it was as water of the brook, that two and a half inches of stiff, treacly Navy rum. And we looked each in the other's face, and we nodded, bright-eyed, burning with bliss.

Moorshed walked aft to the torpedo-tubes and paced back and forth, a captain victorious on his own quarter-deck; and the triumphant day broke over the green-bedded villas of Torquay to show us the magnitude of our victory. There lay the cruisers (I have reason to believe that they had made good their defects). They were each four hundred and forty feet long and sixty-six wide; they held close upon eight hundred men apiece, and they had cost, say, a million and a half the pair. And they were ours, and they did not know it. Indeed, the *Cryptic*, senior ship, was signalling vehement remarks to our address, which we did not notice.

'If you take these glasses, you'll get the general run o' last night's vaccination,' said Pyecroft. 'Each one represents a torpedo got 'ome, as you might say.'

I saw on the *Cryptic*'s port side, as she lay half a mile away across the glassy water, four neat white squares in outline, a white blur in the centre.

'There are five more to starboard. 'Ere's the original!' He handed me a paint-dappled copper stencil-plate, two feet square, bearing in the centre the six-inch initials, 'G.M.'

'Ten minutes ago I'd ha' eulogized about that little trick of ours, but Morgan's performance has short-circuited me. Are you happy, Morgan?'

'Bustin',' said the signalman briefly.

'You may be. Gawd forgive you, Morgan, for as Queen 'Enrietta said to the 'ousemaid, *I* never will. I'd ha' given a year's pay for ten minutes o' your signallin' work this mornin'.'

'I wouldn't 'ave took it up,' was the answer. 'Perishin' 'Eavens above! Look at the *Devolution*'s semaphore!' Two black wooden arms waved from the junior ship's upper bridge. 'They've seen it.'

'*The* mote *on* their neighbour's beam, of course,' said Pyecroft, and read syllable by syllable: ' "Captain Malan to Captain Panke. Is – sten – cilled – frieze your starboard side new Admiralty regulation, or your Number One's private expense?" Now *Cryptic* is saying, "Not understood." Poor old *Crippy*, the *Devolute*'s raggin' 'er sore. "Who is G.M.?" she says. That's fetched the *Cryptic*. She's answerin': "You ought to know. Examine own paintwork." Oh Lord! they're both on to it now. This is balm. This is beginning to be balm. I forgive you, Morgan!'

Two frantic pipes twittered. From either cruiser a whaler dropped into the water and madly rowed round the ship: as a gay-coloured hoist rose to the *Cryptic*'s yardarm: 'Destroyer will close at once. Wish to speak by semaphore.' Then on the bridge semaphore itself: 'Have been trying to attract your attention last half-hour. Send commanding officer aboard at once.'

'Our attention? After all the attention we've given 'er, too,' said Pyecroft. 'What a greedy old woman!' To Moorshed: 'Signal from the *Cryptic*, Sir.'

'Never mind that!' said the boy, peering through his glasses. 'Out dinghy quick, or they'll paint our marks out. Come along!'

By this time I was long past even hysteria. I remember

Pyecroft's bending back, the surge of the driven dinghy, a knot of amazed faces as we skimmed the *Cryptic*'s ram, and the dropped jaw of the midshipman in her whaler when we barged fairly into him.

'Mind my paint!' he yelled.

'You mind mine, snotty,' said Moorshed. 'I was all night putting these little ear-marks on you for the umpires to sit on. Leave 'em alone.'

We splashed past him to the *Devolution*'s boat, where sat no one less than her first lieutenant, a singularly unhandy-looking officer.

'What the deuce is the meaning of this?' he roared, with an accusing forefinger.

'You're sunk, that's all. You've been dead half a tide.'

'Dead, am I? I'll show you whether I'm dead or not, Sir!'

'Well, you may be a survivor,' said Moorshed ingratiatingly, 'though it isn't at all likely.'

The officer choked for a minute. The midshipman crouched up in stern said, half aloud: 'Then I *was* right – last night.'

'Yesh,' I gasped from the dinghy's coal-dust. 'Are you member Torquay Yacht Club?'

'Hell!' said the first lieutenant, and fled away. The *Cryptic*'s boat was already at that cruiser's side, and semaphores flicked zealously from ship to ship. We floated, a minute speck, between the two hulls, while the pipes went for the captain's galley on the *Devolution*.

'That's all right,' said Moorshed. 'Wait till the gangway's down and then board her decently. We oughtn't to be expected to climb up a ship we've sunk.'

Pyecroft lay on his disreputable oars till Captain Malan, full-uniformed, descended the *Devolution*'s side. With due compliments – not acknowledged, I grieve to say – we fell in behind his sumptuous galley, and at last, upon pressing invitation, climbed, black as sweeps all, the lowered gangway of the *Cryptic*. At the top stood as fine a constellation of marine stars as ever sang together of a morning on a King's ship. Everyone who could get within earshot found that his work took him aft.

I counted eleven able seamen polishing the breech-block of the stern nine-point-two, four marines zealously relieving each other at the lifebuoy, six call-boys, nine midshipmen of the watch, exclusive of naval cadets, and the higher ranks past all census.

'If I die o' joy,' said Pyecroft behind his hand, 'remember I died forgivin' Morgan from the bottom of my 'eart, because, like Martha, we 'ave scoffed the better part. You'd better try to come to attention, Sir.'

Moorshed ran his eye voluptuously over the upper deck battery, the huge beam, and the immaculate perspective of power. Captain Panke and Captain Malan stood on the well-browned flash-plates by the dazzling hatch. Precisely over the flagstaff I saw Two Six Seven astern, her black petticoat half hitched up, meekly floating on the still sea. She looked like the pious Abigail who has just spoken her mind, and, with folded hands, sits thanking Heaven among the pieces. I could almost have sworn that she wore black worsted gloves and had a little dry cough. But it was Captain Panke that coughed so austerely. He favoured us with a lecture on uniform, deportment, and the urgent necessity of answering signals from a senior ship. He told us that he disapproved of masquerading, that he loved discipline, and would be obliged by an explanation. And while he delivered himself deeper and more deeply into our hands, I saw Captain Malan wince. He was watching Moorshed's eye.

'I belong to Blue Fleet, Sir. I command Number Two Six Seven,' said Moorshed, and Captain Panke was dumb. 'Have you such a thing as a frame-plan of the *Cryptic* aboard?' He spoke with winning politeness as he opened a small and neatly folded paper.

'I have, sir.' The little man's face was working with passion.

'Ah! Then I shall be able to show you precisely where you were torpedoed last night in' – he consulted the paper with one finely arched eyebrow – 'in nine places. And since the *Devolution* is, I understand, a sister ship' – he bowed slightly toward Captain Malan – 'the same plan –'

I had followed the clear precision of each word with a dumb amazement which seemed to leave my mind abnormally clear. I saw Captain Malan's eye turn from Moorshed and seek that of the *Cryptic*'s commander. And he telegraphed as clearly as Moorshed was speaking: 'My dear friend and brother officer, *I* know Panke; *you* know Panke; *we* know Panke – good little Panke! In less than three Greenwich chronometer seconds Panke will make an enormous ass of himself, and I shall have to put things straight, unless you who are a man of tact and discernment—'

'Carry on.' The Commander's order supplied the unspoken word. The cruiser boiled about her business around us; watch and watch officers together, up to the limit of noise permissible. I saw Captain Malan turn to his senior.

'Come to my cabin!' said Panke gratingly, and led the way. Pyecroft and I stayed still.

'It's all right,' said Pyecroft. 'They daren't leave us loose aboard for one revolution,' and I knew that he had seen what I had seen.

'You, too!' said Captain Malan, returning suddenly. We passed the sentry between white enamelled walls of speckless small-arms, and since that Royal Marine Light Infantryman was visibly suffocating from curiosity, I winked at him. We entered the chintz-adorned, photo-speckled, brass-fendered, tile-stoved main cabin. Moorshed, with a ruler, was demonstrating before the frame-plan of H.M.S. *Cryptic*.

'– making nine stencils in all of my initials G.M.,' I heard him say. 'Further, you will find attached to your rudder, and you, too, Sir' – he bowed to Captain Malan yet again – 'one fourteen-inch Mark IV practice torpedo, as issued to first-class torpedo-boats, properly buoyed. I have sent full particulars by telegraph to the umpires, and have requested them to judge on the facts as they – appear.' He nodded through the large window to the stencilled *Devolution* awink with brass-work in the morning sun, and ceased.

Captain Panke faced us. I remembered that this was only play, and caught myself wondering with what keener agony comes the real defeat.

'Good God, Johnny!' he said, dropping his lower lip like a child, 'this young pup says he has put us both out of action. Inconceivable – eh? My first command of one of the class.

Eh? What shall we do with him? What shall we do with him – eh?'

'As far as I can see, there's no getting over the stencils,' his companion answered.

'Why didn't I have the nets down? Why didn't I have the nets down?' The cry tore itself from Captain Panke's chest as he twisted his hands.

'I suppose we'd better wait and find out what the umpires will say. The Admiral won't be exactly pleased.' Captain Malan spoke very soothingly. Moorshed looked out through the stern door at Two Six Seven. Pyecroft and I, at attention, studied the paintwork opposite. Captain Panke had dropped into his desk chair, and scribbled nervously at a blotting-pad.

Just before the tension became unendurable, he looked at his junior for a lead. 'What – what are you going to do about it, Johnny – eh?'

'Well, if you don't want him, I'm going to ask this young gentleman to breakfast, and then we'll make and mend clothes till the umpires have decided.'

Captain Panke flung out a hand swiftly.

'Come with me,' said Captain Malan. 'Your men had better go back in the dinghy to – their – own – ship.'

'Yes, I think so,' said Moorshed, and passed out behind the captain. We followed at a respectful interval, waiting till they had ascended the ladder.

Said the sentry, rigid as the naked barometer behind him: 'For Gawd's sake! 'Ere, come 'ere! For Gawd's sake! What's 'appened? Oh! come '*ere* an' tell.'

'Tell? You?' said Pyecroft. Neither man's lips moved, and the words were whispers: 'Your ultimate illegitimate grand-children might begin to understand, not you – nor ever will.'

'Captain Malan's galley away, Sir,' cried a voice above; and one replied: 'Then get those two greasers into their dinghy and hoist the blue peter. We're out of action.'

'Can you do it, Sir?' said Pyecroft at the foot of the ladder. 'Do you think it is in the English language, or do you not?'

'I don't think I can, but I'll try. If it takes me two years, I'll try.'

*

There are witnesses who can testify that I have used no artifice. I have, on the contrary, cut away priceless slabs of *opus alexandrinum*. My gold I have lacquered down to dull bronze, my purples overlaid with sepia of the sea, and for hell-hearted ruby and blinding diamond I have substituted pale amethyst and mere jargoon. Because I would say again 'Disregarding the inventions of the Marine Captain whose other name is Gubbins, let a plain statement suffice.'

The Comprehension of Private Copper

The King's Task

After the sack of the City, when Rome was sunk to a name,
In the years when the Lights were darkened, or ever Saint
Wilfrid came,
Low on the borders of Britain, the ancient poets sing,
Between the cliff and the forest there ruled a Saxon king.

Stubborn all were his people, a stark and a jealous horde—
Not to be schooled by the cudgel, scarce to be cowed by the
sword;
Blithe to turn at their pleasure, bitter to cross in their mood,
And set on the ways of their choosing as the hogs of Andred's
Wood . . .

They made them laws in the Witan, the laws of flaying
and fine,
Folkland, common and pannage, the theft and the track of kine;
Statutes of tun and of market for the fish and the malt and
the meal,
The tax on the Bramber packhorse and the tax on the Hastings
keel.
Over the graves of the Druids and over the wreck of Rome
Rudely but deeply they bedded the plinth of the days to come.
Behind the feet of the Legions and before the Northman's ire,
Rudely but greatly begat they the body of state and of shire.
Rudely but greatly they laboured, and their labour stands till
now
If we trace on our ancient headlands the twist of their eight-ox
plough.

The Comprehension of Private Copper

Private Copper's father was a a Southdown shepherd; in early youth Copper had studied under him. Five years' army service had somewhat blunted Private Copper's pastoral instincts, but it occurred to him as a memory of the Chalk that sheep, or in this case buck, do not move towards one across turf, or in this case, the Colesberg kopjes unless a stranger, or in this case an enemy, is in the neighbourhood. Copper, helmet back-first, advanced with caution, leaving his mates of the picket full a mile behind. The picket, concerned for its evening meal, did not protest. A year ago it would have been an officer's command, moving as such. Today it paid casual allegiance to a Canadian, nominally a sergeant, actually a trooper of Irregular Horse, discovered convalescent in Naauwport Hospital, and forthwith employed on odd jobs. Private Copper crawled up the side of a bluish rock-strewn hill thinly fringed with brush a-top, and remembering how he had peered at Sussex conies through the edge of furze-clumps, cautiously parted the dry stems before his face. At the foot of the long slope sat three farmers smoking. To his natural lust for tobacco was added personal wrath because spiky plants were pricking his belly, and Private Copper slid the backsight up to fifteen hundred yards . . .

'Good evening, khaki. Please don't move,' said a voice on his left, and as he jerked his head round he saw entirely down the barrel of a well-kept Lee-Metford protruding from an insignificant tuft of thorn. Very few graven images have moved less than did Private Copper through the next ten seconds.

'It's nearer seventeen hundred than fifteen,' said a young man in an obviously ready-made suit of grey tweed, possessing himself of Private Copper's rifle. 'Thank *you*. We've got a post of thirty-seven men out yonder. You've eleven – eh? We don't want to kill 'em. We have no quarrel with poor uneducated khakis, and we do not want prisoners we do not keep. It is demoralizing to both sides – eh?'

Private Copper did not feel called upon to lay down the conduct of guerilla warfare. This dark-skinned, dark-haired, and dark-eyed stranger was his first intimate enemy. He spoke, allowing for a clipped cadence that recalled to Copper vague memories of Umballa, in precisely the same offensive accent that the young squire of Wilmington had used fifteen years ago when he caught and kicked Alf Copper, a rabbit in each pocket, out of the ditches of Cuckmere. The enemy looked Copper up and down, folded and repocketed a copy of an English weekly which he had been reading, and said: 'You seem an inarticulate sort of swine – like the rest of them – eh?'

'You,' said Copper, thinking, somehow, of the crushing answers he had never given to the young squire, 'are a renegid. Why, you ain't Dutch. You're English, same as me.'

'*No*, khaki. If you cannot talk civilly to a gentleman I will blow your head off.'

Copper cringed, and the action overbalanced him so that he rolled some six or eight feet downhill, under the lee of a rough rock. His brain was working with a swiftness and clarity strange in all his experience of Alf Copper. While he rolled he spoke, and the voice from his own jaws amazed him: 'If you did, 'twouldn't make you any less of a renegid.' As a useful after-thought he added: 'I've sprained my ankle.'

The young man was at his side in a flash. Copper made no motion to rise, but, cross-legged under the rock, grunted: ''Ow much did old Krujer pay you for this? What was you wanted for at 'ome? Where did you desert from?'

'Khaki,' said the young man, sitting down in his turn, 'you are a shade better than your mates. You did not make much more noise than a yoke of oxen when you tried to come up this hill, but you are an ignorant diseased beast like the rest of your people – eh? When you were at the Ragged Schools did they teach you any history, Tommy – 'istory, I mean?'

'Don't need no schoolin' to know a renegid,' said Copper. He had made three yards down the hill – out of sight, unless they could see through rocks, of the enemy's smoking party.

The young man laughed; and tossed the soldier a black sweating stick of 'True Affection'. (Private Copper had not smoked a pipe for three weeks.)

'*You* don't get this – eh?' said the young man. '*We* do. We take it from the trains as we want it. You can keep the cake – you po-ah Tommee.' Copper rammed the good stuff into his long-cold pipe and puffed luxuriously. Two years ago the sister of gunner-guard De Souza, East India Railway, had, at a dance given by the sergeants to the Allahabad Railway Volunteers, informed Copper that she could not think of waltzing with 'a poo-ah Tommee.' Private Copper wondered why that memory should have returned at this hour.

'I'm going to waste a little trouble on you before I send you back to your picket *quite* naked – eh? Then you can say how you were overpowered by twenty of us and fired off your last round – like the men we picked up at the drift playing cards at Stryden's farm – eh? What's your name – eh?'

Private Copper thought for a moment of a faraway house-maid who might still, if the local postman had not gone too far, be interested in his fate. On the other hand, he was, by temperament, economical of the truth. 'Pennycuik,' he said, 'John Pennycuik.'

'Thank you. Well, Mr John Pennycuik, I'm going to teach you a little 'istory, as you'd call it – eh?'

'Ow!' said Copper, stuffing his left hand in his mouth. 'So long since I've smoked I've burned my 'and – an' the pipe's dropped too. No objection to my movin' down to fetch it, is there – Sir?'

'I've got you covered,' said the young man, graciously, and Private Copper, hopping on one leg, because of his sprain, recovered the pipe yet another three yards downhill and squatted under another rock slightly larger than the first. A roundish boulder made a pleasant rest for his captor, who sat cross-legged once more, facing Copper, his rifle across his knee, his hand on the trigger-guard.

'Well, Mr Pennycuik, as I was going to tell you. A little after

146

you were born in your English workhouse, your kind, honourable, brave country, England, sent an English gentleman, who
could not tell a lie, to say that so long as the sun rose and the
rivers ran in their courses the Transvaal would belong to England. Did you ever hear that, khaki – eh?'

'Oh no, Sir,' said Copper. This sentence about the sun and
the rivers happened to be a very aged jest of McBride, the
professional humorist of D Company, when they discussed the
probable length of the war. Copper had thrown beef-tins at
McBride in the grey dawn of many wet and dry camps for
intoning it.

'*Of* course you would not. Now, mann, I tell you, listen.' He
spat aside and cleared his throat. 'Because of that little promise,
my father he moved into the Transvaal and bought a farm – a
little place of twenty or thirty thousand acres, don't – you –
know.'

The tone, in spite of the sing-song cadence fighting with the
laboured parody of the English drawl, was unbearably like the
young Wilmington squire's, and Copper found himself saying:
'I ought to. I've 'elped burn some.'

'Yes, you'll pay for that later. *And* he opened a store.'

'Ho! Shopkeeper was he?'

'The kind you call "Sir" and sweep the floor for, Pennycuik
... You see, in those days one used to believe in the British
Government. My father did. *Then* the Transvaal wiped thee
earth with the English. They beat them six times running. You
know *thatt* – eh?'

'Isn't what we've come 'ere for.'

'*But* my father (he knows better now) kept on believing in
the English. I suppose it was the pretty talk about rivers and
suns that cheated him – eh? Anyhow, he believed in his own
country. Inn his own country. *So* – you see – he was a little
startled when he found himself handed over to the Transvaal
as a prisoner of war. That's what it came to, Tommy – a
prisoner of war. You know what that is – eh? England was too
honourable and too gentlemanly to take trouble. There were no
terms made for my father.'

'So 'e made 'em 'imself. Useful old bird.' Private Copper

147

sliced up another pipeful and looked out across the wrinkled sea of kopjes, through which came the roar of the rushing Orange River, so unlike quiet Cuckmere.

The young man's face darkened. 'I think I shall sjambok you myself when I've quite done with you. *No*, my father (he was a fool) made no terms for eight years — ninety-six months — and for every day of them the Transvaal made his life hell for my father and — his people.'

'I'm glad to hear that,' said the impenitent Copper.

'Are you? You can think of it when I'm taking the skin off your back — eh? . . . My father, he lost everything — everything down to his self-respect. You don't know what *thatt* means — eh?'

'Why?' said Copper. 'I'm smokin' baccy stole by a renegid. Why wouldn't I know?'

If it came to a flogging on that hillside there might be a chance of reprisals. Of course, he might be marched to the Boer camp in the next valley and there operated upon; but Army life teaches no man to cross bridges unnecessarily.

'Yes, after eight years, my father, cheated by your bitch of a country, he found out who was the upper dog in South Africa.'

'That's me,' said Copper valiantly. 'If it takes another 'alf-century, it's me an' the likes of me.'

'You? Heaven help you! You'll be screaming at a wagon-wheel in an hour . . . Then it struck my father that he'd like to shoot the people who'd betrayed him. You — you — *you*! He told his son all about it. He told him never to trust the English. He told him to do them all the harm he could. Mann, I tell you, I don't want much telling. I was born in the Transvaal — I'm a burgher. If my father didn't love the English, by the Lord, mann, I tell you, I hate them from the bottom of my soul.'

The voice quavered and ran high. Once more, for no conceivable reason, Private Copper found his inward eye turned upon Umballa cantonments of a dry dusty afternoon, when the saddle-coloured son of a local hotel-keeper came to the barracks to complain of a theft of fowls. He saw the dark face, the plover's-egg-tinted eyeballs, and the thin excited hands. Above all, he remembered the passionate, queerly-strung words. Slowly he returned to South Africa, using the very sentence his sergeant had used to the poultry man.

'Go on with your complaint. I'm listenin'.'

'Complaint! Complaint about *you*, you ox! We strip and kick your sort by thousands.'

The young man rocked to and fro above the rifle, whose muzzle thus deflected itself from the pit of Private Copper's stomach. His face was dusky with rage.

'Yess, I'm a Transvaal burgher. It took us about twenty years to find out how rotten you were. *We* know and you know it now. Your Army — it is the laughing-stock of the Continent.' He tapped the newspaper in his pocket. 'You think you're going to win, you poor fools! Your people — your own people — your silly rotten fools of people will crawl out of it as they did after Majuba. They are beginning now. Look what your own working classes, the diseased, lying, drinking white stuff that you come out of, are saying.' He thrust the English weekly, doubled at the leading article, on Copper's knee. 'See what dirty dogs your masters are. They do not even back you in your dirty work. *We* cleared the country down to Ladysmith — to Estcourt. *We* cleared the country down to Colesberg.'

'Yes. We 'ad to clean up be'ind you. Messy, I call it.'

'You've had to stop farm-burning because your people daren't do it. They were afraid. You daren't kill a spy. You daren't shoot a spy when you catch him in your own uniform. You daren't touch our loyall people in Cape Town! Your masters won't let you. You will feed our women and children till we are quite ready to take them back. *You* can't put your cowardly noses out of the towns you say you've occupied. *You* daren't move a convoy twenty miles. You think you've done something? You've done nothing, and you've taken a quarter of a million of men to do it! There isn't a nigger in South Africa that doesn't obey us if we lift our finger. You pay the stuff four pounds a month and they lie to you. *We* flog 'em, as I shall flog you.'

He clasped his hands together and leaned forward his out-thrust chin within two feet of Copper's left, or pipe hand.

'Yuss,' said Copper, 'it's a fair knock-out.' The fist landed to a hair on the chin-point, the neck snicked like a gun-lock, and the back of the head crashed on the boulder behind.

Copper grabbed up both rifles, unshipped the cross-bandoliers, drew forth the English weekly, and picking up the lax hands, looked long and intently at the finger-nails.

'No! Not a sign of it there,' he said. ''Is nails are as clean as mine – but he talks just like 'em though. And he's a landlord too! A landed proprietor! Shockin', I call it.'

The arms began to flap with returning consciousness. Private Copper rose up and whispered: 'If you open your head, I'll bash it.' There was no suggestion of sprain in the flung-back left boot. 'Now walk in front of me, both arms perpendicularly elevated. I'm only a third-class shot, so, if you don't object, I'll rest the muzzle of my rifle lightly but firmly on your collar-button – coverin' the serviceable vertebree. If your friends see us thus engaged, you pray – 'ard.'

Private and prisoner staggered downhill. No shots broke the peace of the afternoon, but once the young man checked and was sick.

'There's a lot of things I could say to you,' Copper observed, at the close of the paroxysm, 'but it doesn't matter. Look 'ere, you call me "pore Tommy" again.'

The prisoner hesitated.

'Oh, I ain't goin' to do anythin' *to* you. I'm reconnoiterin' in my own. Say "pore Tommy" 'alf-a-dozen times.'

The prisoner obeyed.

'*That's* what's been puzzlin' me since I 'ad the pleasure o' meetin' you,' said Copper. 'You ain't 'alf-caste, but you talk *chee-chee* – *pukka* bazar chee-chee. *Pro*ceed.'

'Hullo,' said the Sergeant of the picket, twenty minutes later, 'where did you round him up?'

'On the top o' yonder craggy mounting. There's a mob of 'em sitting round their Bibles seventeen 'undred yards (you said it was seventeen 'undred?) t'other side – an' I want some coffee.' He sat down on the smoke-blackened stones by the fire.

''Ow did you get 'im?' said McBride, professional humorist, quietly filching the English weekly from under Copper's armpit.

'On the chin – while 'e was waggin' it at me.'

'What is 'e? 'Nother Colonial rebel to be 'orribly dis-enfranchised, or a Cape Minister, or only a loyal farmer with dynamite in both boots. Tell us all about it, Burjer!'

'You leave my prisoner alone,' said Private Copper. ''E's 'ad losses an' trouble; an' it's in the family too. 'E thought I never read the papers, so 'e kindly lent me his very own *Jerrold's Weekly* – an' 'e explained it to me as patronizin' as a – as a militia subaltern doin' Railway Staff Officer. 'E's a left-over from Majuba – one of the worst kind, an' 'earin' the evidence as I did, I don't exactly blame 'im. It was this way.'

To the picket Private Copper held forth for ten minutes on the life-history of his captive. Allowing for some purple patches, it was an absolutely fair rendering.

'But what I dis-liked was this baccy-priggin' beggar, 'oo's people, on 'is own showin', couldn't 'ave been more than thirty or forty years in the coun – on this Gawd-forsaken dust-'eap, comin' the squire over me. They're all parsons – we know *that*, but parson *an'* squire is a bit too thick for Alf Copper. Why, I caught 'im in the shameful act of trying' to start a aristocracy on a gun an' a wagon an' a *shambuk*! Yes; that's what it was: a bloomin' aristocracy.'

'No, it weren't,' said McBride, at length, on the dirt, above the purloined weekly. 'You're the aristocrat, Alf. Old *Jerrold's* givin' it you 'ot. You're the uneducated 'ireling of a calcallous aristocracy which 'as sold itself to the 'Ebrew financeer. Meantime, Ducky' – he ran his finger down a column of assorted paragraphs – 'you're slakin' your brutal instincks in furious excesses. Shriekin' women an' desolated 'omesteads is what you enjoy, Alf . . . Halloa! What's a smokin' 'ektacomb?'

''Ere! Let's look. 'Aven't seen a proper spicy paper for a year. Good old *Jerrold's*!' Pinewood and Moppet, reservists, flung themselves on McBride's shoulders, pinning him to the ground.

'Lie over your own bloomin' side of the bed, an' we can all look,' he protested.

'They're only po-ah Tommies,' said Copper, apologetically, to the prisoner. 'Po-ah unedicated khakis. *They* don't know what they're fightin' for. They're lookin' for what the diseased, lying, drinkin' white stuff that they come from is sayin' about 'em!'

The prisoner set down his tin of coffee and stared helplessly round the circle.

'I – I don't understand them.'

The Canadian sergeant, picking his teeth with a thorn, nodded sympathetically:

'If it comes to that, *we* don't in my country! . . . Say, boys, when you're through with your English mail you might's well provide an escort for your prisoner. He's waitin'.'

'Arf a mo', Sergeant,' said McBride, still reading. ''Ere's Old Barbarity on the ramp again with some of 'is lady friends, 'oo don't like concentration camps. Wish they'd visit ours. Pine-wood's a married man. He'd know how to be'ave!'

'Well, I ain't goin' to amuse my prisoner alone. 'E's gettin' 'omesick,' cried Copper. 'One of you thieves read out what's vexin' Old Barbarity an' 'is 'arem these days. You'd better listen, Burjer, because, afterwards, I'm goin' to fall out an' perpetrate those nameless barbarities all over you to keep up the reputation of the British Army.'

From that English weekly, to bar out which a large and perspiring staff of Press censors toiled seven days of the week at Cape Town, did Pinewood of the Reserve read unctuously excerpts of the speeches of the accredited leaders of His Majesty's Opposition. The night-picket arrived in the middle of it, but stayed entranced without paying any compliments, till Pinewood had entirely finished the leading article, and several occasional notes.

'Gentlemen of the jury,' said Alf Copper, hitching up what war had left to him of trousers – 'you've 'eard what 'e's been fed up with. *Do* you blame the beggar? 'Cause I don't! . . . Leave 'im alone, McBride. He's my first and only cap-ture, an' I'm goin' to walk 'ome with 'im, ain't I, Ducky? . . . Fall in, Burjer. It's Bermuda, or Umballa, or Ceylon for you – and I'd give a month's pay to be in your little shoes.'

As not infrequently happens, the actual moving off the ground broke the prisoner's nerve. He stared at the tinted hills round him, gasped and began to struggle – kicking, swearing, weeping, and fluttering all together.

'Pore beggar – oh, pore, *pore* beggar!' said Alf, leaning in on one side of him, while Pinewood blocked him on the other.

'Let me go! Let me go! Mann, I tell you, let me go –'

''E screams like a woman!' said McBride. 'They'll 'ear 'im five miles off.'

'There's one or two ought to 'ear 'im – in England,' said Copper, putting aside a wildly waving arm.

'Married, ain't 'e?' said Pinewood. 'I've seen 'em go like this before – just at the last.' *Old* on, old man. No one's goin' to 'urt you.'

The last of the sun threw the enormous shadow of a kopje over the little, anxious, wriggling group.

'Quit that,' said the Sergeant of a sudden. 'You're only making him worse. Hands *up*, prisoner! Now you get a holt of yourself, or this'll go off.'

And indeed the revolver-barrel square at the man's panting chest seemed to act like a tonic; he choked, recovered himself, and fell in between Copper and Pinewood.

As the picket neared the camp it broke into song that was heard among the officers' tents:

> ''E sent us 'is blessin' from London town
>   (The beggar that kep' the cordite down),
> But what do we care if 'e smile or frown,
>   The beggar that kep' the cordite down?
> The mildly nefarious
> Wildly barbarious
>   Beggar that kept the cordite down!'

Said a captain a mile away: 'Why are they singing *that*? We haven't had a mail for a month, have we?'

An hour later the same captain said to his servant: 'Jenkins, I understand the picket have got a – got a newspaper off a prisoner today. I wish you could lay hands on it, Jenkins. Copy of the *Times*, I think.'

'Yes, Sir. Copy of the *Times*, Sir,' said Jenkins, without a quiver, and went forth to make his own arrangements.

'Copy of the *Times*,' said the blameless Alf, from beneath his blanket. 'I ain't a member of the Soldiers' Institoot. Go an' look in the reg'mental Readin'-room – Veldt Row, Kopje Street, second turnin' to the left between 'ere an' Naauwport.'

Jenkins summarized briefly in a tense whisper the thing that Alf Copper need not be.

'But my particular copy of the *Times* is specially pro'ibited by the censor from corruptin' the morals of the Army. Get a written order from K. o' K., properly countersigned, an' I'll think about it.'

'I've got all *you* want,' said Jenkins. ''Urry up. I want to 'ave a squint myself.'

Something gurgled in the darkness, and Private Copper fell back smacking his lips.

'Gawd bless my prisoner, and make me a good boy. Amen. 'Ere you are, Jenkins. It's dirt cheap at a tot.'

⁅ Steam Tactics ⁆

The Necessitarian

I know not in whose hands are laid
   To empty upon earth
From unsuspected ambuscade
   The very Urns of Mirth:

Who bids the Heavenly Lark arise
   And cheer our solemn round –
The Jest beheld with streaming eyes
   And grovellings on the ground;

Who joins the flats of Time and Chance
   Behind the prey preferred,
And thrones on Shrieking Circumstance
   The Sacredly Absurd,

Till Laughter, voiceless through excess,
   Waves mute appeal and sore,
Above the midriff's deep distress,
   For breath to laugh once more.

No creed hath dared to hail him Lord,
   No raptured choirs proclaim,
And Nature's strenuous Overword
   Hath nowhere breathed his name.

Yet, may it be, on wayside jape,
   The selfsame Power bestows
The selfsame power as went to shape
   His Planet or His Rose.

Steam Tactics

I caught sight of their faces as we came up behind the cart in the narrow Sussex lane; but though it was not eleven o'clock, they were both asleep.

That the carrier was on the wrong side of the road made no difference to his language when I rang my bell. He said aloud of motor-cars, and specially of steam ones, all the things which I had read in the faces of superior coachmen. Then he pulled slantwise across me.

There was a vociferous steam air-pump attached to that car which could be applied at pleasure . . .

The cart was removed about a bowshot's length in seven and a quarter seconds, to the accompaniment of parcels clattering. At the foot of the next hill the horse stopped, and the two men came out over the tail-board.

My engineer backed and swung the car, ready to move out of reach.

'The blighted egg-boiler has steam up,' said Mr Hinchcliffe, pausing to gather a large stone. 'Temporize with the beggar, Pye, till the sights come on!'

'I can't leave my 'orse!' roared the carrier; 'but bring 'em up 'ere, an' I'll kill 'em all over again.'

'Good morning, Mr Pyecroft,' I called cheerfully. 'Can I give you a lift anywhere?'

The attack broke up round my fore-wheels.

'Well, we *do* 'ave the knack o' meeting *in puris naturalibus*, as I've so often said.' Mr Pyecroft wrung my hand. 'Yes, I'm on leaf. So's Hinch. We're visiting friends among these kopjes.'

A monotonous bellowing up the road persisted, where the carrier was still calling for corpses.

'That's Agg. He's Hinch's cousin. You aren't fortunit in your family connections, Hinch. 'E's usin' language in derogation of good manners. Go and abolish 'im.'

Henry Salt Hinchcliffe stalked back to the cart and spoke to his cousin. I recall much that the wind bore to me of his words and the carrier's. It seemed as if the friendship of years were dissolving amid throes.

''Ave it your own silly way, then,' roared the carrier, 'an' get into Linghurst on your own silly feet. I've done with you two runagates.' He lashed his horse and passed out of sight still rumbling.

'The fleet's sailed,' said Pyecroft, 'leavin' us on the beach as before. Had you any particular port in your mind?'

'Well, I was going to meet a friend at Instead Wick, but I don't mind –'

'Oh! that'll do as well as anything! We're on leaf, you see.'

'She'll hardly hold four,' said my engineer. I had broken him of the foolish habit of being surprised at things, but he was visibly uneasy.

Hinchcliffe returned, drawn as by ropes to my steam-car, round which he walked in narrowing circles.

'What's her speed?' he demanded of the engineer.

'Twenty-five,' said that loyal man.

'Easy to run?'

'No; very difficult,' was the emphatic answer.

'That just shows that you ain't fit for your ratiug. D'you suppose that a man who earns his livin' by runnin' 30-knot destroyers for a parstime – for a parstime, mark you! – is going to lie down before any blighted land-crabbing steam-pinnace on springs?'

Yet that was what he did. Directly under the car he lay and looked upward into pipes – petrol, steam, and water – with a keen and searching eye.

I telegraphed Mr Pyecroft a question.

'Not – in – the – least,' was the answer. 'Steam gadgets always take him that way. We had a bit of a riot at Parsley Green through his tryin' to show a traction-engine haulin' gipsy-wagons how to turn corners.'

'Tell him everything he wants to know,' I said to the engineer, as I dragged out a rug and spread it on the roadside.

'*He* don't want much showing,' said the engineer. Now, the two men had not, counting the time we took to stuff our pipes, been together more than three minutes.

'This,' said Pyecroft, driving an elbow back into the deep verdure of the hedge-foot, 'is a little bit of all right. Hinch, I shouldn't let too much o' that hot muckings drop in my eyes. Your leaf's up in a fortnight, an' you'll be wantin' 'em.'

'Here!' said Hinchcliffe, still on his back, to the engineer. 'Come here and show me the lead of this pipe.' And the engineer lay down beside him.

'That's all right,' said Mr Hinchcliffe, rising. 'But she's more of a bag of tricks than I thought. Unship this super-structure aft' – he pointed to the back seat – 'and I'll have a look at the forced draught.'

The engineer obeyed with alacrity. I heard him volunteer the fact that he had a brother an artificer in the Navy.

'They couple very well, those two,' said Pyecroft critically, while Hinchcliffe sniffed round the asbestos-lagged boiler and turned on gay jets of steam.

'Now take me up the road,' he said. My man, for form's sake, looked at me.

'Yes, take him,' I said. 'He's all right.'

'No, I'm not,' said Hinchcliffe of a sudden – 'not if I'm expected to judge my water out of a little shaving-glass.'

The water-gauge of that steam-car was reflected on a mirror to the right of the dashboard. I also had found it inconvenient.

'Throw up your arm and look at the gauge under your armpit. Only mind how you steer while you're doing it, or you'll get ditched!' I cried, as the car ran down the road.

'I wonder!' said Pyecroft, musing. 'But, after all, it's your steamin' gadgets he's usin' for his libretto, as you might put it. He said to me after breakfast only this mornin' 'ow he thanked his Maker, on all fours, that he wouldn't see nor smell nor thumb a runnin' bulgine till the nineteenth prox. Now look at him! Only look at 'im!'

We could see, down the long slope of the road, my driver surrendering his seat to Hinchcliffe, while the car flickered generously from hedge to hedge.

'What happens if he upsets?'

'The petrol will light up and the boiler may blow up.'

'How rambunkshus! And' – Pyecroft blew a slow cloud – 'Agg's about three hoops up this mornin', too.'

'What's that to do with us? He's gone down the road,' I retorted.

'Ye – es, but we'll overtake him. He's a vindictive carrier. He and Hinch 'ad words about pig-breeding this morning. O' course, Hinch don't know the elements o' that evolution; but he fell back on 'is naval rank an' office, an' Agg grew peevish. I wasn't sorry to get out of the cart . . . Have you ever considered how, when you an' I meet, so to say, there's nearly always a remarkably hectic day ahead of us! Hullo! Behold the beef-boat returnin'!'

He rose as the car climbed up the slope, and shouted: 'In bow! Way 'nuff!'

'You be quiet!' cried Hinchcliffe, and drew up opposite the rug, his dark face shining with joy. 'She's the Poetry o' Motion! She's the Angel's Dream. She's –' He shut off steam, and the slope being against her, the car slid soberly downhill again.

'What's this? I've got the brake on!' he yelled.

'It doesn't hold backwards,' I said. 'Put her on the mid-link.'

'That's a nasty one for the chief engineer o' the *Djinn*, 31-knot T.B.D.,' said Pyecroft. '*Do* you know what the mid-link is, Hinch?'

Once more the car returned to us; but as Pyecroft stooped to gather up the rug, Hinchcliffe jerked the lever testily, and with prawn-like speed she retired backwards into her own steam.

'Apparently 'e don't,' said Pyecroft. 'What's he done now, Sir?'

'Reversed her. I've done it myself.'

'But he's an engineer.'

For the third time the car manoeuvred up the hill.

'I'll teach you to come alongside properly, if I keep you tiffies out all night!' shouted Pyecroft. It was evidently a quotation. Hinchcliffe's face grew livid, and, his hand ever so slightly working on the throttle, the car buzzed twenty yards uphill.

'That's enough. We'll take your word for it. The mountain will go to Ma'ommed. Stand *fast*!'

Pyecroft and I and the rug marched up where she and Hinchcliffe fumed together.

'Not as easy as it looks – eh, Hinch?'

'It is dead easy. I'm going to drive her to Instead Wick – aren't I?' said the first-class engine-room artificer. I thought of his performances with No. 267 and nodded. After all, it was a small privilege to accord to pure genius.

'But my engineer will stand by – at first,' I added.

'An' you a family man, too,' muttered Pyecroft, swinging himself into the right rear seat. 'Sure to be a remarkably hectic day when we meet.'

We adjusted ourselves and, in the language of the immortal Navy doctor, paved our way towards Linghurst, distant by mile-post $11\frac{3}{4}$ miles.

Mr Hinchcliffe, every nerve and muscle braced, talked only to the engineer, and that professionally. I recalled the time when I, too, had enjoyed the rack on which he voluntarily extended himself.

And the County of Sussex slid by in slow time.

'How cautious is the tiffy-bird!' said Pyecroft.

'Even in a destroyer,' Hinch snapped over his shoulder, 'you ain't expected to con and drive simultaneous. Don't address any remarks to *me*!'

'Pump!' said the engineer. 'Your water's droppin'.'

'*I* know that. Where the Heavens is that blighted by-pass?'

He beat his right or throttle hand madly on the side of the car till he found the bent rod that more or less controls the pump, and, neglecting all else, twisted it furiously.

My engineer grabbed the steering-bar just in time to save us lurching into a ditch.

'If I was a burnin' peacock, with two hundred bloodshot eyes in my shinin' tail, I'd need 'em all on this job!' said Hinch.

'Don't talk! Steer! This ain't the North Atlantic,' Pyecroft replied.

'Blast my stokers! Why, the steam's dropped fifty pounds!' Hinchcliffe cried.

'Fire's blown out,' said the engineer. 'Stop her!'

'Does she do that often?' said Hinch, descending.

'Sometimes.'

'Any time?'

'Any time a cross-wind catches her.'

The engineer produced a match and stooped.

That car (now, thank Heaven, no more than an evil memory) never lit twice in the same fashion. This time she back-fired superbly, and Pyecroft went out over the right rear wheel in a column of rich yellow flame.

'I've seen a mine explode at Bantry – once – prematoor,' he volunteered.

'That's all right,' said Hinchcliffe, brushing down his singed beard with a singed forefinger. (He had been watching too closely.) 'Has she any more little surprises up her dainty sleeve?'

'She hasn't begun yet,' said my engineer, with a scornful cough. 'Someone 'as opened the petrol-supply-valve too wide.'

'Change places with me, Pyecroft,' I commanded, for I remembered that the petrol-supply, the steam-lock, and the forced draught were all controlled from the right rear seat.

'Me? Why? There's a whole switchboard full o' nickel-plated muckin's which I haven't begun to play with yet. The starboard side's crawlin' with 'em.'

'Change, or I'll kill you!' said Hinchcliffe, and he looked like it.

'That's the tiffy all over. When anything goes wrong, blame it on the lower deck. Navigate by your automatic self, then! *I* won't help you any more.'

We navigated for a mile in dead silence.

'Talkin' o' wakes ' said Pyecroft suddenly.

'We weren't,' Hinchcliffe grunted.

'There's some wakes would break a snake's back; but this of yours, so to speak, would fair turn a tapeworm giddy. That's all I wish to observe, Hinch ... Cart at anchor on the port bow. It's Agg!'

Far up the shaded road into secluded Bromlingleigh we saw the carrier's cart at rest before the post-office.

'He's bung in the fairway. How'm I to get past?' said Hinchcliffe. 'There's no room. Here, Pye, come and relieve the wheel!'

'Nay, nay, Pauline. You've made your own bed. You've as good as left your happy home an' family cart to steal it. Now you lie on it.'

'Ring your bell,' I suggested.

'Glory!' said Pyecroft, falling forward into the nape of Hinchcliffe's neck as the car stopped dead.

'Get out o' my back-hair! That must have been the brake I touched off,' Hinchcliffe muttered, and repaired his error tumultuously.

We passed the cart as though we had been all Bruges belfry. Agg, from the post-office door, regarded us with a too pacific eye. I remembered later that the pretty postmistress looked on us pityingly.

Hinchcliffe wiped the sweat from his brow and drew breath. It was the first vehicle that he had passed, and I sympathized with him.

'You needn't grip so hard,' said my engineer. 'She steers as easy as a bicycle.'

'Ho! You suppose I ride bicycles up an' down my engine-room?' was the answer. 'I've other things to think about. She's a terror. She's a whistlin' lunatic. I'd sooner run the old South-Easter at Simonstown than her!'

'One of the nice things they say about her,' I interrupted, 'is that no engineer is needed to run this machine.'

'No. They'd need about seven.'

'"Common-sense only is needed,"' I quoted.

'Make a note of that, Hinch. Just common-sense,' Pyecroft put in.

'And now,' I said, 'we'll have to take in water. There isn't more than a couple of inches of water in the tank.'

'Where d'you get it from?'

'Oh! – cottages and such-like.'

'Yes, but that being so, where does your much-advertised

162

twenty-five miles an hour come in? Ain't a dung-cart more to the point?'

'If you want to go anywhere, I suppose it would be,' I replied.

'*I* don't want to go anywhere. I'm thinkin' of you who've got to live with her. She'll burn her tubes if she loses her water?'

'She will.'

'I've never scorched yet, and I'm not beginnin' now.' He shut off steam firmly. 'Out you get, Pye, an' shove her along by hand.'

'Where to?'

'The nearest water-tank,' was the reply. 'And Sussex is a dry county.'

'She ought to have drag-ropes – little pipe-clayed ones,' said Pyecroft.

We got out and pushed under the hot sun for half-a-mile till we came to a cottage, sparsely inhabited by one child who wept.

'All out haymakin', o' course,' said Pyecroft, thrusting his head into the parlour for an instant. 'What's the evolution now?'

'Skirmish till we find a well,' I said.

'Hmm! But they wouldn't 'ave left that kid without a chaperon, so to say . . . I thought so! Where's a stick?'

A bluish and silent beast of the true old sheepdog breed glided from behind an outhouse and without words fell to work.

Pyecroft kept him at bay with a rake-handle while our party, in rallying-square, retired along the box-bordered brick path to the car.

At the garden gate the dumb devil halted, looked back on the child, and sat down to scratch.

'That's his three-mile limit, thank Heaven!' said Pyecroft. 'Fall in, push-party, and proceed with land-transport o' pinnace. I'll protect your flanks in case this sniffin' flea-bag is tempted beyond 'is strength.'

We pushed off in silence. The car weighed 1200 lb., and even on ball-bearings was a powerful sudorific. From somewhere behind a hedge we heard a gross rustic laugh.

'Those are the beggars we lie awake for, patrollin' the high seas. There ain't a port in China where we wouldn't be better treated. Yes, a Boxer 'ud be ashamed of it,' said Pyecroft.

A cloud of fine dust boomed down the road.

'Some happy craft with a well-found engine-room! How different!' panted Hinchcliffe, bent over the starboard mudguard.

It was a claret-coloured petrol car, and it stopped courteously, as good cars will at sight of trouble.

'Water, only water,' I answered in reply to offers of help.

'There's a lodge at the end of these oak palings. They'll give you all you want. Say I sent you. Gregory – Michael Gregory. Goodbye!'

'Ought to 'ave been in the Service. Prob'ly is,' was Pyecroft's comment.

At that thrice-blessed lodge our water-tank was filled (I dare not quote Mr Hinchcliffe's remarks when he saw the collapsible rubber bucket with which we did it) and we re-embarked. It seemed that Sir Michael Gregory owned many acres, and that his park ran for miles.

'No objection to your going through it,' said the lodge-keeper. 'It'll save you a goodish bit to Instead Wick.'

But we needed petrol, which could be purchased at Pigginfold, a few miles farther up, and so we held to the main road, as our fate had decreed.

'We've come seven miles in fifty-four minutes, so far,' said Hinchcliffe (he was driving with greater freedom and less responsibility), 'and now we have to fill our bunkers. This is worse than the Channel Fleet.'

At Pigginfold, after ten minutes, we refilled our petrol tank and lavishly oiled our engines. Mr Hinchcliffe wished to discharge our engineer on the grounds that he (Mr Hinchcliffe) was now entirely abreast of his work. To this I demurred, for I knew my car. She had, in the language of the road, held up for a day and a half, and by most bitter experience I suspected that her time was very near. Therefore, three miles short of Linghurst, I was less surprised than anyone, excepting always my engineer, when the engines set up a lunatic clucking, and, after two or three kicks, jammed.

'Heaven forgive me all the harsh things I may have said about destroyers in my sinful time!' wailed Hinchcliffe, snapping back the throttle. 'What's worryin' Ada now?'

'The forward eccentric-strap screw's dropped off,' said the engineer, investigating.

'That all? I thought it was a propeller-blade.'

'We must go an' look for it. There isn't another.'

'Not me,' said Pyecroft from his seat. 'Out pinnace, Hinch, an' creep for it. It won't be more than five miles back.'

The two men, with bowed heads, moved up the road.

'Look, like etymologists, don't they? Does she decant her innards often, so to speak?' Pyecroft asked.

I told him the true tale of a race-full of ball bearings strewn four miles along a Hampshire road, and by me recovered in detail. He was profoundly touched.

'Poor Hinch! Poor – poor Hinch!' he said. 'And that's only one of her little games, is it? He'll be homesick for the Navy by night.'

When the search-party doubled back with the missing screw, it was Hinchcliffe who replaced it in less than five minutes, while my engineer looked on admiringly.

'Your boiler's only seated on four little paper-clips,' he said, crawling from beneath her. 'She's a wicker-willow lunch-basket below. She's a runnin' miracle. Have you had this combustible spirit-lamp long?'

I told him.

'And yet you were afraid to come into the *Nightmare*'s engine-room when we were runnin' trials!'

'It's all a matter of taste,' Pyecroft volunteered. 'But I will say for you, Hinch, you've certainly got the hang of her steamin' gadgets in quick time.'

He was driving her very sweetly, but with a worried look in his eye and a tremor in his arm.

'She don't seem to answer her helm somehow,' he said.

'There's a lot of play to the steering-gear,' said my engineer. 'We generally tighten it up every few miles.'

''Like me to stop now? We've run as much as one mile and a half without incident,' he replied tartly.

'Then you're lucky,' said my engineer, bristling in turn.

'They'll wreck the whole turret out o' nasty professional spite in a minute,' said Pyecroft. 'That's the worst o' machinery. Man dead ahead, Hinch — semaphorin' like the flagship in a fit!'

'Amen!' said Hinchcliffe. 'Shall I stop, or shall I cut him down?'

He stopped, for full in the centre of the Linghurst Road stood a person in pepper-and-salt raiment (ready-made), with a brown telegraph envelope in his hands.

'Twenty-three and a half miles an hour,' he began, weighing a small beam-engine of a Waterbury in one red paw. 'From the top of the hill over our measured quarter-mile — twenty-three and a half.'

'You manurial gardener —' Hinchcliffe began. I prodded him warningly from behind, and laid the other hand on Pyecroft's stiffening knee.

'Also — on information received — drunk and disorderly in charge of a motor-car — to the common danger — two men like sailors in appearance,' the man went on.

'Like sailors! ... That's Agg's little *roose*. No wonder he smiled at us,' said Pyecroft.

'I've been waiting for you some time,' the man concluded, folding up the telegram.

'Who's the owner?'

I indicated myself.

'Then I want you as well as the two seafaring men. Drunk and disorderly can be treated summary. You come on.'

My relations with the Sussex constabulary have, so far, been of the best, but I could not love this person.

'Of course you have your authority to show?' I hinted.

'I'll show it you at Linghurst,' he retorted hotly — 'all the authority you want.'

'I only want the badge, or warrant, or whatever it is a plain-clothes man has to show.'

He made as though to produce it, but checked himself, repeating less politely the invitation to Linghurst. The action and the tone confirmed my many-times-tested theory that the bulk of English shoregoing institutions are based on conformable strata of absolutely impervious inaccuracy. I reflected and became aware of a drumming on the back of the front seat that Pyecroft, bowed forward and relaxed, was tapping with his knuckles. The hardly checked fury on Hinchcliffe's brow had given place to a greasy imbecility, and he nodded over the steering-bar. In longs and shorts, as laid down by the pious and immortal Mr Morse, Pyecroft tapped out, 'Sham drunk. Get him in the car.'

'I can't stay here all day,' said the constable.

Pyecroft raised his head. Then was seen with what majesty the British sailor-man envisages a new situation.

'Met gennelman heavy sheeway,' said he. 'Do' tell me British gelman can't give 'ole Brish Navy lif' own blighted ste' cart. Have another drink!'

'I didn't know they were as drunk as all that when they stopped me,' I explained.

'You can say all that at Linghurst,' was the answer. 'Come on.'

'Quite right,' I said. 'But the question is, if you take these two out on the road, they'll fall down or start killing you.'

'Then I'd call on you to assist me in the execution o' my duty.'

'But I'd see you further first. You'd better come with us in the car. I'll turn this passenger out.' (This was my engineer, sitting quite silent.) 'You don't want him, and, anyhow, he'd only be a witness for the defence.'

'That's true,' said the constable. 'But it wouldn't make any odds – at Linghurst.'

My engineer skipped into the bracken like a rabbit. I bade him cut across Sir Michael Gregory's park, and if he caught my friend, to tell him I should probably be rather late for lunch.

'I ain't going to be driven by *him*.' Our destined prey pointed at Hinchcliffe with apprehension.

'Of course not. You take my seat and keep the big sailor in order. He's too drunk to do much. I'll change places with the other one. Only be quick; I want to pay my fine and get it over.'

'That's the way to look at it,' he said, dropping into the left

rear seat. 'We're making quite a lot out o' you motor gentry.'
He folded his arms judicially as the car gathered way under
Hinchcliffe's stealthy hand.

'But *you* aren't driving?' he cried, half rising.

'You've noticed it?' said Pyecroft, and embraced him with
one anaconda-like left arm.

'Don't kill him,' said Hinchcliffe briefly. 'I want to show
him what twenty-three and a quarter is.' We were going a fair
twelve, which was about the car's limit.

Our passenger swore something and then groaned.

'Hush, darling!' said Pyecroft, 'or I'll have to hug you.'

The main road, white under the noon sun, lay broad before
us, running north to Linghurst. We slowed and looked anxiously
for a side track.

'And now,' said I, 'I want to see your authority.'

'The badge of your ratin',' Pyecroft added.

'I'm a constable,' he said, and kicked. Indeed, his boots
would have bewrayed him across half a county's plough; but
boots are not legal evidence.

'I want your authority,' I repeated coldly; 'some evidence
that you are not a common, drunken tramp.'

It was as I had expected. He had forgotten or mislaid his
badge. He had neglected to learn the outlines of the work for
which he received money and consideration; and he expected
me, the taxpayer, to go to infinite trouble to supplement his
deficiencies.

'If you don't believe me, come to Linghurst,' was the burden
of his almost national anthem.

'But I can't run all over Sussex every time a blackmailer
jumps up and says he is a policeman.'

'Why, it's quite close,' he persisted.

''Twon't be – soon,' said Hinchcliffe.

'None of the other people ever made any trouble. To be sure
they was gentlemen,' he cried. 'All I can say is, it may be very
funny, but it ain't fair.'

I laboured with him in this dense fog, but to no end. He had
forgotten his badge, and we were villains for that we did not
cart him to the pub or barracks where he had left it.

Pyecroft listened critically as we spun along the hard road.

'If he was a concentrated Boer, he couldn't expect much more,' he observed. 'Now, suppose I'd been a lady in a delicate state o'health – you'd ha' made me very ill with your doings.'

'I wish I 'ad. 'Ere! 'Elp! 'Elp! Hi!'

The man had seen a constable in uniform fifty yards ahead, where a lane ran into the road, and would have said more but that Hinchcliffe jerked her up that lane with a wrench that nearly capsized us as the constable came running heavily.

It seemed to me that both our guest and his fellow-villain in uniform smiled as we fled down the road easterly betwixt the narrowing hedges.

'You'll know all about it in a little time,' said our guest. 'You've only yourselves to thank for runnin' your 'ead into a trap.' And he whistled ostentatiously.

We made no answer.

'If that man 'ad chose, 'e could have identified me,' he said.

Still we were silent.

'But 'e'll do it later, when you're caught.'

'Not if you go on talking. 'E won't be able to,' said Pyecroft. 'I don't know what traverse you think you're workin', but your duty till you're put in cells for a highway robber is to love, honour, an' cherish *me* most special – performin' all evolutions signalled in rapid time. I tell you this, in case o' anything turnin' up.'

'Don't you fret about things turnin' up,' was the reply.

Hinchcliffe had given the car a generous throttle, and she was well set to work, when, without warning, the road – there are two or three in Sussex like it – turned down and ceased.

'Holy Muckins!' he cried, and stood on both brakes as our helpless tyres slithered over wet grass and bracken – down and down into forest – early British woodland. It was the change of a nightmare, and that all should fit, fifty yards ahead of us a babbling brook barred our way. On the far side a velvet green ride, sprinkled with rabbits and fern, gently sloped upwards and away, but behind us was no hope. Forty horse-power would never have rolled wet pneumatic tyres up that verdurous cliff we had descended.

'H'm!' Our guest coughed significantly. 'A great many cars thinks they can take this road; but they all come back. We walks after 'em at our convenience.'

'Meanin' that the other jaunty is now pursuin' us on his lily feet?' said Pyecroft.

'*Pre*cisely.'

'An' you think,' said Pyecroft (I have no hope to render the scorn of the words), '*that*'ll make any odds? Get out!'

The man obeyed with alacrity.

'See those spars up-ended over there? I mean that wickyup-thing. Hop-poles, then, you rural blighter. Keep on fetching me hop-poles at the double.'

And he doubled, Pyecroft at his heels; for they had arrived at a perfect understanding.

There was a stack of hurdles a few yards down stream, laid aside after sheep-washing; and there were stepping-stones in the brook. Hinchcliffe rearranged these last to make some sort of causeway; I brought up the hurdles; and when Pyecroft and his subaltern had dropped a dozen hop-poles across the stream, laid them down over all.

'Talk o' the Agricultur'l Hall!' he said, mopping his brow – ''tisn't in it with us. The approach to the bridge must now be paved with hurdles, owin' to the squashy nature o' the country. Yes, an' we'd better have one or two on the far side to lead her on to *terror fermior*. Now, Hinch! Give her full steam and 'op along. If she slips off, we're done. Shall I take the wheel?'

'No. This is my job,' said the first-class engine-room artificer. 'Get over the far side, and be ready to catch her if she jibs on the uphill.'

We crossed that elastic structure and stood ready amid the bracken. Hinchcliffe gave her a full steam and she came like a destroyer on her trial. There was a crack, a flicker of white water, and she was in our arms fifty yards up the slope; or rather, we were behind her pushing her madly towards a patch of raw gravel whereon her wheels could bite. Of the bridge remained only a few wildly vibrating hop-poles, and those hurdles which had been sunk in the mud of the approaches.

'She – she kicked out all the loose ones behind her, as she finished with 'em,' Hinchcliffe panted.

'At the Agricultural Hall they would 'ave been fastened down with ribbons,' said Pyecroft. 'But this ain't Olympia.'

'She nearly wrenched the tiller out of my hand. Don't you think I conned her like a cock-angel, Pye?'

'*I* never saw anything like it,' said our guest propitiatingly. 'And now, gentlemen, if you'll let me go back to Linghurst, I promise you you won't hear another word from me.'

'Get in,' said Pyecroft, as we puffed out on to a metalled road once more. 'We 'aven't begun on *you* yet.'

'A joke's a joke,' he replied. 'I don't mind a little bit of a joke myself, but this is going beyond it.'

'Miles an' miles beyond it, if this machine stands up. We'll want water pretty soon.'

Our guest's countenance brightened, and Pyecroft perceived it.

'Let me tell you,' he said earnestly, 'It won't make any difference to you whatever happens. Barrin' a dhow or two Tajurrahway, prizes are scarce in the Navy. Hence we never abandon 'em.'

There was a long silence. Pyecroft broke it suddenly.

'Robert,' he said, 'have you a mother?'

'Yes.'

'Have you a big brother?'

'Yes.'

'An' a little sister?'

'Yes.'

'Robert. Does your mamma keep a dog?'

'Yes. Why?'

'All right, Robert. I won't forget it.'

I looked for an explanation.

'I saw his cabinet photograph in full uniform on the mantelpiece o' that cottage before faithful Fido turned up,' Pyecroft whispered. 'Ain't you glad it's all in the family somehow?'

We filled with water at a cottage on the edge of St Leonard's Forest, and, despite our increasing leakage, made shift to climb the ridge above Instead Wick. Knowing the car as I did, I felt sure that final collapse would not be long delayed. My sole concern was to run our guest well into the wilderness before that came.

On the roof of the world – a naked plateau clothed with young heather – she retired from active life in floods of tears. Her feed-water-heater (Hinchcliffe blessed it and its maker for three minutes) was leaking beyond hope of repair; she had shifted most of her packing, and her water-pump would not lift.

'If I had a bit of piping I could disconnect this tin cartridge-case an' feed direct into the boiler. It 'ud knock down her speed, but we could get on,' said he, and looked hopelessly at the long dun ridges that hove us above the panorama of Sussex. Northward we could see the London haze. Southward, between gaps of the whale-backed Downs, lay the Channel's zinc-blue. But all our available population in that vast survey was one cow and a kestrel.

'It's down hill to Instead Wick. We can run her there by gravity,' I said at last.

'Then he'll only have to walk to the station to get home. Unless we take off 'is boots first,' Pyecroft replied.

'That,' said our guest earnestly, 'would be theft atop of assault and very serious.'

'Oh, let's hang him an' be done,' Hinchcliffe grunted. 'It's evidently what he's sufferin' for.'

Somehow murder did not appeal to us that warm noon. We sat down to smoke in the heather, and presently out of the valley below came the thick beat of a petrol-motor ascending. I paid little attention to it till I heard the roar of a horn that has no duplicate in all the Home Counties.

'That's the man I was going to lunch with!' I cried. 'Hold on!' and I ran down the road.

It was a big, black, black-dashed, tonneaued twenty-four-horse Octopod; and it bore not only Kysh my friend, and Salmon his engineer, but my own man, who for the first time in our acquaintance smiled.

'Did they get you? What did you get? I was coming into Linghurst as witness to character – your man told me what happened – but I was stopped near Instead Wick myself,' cried Kysh.

'What for?'

'Leaving car unattended. An infernal swindle, when you think of the loose carts outside every pub in the county. I was jawing with the police for an hour, but it's no use. They've got it all their own way, and we're helpless.'

Hereupon I told him my tale, and for proof, as we topped the hill, pointed out the little group round my car.

All supreme emotion is dumb. Kysh put on the brake and hugged me to his bosom till I groaned. Then, as I remember, he crooned like a mother returned to her suckling.

'Divine! Divine!' he murmured. 'Command me.'

'Take charge of the situation,' I said. 'You'll find a Mr Pyecroft on the quarter-deck. I'm altogether out of it.'

'He shall stay there. Who am I but the instrument of vengeance in the hands of an overruling Providence? (And I put in fresh sparking-plugs this morning.) Salmon, take that steam-kettle home, somehow. I would be alone.'

'Leggat,' I said to my man, 'help Salmon home with my car.'

'Home? Now? It's hard. It's cruel hard,' said Leggat, almost with a sob.

Hinchcliffe outlined my car's condition briefly to the two engineers. Mr Pyecroft clung to our guest, who stared with affrighted eyes at the palpitating Octopod; and the free wind of high Sussex whimpered across the ling.

'I am quite agreeable to walkin' 'ome all the way on my feet,' said our guest. 'I wouldn't go to any railway station. It 'ud be just the proper finish to our little joke.' He laughed nervously.

'What's the evolution?' said Pyecroft. 'Do we turn over to the new cruiser?'

I nodded, and he escorted our guest to the tonneau with care. When I was in, he sat himself broad-armed on the little flap-seat which controls the door. Hinchcliffe sat by Kysh.

'You drive?' Kysh asked, with the smile that has won him his chequered way through the world.

'Steam only, and I've about had my whack for today, thanks.'

'I see.'

The long, low car slid forward and then dropped like a bullet down the descent our steam toy had so painfully climbed. Our guest's face blanched, and he clutched the back of the tonneau.

'New commander's evidently been trained on a destroyer,' said Hinchcliffe.

'What's 'is wonderful name?' whispered Pyecroft. 'Ho! Well, I'm glad it ain't Saul we've run up against – nor Nimshi, for that matter. This is makin' me feel religious.'

Our impetus carried us half-way up the next slope, where we steadied to a resonant fifteen an hour against the collar.

'What do you think?' I called to Hinchcliffe.

''Taint as sweet as steam, o' course; but for power it's twice the *Furious* against half the *Jaseur* in a head-sea.'

Volumes could not have touched it more exactly. His bright eyes were glued on Kysh's hands juggling with levers behind the discreet backward sloping dash.

'An' what sort of a brake might you use?' he said politely.

'This,' Kysh replied, as the last of the hill shot up to one in eight. He let the car run back a few feet and caught her deftly on the brake, repeating the performance cup and ball fashion. It was like being daped above the Pit at the end of an uncoiled solar plexus. Even Pyecroft held his breath.

'It ain't fair! It ain't fair!' our guest moaned. 'You're makin' me sick.'

'What an ungrateful blighter he is!' said Pyecroft. 'Money couldn't buy you a run like this . . . Do it well overboard!'

'We'll just trundle up the Forest and drop into the Park Row, I think,' said Kysh. 'There's a bit of good going hereabouts.'

He flung a careless knee over the low raking tiller that the ordinary expert puts under his armpit, and down four miles of yellow road, cut through barren waste, the Octopod sang like a six-inch shell.

'Whew! But you know your job,' said Hinchcliffe. 'You're wasted here. I'd give something to have you in my engine-room.'

'He's steering with 'is little hind-legs,' said Pyecroft. 'Stand up and look at him, Robert. You'll never see such a sight again!'

'Nor don't want to,' was our guest's reply. 'Five 'undred pounds wouldn't begin to cover 'is fines even since I've been with him.'

Park Row is reached by one hill which drops three hundred feet in half a mile. Kysh had the thought to steer with his hand down the abyss, but the manner in which he took the curved bridge at the bottom brought my few remaining hairs much nearer the grave.

'We're in Surrey now; better look out,' I said.

'Never mind. I'll roll her into Kent for a bit. We've lots of time; it's only three o'clock.'

'Won't you want to fill your bunkers, or take water, or oil her up?' said Hinchcliffe.

'We don't use water, and she's good for two hundred on one tank o' petrol if she doesn't break down.'

'Two hundred miles from 'ome and mother *and* faithful Fido tonight, Robert,' said Pyecroft, slapping our guest on the knee. 'Cheer up! Why, I've known a destroyer do less.'

We passed with some decency through some towns, till by way of the Hastings road we whirled into Cramberhurst, which is a deep pit.

'Now,' said Kysh, 'we begin.'

'Previous service not reckoned towards pension,' said Pyecroft. 'We are doin' you lavish, Robert.'

'But when's this silly game to finish, any'ow?' our guest snarled.

'Don't worry about the *when* of it, Robert. The *where's* the interestin' point for you just now.'

I had seen Kysh drive before, and I thought I knew the Octopod, but that afternoon he and she were exalted beyond my knowledge. He improvised on the keys – the snapping levers and quivering accelerators – marvellous variations, so that our progress was sometimes a fugue and sometimes a barn-dance, varied on open greens by the weaving of fairy rings. When I protested, all that he would say was: 'I'll hypnotize the fowl! I'll dazzle the rooster!' or other words equally futile. And she – oh! that I could do her justice! – she turned her broad black bows to the westering light, and lifted us high upon hills that we might see and rejoice with her. She whooped into veiled hollows of elm and Sussex oak; she devoured infinite perspectives of park palings; she surged through forgotten hamlets, whose single streets gave back, reduplicated, the clatter of her exhaust, and, tireless, she repeated the motions. Over naked uplands she droned like a homing bee, her shadow lengthening in the sun that she chased to his lair. She nosed up unparochial byways and accommodation-roads of the least accommodation, and put old scarred turf or new-raised molehills under her most marvellous springs with never a jar. And since the King's highway is used for every purpose save traffic, in mid-career she stepped aside for, or flung amazing loops about, the brainless driver, the driverless horse, the drunken carrier, the engaged couple, the female student of the bicycle and her staggering instructor, the pig, the perambulator, and the infant school (where it disembogued yelping on cross-roads), with the grace of Nellie Farren (upon whom be the Peace) and the lithe abandon of all the Vokes family. But at heart she was ever Judic as I remember that Judic long ago – Judic clad in bourgeois black from wrist to ankle, achieving incredible improprieties.

We were silent – Hinchcliffe and Pyecroft through professional appreciation; I with a layman's delight in the expert; and our guest because of fear.

At the edge of the evening she smelt the sea to southward and sheered thither like the strong-winged albatross, to circle enormously amid green flats fringed by martello towers.

'Ain't that Eastbourne yonder?' said our guest, reviving. 'I've a aunt there – she's cook to a J.P. – could identify me.'

'Don't worry her for a little thing like that,' said Pyecroft; and ere he had ceased to praise family love, our unpaid judiciary, and domestic service, the Downs rose between us and the sea, and the Long Man of Hillingdon lay out upon the turf.

'Trevington – up yonder – is a fairly isolated little dorp,' I said, for I was beginning to feel hungry.

'No,' said Kysh. 'He'd get a lift to the railway in no time . . . Besides, I'm enjoying myself . . . Three pounds eighteen and sixpence. Infernal swindle!'

I take it one of his more recent fines was rankling in Kysh's brain; but he drove like the Archangel of the Twilight.

About the longitude of Cassocks, Hinchcliffe yawned. 'Aren't we ever goin' to maroon our Robert? I'm hungry, too.'

'The commodore wants his money back,' I answered.

'If he drives like this habitual, there must be a tidyish little lump owin' to him,' said Pyecroft. 'Well, I'm agreeable.'

'I didn't know it could be done. S'welp me, I didn't,' our guest murmured.

'But you will,' said Kysh. And that was the first and last time he addressed the man.

We ran through Penfield Green, half stupefied with open air, drugged with the relentless boom of the Octopod, and extinct with famine.

'I used to shoot about here,' said Kysh, a few miles farther on. 'Open that gate, please,' and he slowed as the sun touched the sky-line. At this point we left metalled roads and bucked vigorously amid ditches and under trees for twenty minutes.

'Only cross-country car on the market,' he said, as we wheeled into a straw-yard where a lone bull bellowed defiance to our growlings. 'Open that gate, please. I hope the cattle-bridge will stand up.'

'I've took a few risks in my time,' said Pyecroft as timbers cracked beneath us and we entered between thickets, 'but I'm a babe to this man, Hinch.'

'Don't talk to me. Watch *him!* It's a liberal education, as Shakespeare says. Fallen tree on the port bow, Sir.'

'Right! That's my mark. Sit tight!'

She flung up her tail like a sounding whale and buried us in a fifteen-foot deep bridle-path buttressed with the exposed roots of enormous beeches. The wheels leaped from root to rounded boulder, and it was very dark in the shadow of the foliage.

'There ought to be a hammer-pond somewhere about here.' Kysh was letting her down this chute in brakeful spasms.

'Water dead ahead, Sir. Stack o' brushwood on the starboard beam, and – no road,' sang Pyecroft.

'Cr-r-ri-key!' said Hinchcliffe, as the car on a wild cant to the left went astern, screwing herself round the angle of a track that overhung the pond. 'If she only had two propellers, I believe she'd talk poetry. She can do everything else.'

'We're rather on our port wheels now,' said Kysh; 'but I don't think she'll capsize. This road isn't used much by motors.'

'You don't say so,' said Pyecroft. 'What a pity!'

She bored through a mass of crackling brushwood, and emerged into an upward-sloping fern-glade fenced with woods so virgin, so untouched, that William Rufus might have ridden off as we entered. We climbed out of the violet-purple shadows towards the upland where the last of the day lingered. I was filled to my moist eyes with the almost sacred beauty of sense and association that clad the landscape.

'Does 'unger produce 'alluciations?' said Pyecroft in a whisper. 'Because I've just seen a sacred ibis walkin' arm in arm with a British cock-pheasant.'

'What are you panickin' at?' said Hinchcliffe. 'I've been seein' zebra for the last two minutes, but *I* 'aven't complained.'

He pointed behind us, and I beheld a superb painted zebra (Burchell's, I think), following our track with palpitating nostrils. The car stopped, and it fled away.

There was a little pond in front of us from which rose a dome of irregular sticks crowned with a blunt-muzzled beast that sat upon its haunches.

'Is it catching?' said Pyecroft.

'Yes. I'm seeing beaver,' I replied.

'It is here!' said Kysh, with the air and gesture of Captain Nemo, and half turned.

'No – no – no! For 'Eaven's sake – not 'ere!' Our guest gasped like a sea-bathed child, as four efficient hands swung him far out-board on to the turf. The car ran back noiselessly down the slope.

'Look! Look! It's sorcery!' cried Hinchcliffe.

There was a report like a pistol-shot as the beaver dived from the roof of his lodge, but we watched our guest. He was on his knees, praying to kangaroos. Yea, in his bowler hat he kneeled before kangaroos – gigantic, erect, silhouetted against the light – four buck-kangaroos in the heart of Sussex!

And we retrogressed over the velvet grass till our hind-wheels struck well-rolled gravel, leading us to sanity, main roads, and, half an hour later, the 'Grapnel Inn' at Horsham.

After a great meal we poured libations and made burnt-offerings in honour of Kysh, who received our homage graciously, and, by the way, explained a few things in the natural history line that had puzzled us. England is a most marvellous country, but one is not, till one knows the eccentricities of large landowners, trained to accept kangaroos, zebras, or beavers as part of its landscape.

When we went to bed Pyecroft pressed my hand, his voice thick with emotion.

'We owe it to you,' he said. 'We owe it all to you. Didn't I say we never met in *pup-pup-puris naturalibus*, if I may so put it, without a remarkably hectic day ahead of us?'

'That's all right,' I said. 'Mind the candle.' He was tracing smoke-patterns on the wall.

'But what I want to know is whether we'll succeed in acclimatizin' the blighter, or whether Sir William Gardner's keepers 'll kill 'im before 'e gets accustomed to 'is surroundin's?'

Some day, I think, we must go up the Linghurst Road and find out.

⁅ 'Wireless' ⁆

Kaspar's Song in 'Varda'
(*From the Swedish of Stagnelius*)

Eyes aloft, over dangerous places,
   The children follow where Psyche flies,
And, in the sweat of their upturned faces,
   Slash with a net at the empty skies.

So it goes they fall amid brambles,
   And sting their toes on the nettle-tops,
Till after a thousand scratches and scrambles
   They wipe their brows, and the hunting stops.

Then to quiet them comes their father
   And stills the riot of pain and grief,
Saying, 'Little ones, go and gather
   Out of my garden a cabbage leaf.

'You will find on it whorls and clots of
   Dull grey eggs that, properly fed,
Turn, by way of the worm, to lots of
   Radiant Psyches raised from the dead.'

. . .

'Heaven is beautiful, Earth is ugly,'
   The three-dimensioned preacher saith.
So we must not look where the snail and the slug lie
   For Psyche's birth . . . And that is our death!

'Wireless'

'It's a funny thing, this Marconi business, isn't it?' said Mr Shaynor, coughing heavily. 'Nothing seems to make any difference, by what they tell me — storms, hills, or anything; but if that's true we shall know before morning.'

'Of course it's true,' I answered, stepping behind the counter. 'Where's old Mr Cashell?'

'He's had to go to bed on account of his influenza. He said you'd very likely drop in.'

'Where's his nephew?'

'Inside, getting the things ready. He told me that the last time they experimented they put the pole on the roof of one of the big hotels here, and the batteries electrified all the water-supply, and' — he giggled — 'the ladies got shocks when they took their baths.'

'I never heard of that.'

'The hotel wouldn't exactly advertise it, would it? Just now, by what Mr Cashell tells me, they're trying to signal from here to Poole, and they're using stronger batteries than ever. But, you see, he being the guvnor's nephew and all that (and it will be in the papers too), it doesn't matter how they electrify things in this house. Are you going to watch?'

'Very much. I've never seen this game. Aren't you going to bed?'

'We don't close till ten on Saturdays. There's a good deal of influenza in town, too, and there'll be a dozen prescriptions coming in before morning. I generally sleep in the chair here. It's warmer than jumping out of bed every time. Bitter cold, isn't it?'

'Freezing hard. I'm sorry your cough's worse.'

'Thank you. I don't mind cold so much. It's this wind that fair cuts me to pieces.' He coughed again hard and hackingly, as an old lady came in for ammoniated quinine. 'We've just run

181

out of it in bottles, madam,' said Mr Shaynor, returning to the professional tone, 'but if you will wait two minutes, I'll make it up for you, madam.'

I had used the shop for some time, and my acquaintance with the proprietor had ripened into friendship. It was Mr Cashell who revealed to me the purpose and power of Apothecaries' Hall what time a fellow-chemist had made an error in a prescription of mine, had lied to cover his sloth, and when error and lie were brought home to him had written vain letters.

'A disgrace to our profession,' said the thin, mild-eyed man, hotly, after studying the evidence. 'You couldn't do a better service to the profession than report him to Apothecaries' Hall.'

I did so, not knowing what djinns I should evoke; and the result was such an apology as one might make who had spent a night on the rack. I conceived great respect for Apothecaries' Hall, and esteem for Mr Cashell, a zealous craftsman who magnified his calling. Until Mr Shaynor came down from the North his assistants had by no means agreed with Mr Cashell. 'They forget,' said he, 'that, first and foremost, the compounder is a medicine-man. On him depends the physician's reputation. He holds it literally in the hollow of his hand, Sir.'

Mr Shaynor's manners had not, perhaps, the polish of the grocery and Italian warehouse next door, but he knew and loved his dispensary work in every detail. For relaxation he seemed to go no farther afield than the romance of drugs – their discovery, preparation, packing, and export – but it led him to the ends of the earth, and on this subject, and the Pharmaceutical Formulary, and Nicholas Culpepper, most confident of physicians, we met.

Little by little I grew to know something of his beginnings and his hopes – of his mother, who had been a school-teacher in one of the northern counties, and of his red-headed father, a small job-master at Kirby Moors, who died when he was a child; of the examinations he had passed and of their exceeding and increasing difficulty; of his dreams of a shop in London; of his hate for the price-cutting Co-operative stores; and, most interesting, of his mental attitude towards customers.

'There's a way you get into,' he told me, 'of serving them carefully, and I hope, politely, without stopping your own thinking. I've been reading Christy's *New Commercial Plants* all this autumn, and that needs keeping your mind on it, I can tell you. So long as it isn't a prescription, of course, I can carry as much as half a page of Christy in my head, and at the same time I could sell out all that window twice over, and not a penny wrong at the end. As to prescriptions, I think I could make up the general run of 'em in my sleep, almost.'

For reasons of my own, I was deeply interested in Marconi experiments at their outset in England; and it was of a piece with Mr Cashell's unvarying thoughtfulness that, when his nephew the electrician appropriated the house for a long-range installation, he should, as I have said, invite me to see the result.

The old lady went away with her medicine, and Mr Shaynor and I stamped on the tiled floor behind the counter to keep ourselves warm. The shop, by the light of the many electrics, looked like a Paris-diamond mine, for Mr Cashell believed in all the ritual of his craft. Three superb glass jars – red, green, and blue – of the sort that led Rosamund to parting with her shoes – blazed in the broad plate-glass windows, and there was a confused smell of orris, Kodak films, vulcanite, tooth-powder, sachets, and almond-cream in the air. Mr Shaynor fed the dispensary stove, and we sucked cayenne-pepper jujubes and menthol lozenges. The brutal east wind had cleared the streets, and the few passers-by were muffled to their puckered eyes. In the Italian warehouse next door some gay feathered birds and game, hung upon hooks, sagged to the wind across the left edge of our window-frame.

'They ought to take these poultry in – all knocked about like that,' said Mr Shaynor. 'Doesn't it make you feel fair perishing? See that old hare! The wind's nearly blowing the fur off him.'

I saw the belly-fur of the dead beast blown apart in ridges and streaks as the wind caught it, showing bluish skin underneath. 'Bitter cold,' said Mr Shaynor, shuddering. 'Fancy going out on a night like this! Oh, here's young Mr Cashell.'

The door of the inner office behind the dispensary opened, and an energetic, spade-bearded man stepped forth, rubbing his hands.

'I want a bit of tin-foil, Shaynor,' he said. 'Good evening. My uncle told me you might be coming.' This to me, as I began the first of a hundred questions.

'I've everything in order,' he replied. 'We're only waiting until Poole calls us up. Excuse me a minute. You can come in whenever you like – but I'd better be with the instruments. Give me that tin-foil. Thanks.'

While we were talking, a girl – evidently no customer – had come into the shop, and the face and bearing of Mr Shaynor changed. She leaned confidently across the counter.

'But I can't,' I heard him whisper uneasily – the flush on his cheek was dull red, and his eyes shone like a drugged moth's. 'I can't. I tell you I'm alone in the place.'

'No, you aren't. Who's *that*? Let him look after it for half an hour. A brisk walk will do you good. Ah, come now, John.'

'But he isn't –'

'I don't care. I want you to; we'll only go round by St Agnes. If you don't –'

He crossed to where I stood in the shadow of the dispensary counter, and began some sort of broken apology about a lady-friend.

'Yes,' she interrupted. 'You take the shop for half an hour – to oblige *me*, won't you?'

She had a singularly rich and promising voice that well matched her outline.

'All right,' I said. 'I'll do it – but you'd better wrap yourself up, Mr Shaynor.'

'Oh, a brisk walk ought to help me. We're only going round by the church.' I heard him cough grievously as they went out together.

I refilled the stove, and, after reckless expenditure of Mr Cashell's coal, drove some warmth into the shop. I explored many of the glass-knobbed drawers that lined the walls, tasted some disconcerting drugs, and, by the aid of a few cardamoms,

ground ginger, chloric-ether, and dilute alcohol, manufactured a
new and wildish drink, of which I bore a glassful to young Mr
Cashell, busy in the back office. He laughed shortly when I told
him that Mr Shaynor had stepped out – but a frail coil of wire
held all his attention, and he had no word for me bewildered
among the batteries and rods. The noise of the sea on the
beach began to make itself heard as the traffic in the street
ceased. Then briefly, but very lucidly, he gave me the names
and uses of the mechanism that crowded the tables and the
floor.

'When do you expect to get the message from Poole?' I
demanded, sipping my liquor out of a graduated glass.

'About midnight, if everything is in order. We've got our
installation-pole fixed to the roof of the house. I shouldn't
advise you to turn on a tap or anything tonight. We've connected
up with the plumbing, and all the water will be electrified.' He
repeated to me the history of the agitated ladies at the hotel at
the time of the first installation.

'But what *is* it?' I asked. 'Electricity is out of my beat
altogether.'

'Ah, if you knew *that* you'd know something nobody knows.
It's just It – what we call Electricity, but the magic – the
manifestations – the Hertzian waves – are all revealed by *this*.
The coherer, we call it.'

He picked up a glass tube not much thicker than a ther-
mometer, in which, almost touching, were two tiny silver plugs,
and between them an infinitesimal pinch of metallic dust.
'That's all,' he said, proudly, as though himself responsible for
the wonder. 'That is the thing that will reveal to us the Powers
– whatever the Powers may be – at work – through space – a
long distance away.'

Just then Mr Shaynor returned alone and stood coughing his
heart out on the mat.

'Serves you right for being such a fool,' said young Mr
Cashell, as annoyed as myself at the interruption. 'Never mind
– we've all the night before us to see wonders.'

Shaynor clutched the counter, his handkerchief to his lips.
When he brought it away I saw two bright red stains.

'I — I've got a bit of a rasped throat from smoking cigarettes,' he panted. 'I think I'll try a cubeb.'

'Better take some of this. I've been compounding while you've been away.' I handed him the brew.

' 'Twon't make me drunk, will it? I'm almost a teetotaller. My word! That's grateful and comforting.'

He set down the empty glass to cough afresh.

'Brr! But it was cold out there! I shouldn't care to be lying in my grave a night like this. Don't *you* ever have a sore throat from smoking?' He pocketed the handkerchief after a furtive peep.

'Oh, yes, sometimes,' I replied, wondering, while I spoke, into what agonies of terror I should fall if ever I saw those bright-red danger-signals under my nose. Young Mr Cashell among the batteries coughed slightly to show that he was quite ready to continue his scientific explanations, but I was thinking still of the girl with the rich voice and the significantly cut mouth, at whose command I had taken charge of the shop. It flashed across me that she distantly resembled the seductive shape on a gold-framed toilet-water advertisement whose charms were unholily heightened by the glare from the red bottle in the window. Turning to make sure, I saw Mr Shaynor's eyes bent in the same direction, and by instinct recognized that the flamboyant thing was to him a shrine. 'What do you take for your — cough?' I asked.

'Well, I'm the wrong side of the counter to believe much in patent medicines. But there are asthma cigarettes and there are pastilles. To tell you the truth, if you don't object to the smell, which is very like incense, I believe, though I'm not a Roman Catholic, Blaudett's Cathedral Pastilles relieve me as much as anything.'

'Let's try.' I had never raided a chemist's shop before, so I was thorough. We unearthed the pastilles — brown, gummy cones of benzoin — and set them alight under the toilet-water advertisement, where they fumed in thin blue spirals.

'Of course,' said Mr Shaynor, to my question, 'what one uses in the shop for one's self comes out of one's pocket. Why, stock-taking in our business is nearly the same as with jewellers

– and I can't say more than that. But one gets them' – he pointed to the pastille-box – 'at trade prices.' Evidently the censing of the gay, seven-tinted wench with the teeth was an established ritual which cost something.

'And when do we shut up shop?'

'We stay like this all night. The guv – old Mr Cashell – doesn't believe in locks and shutters as compared with electric light. Besides, it brings trade. I'll just sit here in the chair by the stove and write a letter, if you don't mind. Electricity isn't my prescription.'

The energetic young Mr Cashell snorted within, and Shaynor settled himself up in his chair over which he had thrown a staring red, black, and yellow Austrian jute blanket, rather like a table-cover. I cast about, amid patent-medicine pamphlets, for something to read, but finding little, returned to the manufacture of the new drink. The Italian warehouse took down its game and went to bed. Across the street blank shutters flung back the gaslight in cold smears; the dried pavement seemed to rough up in goose-flesh under the scouring of the savage wind, and we could hear, long ere he passed, the police-man flapping his arms to keep himself warm. Within, the flavours of cardamoms and chloric-ether disputed those of the pastilles and a score of drugs and perfume and soap scents. Our electric lights, set low down in the windows before the tun-bellied Rosamund jars, flung inward three monstrous daubs of red, blue, and green, that broke into kaleidoscopic lights on the facetted knobs of the drug-drawers, the cut-glass scent flagons, and the bulbs of the sparklet bottles. They flushed the white-tiled floor in gorgeous patches: splashed along the nickel-silver counter-rails, and turned the polished mahogany counter-panels to the likeness of intricate grained marbles – slabs of porphyry and malachite. Mr Shaynor unlocked a drawer, and ere he began to write, took out a meagre bundle of letters. From my place by the stove, I could see the scalloped edges of the paper with a flaring monogram in the corner and could even smell the reek of chypre. At each page he turned toward the toilet-water lady of the advertisement and devoured her with over-luminous eyes. He had drawn the Austrian blanket over his shoulders, and among those warring lights he looked more than ever the incarnation of a drugged moth – a tiger-moth as I thought.

He put his letter into an envelope, stamped it with stiff mechanical movements, and dropped it in the drawer. Then I became aware of the silence of a great city asleep – the silence that underlaid the even voice of the breakers along the sea-front – a thick, tingling quiet of warm life stilled down for its appointed time, and unconsciously I moved about the glittering shop as one moves in a sick-room. Young Mr Cashell was adjusting some wire that crackled from time to time with the tense, knuckle-stretching sound of the electric spark. Upstairs, where a door shut and opened swiftly, I could hear his uncle coughing abed.

'Here,' I said, when the drink was properly warmed, 'take some of this, Mr Shaynor.'

He jerked in his chair with a start and a wrench, and held out his hand for the glass. The mixture, of a rich port-wine colour, frothed at the top.

'It looks,' he said, suddenly, 'it looks – those bubbles – like a string of pearls winking at you – rather like the pearls round that young lady's neck.' He turned again to the advertisement where the female in the dove-coloured corset had seen fit to put on all her pearls before she cleaned her teeth.

'Not bad, is it?' I said.

'Eh?'

He rolled his eyes heavily full on me, and, as I stared, I beheld all meaning and consciousness die out of the swiftly dilating pupils. His figure lost its stark rigidity, softened into the chair, and, chin on chest, hands dropped before him, he rested open-eyed, absolutely still.

'I'm afraid I've rather cooked Shaynor's goose,' I said, bearing the fresh drink to young Mr Cashell. 'Perhaps it was the chloric-ether.'

'Oh, he's all right.' The spade-bearded man glanced at him pityingly. 'Consumptives go off in those sort of doses very often. It's exhaustion . . . I don't wonder. I daresay the liquor will do him good. It's grand stuff,' he finished his share appreciatively. 'Well, as I was saying – before he interrupted – about this little coherer. The pinch of dust, you see, is nickel-filings. The Hertzian waves, you see, come out of space from the station that despatches 'em, and all these little particles are attracted together – cohere, we call it – for just so long as the current passes through them. Now, it's important to remember that the current is an induced current. There are a good many kinds of induction –'

'Yes, but what *is* induction?'

'That's rather hard to explain untechnically. But the long and the short of it is that when a current of electricity passes through a wire there's a lot of magnetism present round that wire; and if you put another wire parallel to, and within what we call its magnetic field – why then, the second wire will also become charged with electricity.'

'On its own account?'

'On its own account.'

'Then let's see if I've got it correctly. Miles off, at Poole, or wherever it is –'

'It will be anywhere in ten years.'

'You've got a charged wire –'

'Charged with Hertzian waves which vibrate, say, two hundred and thirty million times a second.' Mr Cashell snaked his forefinger rapidly through the air.

'All right – a charged wire at Poole, giving out these waves into space. Then this wire of yours sticking out into space – on the roof of the house – in some mysterious way gets charged with those waves from Poole –'

'Or anywhere – it only happens to be Poole tonight.'

'And those waves set the coherer at work just like an ordinary telegraph-office ticker?'

'No! That's where so many people make the mistake. The Hertzian waves wouldn't be strong enough to work a great heavy Morse instrument like ours. They can only just make that dust cohere, and while it coheres (a little while for a dot and a longer while for a dash) the current from this battery – the home battery' – he laid his hand on the thing – 'can get through to the Morse printing-machine to record the dot or dash. Let me make it clearer. Do you know anything about steam?'

'Very little. But go on.'

'Well, the coherer is like a steam-valve. Any child can open a valve and start a steamer's engines, because a turn of the hand lets in the main steam, doesn't it? Now, this home battery here ready to print is the main steam. The coherer is the valve, always ready to be turned on. The Hertzian wave is the child's hand that turns it.'

'I see. That's marvellous.'

'Marvellous, isn't it? And, remember, we're only at the beginning. There's nothing we shan't be able to do in ten years. I want to live – my God, how I want to live, and see it develop?' He looked through the door at Shaynor breathing lightly in his chair. 'Poor beast! And he wants to keep company with Fanny Brand.'

'Fanny *who*?' I said, for the name struck an obscurely familiar chord in my brain – something connected with a stained handkerchief, and the word 'arterial'.

'Fanny Brand – the girl you kept shop for.' He laughed. 'That's all I know about her, and for the life of me I can't see what Shaynor sees in her, or she in him.'

'*Can't* you see what he sees in her?' I insisted.

'Oh, yes, if *that's* what you mean. She's a great, big, fat lump of a girl, and so on. I suppose that's why he's so crazy after her. She isn't his sort. Well, it doesn't matter. My uncle says he's bound to die before the year's out. Your drink's given him a good sleep, at any rate.' Young Mr Cashell could not catch Mr Shaynor's face, which was half turned to the advertisement.

I stoked the stove anew, for the room was growing cold, and lighted another pastille. Mr Shaynor in his chair, never moving, looked through and over me with eyes as wide and lustreless as those of a dead hare.

'Poole's late,' said young Mr Cashell, when I stepped back. 'I'll just send them a call.'

He pressed a key in the semi-darkness, and with a rending crackle there leaped between two brass knobs a spark, streams of sparks, and sparks again.

'Grand, isn't it? *That's* the Power – our unknown Power – kicking and fighting to be let loose,' said young Mr Cashell. 'There she goes – kick – kick – kick into space. I never get over the strangeness of it when I work a sending-machine – waves going into space, you know. T. R. is our call. Poole ought to answer with L. L. L.'

We waited two, three, five minutes. In that silence, of which the boom of the tide was an orderly part, I caught the clear *'kiss – kiss – kiss'* of the halliards on the roof, as they were blown against the installation-pole.

'Poole is not ready. I'll stay here and call you when he is.'

I returned to the shop, and set down my glass on a marble slab with a careless clink. As I did so, Shaynor rose to his feet, his eyes fixed once more on the advertisement, where the young woman bathed in the light from the red jar simpered pinkly over her pearls. His lips moved without cessation. I stepped nearer to listen. 'And threw – and threw – and threw,' he repeated, his face all sharp with some inexplicable agony.

I moved forward astonished. But it was then he found words – delivered roundly and clearly. These:

And threw warm gules on Madeleine's young breast.

The trouble passed off his countenance, and he returned lightly to his place, rubbing his hands.

It had never occurred to me, though we had many times discussed reading and prize-competitions as a diversion, that Mr Shaynor ever read Keats, or could quote him at all appositely. There was, after all, a certain stained-glass effect of light on the high bosom of the highly-polished picture which might, by stretch of fancy, suggest, as a vile chromo recalls some incomparable canvas, the line he had spoken. Night, my drink, and solitude were evidently turning Mr Shaynor into a poet. He sat down again and wrote swiftly on his villainous note-paper, his lips quivering.

I shut the door into the inner office and moved up behind him. He made no sign that he saw or heard. I looked over his shoulder, and read, amid half-formed words, sentences, and wild scratches:

> – Very cold it was. Very cold
> The hare – the hare – the hare –
> The birds –

He raised his head sharply, and frowned toward the blank shutters of the poulterer's shop where they jutted out against our window. Then one clear line came:

> The hare, in spite of fur, was very cold.

The head, moving machine-like, turned right to the advertisement where the Blaudett's Cathedral pastille reeked abominably. He grunted, and went on:

> Incense in a censer –
> Before her darling picture framed in gold –
> Maiden's picture – angel's portrait –

'Hsh!' said Mr Cashell guardedly from the inner office, as though in the presence of spirits. 'There's something coming through from somewhere; but it isn't Poole.' I heard the crackle of sparks as he depressed the keys of the transmitter. In my own brain, too, something crackled, or it might have been the hair on my head. Then I heard my own voice, in a harsh whisper: 'Mr Cashell, there is something coming through here, too. Leave me alone till I tell you.'

'But I thought you'd come to see this wonderful thing – Sir,' indignantly at the end.

'Leave me alone till I tell you. Be quiet.'

I watched – I waited. Under the blue-veined hand – the dry hand of the consumptive – came away clear, without erasure:

> And my weak spirit fails
> To think how the dead must freeze –

he shivered as he wrote –

> Beneath the churchyard mould.

192

Then he stopped, laid the pen down, and leaned back.

For an instant, that was half an eternity, the shop spun before me in a rainbow-tinted whirl, in and through which my own soul most dispassionately considered my own soul as that fought with an over-mastering fear. Then I smelt the strong smell of cigarettes from Mr Shaynor's clothing, and heard, as though it had been the rending of trumpets, the rattle of his breathing. I was still in my place of observation, much as one would watch a rifle-shot at the butts, half-bent, hands on my knees, and head within a few inches of the black, red, and yellow blanket of his shoulder. I was whispering encouragement, evidently to my other self, sounding sentences, such as men pronounce in dreams.

'If he has read Keats, it proves nothing. If he hasn't – like causes *must* beget like effects. There is no escape from this law. *You* ought to be grateful that you know "St Agnes' Eve" without the book; because, given the circumstances, such as Fanny Brand, who is the key of the enigma, and approximately represents the latitude and longitude of Fanny Brawne; allowing also for the bright red colour of the arterial blood upon the handkerchief, which was just what you were puzzling over in the shop just now; and counting the effect of the professional environment, here almost perfectly duplicated – the result is logical and inevitable. As inevitable as induction.'

Still, the other half of my soul refused to be comforted. It was cowering in some minute and inadequate corner – at an immense distance.

Hereafter, I found myself one person again, my hands still gripping my knees, and my eyes glued on the page before Mr Shaynor. As dreamers accept and explain the upheaval of landscapes and the resurrection of the dead, with excerpts from the evening hymn or the multiplication-table, so I had accepted the facts, whatever they might be, that I should witness, and had devised a theory, sane and plausible to my mind, that explained them all. Nay, I was even in advance of my facts, walking hurriedly before them, assured that they would fit my theory. And all that I now recall of that epoch-making theory are the lofty words: 'If he has read Keats it's the chloric-ether. If he hasn't, it's the identical bacillus, or Hertzian wave of tuberculosis, *plus* Fanny Brand and the professional status which, in conjunction with the main-stream of subconscious thought common to all mankind, has thrown up temporarily an induced Keats.'

Mr Shaynor returned to his work, erasing and rewriting as before with swiftness. Two or three blank pages he tossed aside. Then he wrote, muttering:

> The little smoke of a candle that goes out.

'No,' he muttered. 'Little smoke – little smoke – little smoke. What else?' He thrust his chin forward toward the advertisement, whereunder the last of the Blaudett's Cathedral pastilles fumed in its holder. 'Ah!' Then with relief:

> The little smoke that dies in moonlight cold

Evidently he was snared by the rhymes of his first verse, for he wrote and rewrote 'gold – cold – mould' many times. Again he sought inspiration from the advertisement, and set down, without erasure, the line I had overheard: –

> And threw warm gules on Madeleine's young breast.

As I remembered the original it is 'fair' – a trite word – instead of 'young', and I found myself nodding approval, though I admitted that the attempt to reproduce 'its little smoke in pallid moonlight died' was a failure.

Followed without a break ten or fifteen lines of bald prose – the naked soul's confession of its physical yearning for its beloved – unclean as we count uncleanliness; unwholesome, but human exceedingly; the raw material, so it seemed to me in that hour and in that place, whence Keats wove the twenty-sixth, seventh, and eighth stanzas of his poem. Shame I had none in overseeing this revelation; and my fear had gone with the smoke of the pastille.

'That's it,' I murmured. 'That's how it's blocked out. Go on! Ink it in, man. Ink it in!'

'Wireless'

Mr Shaynor returned to broken verse wherein 'loveliness' was made to rhyme with a desire to look upon 'her empty dress'. He picked up a fold of the gay, soft blanket, spread it over one hand, caressed it with infinite tenderness, thought, muttered, traced some snatches which I could not decipher, shut his eyes drowsily, shook his head, and dropped the stuff. Here I found myself at fault, for I could not then see (as I do now) in what manner a red, black, and yellow Austrian blanket coloured his dreams.

In a few minutes he laid aside his pen, and, chin on hand, considered the shop with thoughtful and intelligent eyes. He threw down the blanket, rose, passed along a line of drug-drawers, and read the names on the labels aloud. Returning, he took from his desk Christy's *New Commercial Plants* and the old Culpepper that I had given him, opened and laid them side by side with a clerky air, all trace of passion gone from his face, read first in one and then in the other, and paused with pen behind his ear.

'What wonder of Heaven's coming now?' I thought.

'Manna – manna – manna,' he said at last, under wrinkled brows. 'That's what I wanted. Good! Now then! Now then! Good! Good! Oh, by God, that's good!' His voice rose and he spoke rightly and fully without a falter:

> Candied apple, quince and plum and gourd,
> And jellies smoother than the creamy curd,
> And lucent syrups tinct with cinnamon,
> Manna and dates in Argosy transferred
> From Fez; and spiced dainties, every one
> From silken Samarcand to cedared Lebanon.

He repeated it once more, using 'blander' for 'smoother' in the second line; then wrote it down without erasure, but this time (my set eyes missed no stroke of any word) he substituted 'soother' for his atrocious second thought, so that it came away under his hand as it is written in the book – as it is written in the book.

A wind went shouting down the street, and on the heels of the wind followed a spurt and rattle of rain.

After a smiling pause – and good right had he to smile – he began anew, always tossing the last sheet over his shoulder:

> The sharp rain falling on the window-pane,
> Rattling sleet – the wind-blown sleet.

Then prose: 'It is very cold of mornings when the wind brings rain and sleet with it. I heard the sleet on the window-pane outside, and thought of you, my darling. I am always thinking of you. I wish we could both run away like two lovers into the storm and get that little cottage by the sea which we are always thinking about, my own dear darling. We could sit and watch the sea beneath our windows. It would be a fairyland all of our own – a fairy sea – a fairy sea . . .'

He stopped, raised his head, and listened. The steady drone of the Channel along the sea-front that had borne us company so long leaped up a note to the sudden fuller surge that signals the change from ebb to flood. It beat in like the change of step throughout an army – this renewed pulse of the sea – and filled our ears till they, accepting it, marked it no longer.

> A fairyland for you and me
> Across the foam – beyond . . .
> A magic foam, a perilous sea.

He grunted again with effort and bit his underlip. My throat dried, but I dared not gulp to moisten it lest I should break the spell that was drawing him nearer and nearer to the high-water mark but two of the sons of Adam have reached. Remember that in all the millions permitted there are no more than five – five little lines – of which one can say: 'These are the pure Magic. These are the clear Vision. The rest is only poetry.' And Mr Shaynor was playing hot and cold with two of them!

I vowed no unconscious thought of mine should influence the blindfold soul, and pinned myself desperately to the other three, repeating and re-repeating:

'Wireless'

> A savage spot as holy and enchanted
> As e'er beneath a waning moon was haunted
> By woman wailing for her demon lover.

But though I believed my brain thus occupied, my every sense hung upon the writing under the dry, bony hand, all brown-fingered with chemicals and cigarette-smoke.

> Our windows fronting on the dangerous foam,

(he wrote, after long, irresolute snatches), and then –

> Our open casements facing desolate seas
> Forlorn – forlorn –

Here again his face grew peaked and anxious with that sense of loss I had first seen when the Power snatched him. But this time the agony was tenfold keener. As I watched it mounted like mercury in the tube. It lighted his face from within till I thought the visibly scourged soul must leap forth naked between his jaws, unable to endure. A drop of sweat trickled from my forehead down my nose and splashed on the back of my hand.

> Our windows facing on the desolate seas
> And pearly foam of magic fairyland –

'Not yet – not yet,' he muttered, 'wait a minute. *Please* wait a minute. I shall get it then –

> Our magic windows fronting the sea,
> The dangerous foam of desolate seas . . .
> For aye.

Ouh, my God!'

From head to heel he shook – shook from the marrow of his bones outwards – then leaped to his feet with raised arms, and slid the chair screeching across the tiled floor where it struck the drawers behind and fell with a jar. Mechanically, I stooped to recover it.

As I rose, Mr Shaynor was stretching and yawning at leisure.

'I've had a bit of a doze,' he said. 'How did I come to knock the chair over? You look rather –'

'The chair startled me,' I answered. 'It was so sudden in this quiet.'

Young Mr Cashell behind his shut door was offendedly silent.

'I suppose I must have been dreaming,' said Mr Shaynor.

'I suppose you must,' I said. 'Talking of dreams – I – I noticed you writing – before –'

He flushed consciously.

'I meant to ask you if you've ever read anything written by a man called Keats.'

'Oh! I haven't much time to read poetry, and I can't say that I remember the name exactly. Is he a popular writer?'

'Middling. I thought you might know him because he's the only poet who was ever a druggist. And he's rather what's called the lover's poet.'

'Indeed. I must dip into him. What did he write about?'

'A lot of things. Here's a sample that may interest you.'

Then and there, carefully, I repeated the verse he had twice spoken and once written not ten minutes ago.

'Ah! Anybody could see he was a druggist from that line about the tinctures and syrups. It's a fine tribute to our profession.'

'I don't know,' said young Mr Cashell, with icy politeness, opening the door one half-inch, 'if you still happen to be interested in our trifling experiments. But, should such be the case –'

I drew him aside, whispering, 'Shaynor seemed going off into some sort of fit when I spoke to you just now. I thought, even at the risk of being rude, it wouldn't do to take you off your instruments just as the call was coming through. Don't you see?'

'Granted – granted as soon as asked,' he said, unbending. 'I *did* think it a shade odd at the time. So that was why he knocked the chair down?'

'I hope I haven't missed anything,' I said.

'I'm afraid I can't say that, but you're just in time for the end of a rather curious performance. You can come in too, Mr Shaynor. Listen, while I read it off.'

The Morse instrument was ticking furiously. Mr Cashell interpreted: '*"K.K.V. Can make nothing of your signals."*' A pause. '*"M.M.V. M.M.V. Signals unintelligible. Purpose anchor Sandown Bay. Examine instruments tomorrow."* Do you know what that means? It's a couple of men–o'–war working Marconi signals off the Isle of Wight. They are trying to talk to each other. Neither can read the other's messages, but all their messages are being taken in by our receiver here. They've been going on for ever so long. I wish you could have heard it.'

'How wonderful!' I said. 'Do you mean we're overhearing Portsmouth ships trying to talk to each other – that we're eavesdropping across half South England?'

'Just that. Their transmitters are all right, but their receivers are out of order, so they only get a dot here and a dash there. Nothing clear.'

'Why is that?'

'God knows – and Science will know tomorrow. Perhaps the induction is faulty; perhaps the receivers aren't tuned to receive just the number of vibrations per second that the transmitter sends. Only a word here and there. Just enough to tantalize.'

Again the Morse sprang to life.

'That's one of 'em complaining now. Listen: "*Disheartening – most disheartening.*" It's quite pathetic. Have you ever seen a spiritualistic seance? It reminds me of that sometimes – odds and ends of messages coming out of nowhere – a word here and there – no good at all.'

'But mediums are all impostors,' said Mr Shaynor, in the doorway, lighting an asthma–cigarette. 'They only do it for the money they can make. I've seen 'em.'

'Here's Poole, at last – clear as a bell. L.L.L. *Now* we shan't be long.' Mr Cashell rattled the keys merrily. 'Anything you'd like to tell 'em?'

'No, I don't think so,' I said. 'I'll go home and get to bed. I'm feeling a little tired.'

❴ The Army of a Dream ❵

Song of the Old Guard

And thou shalt make a candlestick of pure gold: of beaten work
shall the candlestick be made: his shaft and its branches, his bowls,
his knops, and his flowers, shall be the same ...

And there shall be a knop under two branches of the same, and a
knop under two branches of the same, and a knop under two branches
of the same, according to the six branches that proceed out of the
candlestick ... Their knops and their branches shall be the same.

Exodus

'Know this, my brethren, Heaven is clear
    And all the clouds are gone –
The Proper Sort shall flourish now,
    Good times are coming on' –
The evil that was threatened late
    To all of our degree,
Hath passed in discord and debate,
    And, *Hey then up go we!*

A common people strove in vain
    To shame us unto toil,
But they are spent and we remain,
    And we shall share the spoil
According to our several needs
    As Beauty shall decree,
As Age ordains or Birth concedes,
    And, *Hey then up go we!*

And they that with accursèd zeal
    Our Service would amend,
Shall own the odds and come to heel
    Ere worse befall their end:
For though no naked word be wrote
    Yet plainly shall they see
What pinneth Orders to their coat,
    And, *Hey then up go we!*

The Army of a Dream

Our doorways that, in time of fear,
  We opened overwide
Shall softly close from year to year
  Till all be purified;
For though no fluttering fan be heard
  Nor chaff be seen to flee –
The Lord shall winnow the Lord's
    Preferred –
    And, *Hey then up go we!*

Our altars which the heathen brake
  Shall rankly smoke anew,
And anise, mint, and cummin take
  Their dread and sovereign due,
Whereby the buttons of our trade
  Shall all restorèd be
With curious work in gilt and braid,
    And, *Hey then up go we!*

Then come, my brethren, and prepare
  The candlesticks and bells,
The scarlet, brass, and badger's hair
  Wherein our Honour dwells,
And straitly fence and strictly keep
  The Ark's integrity
Till Armageddon break our sleep . . .
    And, *Hey then up go we!*

The Army of a Dream

Part I

I sat down in the Club smoking-room to fill a pipe.

It was entirely natural that I should be talking to 'Boy' Bayley.
We had met first, twenty odd years ago, at the Indian mess of
the Tyneside Tail-twisters. Our last meeting, I remembered,
had been at the Mount Nelson Hotel, which was by no means
India, and there we had talked half the night. Boy Bayley had
gone up that week to the front, where I think he stayed a long,
long time.

But now he had come back.

'Are you still a Tynesider?' I asked.

'I command the Imperial Guard Battalion of the old regiment, my son,' he replied.

'Guard which? They've been Fusiliers since Fontenoy. Don't
pull my leg, Boy.'

'I said Guard, not Guard-s. The I.G. Battalion of the Tail-
twisters. Does that make it any clearer?'

'Not in the least.'

'Then come over to mess and see for yourself. We aren't a
step from barracks. Keep on my right side. I'm – I'm a bit deaf
on the near.'

We left the Club together and crossed the street to a vast
four-storied pile, which more resembled a Rowton lodging-
house than a barrack. I could see no sentry at the gates.

'There ain't any,' said the Boy lightly. He led me into a
many-tabled restaurant full of civilians and grey-green uniforms. At one end of the room, on a slightly raised dais, stood a
big table.

'Here we are! We usually lunch here and dine in mess by
ourselves. These are our chaps – but what am I thinking of?

You must know most of 'em. Devine's my second in command now. There's old Luttrell – remember him at Cherat? – Burgard, Verschoyle (you were at school with him), Harrison, Pigeon, and Kyd.'

With the exception of the last I knew them all, but I could not remember that they had all been Tynesiders.

'I've never seen this sort of place,' I said, looking round. 'Half the men here are in plain clothes, and what are those women and children doing?'

'Eating, I hope,' Boy Bayley answered. 'Our canteens would never pay if it wasn't for the Line and Militia trade. When they were first started people looked on 'em rather as catsmeat-shops; but we got a duchess or two to lunch in 'em, and they've been grossly fashionable since.'

'So I see,' I answered. A woman of the type that shops at the Stores came up the room looking about her. A man in the dull-grey uniform of the corps rose up to meet her, piloted her to a place between three other uniforms, and there began a very merry little meal.

'I give it up,' I said. 'This is guilty splendour that I don't understand.'

'Quite simple,' said Burgard across the table. 'The barrack supplies breakfast, dinner, and tea on the Army scale to the Imperial Guard (which we call I.G.) when it's in barracks as well as to the Line and Militia. They can all invite their friends if they choose to pay for them. That's where we make our profits. Look!'

Near one of the doors were four or five tables crowded with workmen in the raiment of their callings. They ate steadily, but found time to jest with the uniforms about them; and when one o'clock clanged from a big half-built block of flats across the street, filed out.

'Those,' Devine explained, 'are either our Line or Militia men, as such entitled to the regulation whack at regulation cost. It's cheaper than they could buy it; an' they meet their friends too. A man'll walk a mile in his dinner-hour to mess with his own lot.'

'Wait a minute,' I pleaded. 'Will you tell me what those

plumbers and plasterers and bricklayers, that I saw go out just now, have to do with what I was taught to call the Line?'

'Tell him,' said the Boy over his shoulder to Burgard. He was busy talking with the large Verschoyle, my old schoolmate.

'The Line comes next to the Guard. The Linesman's generally a town-bird who can't afford to be a Volunteer. He has to go into camp in an Area for two months his first year, six weeks his second, and a month the third. He gets about five bob a week the year round for that and for being on duty two days of the week, and for being liable to be ordered out to help the Guard in a row. He needn't live in barracks unless he wants to, and he and his family can feed at the regimental canteen at usual rates. The women like it.'

'All this,' I said politely, but intensely, 'is the raving of delirium. Where may your precious recruit who needn't live in barracks learn his drill?'

'At his precious school, my child, like the rest of us. The notion of allowing a human being to reach his twentieth year before asking him to put his feet in the first position *was* raving lunacy if you like!' Boy Bayley dived back into the conversation.

'Very good,' I said meekly. 'I accept the virtuous plumber who puts in two months of his valuable time at Aldershot –'

'Aldershot!' The table exploded. I felt a little annoyed.

'A camp in an Area is not exactly Aldershot,' said Burgard. 'The Line isn't exactly what you fancy. Some of them even come to *us!*'

'You recruit from 'em?'

'I beg your pardon,' said Devine with mock solemnity. 'The Guard doesn't recruit. It selects.'

'It would,' I said, 'with a Spiers and Pond restaurant; pretty girls to play with; and –'

'A room apiece, four bob a day and all found,' said Verschoyle. 'Don't forget that.'

'Of course!' I said. 'It probably beats off recruits with a club.'

'No, with the ballot-box,' said Verschoyle, laughing. 'At least in all R.C. companies.'

'I didn't know Roman Catholics were so particular,' I ventured.

They grinned. 'R.C. companies,' said the Boy, 'mean Right of Choice. When a company has been very good and pious for a long time it may, if the C.O. thinks fit, choose its own men – all same one-piece Club. All our companies are R.C.'s, and, as the battalion is making up a few vacancies ere starting once more on the wild and trackless "heef" into the Areas, the Linesman is here in force today sucking up to our non-coms.'

'Would someone mind explaining to me the meaning of every other word you've used,' I said. 'What's a trackless "heef"? What's an Area? What's everything generally?' I asked.

'Oh, "heef's" part of the British Constitution,' said the Boy. 'It began long ago when they first mapped out the big military manoeuvring grounds – we call 'em Areas for short – where the I.G. spend two-thirds of their time and the other regiments get their training. It was slang originally for beef on the hoof, because in the Military Areas two-thirds of your meat-rations at least are handed over to you on the hoof, and you make your own arrangements. The word "heef" became a parable for camping in the Military Areas and all its miseries. There are two Areas in Ireland, one in Scotland, and a sort of parade-ground in the Lake District; but the real working Areas are in India, Africa, and Australia, and so on.'

'And what do you do there?'

'We "heef" under service conditions, which are rather like hard work. We "heef" in an English Area for about a year, coming into barracks for one month to make up wastage. Then we may "heef" foreign for another year or eighteen months. Then we do sea-time in the war boats –'

'*What-t?*' I said.

'Sea-time,' Bayley repeated. 'Just like Marines, to learn about the big guns and how to embark and disembark quick. Then we come back to our territorial headquarters for six months, to educate the Line and Volunteer camps, to go to Hythe, to keep abreast of any new ideas, and then we fill up vacancies. We call those six months "Schools". Then we begin all over again, thus: Home "heef", foreign "heef", sea-time, schools.

"Heefing" isn't precisely luxurious, but it's on "heef" that we make our head-money.'

'Or lose it,' said the sallow Pigeon, and all laughed, as men will, at regimental jokes.

'The Dove never lets me forget that,' said Boy Bayley. 'It happened last March. We were out in the Second Northern Area at the top end of Scotland where a lot of those silly deer-forests used to be. I'd sooner "heef" in the middle of Australia myself – or Athabasca, with all respect to The Dove; he's a native of those parts. We were camped somewhere near Caithness, and the Armity (that's the combined Navy and Army Board which runs our show) sent us about eight hundred raw remounts to break in to keep us warm.'

'Why horses for a foot regiment?'

'I.G.'s don't foot it unless they're obliged to. No have gee-gee how can move? I'll show you later. Well, as I was saying, we broke those beasts in on compressed forage and small box-spurs, and then we started across Scotland to Applecross to hand 'em over to a horse-depot there. It was snowing cruel, and we didn't know the country overmuch. You remember the 30th – the old East Lancashire – at Mian Mir? Their Guard Battalion had been "heefing" round those parts for six months. We thought they'd be snowed up all quiet and comfy, but Burden, their C.O., got wind of our coming, and sent spies in to Eschol.'

'Confound him!' said Luttrell, who was fat and well-liking. 'I entertained one of 'em – in a red worsted comforter – under Bean Derig. He said he was a crofter. 'Gave him a drink too.'

'I don't mind admitting,' said the Boy, 'that, what with the cold and the remounts, we were moving rather base-over-apex. Burden bottled us under Sghurr Mhor in a snowstorm. He stampeded half the horses, cut off a lot of us in a snow-bank, and generally rubbed our noses in the dirt.'

'Was he allowed to do that?' I said.

'There is no peace in a Military Area. If we'd beaten him off or got away without losing anyone, we'd have been entitled to a day's pay from every man engaged against us. But we didn't. He cut off fifty of ours, held 'em as prisoners for the regulation

206

three days, and then sent in his bill – three days' pay for each man taken. Fifty men at twelve bob a head, plus five pounds for The Dove as a captured officer, and Kyd here, his junior, three, made about forty quid to Burden and Co. They crowed over us horrid.'

'Couldn't you have appealed to an umpire or – or something?'

'We could, but we talked it over with the men and decided to pay and look happy. We were fairly had. The 30th knew every foot of Sghurr Mhor. I spent three days huntin' 'em in the snow, but they went off on our remounts about twenty mile that night.'

'Do you always do this sham-fight business?' I asked.

'Once inside an Area you must look after yourself; but I tell you that a fight which means that every man-Jack of us may lose a week's pay isn't so dam-sham after all. It keeps the men nippy. Still, in the long run, it's like whist on a P. and O. It comes out fairly level if you play long enough. Now and again, though, one gets a present – say, when a Line regiment's out on the "heef", and signifies that it's ready to abide by the rules of the game. You mustn't take head-money from a Line regiment in an Area unless it says that it'll play you; but, after a week or two, those clever Linesmen always think they see a chance of making a pot, and send in their compliments to the nearest I.G. Then the fun begins. We caught a Line regiment single-handed about two years ago in Ireland – caught it on the hop between a bog and a beach. It had just moved in to join its brigade, and we made a forty-two-mile march in fourteen hours, and cut it off, lock, stock, and barrel. It went to ground like a badger – I *will* say those Line regiments can dig – but we got out privily by night and broke up the only road it could expect to get its baggage and company-guns along. Then we blew up a bridge that some Sappers had made for experimental purposes (*they* were rather stuffy about it) on its line of retreat, while we lay up in the mountains and signalled for the A.C. of those parts.'

'Who's an A.C.?' I asked.

'The Adjustment Committee – the umpires of the Military Areas. They're a set of superannuated old aunts of colonels kept for the purpose, but they occasionally combine to do justice. Our A.C. came, saw our dispositions, and said it was a sanguinary massa*cree* for the Line, and that we were entitled to our full pound of flesh – head-money for one whole regiment, with equipment, four company-guns, and all kit! At Line rates this worked out as one fat cheque for two hundred and fifty. Not bad!'

'But we had to pay the Sappers seventy-four quid for blowing their patent bridge to pieces,' Devine interpolated. 'That was a swindle.'

'That's true,' the Boy went on, 'but the Adjustment Committee gave our helpless victims a talking to that was worth another hundred to hear.'

'But isn't there a lot of unfairness in this head-money system?' I asked.

''Can't have everything perfect,' said the Boy. 'Head-money is an attempt at payment by results, and it gives the men a direct interest in their job. Three times out of five, of course, the A.C. will disallow both sides' claim, but there's always the chance of bringing off a coup.'

'Do all regiments do it?'

'Heavily. The Line pays a bob per prisoner and the Militia ninepence, not to mention side-bets which are what really keep the men keen. It isn't supposed to be done by the Volunteers, but they gamble worse than anyone. Why, the very kids do it when they go to First Camp at Aldershot or Salisbury.'

'Head-money's a national institution – like betting,' said Burgard.

'I should say it was,' said Pigeon suddenly. 'I was roped in the other day as an Adjustment Committee by the Kemptown Board School. I was riding under the Brighton racecourse, and I heard the whistle goin' for umpire – the regulation, two longs and two shorts. I didn't take any notice till an infant about a yard high jumped up from a furze-patch and shouted: "Guard! Guard! Come 'ere! I want you *per*-fessionally. Alf says 'e ain't outflanked. Ain't 'e a liar? Come an' look 'ow I've posted my men." You bet I looked! The young demon trotted by my stirrup and showed me his whole army (twenty of 'em) laid out under cover as nicely as you please round a cowhouse in a hollow. He kept on shouting: "I've drew Alf into there. 'Is persition ain't tenable. Say it ain't tenable, Guard!" I rode round the position, and Alf with his army came out of his cowhouse an' sat on the roof and protested like a – like a Militia Colonel; but the facts were in favour of my friend and I umpired according. Well, Alf abode by my decision. I explained it to him at length, and he solemnly paid up his head-money – farthing points if you please!'

'Did they pay you umpire's fee?' said Kyd. 'I umpired a whole afternoon once for a village school at home, and they stood me a bottle of hot ginger beer.'

'I compromised on a halfpenny – a sticky one – or I'd have hurt their feelings,' said Pigeon gravely. 'But I gave 'em sixpence back.'

'How were they manoeuvring and what with?' I asked.

'Oh, by whistle and hand-signal. They had the dummy Board School guns and flags for positions, but they were rushing their attack much too quick for that open country. I told 'em so, and they admitted it.'

'But who taught 'em?' I said.

'They had learned in their schools, of course, like the rest of us. They were all of 'em over ten; and squad-drill begins when they're eight. They knew their company-drill a heap better than they knew their King's English.'

'How much drill do the boys put in?' I asked.

'All boys begin physical-drill to music in the Board Schools when they're six; squad-drill, one hour a week, when they're eight; company-drill when they're ten, for an hour and a half a week. Between ten and twelve they get battalion-drill of a sort. They take the rifle at twelve and record their first target-score at thirteen. That's what the Code lays down. But it's worked very loosely so long as a boy comes up to the standard of his age.'

'In Canada we don't need your physical drill. We're born fit,' said Pigeon, 'and our ten-year-olds could knock spots out of your twelve-year-olds.'

'I may as well explain,' said the Boy, 'that The Dove is our "swop" officer. He's an untamed Huskie from Nootka Sound when he's at home. An I.G. Corps exchanges one officer every two years with a Canadian or Australian or African Guard Corps. We've had a year of our Dove, an' we shall be sorry to lose him. He humbles our insular pride. Meantime, Morten, our "swop" in Canada, keeps the ferocious Canuck humble. When Pig goes we shall swop Kyd, who's next on the roster, for a Cornstalk or a Maori. But about the education-drill. A boy can't attend First Camp, as we call it, till he is a trained boy and holds his First Musketry certificate. The Education Code says he must be fourteen, and the boys usually go to First Camp at about that age. Of course, they've been to their little private camps and Boys' Fresh Air Camps and public school picnics while they were at school, but First Camp is where the young drafts all meet – generally at Aldershot in this part of the world. First Camp lasts a week or ten days, and the boys are looked over for vaccination and worked lightly in brigades with lots of blank cartridge. Second Camp – that's for the fifteen to eighteen-year-olds – lasts ten days or a fortnight, and that includes a final medical examination. Men don't like to be chucked out on medical certificate much – nowadays. I assure you Second Camp, at Salisbury, say, is an experience for a young I.G. Officer. We're told off to 'em in rotation. A wilderness of monkeys isn't in it. The kids are apt to think 'emselves soldiers, and we have to take the edge off 'em with lots of picquet-work and night attacks.'

'And what happens after Second Camp?'

'It's hard to explain. Our system is so illogical. Theoretically, the boys needn't show up for the next three or four years after Second Camp. They are supposed to be making their way in life. Actually, the young doctor or lawyer or engineer joins a Volunteer battalion that sticks to the minimum of camp – ten days per annum. That gives him a holiday in the open air, and now that men have taken to endowing their Volunteer drill-halls with baths and libraries he finds, if he can't run to a Club, that his own drill-hall is an efficient substitute. He meets men there who'll be useful to him later, and he keeps himself in touch with what's going on while he's studying for his profession. The town-birds – such as the chemist's assistant, clerk, plumber, mechanic, electrician, and so forth – generally put in for their town Volunteer corps as soon as they begin to walk out with the girls. They like takin' their true-loves to our restaurants. Look yonder!' I followed his gaze, and saw across the room a man and a maid at a far table, forgetting in each other's eyes the good food on their plates.

'So it is,' said I. 'Go ahead.'

'Then, too, we have some town Volunteer corps that lay themselves out to attract promising youths of nineteen or twenty, and make much of 'em on condition that they join their Line battalion and play for their county. Under the new county qualifications – birth or three years' residence – that means a great deal in League matches, and the same in County cricket.'

'By Jove, that's a good notion,' I cried. 'Who invented it?'

'C. B. Fry – long ago. He said, in his paper, that County cricket and County volunteering ought to be on the same footing – unpaid and genuine. "No cricketer no corps. No corps no cricketer" was his watchword. There was a row among the pro's at first, but C. B. won, and later the League had to come in. They said at first it would ruin the gate; but when County matches began to be *pukka* county, *plus* inter-regimental, affairs the gate trebled, and as two-thirds of the gate goes to the regiments supplying the teams some Volunteer corps fairly wallow in cash. It's all unofficial, of course, but League Corps, as they call 'em, can take their pick of the Second Camper. Some corps ask ten guineas entrance-fee, and get it too, from the young bloods that want to shine in the arena. I told you we catered for all tastes. Now, as regards the Line proper, I believe the young artisan and mechanic puts in for that before he marries. He likes the two months' "heef" in his first year, and five bob a week is something to go on with between times.'

'Do they follow their trade while they're in the Line?' I demanded.

'Why not? How many well-paid artisans work more than four days a week anyhow? Remember a Linesman hasn't to be drilled in your sense of the word. He must have had at least eight years' grounding in that, as well as two or three years in his Volunteer battalion. He can sleep where he pleases. He can't leave town-limits without reporting himself, of course, but he can get leave if he wants it. He's on duty two days in the week as a rule, and he's liable to be invited out for garrison duty down the Mediterranean, but his benefit societies will insure him against that. I'll tell you about that later. If it's a hard winter and trade's slack, a lot of the bachelors are taken into the I.G. barracks (while the I.G. is out on the "heef") for theoretical instruction. Oh, I assure you the Line hasn't half a bad time of it.'

'Amazing!' I murmured. 'And what about the others?'

'The Volunteers? Observe the beauty of our system. We're a free people. We get up and slay the man who says we aren't. But as a little detail we never mention, if we don't volunteer in some corps or another – as combatants if we're fit, as non-combatants if we ain't – till we're thirty-five – we don't vote, and we don't get poor-relief, and the women don't love us.'

'Oh, that's the compulsion of it?' said I.

Bayley inclined his head gravely. 'That, Sir, is the compulsion. We voted the legal part of it ourselves in a fit of panic, and we have not yet rescinded our resolution! The women attend to the unofficial penalties. But being free British citizens –'

'*And* snobs,' put in Pigeon.

'The point is well taken, Pij – we have supplied ourselves with every sort and shape and make of Volunteer corps that you can imagine, and we've mixed the whole show up with our Oddfellows and our I.O.G.T.'s and our Buffaloes, and our Burkes and our Debretts, not to mention Leagues and Athletic Clubs, till you can't tell t'other from which. You remember the young pup who used to look on soldiering as a favour done to his ungrateful country – the gun-poking, ferret-pettin', landed gentleman's offspring – the suckin' Facey Romford? Well, he generally joins a Foreign Service Corps when he leaves college.'

'Can Volunteers go foreign then?'

'Can't they just, if their C.O. *or* his wife has influence! The Armity will always send a well-connected F.S. corps out to help a Guard battalion in a small campaign. Otherwise F.S. corps make their own arrangements about camps. You see, the Military Areas are always open. They can "heef" there (and gamble on head-money) as long as their finances run to it; or they can apply to do sea-time in the ships. It's a cheap way for a young man to see the world, and if he's any good he can try to get into the Guard later.'

'The main point,' said Pigeon, 'is that F.S. corps are "swagger" – the correct thing. It 'ud never do to be drawn for the Militia, don't you know,' he drawled, trying to render the English voice.

'That's what happens to a chap who doesn't volunteer,' said Bayley. 'Well, after the F.S. corps (we've about forty of 'em) come our territorial Volunteer battalions, and a man who can't suit himself somewhere among 'em must be a shade difficult. We've got those "League" corps I was talking about; and those studious corps that just scrape through their ten days' camp; and we've crack corps of highly-paid mechanics who can afford a two months' "heef" in an interesting Area every other year; and we've senior and junior scientific corps of earnest boiler-makers and fitters and engineers who read papers on high explosives, and do their "heefing" in a wet picket-boat – mine-droppin' – at the ports. Then we've heavy artillery – recruited from the big manufacturing towns and shipbuilding yards – and ferocious hard-ridin' Yeomanry (they *can* ride – now), genteel, semi-genteel, and Hooligan corps, and so on and so forth till you come to the Home Defence Establishment – the young chaps knocked out under medical certificate at the Second Camp, but good enough to sit behind hedges or clean up camp, and the old was-birds who've served their time but don't care to drop out of the fun of the yearly camps and the halls. They call 'emselves veterans and do fancy-shooting at Bisley, but, between you and me, they're mostly Fresh Air Benefit Clubs. They contribute to the Volunteer journals and tell the Guard that it's no good. But I like 'em. I shall be one of 'em some day – a copper-nosed was-bird! ... So you see we're mixed to a degree on the Volunteer side.'

'It sounds that way,' I ventured.

'You've overdone it, Bayley,' said Devine. 'You've missed

our one strong point.' He turned to me and continued: 'It's embarkation. The Volunteers may be as mixed as the Colonel says, but they *are* trained to go down to the sea in ships. You ought to see a big Bank Holiday roll-out! We suspend most of the usual railway traffic and turn on the military time-table – say on Friday at midnight. By 4 a.m. the trains are running from every big centre in England to the nearest port at two-minute intervals. As a rule, the Armity meets us at the other end with shipping of sorts – fleet-reserves or regular men-of-war or hulks – anything you can stick a gang-plank to. We pile the men on to the troop-decks, stack the rifles in the racks, send down the sea-kit, steam about for a few hours, and land 'em somewhere. It's a good notion, because our army to be any use *must* be an army of embarkation. Why, last Whit Monday we had – how many were down at the dock-edge in the first eight hours? Kyd, you're the Volunteer enthusiast last from school.'

'In the first ten hours over a hundred and eighteen thousand,' said Kyd across the table, 'with thirty-six thousand actually put in and taken out of ship. In the whole thirty-six hours we had close on ninety thousand men on the water and a hundred and thirty-three thousand on the quays fallen in with their sea-kit.'

'That must have been a sight,' I said.

'One didn't notice it much. It was scattered between Chatham, Dover, Portsmouth, Plymouth, Bristol, Liverpool, and so on, merely to give the inland men a chance to get rid of their breakfasts. We don't like to concentrate and try a big embarkation at any one point. It makes the Continent jumpy. Otherwise,' said Kyd, 'I believe we could get two hundred thousand men, with their kits, away on one tide.'

'What d'you want with so many?' I asked.

'*We* don't want one of 'em; but the Continent used to point out, every time relations were strained, that nothing would be easier than to raid England if they got command of the sea for a week. After a few years some genius discovered that it cut both ways, an' there was no reason why we, who are supposed to command the sea and own a few ships, should not organize our little raids in case of need. The notion caught on among the Volunteers – they were getting rather sick of manoeuvres on dry land – and since then we haven't heard so much about raids from the Continent,' said Bayley.

'It's the offensive–defensive,' said Verschoyle, 'that they talk so much about. We learned it *all* from the Continent – bless 'em! They insisted on it so.'

'No, we learned it from the Fleet,' said Devine. 'The Mediterranean Fleet landed ten thousand marines and sailors, with guns, in twenty minutes once at manoeuvres. That was long ago. I've seen the Fleet Reserve, and a few paddle-steamers hired for the day, land twenty-five thousand Volunteers at Bantry in four hours – half the men sea-sick too. You've no notion what a difference that sort of manoeuvre makes in the calculations of our friends on the mainland. The Continent knows what invasion means. It's like dealing with a man whose nerve has been shaken. It doesn't cost much after all, and it makes us better friends with the great European family. We're as thick as thieves now.'

'Where does the Imperial Guard come in in all this gorgeousness,' I asked. 'You're unusual modest about yourselves.'

'As a matter of fact, we're supposed to go out and stay out. We're the permanently mobilized lot. I don't think there are more than eight I.G. battalions in England now. We're a hundred battalions all told. Mostly on the "heef" in India, Africa, and so forth.'

'A hundred thousand. Isn't that small allowance?' I suggested.

'You think so? One hundred thousand *men*, without a single case of venereal, and an average sick list of two per cent, permanently on a war footing? Well, perhaps you're right, but it's a useful little force to begin with while the others are getting ready. There's the native Indian Army also, which isn't a broken reed, and, since "no Volunteer no Vote" is the rule throughout the Empire, you will find a few men in Canada, Australia, and elsewhere, that are fairly hefty in their class.'

'But a hundred thousand isn't enough for garrison duty,' I persisted.

'A hundred thousand *sound* men, not sick boys, go quite a way,' said Pigeon.

'We expect the Line to garrison the Mediterranean Ports and thereabouts,' said Bayley. 'Don't sneer at the mechanic. He's deuced good stuff. He isn't rudely ordered out, because this ain't a military despotism, and we have to consider people's feelings. The Armity usually brackets three Line regiments together, and calls for men for six months or a year for Malta, Gib, or elsewhere, at a bob a day. Three battalions will give you nearly a whole battalion of bachelors between 'em. You fill up deficiencies with a call on the territorial Volunteer battalion, and away you go with what we call a Ports battalion. What's astonishing in that? Remember that in this country, where fifty per cent of the able-bodied males have got a pretty fair notion of soldiering, and, which is more, have all camped out in the open, you wake up the spirit of adventure in the young.'

'Not much adventure at Malta, Gib, or Cyprus,' I retorted. 'Don't they get sick of it?'

'But you don't realize that we treat 'em rather differently from the soldier of the past. You ought to go and see a Ports battalion drawn from a manufacturing centre growin' vines in Cyprus in its shirt sleeves; and at Gib, and Malta, of course, the battalions are working with the Fleet half the time.'

'It seems to me,' I said angrily, 'you are knocking *esprit de corps* on the head with all this Army-Navy jumble. It's as bad as –'

'I know what you're going to say. As bad as what Kitchener used to do when he believed that a thousand details picked up on the veldt were as good as a column of two regiments. In the old days, when drill was a sort of holy sacred art learned in old age, you'd be quite right. But remember *our* chaps are broke to drill from childhood, and the theory we work on is that a thousand trained Englishmen ought to be about as good as another thousand trained Englishmen. We've enlarged our horizon, that's all. Some day the Army and the Navy will be interchangeable.'

'You've enlarged it enough to fall out of, I think. Now where in all this mess of compulsory Volunteers –?'

'My dear boy, there's no compulsion. You've *got* to be drilled when you're a child, same as you've got to learn to read; and if you don't pretend to serve in some corps or other till you're thirty-five or medically chucked, you rank with lunatics, women, and minors. That's fair enough.'

'Compulsory conscripts,' I continued. 'Where, as I was going to say, does the Militia come in?'

'As I have said – for the men who can't afford volunteering. The Militia is recruited by ballot – pretty comprehensively too. Volunteers are exempt, but most men not otherwise accounted for are bagged by the Militia. They have to put in a minimum three weeks' camp every other year, and they get fifteen bob a week and their keep when they're at it, and some sort of a yearly fee, I've forgotten how much. 'Tisn't a showy service, but it's very useful. It keeps the mass of the men between twenty-five, say, and thirty-five moderately fit, and gives the Armity an excuse for having more equipment ready – in case of emergencies.'

'I don't think you're quite fair on the Militia,' drawled Verschoyle. 'They're better than we give 'em credit for. Don't you remember the Middle Moor Collieries strike?'

'Tell me,' I said quickly. Evidently the others knew.

'We-ell, it was no end of a pitmen's strike about eight years ago. There were twenty-five thousand men involved – Militia, of course. At the end of the first month – October – when things were looking rather blue, one of those clever Labour leaders got hold of the Militia Act and discovered that any Militia regiment could, by a two-thirds vote, go on "heef" in a Military Area in addition to its usual biennial camp. Two-and-twenty battalions of Geordies solemnly applied, and they were turned loose into the Irish and Scotch Areas under an I.G. Brigadier who had private instructions to knock clinkers out of 'em. But the pitman is a strong and agile bird. He throve on snowdrifts and entrenching and draggin' guns through heather. *He* was being fed and clothed for nothing, besides having a chance of making head-money, and his strike-pay was going clear to his wife and family. You see? Wily man. But wachta-bittje! When that "heef" finished in December the strike was still on. *Then* that same Labour leader found out, from the same Act, that if at any time more than thirty or forty men of a

Militia regiment wished to volunteer to do sea-time and study
big guns in the Fleet they were in no wise to be discouraged,
but were to be taken on as opportunity offered and paid a bob a
day. Accordingly, about January, Geordie began volunteering
for sea-time – seven and eight hundred men out of each regiment. Anyhow it made up seventeen thousand men! It was a
splendid chance and the Armity jumped at it. The Home and
Channel Fleets and the North Sea and Cruiser Squadrons were
strengthened with lame ducks from the Fleet Reserve, and
between 'em with a little stretching and pushing they accommodated all of that young division.'

'Yes, but you've forgotten how we lied to the Continent
about it. All Europe wanted to know what the dooce we were
at,' said Boy Bayley, 'and the wretched Cabinet had to stump
the country in the depths of winter explaining our new system
of poor-relief. I beg your pardon, Verschoyle.'

'The Armity improvised naval manoeuvres between Gib and
Land's End, with frequent coalings and landings; ending in a
cruise round England that fairly paralysed the pitmen. The
first day out they wanted the Fleet stopped while they went
ashore and killed their Labour leader, but they couldn't be
obliged. Then they wanted to mutiny over the coaling – it was
too like their own job. Oh, they had a lordly time! They came
back – the combined Fleets anchored off Hull – with a nautical
hitch to their breeches. They'd had a free fight at Gib with the
Ports battalion there; they cleared out the town of Lagos; and
they'd fought a pitched battle with the dockyard-mateys at
Devonport. So they'd done 'emselves well, but they didn't want
any more military life for a bit.'

'And the strike?'

'That ended, all right enough, when the strike-money came
to an end. The pit-owners were furious. They said the Armity
had wilfully prolonged the strike, and asked questions in the
House. The Armity said that they had taken advantage of the
crisis to put a six months' polish on fifteen thousand fine
young men, and if the masters cared to come out on the same
terms they'd be happy to do the same by them.'

'And then?'

'Palaver done set,' said Bayley. 'Everybody laughed.'

'I don't quite understand about this sea-time business,' I said. 'Is the Fleet open to take any regiment aboard?'

'Rather. The I.G. must, the Line can, the Militia may, and the Volunteers do put in sea-time. The Coast Volunteers began it, and the fashion is spreading inland. Under certain circumstances, as Verschoyle told you, a Volunteer or Militia regiment can vote whether it "heefs" wet or dry. If it votes wet and has influence (like some F.S. corps), it can sneak into the Channel or the Home Fleet and do a cruise round England or to Madeira or the North Sea. The regiment, of course, is distributed among the ships, and the Fleet dry-nurse 'em. It rather breaks up shore discipline, but it gives the inland men a bit of experience and, of course, it gives us a fairish supply of men behind the gun, in event of any strain on the Fleet. Some coast corps make a speciality of it, and compete for embarking and disembarking records. I believe some of the Tyneside engineerin' corps put ten per cent of their men through the Fleet engine-rooms. But there's no need to stay talking here all the afternoon. Come and see the I.G. in his lair – the miserable conscript driven up to the colours at the point of the bayonet.'

Part II

The great hall was emptying apace as the clocks struck two, and we passed out through double doors into a huge reading and smoking room, blue with tobacco and buzzing with voices.

'We're quieter as a rule,' said the Boy. 'But we're filling up vacancies today. Hence the anxious faces of the Line and Militia. Look!' There were four tables against the walls, and at each stood a crowd of uniforms. The centres of disturbance were non-commissioned officers who, seated, growled and wrote down names.

'Come to my table,' said Burgard. 'Well, Purvis, have you ear-marked our little lot?'

'I've been tellin' 'em for the last hour we've only twenty-three vacancies,' was the sergeant's answer. 'I've taken nearly fifty for Trials, and this is what's left.' Burgard smiled.

'I'm very sorry,' he said to the crowd, 'but C Company's full.'

'Excuse me, Sir,' said a man, 'but wouldn't sea-time count in my favour? I've put in three months with the Fleet. Small quick-firers, Sir? Company guns? Any sort of light machinery?'

'Come away,' said a voice behind. 'They've chucked the best farrier between Hull and Dewsbury. 'Think they'll take *you* an' your potty quick-firers?'

The speaker turned on his heel and swore.

'Oh, damn the Guard, by all means,' said Sergeant Purvis, collecting his papers. 'D'you suppose it's any pleasure to *me* to reject chaps of your build and make? Vote us a second Guard battalion and we'll accommodate you. Now, you can come into Schools and watch Trials if you like.'

Most of the men accepted his invitation, but a few walked away angrily. I followed from the smoking-room across a wide corridor into a riding-school, under whose roof the voices of the few hundred assembled wandered in lost echoes.

'I'll leave you, if you don't mind,' said Burgard. 'Company officers aren't supposed to assist at these games. Here, Matthews!' He called to a private and put me in his charge.

In the centre of the vast floor my astonished eyes beheld a group of stripped men; the pink of their bodies startling the tan.

'These are our crowd,' said Matthews. 'They've been vetted, an' we're putting 'em through their paces.'

'They don't look a bit like raw material,' I said.

'No, we don't use either raw men or raw meat for that matter in the Guard,' Matthews replied. 'Life's too short.'

Purvis stepped forward and barked in the professional manner. It was physical drill of the most searching, checked only when he laid his hand over some man's heart.

Six or seven, I noticed, were sent back at this stage of the game. Then a cry went up from a group of privates standing near the line of contorted figures. 'White, Purvis, white! Number Nine is spitting white!'

'I know it,' said Purvis. 'Don't you worry.'

'Unfair!' murmured the man who understood quick-firers.

'If I couldn't shape better than that I'd hire myself out to wheel a perambulator. He's cooked.'

'Nah,' said the intent Matthews. 'He'll answer to a month's training like a horse. It's only suet. *You've* been training for this, haven't you?'

'Look at me,' said the man simply.

'Yes. You're overtrained,' was Matthews' comment. 'The Guard isn't a circus.'

'Guns!' roared Purvis, as the men broke off and panted. 'Number off from the right. Fourteen is one, three is two, eleven's three, twenty and thirty-nine are four and five, and five is six.' He was giving them their numbers at the guns as they struggled into their uniforms. In like manner he told off three other gun-crews, and the remainder left at the double, to return through the farther doors with four light quick-firers jerking at the end of man-ropes.

'Knock down and assemble against time!' Purvis called.

The audience closed in a little as the crews flung themselves on the guns, which melted, wheel by wheel, beneath their touch.

'I've never seen anything like this,' I whispered.

'Huh!' said Matthews scornfully. 'They're always doin' it in the Line and Militia drill halls. It's only circus-work.'

The guns were assembled again and someone called the time. Then followed ten minutes of the quickest feeding and firing with dummy cartridges that was ever given man to behold.

'They look as if they might amount to something – this draft,' said Matthews softly.

'What might you teach 'em after this, then?' I asked.

'To be Guard,' said Matthews.

'Spurs!' cried Purvis, as the guns disappeared through the doors into the stables. Each man plucked at his sleeve, and drew up first one heel and then the other.

'What the deuce are they doing?' I said.

'This,' said Matthews. He put his hand to a ticket-pocket inside his regulation cuff, showed me two very small black box-spurs: drawing up a gaitered foot he snapped them into the box in the heel, and when I had inspected snapped them out again.

'That's all the spur you really need,' he said.

Then horses were trotted out into the school barebacked, and the neophytes were told to ride.

Evidently the beasts knew the game and enjoyed it, for they would not make it easy for the men.

A heap of saddlery was thrown in a corner, and from this each man, as he captured his mount, made shift to draw proper equipment, while the audience laughed, derided, or called the horses towards them.

It was, most literally, wild horseplay, and by the time it was finished the recruits and the company were weak with fatigue and laughter.

'That'll do,' said Purvis, while the men rocked in their saddles. 'I don't see any particular odds between any of you. C Company! Does anybody here know anything against any of these men?'

'That's a bit of the Regulations,' Matthews whispered. 'Just like forbiddin' the banns in church. Really it was all settled long ago when the names first came up.'

There was no answer.

'You'll take 'em as they stand?'

There was a grunt of assent.

'Very good. There's forty men for twenty-three billets.' He turned to the sweating horsemen. 'I must put you into the Hat.'

With great ceremony and a shower of company jokes that I did not follow, an enormous Ally Sloper top-hat was produced, into which numbers and blanks were dropped, and the whole was handed round to the riders by a private, evidently the joker of C Company.

Matthews gave me to understand that each company owned a cherished receptacle (sometimes not a respectable one) for the papers of the final drawing. He was telling me how his company had once stolen the Sacred Article used by D Company for this purpose and of the riot that followed, when through the west door of the schools entered a fresh detachment of stripped men, and the arena was flooded with another company.

Said Matthews as we withdrew, 'Each company does Trials their own way. B Company is all for teaching men how to cook and camp. D Company keeps 'em to horse-work mostly. We call D the circus-riders and B the cooks. They call us the gunners.'

'An' you've rejected *me*,' said the man who had done sea-time, pushing out before us. 'The Army's goin' to the dogs!'

I stood in the corridor looking for Burgard.

'Come up to my room and have a smoke,' said Matthews, Private of the Imperial Guard.

We climbed two flights of stone stairs ere we reached an immense landing flanked with numbered doors. Matthews pressed a spring-latch and led me into a little cabin-like room. The cot was a standing bunk, with drawers beneath. On the bed lay a brilliant blanket; by the bed head was an electric light and a shelf of books: a writing table stood in the window, and I dropped into a low wicker chair.

'This is a cut above subaltern's quarters,' I said, surveying the photos, the dhurri on the floor, the rifle in its rack, the field-kit hung up behind the door, and the knicknacks on the walls.

'The Line bachelors use 'em while we're away; but they're nice to come back to after "heef".' Matthews passed me his cigarette-case.

'Where have you "heefed"?' I said.

'In Scotland, Central Australia, and North-Eastern Rhodesia and the North-West Indian front.'

'What's your service?'

'Four years. I'll have to go in a year. I got in when I was twenty-two – by a fluke – from the Militia direct – on Trials.'

'Trials like those we just saw?'

'Not so severe. There was less competition then. I hoped to get my stripes, but there's no chance.'

'Why?'

'I haven't the knack of handling men. Purvis let me have a half-company for a month in Rhodesia – over towards Lake Ngami. I couldn't work 'em properly. It's a gift.'

'Do colour-sergeants handle half-companies with you?'

'They can command 'em on the "heef". We've only four company officers – Burgard, Luttrell, Kyd, and Harrison. Pigeon's our swop, and he's in charge of the ponies. Burgard got his company on the "heef". You see Burgard had been a lieutenant in the Line, but he came into the Guard on Trials like the men. *He* could command. They tried him in India with a wing of the battalion for three months. He did well, so he got his company. That's what made me hopeful. But it's a gift, you see – managing men – and so I'm only a senior private. They let ten per cent of us stay on for two years extra after our three are finished – to polish the others.'

'Aren't you even a corporal?'

'We haven't corporals, or lances for that matter, in the Guard. As a senior private I'd take twenty men into action; but one Guard don't tell another how to clean himself. You've learned that before you apply . . . Come in!'

There was a knock at the door, and Burgard entered, removing his cap.

'I thought you'd be here,' he said, as Matthews vacated the other chair and sat on the bed. 'Well, has Matthews told you all about it? How did our Trials go, Matthews?'

'Forty names in the Hat, Sir, at the finish. They'll make a fairish lot. Their gun-tricks weren't bad; but D Company has taken the best horsemen – as usual.'

'Oh, I'll attend to that on "heef". Give me a man who can handle company-guns and I'll engage to make him a horse-master. D Company will end by thinkin' 'emselves Captain Pigeon's private cavalry some day.'

I had never heard a private and a captain talking after this fashion, and my face must have betrayed my astonishment, for Burgard said:

'These are not our parade manners. In our rooms, as we say in the Guard, all men are men. Outside we are officers and men.'

'I begin to see,' I stammered. 'Matthews was telling me that sergeants handled half-companies and rose from the ranks – and I don't see that there are any lieutenants – and your companies appear to be two hundred and fifty strong. It's a shade confusing to the layman.'

Burgard leaned forward didactically. 'The Regulations lay down that every man's capacity for command must be tested to the uttermost. We construe that very literally when we're on the "heef". F'r instance, any man can apply to take the command next above him, and if a man's too shy to ask, his company officer must see that he gets his chance. A sergeant is given a wing of the battalion to play with for three weeks, a month, or six weeks – according to his capacity, and turned adrift in an Area to make his own arrangements. That's what Areas are for – and to experiment in. A good gunner – a private very often – has all four company-guns to handle through a week's fight, acting for the time as the major. Majors of Guard battalions (Verschoyle's our major) are supposed to be responsible for the guns, by the way. There's nothing to prevent any man who has the gift working his way up to the experimental command of the battalion on "heef". Purvis, my colour-sergeant, commanded the battalion for three months at the back of Coolgardie, an' very well he did it. Bayley 'verted to company officer for the time being an' took Harrison's company, and Harrison came over to me as my colour-sergeant. D'you see? Well, Purvis is down for a commission when there's a vacancy. He's been thoroughly tested, and we all like him. Two other sergeants have passed that three months' trial in the same way (just as second mates go up for extra master's certificate). They have E.C. after their names in the Army List. That shows they're capable of taking command in event of war. The result of our system is that you could knock out every single officer of a Guard battalion early in the day, and the wheels 'ud still go forward, *not* merely round. We're allowed to fill up half our commissioned list from the ranks direct. *Now* d'you see why there's such a rush to get into a Guard battalion?'

'Indeed I do. Have you commanded the regiment experimentally?'

'Oh, time and again,' Burgard laughed. 'We've all had our E.C. turn.'

'Doesn't the chopping and changing upset the men?'

'It takes something to upset the Guard. Besides, they're all in the game together. They give each other a fair show, you may be sure.'

'That's true,' said Matthews. 'When I went to Ngami with my – with the half-company,' he sighed, 'they helped me all they knew. But it's a gift – handling men. I found *that* out.'

'I know you did,' said Burgard softly. 'But you found it out in time, which is the great thing. You see,' he turned to me, 'with our limited strength we can't afford to have a single man who isn't more than up to any duty – in reason. Don't you be led away by what you saw at Trials just now. The Volunteers and the Militia have all the monkey-tricks of the trade – such as mounting and dismounting guns, and making fancy scores and doing record marches; but they need a lot of working up before they can pull their weight in the boat.'

There was a knock at the door. A note was handed in. Burgard read it and smiled.

'Bayley wants to know if you'd care to come with us to the Park and see the kids. It's only a Saturday afternoon walk-round before the taxpayer ... Very good. If you'll press the button we'll try to do the rest.'

He led me by two flights of stairs up an iron stairway that gave on a platform, not unlike a ship's bridge, immediately above the barrelled glass roof of the riding-school. Through a ribbed ventilator I could see B Company far below watching some men who chased sheep. Burgard unlocked a glass-fronted fire-alarm arrangement flanked with dials and speaking-tubes, and bade me press the centre button.

Next moment I should have fallen through the riding-school roof if he had not caught me; for the huge building below my feet thrilled to the multiplied purring of electric bells. The men in the school vanished like minnows before a shadow, and above the stamp of booted feet on staircases I heard the neighing of many horses.

'What in the world have I done?' I gasped.

'Turned out the Guard – horse, foot, and guns!'

A telephone bell rang imperiously. Burgard snatched up the receiver.

'Yes, Sir ... *What*, Sir ... I never heard they said that,' he laughed, 'but it would be just like 'em. In an hour and a half? Yes, Sir. Opposite the Statue? Yes, Sir.'

He turned to me with a wink as he hung up.

'Bayley's playing up for you. Now you'll see some fun.'

'Who's going to catch it?' I demanded.

'Only our local Foreign Service Corps. Its C.O. has been boasting that it's *en état de partir*, and Bayley's going to take him at his word and have a kit-inspection this afternoon in the Park. I must tell their drill-hall. Look over yonder between that brewery chimney and the mansard roof!'

He readdressed himself to the telephone, and I kept my eye on the building to the southward. A Blue Peter climbed up to the top of the flagstaff that crowned it and blew out in the summer breeze. A black storm-cone followed.

'Inspection for F.S. corps acknowledged, Sir,' said Burgard down the telephone. 'Now we'd better go to the riding-school. The battalion falls in there. I have to change, but you're free of the corps. Go anywhere. Ask anything. In another ten minutes we're off.'

I lingered for a little looking over the great city, its huddle of houses and the great fringe of the Park, all framed between the open windows of this dial-dotted eyrie.

When I descended the halls and corridors were as hushed as they had been noisy, and my feet echoed down the broad tiled staircases. On the third floor, Matthews, gaitered and armed, overtook me smiling.

'I thought you might want a guide,' said he. 'We've five minutes yet,' and piloted me to the sun-splashed gloom of the riding-school. Three companies were in close order on the tan. They moved out at a whistle, and as I followed in their rear I was overtaken by Pigeon on a rough black mare.

'Wait a bit,' he said, 'till the horses are all out of stables, and come with us. D Company is the only mounted one just now. We do it to amuse the taxpayer,' he explained, above the noise of horses on the tan.

'Where are the guns?' I asked, as the mare lipped my coat-collar.

'Gone ahead long ago. They come out of their own door at the back of barracks. We don't haul guns through traffic more than we can help ... If Belinda breathes down your neck smack her. She'll be quiet in the streets. She loves lookin' into the shop-windows.'

The mounted company clattered through vaulted concrete corridors in the wake of the main body, and filed out into the crowded streets.

When I looked at the townsfolk on the pavement, or in the double-decked trams, I saw that the bulk of them saluted, not grudgingly or of necessity, but in a light-hearted, even flippant fashion.

'Those are Line and Militia men,' said Pigeon. 'That old chap in the top-hat by the lamp-post is an ex-Guardee. That's why he's saluting in slow time. No, there's no regulation governing these things, but we've all fallen into the way of it somehow. Steady, mare!'

'I don't know whether I care about this aggressive militarism,' I began, when the company halted, and Belinda almost knocked me down. Looking forward I saw the badged cuff of a policeman upraised at a crossing, his back towards us.

'Horrid aggressive, ain't we?' said Pigeon with a chuckle when we moved on again and overtook the main body. Here I caught the strains of the band, which Pigeon told me did not accompany the battalion on 'heef', but lived in barracks and made much money by playing at parties in town.

'If we want anything more than drums and fifes on "heef" we sing,' said Pigeon. 'Singin' helps the wind.'

I rejoiced to the marrow of my bones thus to be borne along on billows of surging music among magnificent men, in sunlight, through a crowded town whose people, I could feel, regarded us with comradeship, affection – and more.

'By Jove,' I said at last, watching the eyes about us, 'these people are looking us over as if we were horses.'

'Why not? They know the game.'

The eyes on the pavement, in the trams, the cabs, at the upper windows, swept our lines back and forth with a weighed intensity of regard which at first seemed altogether new to me, till I recalled just such eyes, a thousand of them, at manoeuvres in the Channel when one crowded battleship drew past its sister at biscuit-toss range. Then I stared at the ground overborne by those considering eyes.

Suddenly the music changed to the wail of the Dead March in *Saul*, and once more – we were crossing a large square – the regiment halted.

'Damn!' said Pigeon, glancing behind him at the mounted company. 'I believe they save up their Saturday corpses on purpose.'

'What is it?' I asked.

'A dead Volunteer. We must play him through.'

Again I looked forward and saw the top of a hearse, followed by two mourning coaches, boring directly up the halted regiment, which opened out company by company to let it through.

'But they've got the whole blessed square to funeralize in!' I exclaimed. 'Why don't they go round?'

'Not so,' Pigeon replied. 'In this city it's the Volunteer's perquisite to be played through by any corps he happens to meet on his way to the cemetery. And they make the most of it. You'll see.'

I heard the order, 'Rest on your arms', run before the poor little procession as the men opened out. The driver pulled the black Flanders beasts into a more than funeral crawl, and in the first mourning-coach I saw the tearful face of a fat woman (his mother, doubtless), a handkerchief pressed to one eye, but the other rolling vigilantly, alight with proper pride. Last came a knot of uniformed men – privates, I took it – of the dead one's corps.

Said a man in the crowd beside us to the girl on his arm, 'There, Jenny! That's what I'll get if I have the luck to meet 'em when my time comes.'

'You an' your luck,' she snapped. ''Ow can you talk such silly nonsense?'

'Played through by the Guard,' he repeated slowly. 'The undertaker 'oo could guarantee *that*, mark you, for all his customers – well 'e'd monopolize the trade, is all I can say. See the horses passagin' sideways!'

'She done it a purpose,' said the woman with a sniff.

'An' I only hope you'll follow her example. Just as long as you think I'll keep, too.'

We reclosed when the funeral had left us twenty paces behind. A small boy stuck his head out of a carriage and watched us jealously.

'Amazing! amazing!' I murmured. 'Is it regulation?'

'No. Town-custom. It varies a little in different cities, but the people value being played through more than most things, I imagine. Duddell, the big Ipswich manufacturer – he's a Quaker – tried to bring in a bill to suppress it as unchristian.' Pigeon laughed.

'And?'

'It cost him his seat next election. You see, we're all in the game.'

We reached the Park without further adventure, and found the four company-guns with their spike teams and single drivers waiting for us. Many people were gathered here, and we were halted, so far as I could see, that they might talk with the men in the ranks. The officers broke into groups.

'Why on earth didn't you come along with me?' said Boy Bayley at my side. 'I was expecting you.'

'Well, I had a delicacy about brigading myself with a colonel at the head of his regiment, so I stayed with the rear company and the horses. It's all too wonderful for any words. What's going to happen next?'

'I've handed over to Verschoyle, who will amuse and edify the school-children while I take you round our kindergarten. Don't kill any one, Vee. Are you goin' to charge 'em?'

Old Verschoyle hitched his big shoulder and nodded precisely as he used to do at school. He was a boy of few words grown into a kindly taciturn man.

'Now!' Bayley slid his arm through mine and led me across a riding road towards a stretch of rough common (singularly out of place in a park) perhaps three-quarters of a mile long and half as wide. On the encircling rails leaned an almost unbroken line of men and women – the women outnumbering the men. I saw the Guard battalion move up the road flanking the common and disappear behind the trees.

As far as the eye could range through the mellow English haze the ground inside the railings was dotted with boys in and out of uniform, armed and unarmed. I saw squads here, half-companies there; then three companies in an open space, wheeling with stately steps; a knot of drums and fifes near the railings unconcernedly slashing its way across popular airs, and a batch of gamins labouring through some extended attack destined to be swept aside by a corps crossing the ground at the double. They broke out of furze bushes, ducked over hollows and bunkers, held or fell away from hillocks and rough sandbanks till the eye wearied of their busy legs.

Bayley took me through the railings, and gravely returned the salute of a freckled twelve-year-old near by.

'What's your corps?' said the Colonel of that Imperial Guard battalion to that child.

'Eighth District Board School, Fourth Standard, Sir. We aren't out today.' Then, with a twinkle, 'I go to First Camp next year.'

'What are those boys yonder – that squad at the double?'

'Jew-boys, sir. Jewish Voluntary Schools, Sir.'

'And that full company extending behind the three elms to the south-west?'

'Private day-schools, Sir, I think. Judging distance, Sir.'

'Can you come with us?'

'Certainly, Sir.'

'Here's the raw material at the beginning of the process,' said Bayley to me.

We strolled on towards the strains of 'A Bicycle Built for Two', breathed jerkily into a mouth-organ by a slim maid of fourteen. Some dozen infants with clenched fists and earnest legs were swinging through the extension movements which that tune calls for. A stunted hawthorn overhung the little group, and from a branch a dirty white handkerchief flapped in the breeze. The girl blushed, scowled, and wiped the mouth-organ on her sleeve as we came up.

'We're all waiting for our big bruvvers,' piped up one bold person in blue breeches – seven if he was a day.

'It keeps 'em quieter, Sir,' the maiden lisped. 'The others are with the regiments.'

'Yeth, and they've all lots of blank for *you*,' said the gentleman in blue breeches ferociously.

'Oh, Artie! 'Ush!' the girl cried.

'But why have they lots of blank for *us*?' Bayley asked. Blue Breeches stood firm.

''Cause — 'cause the Guard's goin' to fight the Schools this afternoon; but my big bruvver says they'll be dam-well surprised.'

'Ar*tie*!' The girl leaped towards him. 'You know your ma said I was to smack —'

'Don't, please don't,' said Bayley, pink with suppressed mirth. 'It was all my fault. I must tell old Verschoyle this. I've surprised his plan out of the mouths of babes and sucklings.'

'What plan?' I asked.

'Old Vee has taken the báttalion up to the top of the common, and he told me he meant to charge down through the kids; but they're on to him already. He'll be scuppered. The Guard will be scuppered.'

Here Blue Breeches, overcome by the reproof of his fellows, began to weep.

'I didn't tell,' he roared. 'My big bruvver *he* knew when he saw them go up the road ...'

'Never mind! Never mind, old man,' said Bayley soothingly. 'I'm not fighting today. It's all right.'

He rightened it yet further with sixpence, and left that band loudly at feud over the spoil.

'Oh, Vee! Vee the strategist,' he chuckled. 'We'll pull Vee's leg tonight.'

Our freckled friend of the barriers doubled up behind us.

'So you know that my battalion is charging down the ground?' Bayley demanded.

'Not for certain, Sir, but we're preparin' for the worst,' he answered with a cheerful grin. 'They allow the Schools a little blank ammunition after we've passed the Third Standard; and we nearly always bring it on to the ground of Saturdays.'

'The deuce you do! Why?'

'On account of those amateur Volunteer corps, Sir. They're always experimentin' upon us, Sir, comin' over from their ground an' developin' attacks on our flanks. Oh, it's chronic 'ere of a Saturday sometimes, unless you flag yourself.'

I followed his eye and saw white flags fluttering before a drum and fife band and a knot of youths in sweaters gathered round the dummy breech of a four-inch gun which they were feeding at express rates.

'The attacks don't interfere with you if you flag yourself, Sir,' the boy explained. 'That's a Second Camp team from the Technical Schools loading against time for a bet.'

We picked our way deviously through the busy groups. Apparently it was not etiquette to notice a Guard officer, and the youths at the twenty-five-pounder were far too busy to look up. I watched the cleanly finished hoist and shove-home of the full-weight shell from a safe distance, when I became aware of a change among the scattered boys on the common, who disappeared behind the hillocks to an accompaniment of querulous whistles. A boy or two on bicycles dashed from corps to corps, and on their arrival each corps seemed to fade away.

The youths at loading practice did not pause for the growing hush round them, nor did the drum and fife band drop a single note. Bayley exploded afresh. 'The Schools are preparing for our attack, by Jove! I wonder who's directin' 'em. Do *you* know?'

The warrior of the Eighth District looked up shrewdly.

'I saw Mr Cameron speaking to Mr Levitt just as the Guard went up the road. 'E's our 'ead-master, Mr Cameron, but Mr Levitt, of the Sixth District, is actin' as senior officer on the ground this Saturday. Most likely Mr Levitt is commandin'.'

'How many corps are there here?' I asked.

'Oh, bits of lots of 'em – thirty or forty p'r'aps, Sir. But the whistles says they've all got to rally on the Board Schools. 'Ark! There's the whistle for the Private Schools! They've been called up the ground at the double.'

'Stop!' cried a bearded man with a watch, and the crews dropped beside the breech wiping their brows and panting.

'Hullo! there's some attack on the Schools,' said one. 'Well, Marden, you owe me three half-crowns. I've beaten your record. Pay up!'

The boy beside us tapped his foot fretfully as he eyed his

companions melting among the hillocks, but the gun-team adjusted their bets without once looking up.

The ground rose a little to a furze-crowned ridge in the centre so that I could not see the full length of it, but I heard a faint bubble of blank in the distance.

'The Saturday allowance,' murmured Bayley. 'War's begun, but it wouldn't be etiquette for us to interfere. What are you saying, my child?'

'Nothin', Sir, only – only I don't think the Guard will be able to come through on so narrer a front, Sir. They'll all be jammed up be'ind the ridge if *we*'ve got there in time. It's awful sticky for guns at the end of our ground, Sir.'

'I'm inclined to think you're right, Moltke. The Guard is hung up: distinctly so. Old Vee will have to cut his way through. What a pernicious amount of blank the kids seem to have!'

It was quite a respectable roar of battle that rolled among the hillocks for ten minutes, always out of our sight. Then we heard the 'Cease fire' over the ridge.

'They've sent for the Umpires,' the Board School boy squeaked, dancing on one foot. 'You've been hung up, Sir. I – I thought the sand-pits 'ud stop you.'

Said one of the jerseyed hobbledehoys at the gun, slipping on his coat: 'Well, that's enough for this afternoon. I'm off,' and moved to the railings without even glancing towards the fray.

'I anticipate the worst,' said Bayley with gravity after a few minutes. 'Hullo! Here comes my disgraced corps.'

The Guard was pouring over the ridge – a disorderly mob – horse, foot, and guns mixed, while from every hollow of the ground about rose small boys cheering shrilly. The outcry was taken up by the parents at the railings, and spread to a complete circle of cheers, handclappings, and waved handkerchiefs.

Our Eighth District private cast away restraint and openly capered. 'We got 'em! We got 'em!' he squealed.

The grey-green flood paused a fraction of a minute and drew itself into shape, coming to rest before Bayley. Verschoyle saluted.

'Vee, Vee,' said Bayley. 'Give me back my legions! Well, I hope you're proud of yourself.'

'The little beasts were ready for us. Deuced well posted too,' Verschoyle replied. 'I wish you'd seen that first attack on our flank. Rather impressive. Who warned 'em?'

'I don't know. I got my information from a baby in blue plush breeches. Did they do well?'

'Very decently indeed. I've complimented their C.O. and buttered the whole boiling.' He lowered his voice. 'As a matter o' fact, I halted five good minutes to give 'em time to get into position.'

'Well, now we can inspect our Foreign Service corps. We shan't need the men for an hour, Vee.'

'Very good, Sir. Colour-sergeants!' cried Verschoyle, raising his voice, and the cry ran from company to company. Whereupon the officers left their men, people began to climb over the railings, and the regiment dissolved among the spectators and the school corps of the city.

' 'No sense keeping men standing when you don't need 'em,' said Bayley. 'Besides, the Schools learn more from our chaps in an afternoon than they can pick up in a month's drill. Look at those Board-schoolmaster captains buttonholing old Purvis on the art of war!'

' 'Wonder what the evening papers 'll say about this,' said Pigeon.

'You'll know in half an hour,' Burgard laughed. 'What possessed you to take your ponies across the sand-pits, Pij?'

'Pride. Silly pride,' said the Canadian.

We crossed the common to a very regulation parade-ground overlooked by a statue of Our Queen. Here were carriages, many and elegant, filled with pretty women, and the railings were lined with frockcoats and top hats. 'This is distinctly social,' I suggested to Kyd.

'Ra-ather. Our F.S. corps is nothing if not correct, but Bayley 'll sweat 'em all the same.'

I saw six companies drawn up for inspection behind lines of long sausage-shaped kit-bags. A band welcomed us with 'A Life on the Ocean Wave'.

'What cheek!' muttered Verschoyle. 'Give 'em beans, Bayley.'

'I intend to,' said the Colonel grimly. 'Will each of you fellows take a company, please, and inspect 'em faithfully. *En état de partir* is their little boast, remember. When you've finished you can give 'em a little pillow-fighting.'

'What does the single cannon on those men's sleeves mean?' I asked.

'That they're big-gun men, who've done time with the Fleet,' Bayley returned. 'Any F.S. corps that has over twenty per cent big-gun men thinks itself entitled to play "A Life on the Ocean Wave" – when it's out of hearing of the Navy.'

'What beautiful stuff they are! What's their regimental average?'

'It ought to be five eight, height, thirty-eight, chest, and twenty-four years, age. What is it?' Bayley asked of a private.

'Five nine and half, Sir, thirty-nine, twenty-four and a half,' was the reply, and he added insolently, '*En état de partir*.' Evidently that F.S. corps was on its mettle ready for the worst.

'What about their musketry average?' I went on.

'Not my pidgin,' said Bayley. 'But they wouldn't be in the corps a day if they couldn't shoot; I know *that* much. Now I'm going to go through 'em for socks and slippers.'

The kit-inspection exceeded anything I had ever dreamed. I drifted from company to company while the Guard officers oppressed them. Twenty per cent, at least, of the kits were shovelled out on the grass and gone through in detail.

'What have they got jumpers and ducks for?' I asked of Harrison.

'For Fleet work, of course. *En état de partir* with an F.S. corps means they are amphibious.'

'Who gives 'em their kit – Government?'

'There is a Government allowance, but no C.O. sticks to it. It's the same as paint and gold-leaf in the Navy. It comes out of someone's pockets. How much does your kit cost you?' – this to the private in front of us.

'About ten or fifteen quid every other year, I suppose,' was the answer.

'Very good. Pack your bag – quick.'

The man knelt, and with supremely deft hands returned all to the bag, lashed and tied it, and fell back.

'Arms,' said Harrison. 'Strip and show ammunition.'

The man divested himself of his rolled greatcoat and haversack with one wriggle, as it seemed to me; a twist of a screw removed the side plate of the rifle breech (it was not a bolt action). He handed it to Harrison with one hand, and with the other loosed his clip-studded belt.

'What baby cartridges!' I exclaimed. 'No bigger than bulleted breech-caps.'

'They're the regulation .256,' said Harrison. 'No one has complained of 'em yet. They expand a bit when they arrive . . . Empty your bottle, please, and show your rations.'

The man poured out his water-bottle and showed a two-inch emergency tin.

Harrison passed on to the next, but I was fascinated by the way in which the man re-established himself amid his straps and buckles, asking no help from either side.

'How long does it take you to prepare for inspection?' I asked him.

'Well, I got ready this afternoon in twelve minutes,' he smiled. 'I didn't see the storm-cone till half-past three. I was at the Club.'

'Weren't a good many of you out of town?'

'Not *this* Saturday. We knew what was coming. You see, if we pull through the inspection we may move up one place on the roster for foreign service . . . You'd better stand back. We're going to pillow-fight.'

The companies stooped to the stuffed kitbags, doubled with them variously, piled them in squares and mounds, passed them from shoulder to shoulder like buckets at a fire, and repeated the evolution.

'What's the idea?' I asked of Verschoyle, who, arms folded behind him, was controlling the display. Many women had descended from the carriages, and were pressing in about us admiringly.

'For one thing, it's a fair test of wind and muscle, and for another it saves time at the docks. We'll suppose this first company to be drawn up on the dock-head and those five others still in the troop-train. How would you get their kit into the ship?'

'Fall 'em all in on the platform, march 'em to the gangways,' I answered, 'and trust to Heaven and a fatigue party to gather the baggage and drunks in later.'

'Ye-es, and have half of it sent by the wrong trooper. I know *that* game,' Verschoyle drawled. 'We don't play it any more. Look!'

He raised his voice, and five companies, glistening a little and breathing hard, formed at right angles to the sixth, each man embracing his sixty-pound bag.

'Pack away!' cried Verschoyle, and the great bean-bag game (I can compare it to nothing else) began. In five minutes every bag was passed along either arm of the T and forward down the sixth company, who passed, stacked, and piled them in a great heap. These were followed by the rifles, belts, greatcoats, and knapsacks, so that in another five minutes the regiment stood, as it were, stripped clean.

'Of course on a trooper there'd be a company below stacking the kit away,' said Verschoyle, 'but that wasn't so bad.'

'Bad!' I cried. 'It was miraculous!'

'Circus-work – all circus-work!' said Pigeon. 'It won't prevent 'em bein' as sick as dogs when the ship rolls.' The crowd round us applauded, while the men looked meekly down their self-conscious noses.

A little grey-whiskered man trotted up to the Boy.

'Have we made good, Bayley?' he said. 'Are we *en état de partir*?'

'That's what I shall report,' said Bayley, smiling.

'I thought my bit o' French 'ud draw you,' said the little man, rubbing his hands.

'Who is he?' I whispered to Pigeon.

'Ramsay, their C.O. An old Guard captain. A keen little devil. They say he spends six hundred a year on the show. He used to be in the Lincolns till he came into his property.'

'Take 'em home an' make 'em drunk,' I heard Bayley say. 'I suppose you'll have a dinner to celebrate. But you may as well tell the officers of E Company that I don't think much of them. I shan't report it, but their men were all over the shop.'

'Well, they're young, you see,' Colonel Ramsay began.

'You're quite right. Send 'em to me and I'll talk to 'em. Youth is the time to learn.'

'Six hundred a year?' I repeated to Pigeon. 'That must be an awful tax on a man. Worse than in the old volunteering days.'

'That's where you make your mistake,' said Verschoyle. 'In the old days a man had to spend his money to coax his men to drill because they weren't the genuine article. You know what I mean. They made a favour of putting in drills, didn't they? And they were, most of 'em, the children we have to take over at Second Camp, weren't they? Well, now that a C.O. is sure of his *men*, now that he hasn't to waste himself in conciliatin', an' bribin', an' beerin' *kids*, he doesn't care what he spends on his corps, because every pound tells. Do you understand?'

'I see what you mean, Vee. Having the male material guaranteed –'

'And trained material at that,' Pigeon put in. 'Eight years in the schools, remember, as well as –'

'Precisely. A man rejoices in working them up. That's as it should be,' I said.

'Bayley's saying the very same to those F.S. pups,' said Verschoyle.

The Boy was behind us, between two young F.S. officers, a hand on the shoulder of each.

'Yes, that's all doocid interesting,' he growled paternally. 'But you forget, my sons, now that your men are bound to serve, you're trebly bound to put a polish on 'em. You've let your company simply go to seed. Don't try and explain. I've told all those lies myself in my time. It's only idleness. *I* know. Come and lunch with me tomorrow and I'll give you a wrinkle or two in barracks.' He turned to me:

'Suppose we pick up Vee's defeated legion and go home. You'll dine with us tonight. Goodbye, Ramsay. Yes, you're *en état de partir*, right enough. You'd better get Lady Gertrude to talk to the Armity if you want the corps sent foreign. I'm no politician.'

We strolled away from the great white statue of The Widow, with sceptre, orb, and crown, that looked toward the city, and regained the common, where the Guard battalion walked with the female of its species and the children of all its relatives. At sight of the officers the uniforms began to detach themselves and gather in companies. A Board School corps was moving off the ground, headed by its drums and fifes, which it assisted with song. As we drew nearer we caught the words, for they were launched with intention:

> ''Oo is it mashes the country nurse?
> The Guardsman!
> 'Oo is it takes the lydy's purse?
> The Guardsman!
> Calls for a drink, and a mild cigar,
> Batters a sovereign down on the bar,
> Collars the change and says "Ta-ta!"
> The Guardsman!'

'Why, that's one of old Jemmy Fawne's songs. I haven't heard it in ages,' I began.

'Little devils!' said Pigeon.

'Speshul! Extra Speshul! Sports Edition!' a newsboy cried. ''Ere y'are, Captain. Defeat o' the Guard!'

'I'll buy a copy,' said the Boy, as Pigeon blushed wrathfully. 'I must, to see how The Dove lost his mounted company.' He unfolded the flapping sheet and we crowded round it.

'"*Complete Rout of the Guard*",' he read. '"*Too Narrow a Front.*" That's one for you, Vee! "*Attack anticipated by Mr Levitt, B.A.*" Aha! "*The Schools Stand Fast*".'

'Here's another version,' said Kyd, waving a tinted sheet. '"*To your Tents, O Israel! The Hebrew Schools stop the Mounted Troops.*" Pij, were you scuppered by Jew-boys?'

'"*Umpires Decide all Four Guns Lost*",' Bayley went on. 'By Jove, there'll have to be an inquiry into this regrettable incident, Vee!'

'I'll never try to amuse the kids again,' said the baited Verschoyle. 'Children and newspapers are low things . . . And I was hit on the nose by a wad, too. They oughtn't to be allowed blank ammunition.'

So we leaned against the railings in the warm twilight haze

while the battalion, silently as a shadow, formed up behind us ready to be taken over. The heat, the hum of the great city, as it might have been the hum of a camped army, the creaking of the belts, and the well-known faces bent above them, brought back to me the memory of another evening, years ago, when Verschoyle and I waited for news of guns missing in no sham fight.

'A regular Sanna's Post, isn't it?' I said at last. 'D'you remember, Vee – by the market-square – that night when the wagons went out?'

Then it came upon me, with no horror, but a certain mild wonder, that we had waited, Vee and I, that night for the body of Boy Bayley; and that Vee himself had died of typhoid in the spring of 1902. The rustling of the papers continued, but Bayley, shifting slightly, revealed to me the three-day-old wound on his left side that had soaked the ground about him. I saw Pigeon fling up a helpless arm as to guard himself against a spatter of shrapnel, and Luttrell with a foolish tight-lipped smile lurched over all in one jointless piece. Only old Vee's honest face held steady for awhile against the darkness that had swallowed up the battalion behind us. Then his jaw dropped and the face stiffened, so that a fly made bold to explore the puffed and scornful nostril.

I waked brushing a fly from my nose, and saw the Club waiter lay out the evening papers on the table.

⁅ 'They' ⁆

The Return of the Children

Neither the harps nor the crowns amused, nor the cherubs'
                              dove-winged races –
Holding hands forlornly the Children wandered beneath the
                                        Dome;
Plucking the radiant robes of the passers-by, and with pitiful
                                          faces
Begging what Princes and Powers refused: – 'Ah, please will
                              you let us go home?'

Over the jewelled floor, nigh weeping, ran to them Mary
                              the Mother,
Kneeled and caressed and made promise with kisses, and drew
                        them along to the gateway –
Yea, the all-iron unbribeable Door which Peter must guard
                              and none other.
Straightway She took the Keys from his keeping, and opened
                        and freed them straightway.

Then to Her Son, Who had seen and smiled, She said: 'On
                        the night that I bore Thee
What didst Thou care for a love beyond mine or a heaven that
                              was not my arm?
Didst Thou push from the nipple, O Child, to hear the angels
                              adore Thee?
When we two lay in the breath of the kine?' And he said: –
                        'Thou hast done no harm.'

So through the Void the Children ran homeward merrily hand in hand,
Looking neither to left nor right where the breathless Heavens stood
                                        still;
And the Guards of the Void resheathed their swords, for they
                        heard the Command:
'Shall I that have suffered the children to come to me hold
                        them against their will?'

242

'They'

One view called me to another; one hill top to its fellow, half across the county, and since I could answer at no more trouble than the snapping forward of a lever, I let the county flow under my wheels. The orchid-studded flats of the East gave way to the thyme, ilex, and grey grass of the Downs; these again to the rich cornland and fig-trees of the lower coast, where you carry the beat of the tide on your left hand for fifteen level miles; and when at last I turned inland through a huddle of rounded hills and woods I had run myself clean out of my known marks. Beyond that precise hamlet which stands godmother to the capital of the United States, I found hidden villages where bees, the only things awake, boomed in eighty-foot lindens that overhung grey Norman churches; miraculous brooks diving under stone bridges built for heavier traffic than would ever vex them again; tithe-barns larger than their churches, and an old smithy that cried out aloud how it had once been a hall of the Knights of the Temple. Gipsies I found on a common where the gorse, bracken, and heath fought it out together up a mile of Roman road; and a little farther on I disturbed a red fox rolling dog-fashion in the naked sunlight.

As the wooded hills closed about me I stood up in the car to take the bearings of that great Down whose ringed head is a landmark for fifty miles across the low countries. I judged that the lie of the country would bring me across some westward-running road that went to his feet, but I did not allow for the confusing veils of the woods. A quick turn plunged me first into a green cutting brim-full of liquid sunshine, next into a gloomy tunnel where last year's dead leaves whispered and scuffled about my tyres. The strong hazel stuff meeting overhead had not been cut for a couple of generations at least, nor had any axe helped the moss-cankered oak and beech to spring above them. Here the road changed frankly into a carpeted ride on whose brown velvet spent primrose-clumps showed like jade, and a few sickly, white-stalked blue-bells nodded together. As the slope favoured I shut off the power and slid over the whirled leaves, expecting every moment to meet a keeper; but I only heard a jay, far off, arguing against the silence under the twilight of the trees.

Still the track descended. I was on the point of reversing and working my way back on the second speed ere I ended in some swamp, when I saw sunshine through the tangle ahead and lifted the brake.

It was down again at once. As the light beat across my face my fore-wheels took the turf of a great still lawn from which sprang horsemen ten feet high with levelled lances, monstrous peacocks, and sleek round-headed maids of honour – blue, black, and glistening – all of clipped yew. Across the lawn – the marshalled woods besieged it on three sides – stood an ancient house of lichened and weather-worn stone, with mullioned windows and roofs of rose-red tile. It was flanked by semi-circular walls, also rose-red, that closed the lawn on the fourth side, and at their feet a box hedge grew man-high. There were doves on the roof about the slim brick chimneys, and I caught a glimpse of an octagonal dove-house behind the screening wall.

Here, then, I stayed; a horseman's green spear laid at my breast; held by the exceeding beauty of that jewel in that setting.

'If I am not packed off for a trespasser, or if this knight does not ride a wallop at me,' thought I, 'Shakespeare and Queen Elizabeth at least must come out of that half-open garden door and ask me to tea.'

A child appeared at an upper window, and I thought the little thing waved a friendly hand. But it was to call a companion, for presently another bright head showed. Then I heard a laugh among the yew-peacocks, and turning to make sure (till then I had been watching the house only) I saw the silver of a fountain behind a hedge thrown up against the sun. The doves on the roof cooed to the cooing water; but between the two notes I caught the utterly happy chuckle of a child absorbed in some light mischief.

The garden door – heavy oak sunk deep in the thickness of the wall – opened further: a woman in a big garden hat set her foot slowly on the time-hollowed stone step and as slowly walked across the turf. I was forming some apology when she lifted up her head and I saw that she was blind.

'I heard you,' she said. 'Isn't that a motor-car?'

'I'm afraid I've made a mistake in my road. I should have turned off up above – I never dreamed –' I began.

'But I'm very glad. Fancy a motor-car coming into the garden! It will be such a treat –' She turned and made as though looking about her. 'You – you haven't seen anyone, have you – perhaps?'

'No one to speak to, but the children seemed interested at a distance.'

'Which?'

'I saw a couple up at the window just now, and I think I heard a little chap in the grounds.'

'Oh, lucky you!' she cried, and her face brightened. 'I hear them, of course, but that's all. You've seen them and heard them?'

'Yes,' I answered. 'And if I know anything of children, one of them's having a beautiful time by the fountain yonder. Escaped, I should imagine.'

'You're fond of children?'

I gave her one or two reasons why I did not altogether hate them.

'Of course, of course,' she said. 'Then you understand. Then you won't think it foolish if I ask you to take your car through the gardens, once or twice – quite slowly. I'm sure they'd like to see it. They see so little, poor things. One tries to make their life pleasant, but –' she threw out her hands towards the woods. 'We're so out of the world here.'

'That will be splendid,' I said. 'But I can't cut up your grass.'

She faced to the right. 'Wait a minute,' she said. 'We're at the South gate, aren't we? Behind those peacocks there's a flagged path. We call it the Peacocks' Walk. You can't see it from here, they tell me, but if you squeeze along by the edge of the wood you can turn at the first peacock and get on to the flags.'

It was sacrilege to wake that dreaming house-front with the clatter of machinery, but I swung the car to clear the turf, brushed along the edge of the wood and turned in on the broad stone path where the fountain-basin lay like one star-sapphire.

'May I come too?' she cried. 'No, please don't help me. They'll like it better if they see me.'

She felt her way lightly to the front of the car, and with one foot on the step she called: 'Children, oh, children! Look and see what's going to happen!'

The voice would have drawn lost souls from the Pit, for the yearning that underlay its sweetness, and I was not surprised to hear an answering shout behind the yews. It must have been the child by the fountain, but he fled at our approach, leaving a little toy boat in the water. I saw the glint of his blue blouse among the still horsemen.

Very disposedly we paraded the length of the walk and at her request backed again. This time the child had got the better of his panic, but stood far off and doubting.

'The little fellow's watching us,' I said. 'I wonder if he'd like a ride.'

'They're very shy still. Very shy. But, oh, lucky you to be able to see them! Let's listen.'

I stopped the machine at once, and the humid stillness, heavy with the scent of box, cloaked us deep. Shears I could hear where some gardener was clipping; a mumble of bees and broken voices that might have been the doves.

'Oh, unkind!' she said weariedly.

'Perhaps they're only shy of the motor. The little maid at the window looks tremendously interested.'

'Yes?' She raised her head. 'It was wrong of me to say that. They are really fond of me. It's the only thing that makes life worth living – when they're fond of you, isn't it? I daren't think what the place would be without them. By the way, is it beautiful?'

'I think it is the most beautiful place I have ever seen.'

'So they all tell me. I can feel it, of course, but that isn't quite the same thing.'

'Then have you never —?' I began, but stopped abashed.

'Not since I can remember. It happened when I was only a few months old, they tell me. And yet I must remember something, else how could I dream about colours. I see light in my dreams, and colours, but I never see *them*. I only hear them just as I do when I'm awake.'

'It's difficult to see faces in dreams. Some people can, but most of us haven't the gift,' I went on, looking up at the window where the child stood all but hidden.

'I've heard that too,' she said. 'And they tell me that one never sees a dead person's face in a dream. Is that true?'

'I believe it is — now I come to think of it.'

'But how is it with yourself — yourself?' The blind eyes turned towards me.

'I have never seen the faces of my dead in any dream,' I answered.

'Then it must be as bad as being blind.'

The sun had dipped behind the woods and the long shades were possessing the insolent horsemen one by one. I saw the light die from the top of a glossy-leaved lance and all the brave hard green turned to soft black. The house, accepting another day at end, as it had accepted an hundred thousand gone, seemed to settle deeper into its rest among the shadows.

'Have you ever wanted to?' she said after the silence.

'Very much sometimes,' I replied. The child had left the window as the shadows closed upon it.

'Ah! So've I, but I don't suppose it's allowed ... Where d'you live?'

'Quite the other side of the county — sixty miles and more, and I must be going back. I've come without my big lamp.'

'But it's not dark yet. I can feel it.'

'I'm afraid it will be by the time I get home. Could you lend me someone to set me on my road at first? I've utterly lost myself.'

'I'll send Madden with you to the cross-roads. We are so out of the world, I don't wonder you were lost! I'll guide you round to the front of the house; but you will go slowly, won't you, till you're out of the grounds? It isn't foolish, do you think?'

'I promise you I'll go down like this,' I said, and let the car start herself down the flagged path.

We skirted the left wing of the house, whose elaborately cast lead guttering alone was worth a day's journey; passed under a great rose-grown gate in the red wall, and so round to the high front of the house which in beauty and stateliness as much excelled the back as that all others I had seen.

'Is it so very beautiful?' she said wistfully when she heard my raptures. 'And you like the lead-figures too? There's the old azalea garden behind. They say that this place must have been made for children. Will you help me out, please? I should like to come with you as far as the cross-roads, but I mustn't leave them. Is that you, Madden? I want you to show this gentleman the way to the cross-roads. He has lost his way but – he has seen them.'

A butler appeared noiselessly at the miracle of old oak that must be called the front door, and slipped aside to put on his hat. She stood looking at me with open blue eyes in which no sight lay, and I saw for the first time that she was beautiful.

'Remember,' she said quietly, 'if you are fond of them you will come again,' and disappeared within the house.

The butler in the car said nothing till we were nearly at the lodge gates, where catching a glimpse of a blue blouse in a shrubbery I swerved amply lest the devil that leads little boys to play should drag me into child-murder.

'Excuse me,' he asked of a sudden, 'but why did you do that, Sir?'

'The child yonder.'

'Our young gentleman in blue?'

'Of course.'

'He runs about a good deal. Did you see him by the fountain, Sir?'

'Oh, yes, several times. Do we turn here?'

'Yes, Sir. And did you 'appen to see them upstairs too?'

'At the upper window? Yes.'

'Was that before the mistress came out to speak to you, Sir?'

'A little before that. Why d'you want to know?'

He paused a little. 'Only to make sure that — that they had seen the car, Sir, because with children running about, though I'm sure you're driving particularly careful, there might be an accident. That was all, Sir. Here are the cross-roads. You can't miss your way from now on. Thank you, Sir, but that isn't *our* custom, not with —'

'I beg your pardon,' I said, and thrust away the British silver.

'Oh, it's quite right with the rest of 'em as a rule. Goodbye, Sir.'

He retired into the armour-plated conning tower of his caste and walked away. Evidently a butler solicitous for the honour of his house, and interested, probably through a maid, in the nursery.

Once beyond the signposts at the cross-roads I looked back, but the crumpled hills interlaced so jealously that I could not see where the house had lain. When I asked its name at a cottage along the road, the fat woman who sold sweetmeats there gave me to understand that people with motor-cars had small right to live — much less to 'go about talking like carriage folk'. They were not a pleasant-mannered community.

When I retraced my route on the map that evening I was little wiser. Hawkin's Old Farm appeared to be the Survey title of the place, and the old County Gazetteer, generally so ample, did not allude to it. The big house of those parts was Hodnington Hall, Georgian with early Victorian embellishments, as an atrocious steel engraving attested. I carried my difficulty to a neighbour — a deep-rooted tree of that soil — and he gave me a name of a family which conveyed no meaning.

A month or so later — I went again, or it may have been that my car took the road of her own volition. She over-ran the fruitless Downs, threaded every turn of the maze of lanes below the hills, drew through the high-walled woods, impenetrable in their full leaf, came out at the cross-roads where the butler had left me, and a little farther on developed an internal trouble which forced me to turn her in on a grass way-waste that cut into a summer-silent hazel wood. So far as I could make sure by the sun and a six-inch Ordnance map, this should be the road flank of that wood which I had first explored from the heights above. I made a mighty serious business of my repairs and a glittering shop of my repair kit, spanners, pump, and the like, which I spread out orderly upon a rug. It was a trap to catch all childhood, for on such a day, I argued, the children would not be far off. When I paused in my work I listened, but the wood was so full of the noises of summer (though the birds had mated) that I could not at first distinguish these from the tread of small cautious feet stealing across the dead leaves. I rang my bell in an alluring manner, but the feet fled, and I repented, for to a child a sudden noise is very real terror. I must have been at work half an hour when I heard in the wood the voice of the blind woman crying: 'Children, oh children! Where are you?' and the stillness made slow to close on the perfection of that cry. She came towards me, half feeling her way between the tree boles, and though a child it seemed clung to her skirt, it swerved into a leafage like a rabbit as she drew nearer.

'Is that you?' she said, 'from the other side of the county?'

'Yes, it's me from the other side of the county.'

'Then why didn't you come through the upper woods? They were there just now.'

'They were here a few minutes ago. I expect they knew my car had broken down, and came to see the fun.'

'Nothing serious, I hope? How do cars break down?'

'In fifty different ways. Only mine has chosen the fifty-first.'

She laughed merrily at the tiny joke, cooed with delicious laughter, and pushed her hat back.

'Let me hear,' she said.

'Wait a moment,' I cried, 'and I'll get you a cushion.'

She set her foot on the rug all covered with spare parts, and stooped over it eagerly. 'What delightful things!' The hands through which she saw glanced in the chequered sunlight. 'A box here – another box! Why you've arranged them like playing shop!'

'I confess now that I put it out to attract them. I don't need half those things really.'

'How nice of you! I heard your bell in the upper wood. You say they were here before that?'

'I'm sure of it. Why are they so shy? That little fellow in blue who was with you just now ought to have got over his fright. He's been watching me like a Red Indian.'

'It must have been your bell,' she said. 'I heard one of them go past me in trouble when I was coming down. They're shy – so shy even with me.' She turned her face over her shoulder and cried again: 'Children, oh, children! Look and see!'

'They must have gone off together on their own affairs,' I suggested, for there was a murmur behind us of lowered voices broken by the sudden squeaking giggles of childhood. I returned to my tinkerings and she learned foward, her chin on her hand, listening interestedly.

'How many are they?' I said at last. The work was finished, but I saw no reason to go.

Her forehead puckered a little in thought. 'I don't quite know,' she said simply. 'Sometimes more – sometimes less. They come and stay with me because I love them, you see.'

'That must be very jolly,' I said, replacing a drawer, and as I spoke I heard the inanity of my answer.

'You – you aren't laughing at me,' she cried. 'I – I haven't any of my own. I never married. People laugh at me sometimes about them because – because –'

'Because they're savages,' I returned. 'It's nothing to fret for. That sort laugh at everything that isn't in their own fat lives.'

'I don't know. How should I? I only don't like being laughed at about *them*. It hurts; and when one can't see . . . I don't want to seem silly,' her chin quivered like a child's as she spoke, 'but we blindies have only one skin, I think. Everything outside hits straight at our souls. It's different with you. You've such good defences in your eyes – looking out – before anyone can really pain you in your soul. People forget that with us.'

I was silent reviewing that inexhaustible matter – the more than inherited (since it is also carefully taught) brutality of the Christian peoples, beside which the mere heathendom of the West Coast nigger is clean and restrained. It led me a long distance into myself.

'Don't do that!' she said of a sudden, putting her hands before her eyes.

'What?'

She made a gesture with her hand.

'That! It's – it's all purple and black. Don't! That colour hurts.'

'But, how in the world do you know about colours?' I exclaimed, for here was a revelation indeed.

'Colours as colours?' she asked.

'No. *Those* Colours which you saw just now.'

'You know as well as I do,' she laughed, 'else you wouldn't have asked that question. They aren't in the world at all. They're in *you* – when you went so angry.'

'D'you mean a dull purplish patch, like port wine mixed with ink?' I said.

'I've never seen ink or port wine, but the colours aren't mixed. They are separate – all separate.'

'Do you mean black streaks and jags across the purple?'

She nodded. 'Yes – if they are like this,' and zig-zagged her finger again, 'but it's more red than purple – that bad colour.'

'And what are the colours at the top of the – whatever you see?'

Slowly she leaned forward and traced on the rug the figure of the Egg itself.

'I see them so,' she said, pointing with a grass stem, 'white, green, yellow, red, purple, and when people are angry or bad, black across the red – as you were just now.'

'Who told you anything about it – in the beginning?' I demanded.

'About the colours? No one. I used to ask what colours were when I was little – in table-covers and curtains and carpets, you see – because some colours hurt me and some made me happy. People told me; and when I got older that was how I saw people.' Again she traced the outline of the Egg which it is given to very few of us to see.

'All by yourself?' I repeated.

'All by myself. There wasn't anyone else. I only found out afterwards that other people did not see the Colours.'

She leaned against the tree-bole plaiting and unplaiting chance-plucked grass stems. The children in the wood had drawn nearer. I could see them with the tail of my eye frolicking like squirrels.

'Now I am sure you will never laugh at me,' she went on after a long silence. 'Nor at *them*.'

'Goodness! No!' I cried, jolted out of my train of thought. 'A man who laughs at a child – unless the child is laughing too – is a heathen!'

'I didn't mean that, of course. You'd never laugh *at* children, but I thought – I used to think – that perhaps you might laugh about *them*. So now I beg your pardon . . . What are you going to laugh at?'

I had made no sound, but she knew.

'At the notion of your begging my pardon. If you had done your duty as a pillar of the State and a landed proprietress you ought to have summoned me for trespass when I barged through your woods the other day. It was disgraceful of me – inexcusable.'

She looked at me, her head against the tree trunk – long and steadfastly – this woman who could see the naked soul.

'How curious,' she half whispered. 'How very curious.'

'Why, what have I done?'

'You don't understand . . . and yet you understand about the Colours. Don't you understand?'

She spoke with a passion that nothing had justified, and I faced her bewilderedly as she rose. The children had gathered themselves in a roundel behind a bramble bush. One sleek head bent over something smaller, and the set of the little shoulders told me that fingers were on lips. They, too, had some child's tremendous secret. I alone was hopelessly astray there in the broad sunlight.

'No,' I said, and shook my head as though the dead eyes could note. 'Whatever it is, I don't understand yet. Perhaps I shall later – if you'll let me come again.'

'You will come again,' she answered. 'You will surely come again and walk in the wood.'

'Perhaps the children will know me well enough by that time

to let me play with them – as a favour. You know what children are like.'

'It isn't a matter of favour but of right,' she replied, and while I wondered what she meant, a dishevelled woman plunged round the bend of the road, loose-haired, purple, almost lowing with agony as she ran. It was my rude, fat friend of the sweetmeat shop. The blind woman heard and stepped forward. 'What is it, Mrs Madehurst?' she asked.

The woman flung her apron over her head and literally grovelled in the dust, crying that her grandchild was sick to death, that the local doctor was away fishing, that Jenny the mother was at her wits' end, and so forth, with repetitions and bellowings.

'Where's the next nearest doctor?' I asked between paroxysms.

'Madden will tell you. Go round to the house and take him with you. I'll attend to this. Be quick!' She half supported the fat woman into the shade. In two minutes I was blowing all the horns of Jericho under the front of the House Beautiful, and Madden, in the pantry, rose to the crisis like a butler and a man.

A quarter of an hour at illegal speeds caught us a doctor five miles away. Within the half-hour we had decanted him, much interested in motors, at the door of the sweetmeat shop, and drew up the road to await the verdict.

'Useful things cars,' said Madden, all man and no butler. 'If I'd had one when mine took sick she wouldn't have died.'

'How was it?' I asked.

'Croup. Mrs Madden was away. No one knew what to do. I drove eight miles in a tax cart for the doctor. She was choked when we came back. This car 'd ha' saved her. She'd have been close on ten now.'

'I'm sorry,' I said. 'I thought you were rather fond of children from what you told me going to the cross-roads the other day.'

'Have you seen 'em again, Sir – this mornin'?'

'Yes, but they're well broke to cars. I couldn't get any of them within twenty yards of it.'

He looked at me carefully as a scout considers a stranger – not as a menial should lift his eyes to his divinely appointed superior.

'I wonder why,' he said just above the breath that he drew. We waited on. A light wind from the sea wandered up and down the long lines of the woods, and the wayside grasses, whitened already with summer dust, rose and bowed in sallow waves.

A woman, wiping the suds off her arms, came out of the cottage next the sweetmeat shop.

'I've be'n listenin' in de back-yard,' she said cheerily. 'He says Arthur's unaccountable bad. Did ye hear him shruck just now? Unaccountable bad. I reckon t'will come Jenny's turn to walk in de wood nex' week along, Mr Madden.'

'Excuse me, Sir, but your lap-robe is slipping,' said Madden deferentially. The woman started, dropped a curtsey, and hurried away.

'What does she mean by "walking in the wood"?' I asked.

'It must be some saying they use hereabouts. I'm from Norfolk myself,' said Madden. 'They're an independent lot in this county. She took you for a chauffeur, Sir.'

I saw the Doctor come out of the cottage followed by a draggle-tailed wench who clung to his arm as though he could make treaty for her with Death. 'Dat sort,' she wailed – 'dey're just as much to us dat had 'em as if dey was lawful born. Just as much – just as much! An' God he'd be just as pleased if you saved 'un, Doctor. Don't take it from me. Miss Florence will tell ye de very same. Don't leave 'im Doctor!'

'I know, I know,' said the man; 'but he'll be quiet for a while now. We'll get the nurse and the medicine as fast as we can.' He signalled me to come forward with the car, and I strove not to be privy to what followed; but I saw the girl's face, blotched and frozen with grief, and I felt the hand without a ring clutching at my knees when we moved away.

The Doctor was a man of some humour, for I remember he claimed my car under the Oath of Aesculapius, and used it and me without mercy. First we convoyed Mrs Madehurst and the blind woman to wait by the sick bed till the nurse should come.

Next we invaded a neat county town for prescriptions (the
Doctor said the trouble was cerebro-spinal meningitis), and
when the County Institute, banked and flanked with scared
market cattle, reported itself out of nurses for the moment we
literally flung ourselves loose upon the county. We conferred
with the owners of great houses – magnates at the ends of
overarching avenues whose big-boned womenfolk strode away
from their tea-tables to listen to the imperious Doctor. At last a
white-haired lady sitting under a cedar of Lebanon and sur-
rounded by a court of magnificent Borzois – all hostile to
motors – gave the Doctor, who received them as from a princess,
written orders which we bore many miles at top speed, through
a park, to a French nunnery, where we took over in exchange a
pallid-faced and trembling Sister. She knelt at the bottom of
the tonneau telling her beads without pause till, by short cuts of
the Doctor's invention, we had her to the sweetmeat shop once
more. It was a long afternoon crowded with mad episodes that
rose and dissolved like the dust of our wheels; cross-sections of
remote and incomprehensible lives through which we raced at
right angles; and I went home in the dusk, wearied out, to
dream of the clashing horns of cattle; round-eyed nuns walking
in a garden of graves; pleasant tea-parties beneath shaded trees;
the carbolic-scented, grey-painted corridors of the County
Institute; the steps of shy children in the wood, and the hands
that clung to my knees as the motor began to move.

I had intended to return in a day or two, but it pleased Fate to
hold me from that side of the county, on many pretexts, till the
elder and the wild rose had fruited. There came at last a brilliant
day, swept clear from the south-west, that brought the hills
within hand's reach – a day of unstable airs and high filmy
clouds. Through no merit of my own I was free, and set the car
for the third time on that known road. As I reached the crest of
the Downs I felt the soft air change, saw it glaze under the sun;
and, looking down at the sea, in that instant beheld the blue of
the Channel turn through polished silver and dulled steel to
dingy pewter. A laden collier hugging the coast steered outward
for deeper water, and, across copper-coloured haze, I saw sails

rise one by one on the anchored fishing-fleet. In a deep dene behind me an eddy of sudden wind drummed through sheltered oaks, and spun aloft the first dry sample of autumn leaves. When I reached the beach road the sea-fog fumed over the brickfields, and the tide was telling all the groins of the gale beyond Ushant. In less than an hour summer England vanished in chill grey. We were again the shut island of the North, all the ships of the world bellowing at our perilous gates; and between their outcries ran the piping of bewildered gulls. My cap dripped moisture, the folds of the rug held it in pools or sluiced it away in runnels, and the salt-rime stuck to my lips.

Inland the smell of autumn loaded the thickened fog among the trees, and the drip became a continuous shower. Yet the late flowers – mallow of the wayside, scabious of the field, and dahlia of the garden – showed gay in the mist, and beyond the sea's breath there was little sign of decay in the leaf. Yet in the villages the house doors were all open, and bare-legged, bare-headed children sat at ease on the damp doorsteps to shout 'pip-pip' at the stranger.

I made bold to call at the sweetmeat shop, where Mrs Madehurst met me with a fat woman's hospitable tears. Jenny's child, she said, had died two days after the nun had come. It was, she felt, best out of the way, even though insurance offices, for reasons which she did not pretend to follow, would not willingly insure such stray lives. 'Not but what Jenny didn't tend to Arthur as though he'd come all proper at de end of de first year – like Jenny herself.' Thanks to Miss Florence, the child had been buried with a pomp which, in Mrs Madehurst's opinion, more than covered the small irregularity of its birth. She described the coffin, within and without, the glass hearse, and the evergreen lining of the grave.

'But how's the mother?' I asked.

'Jenny? Oh, she'll get over it. I've felt dat way with one or two o' my own. She'll get over. She's walkin' in de wood now.'

'In this weather?'

Mrs Madehurst looked at me with narrowed eyes across the counter.

'I dunno but it opens de 'eart like. Yes, it opens de 'eart.

Dat's where losin' and bearin' comes so alike in de long run, we do say.'

Now the wisdom of the old wives is greater than that of all the Fathers, and this last oracle sent me thinking so extendedly as I went up the road, that I nearly ran over a woman and a child at the wooded corner by the lodge gates of the House Beautiful.

'Awful weather!' I cried, as I slowed dead for the turn.

'Not so bad,' she answered placidly out of the fog. 'Mine's used to 'un. You'll find yours indoors, I reckon.'

Indoors, Madden received me with professional courtesy, and kind inquiries for the health of the motor, which he would put under cover.

I waited in a still, nut-brown hall, pleasant with late flowers and warmed with a delicious wood fire – a place of good influence and great peace. (Men and women may sometimes, after great effort, achieve a creditable lie; but the house, which is their temple, cannot say anything save the truth of those who have lived in it.) A child's cart and a doll lay on the black-and-white floor, where a rug had been kicked back. I felt that the children had only just hurried away – to hide themselves, most like – in the many turns of the great adzed staircase that climbed statelily out of the hall, or to crouch at gaze behind the lions and roses of the carven gallery above. Then I heard her voice above me, singing as the blind sing – from the soul:

'In the pleasant orchard-closes.'

And all my early summer came back at the call.

'In the pleasant orchard-closes,
God bless all our gains say we –
But may God bless all our losses,
Better suits with our degree.'

She dropped the marring fifth line, and repeated –

'Better suits with our degree!'

I saw her lean over the gallery, her linked hands white as pearl against the oak.

'Is that you – from the other side of the county?' she called.

'Yes, me – from the other side of the county,' I answered, laughing.

'What a long time before you had to come here again.' She ran down the stairs, one hand lightly touching the broad rail. 'It's two months and four days. Summer's gone!'

'I meant to come before, but Fate prevented.'

'I knew it. Please do something to that fire. They won't let me play with it, but I can feel it's behaving badly. Hit it!'

I looked on either side of the deep fireplace, and found but a half-charred hedge-stake with which I punched a black log into flame.

'It never goes out, day or night,' she said, as though explaining. 'In case anyone comes in with cold toes, you see.'

'It's even lovelier inside than it was out,' I murmured. The red light poured itself along the age-polished dusky panels till the Tudor roses and lions of the gallery took colour and motion. An old eagle-topped convex mirror gathered the picture into its mysterious heart, distorting afresh the distorted shadows, and curving the gallery lines into the curves of a ship. The day was shutting down in half a gale as the fog turned to stringy scud. Through the uncurtained mullions of the broad window I could see valiant horsemen of the lawn rear and recover against the wind that taunted them with legions of dead leaves.

'Yes, it must be beautiful,' she said. 'Would you like to go over it? There's still light enough upstairs.'

I followed her up the unflinching, wagon-wide staircase to the gallery whence opened the thin fluted Elizabethan doors.

'Feel how they put the latch low down for the sake of the children.' She swung a light door inward.

'By the way, where are they?' I asked. 'I haven't even heard them today.'

She did not answer at once. Then, 'I can only hear them,' she replied softly. 'This is one of their rooms – everything ready, you see.'

She pointed into a heavily-timbered room. There were little low gate tables and children's chairs. A doll's house, its hooked front half open, faced a great dappled rocking-horse, from whose padded saddle it was but a child's scramble to the broad window-seat overlooking the lawn. A toy gun lay in a corner beside a gilt wooden cannon.

'Surely they've only just gone,' I whispered. In the failing light a door creaked cautiously. I heard the rustle of a frock and the patter of feet – quick feet through a room beyond.

'I heard that,' she cried triumphantly. 'Did you? Children, oh, children! Where are you?'

The voice filled the walls that held it lovingly to the last perfect note, but there came no answering shout such as I had heard in the garden. We hurried on from room to oak-floored room; up a step here, down three steps there; among a maze of passages; always mocked by our quarry. One might as well have tried to work an unstopped warren with a single ferret. There were bolt-holes innumerable – recesses in walls, embrasures of deep slitten windows now darkened, whence they could start up behind us; and abandoned fireplaces, six feet deep in the masonry, as well as the tangle of communicating doors. Above all, they had the twilight for their helper in our game. I had caught one or two joyous chuckles of evasion, and once or twice had seen the silhouette of a child's frock against some darkening window at the end of a passage; but we returned empty-handed to the gallery, just as a middle-aged woman was setting a lamp in its niche.

'No, I haven't seen her either this evening, Miss Florence,' I heard her say, 'but that Turpin he says he wants to see you about his shed.'

'Oh, Mr Turpin must want to see me very badly. Tell him to come to the hall, Mrs Madden.'

I looked down into the hall whose only light was the dulled fire, and deep in the shadow I saw them at last. They must have slipped down while we were in the passages, and now thought themselves perfectly hidden behind an old gilt leather screen. By child's law, my fruitless chase was as good as an introduction, but since I had taken so much trouble I resolved to force them to come forward later by the simple trick, which children detest, of pretending not to notice them. They lay close, in a little huddle, no more than shadows except when a quick flame betrayed an outline.

'And now we'll have some tea,' she said. 'I believe I ought to have offered it you at first, but one doesn't arrive at manners somehow when one lives alone and is considered – h'm – peculiar.' Then with very pretty scorn, 'Would you like a lamp to see to eat by?'

'The firelight's much pleasanter, I think.' We descended into that delicious gloom and Madden brought tea.

I took my chair in the direction of the screen ready to surprise or be surprised as the game should go, and at her permission, since a hearth is always sacred, bent forward to play with the fire.

'Where do you get these beautiful short faggots from?' I asked idly. 'Why, they are tallies!'

'Of course,' she said. 'As I can't read or write I'm driven back on the early English tally for my accounts. Give me one and I'll tell you what it meant.'

I passed her an unburned hazel-tally, about a foot long, and she ran her thumb down the nicks.

'This is the milk-record for the home farm for the month of April last year, in gallons,' said she. 'I don't know what I should have done without tallies. An old forester of mine taught me the system. It's out of date now for everyone else; but my tenants respect it. One of them's coming now to see me. Oh, it doesn't matter. He has no business here out of office hours. He's a greedy, ignorant man – very greedy or – he wouldn't come here after dark.'

'Have you much land then?'

'Only a couple of hundred acres in hand, thank goodness. The other six hundred are nearly all let to folk who knew my folk before me, but this Turpin is quite a new man – and a highway robber.'

'But are you sure I shan't be –?'

'Certainly not. You have the right. He hasn't any children.'

'Ah, the children!' I said, and slid my low chair back till it nearly touched the screen that hid them. 'I wonder whether they'll come out for me.'

There was a murmur of voices – Madden's and a deeper note – at the low, dark side door, and a ginger-headed, canvas-gaitered giant of the unmistakable tenant-farmer type stumbled or was pushed in.

'Come to the fire, Mr Turpin,' she said.

'If – if you please, Miss, I'll – I'll be quite as well by the door.' He clung to the latch as he spoke like a frightened child. Of a sudden I realized that he was in the grip of some almost overpowering fear.

'Well?'

'About that new shed for the young stock – that was all. These first autumn storms settin' in ... but I'll come again, Miss.' His teeth did not chatter much more than the door latch.

'I think not,' she answered levelly. 'The new shed – m'm. What did my agent write you on the 15th?'

'I – fancied p'raps that if I came to see you – ma – man to man like, Miss. But –'

His eyes rolled into every corner of the room wide with horror. He half opened the door through which he had entered, but I noticed it shut again – from without and firmly.

'He wrote what I told him,' she went on. 'You are overstocked already. Dunnett's Farm never carried more than fifty bullocks – even in Mr Wright's time. And *he* used cake. You've sixty-seven and you don't cake. You've broken the lease in that respect. You're dragging the heart out of the farm.'

'I'm – I'm getting some minerals – superphosphates – next week. I've as good as ordered a truck-load already. I'll go down to the station tomorrow about 'em. Then I can come and see you man to man like, Miss, in the daylight ... That gentleman's not going away, is he?' He almost shrieked.

I had only slid the chair a little farther back, reaching behind me to tap on the leather of the screen, but he jumped like a rat.

'No. Please attend to me, Mr Turpin.' She turned in her chair and faced him with his back to the door. It was an old and sordid little piece of scheming that she forced from him – his plea for the new cow-shed at his landlady's expense, that he might with the covered manure pay his next year's rent out of the valuation after, as she made clear, he had bled the enriched pastures to the bone. I could not but admire the intensity of his greed, when I saw him out-facing for its sake whatever terror it was that ran wet on his forehead.

I ceased to tap the leather – was, indeed, calculating the cost of the shed – when I felt my relaxed hand taken and turned softly between the soft hands of a child. So at last I triumphed. In a moment I would turn and acquaint myself with those quick-footed wanderers . . .

The little brushing kiss fell in the centre of my palm – as a gift on which the fingers were, once, expected to close: as the all-faithful half-reproachful signal of a waiting child not used to neglect even when grown-ups were busiest – a fragment of the mute code devised very long ago.

Then I knew. And it was as though I had known from the first day when I looked across the lawn at the high window.

I heard the door shut. The woman turned to me in silence, and I felt that she knew.

What time passed after this I cannot say. I was roused by the fall of a log, and mechanically rose to put it back. Then I returned to my place in the chair very close to the screen.

'Now you understand,' she whispered, across the packed shadows.

'Yes, I understand – now. Thank you.'

'I – I only hear them.' She bowed her head in her hands. 'I have no right, you know – no other right. I have neither borne nor lost – neither borne nor lost!'

'Be very glad then,' said I, for my soul was torn open within me.

'Forgive me!'

She was still, and I went back to my sorrow and my joy.

'It was because I loved them so,' she said at last, brokenly. '*That* was why it was, even from the first – even before I knew that they – they were all I should ever have. And I loved them so!'

She stretched out her arms to the shadows and the shadows within the shadow.

'They came because I loved them – because I needed them. I – I must have made them come. Was that wrong, think you?'

'No – no.'

'I – I grant you that the toys and – and all that sort of thing were nonsense, but – but I used to so hate empty rooms myself when I was little.' She pointed to the gallery. 'And the passages all empty . . . And how could I ever bear the garden door shut? Suppose –'

'Don't! For pity's sake, don't!' I cried. The twilight had brought a cold rain with gusty squalls that plucked at the leaded windows.

'And the same thing with keeping the fire in all night. *I* don't think it so foolish – do you?'

I looked at the broad brick hearth, saw, through tears I believe, that there was no unpassable iron on or near it, and bowed my head.

'I did all that, and lots of other things – just to make believe. Then they came. I heard them, but I didn't know that they were not mine by right till Mrs Madden told me –'

'The butler's wife? What?'

'One of them – I heard – she saw. And knew. Hers! *Not* for me. I didn't know at first. Perhaps I was jealous. Afterwards, I began to understand that it was only because I loved them, not because – . . . Oh, you *must* bear or lose,' she said piteously. 'There is no other way – and yet they love me. They must! Don't they?'

There was no sound in the room except the lapping voices of the fire, but we two listened intently, and she at least took comfort from what she heard. She recovered herself and half rose. I sat still in my chair by the screen.

'Don't think me a wretch to whine about myself like this, but – but I'm all in the dark, you know, and *you* can see.'

In truth I could see, and my vision confirmed me in my resolve, though that was like the very parting of spirit and flesh. Yet a little longer I would stay since it was the last time.

'You think it is wrong, then?' she cried sharply, though I had said nothing.

'Not for you. A thousand times no. For you it is right . . . I am grateful to you beyond words. For me it would be wrong. For me only . . .'

'They'

'Why?' she said, but passed her hand before her face as she had done at our second meeting in the wood. 'Oh, I see,' she went on simply as a child. 'For you it would be wrong.' Then with a little indrawn laugh, 'and, d'you remember, I called you lucky – once – at first. You who must never come here again!'

She left me to sit a little longer by the screen, and I heard the sound of her feet die out along the gallery above.

⦃ Mrs Bathurst ⦄

From Lyden's 'Irenius'
(Act III, Sc. II)

GOW: Had it been your Prince instead of a groom caught in this noose
there's not an astrologer of the city –

PRINCE: Sacked! Sacked! We were a city yesterday.

GOW: So be it, but I was not governor. Not an astrologer, but would
ha' sworn he'd foreseen it at the last versary of Venus, when Vulcan
caught her with Mars in the house of stinking Capricorn. But since
'tis Jack of the Straw that hangs, the forgetful stars had it not on
their tablets.

PRINCE: Another life! Were there any left to die? How did the poor
fool come by it?

GOW: *Simpliciter* thus. She that damned him to death knew not that
she did it, or would have died ere she had done it. For she loved
him. He that hangs him does so in obedience to the Duke, and asks
no more than 'Where is the rope?' The Duke, very exactly he hath
told us, works God's will, in which holy employ he's not to be
questioned. We have then left upon this finger, only Jack whose
soul now plucks the left sleeve of Destiny in Hell to overtake why
she clapped him up like a fly on a sunny wall. Whuff! Soh!

PRINCE: Your cloak, Ferdinand. I'll sleep now.

FERDINAND: Sleep, then . . . He too, loved his life?

GOW: He was born of woman . . . but at the end threw life from him,
like your Prince, for a little sleep . . . 'Have I any look of a King?'
said he, clanking his chain – 'to be so baited on all sides by Fortune,
that I must e'en die now to live with myself one day longer.' I left
him railing at Fortune and woman's love.

FERDINAND: Ah, woman's love!

Mrs Bathurst

(*Aside*) Who knows not Fortune, glutted on easy thrones,
     Stealing from feasts as rare to coneycatch,
     Privily in the hedgerows for a clown
     With that same cruel-lustful hand and eye,
     Those nails and wedges, that one hammer and lead,
     And the very gerb of long-stored lightnings loosed
     Yesterday 'gainst some King.

Mrs Bathurst

The day that I chose to visit H.M.S. *Peridot* in Simon's Bay was the day that the Admiral had chosen to send her up the coast. She was just steaming out to sea as my train came in, and since the rest of the Fleet were either coaling or busy at the rifle-ranges a thousand feet up the hill, I found myself stranded, lunchless, on the sea-front with no hope of return to Cape Town before 5 p.m. At this crisis I had the luck to come across my friend Inspector Hooper, Cape Government Railways, in command of an engine and a brake-van chalked for repair.

'If you get something to eat,' he said, 'I'll run you down to Glengariff siding till the goods comes along. It's cooler there than here, you see.'

I got food and drink from the Greeks who sell all things at a price, and the engine trotted us a couple of miles up the line to a bay of drifted sand and a plank-platform half buried in sand not a hundred yards from the edge of the surf. Moulded dunes, whiter than any snow, rolled far inland up a brown and purple valley of splintered rocks and dry scrub. A crowd of Malays hauled at a net beside two blue and green boats on the beach; a picnic party danced and shouted barefoot where a tiny river trickled across the flat, and a circle of dry hills, whose feet were set in sands of silver, locked us in against a seven-coloured sea. At either horn of the bay the railway line cut just above high-water mark, ran round a shoulder of piled rocks and disappeared.

'You see there's always a breeze here,' said Hooper, opening the door as the engine left us in the siding on the sand, and the strong south-easter buffeting under Elsie's Peak dusted sand into our tickey beer. Presently he sat down to a file full of spiked documents. He had returned from a long trip up-country, where he had been reporting on damaged rolling-stock, as far away as Rhodesia. The weight of the bland wind on my eyelids; the song of it under the car roof, and high up among the rocks; the drift of fine grains chasing each other musically ashore; the tramp of the surf; the voices of the picnickers; the rustle of Hooper's file, and the presence of the assured sun, joined with the beer to cast me into magical slumber. The hills of False Bay were just dissolving into those of fairyland when I heard footsteps on the sand outside, and the clink of our couplings.

'Stop that!' snapped Hooper, without raising his head from his work. 'It's those dirty little Malay boys, you see: they're always playing with the trucks . . .'

'Don't be hard on 'em. The railway's a general refuge in Africa,' I replied.

'"Tis – up-country at any rate. That reminds me,' he felt in his waistcoat-pocket, 'I've got a curiosity for you from Wankies – beyond Bulawayo. It's more of a souvenir perhaps than –'

'The old hotel's inhabited,' cried a voice. 'White men, from the language. Marines to the front! Come on, Pritch. Here's your Belmont. Wha – i – i!'

The last word dragged like a rope as Mr Pyecroft ran round to the open door, and stood looking up into my face. Behind him an enormous Sergeant of Marines trailed a stalk of dried seaweed, and dusted the sand nervously from his fingers.

'What are you doing here?' I asked. 'I thought the *Hierophant* was down the coast?'

'We came in last Tuesday – from Tristan d'Acunha – for overhaul, and we shall be in dockyard 'ands for two months, with boiler-seatings.'

'Come and sit down.' Hooper put away the file.

'This is Mr Hooper of the Railway,' I exclaimed, as Pyecroft turned to haul up the black-moustached sergeant.

'This is Sergeant Pritchard of the *Agaric*, an old shipmate,' said he. 'We were strollin' on the beach.' The monster blushed and nodded. He filled up one side of the van when he sat down.

'And this is my friend, Mr Pyecroft,' I added to Hooper, already busy with the extra beer which my prophetic soul had bought from the Greeks.

'*Moi aussi*,' quoth Pyecroft, and drew out beneath his coat a labelled quart bottle.

'Why, it's Bass!' cried Hooper.

'It was Pritchard,' said Pyecroft. 'They can't resist him.'

'That's not so,' said Pritchard mildly.

'Not *verbatim* per'aps, but the look in the eye came to the same thing.'

'Where was it?' I demanded.

'Just on beyond here – at Kalk Bay. She was slappin' a rug in a back verandah. Pritch 'adn't more than brought his batteries to bear, before she stepped indoors an' sent it flyin' over the wall.'

Pyecroft patted the warm bottle.

'It was all a mistake,' said Pritchard. 'I shouldn't wonder if she mistook me for Maclean. We're about of a size.'

I had heard householders of Muizenburg, St James's, and Kalk Bay complain of the difficulty of keeping beer or good servants at the seaside, and I began to see the reason. None the less, it was excellent Bass, and I too drank to the health of that large-minded maid.

'It's the uniform that fetches 'em, an' they fetch it,' said Pyecroft. 'My simple navy blue is respectable, but not fascinatin'. Now Pritch in 'is Number One rig is always "purr Mary, on the terrace" – *ex officio* as you might say.'

'She took me for Maclean, I tell you,' Pritchard insisted. 'Why – why – to listen to him you wouldn't think that only yesterday –'

'Pritch,' said Pyecroft, 'be warned in time. If we begin tellin' what we know about each other we'll be turned out of the pub. Not to mention aggravated desertion on several occasions –'

'Never anything more than absence without leaf – I defy you to prove it,' said the Sergeant hotly. 'An' if it comes to that, how about Vancouver in '87?'

'How about it? Who pulled bow in the gig going ashore? Who told Boy Niven . . .?'

'Surely you were court-martialled for that?' I said. The story of Boy Niven who lured seven or eight able-bodied seamen and marines into the woods of British Columbia used to be a legend of the Fleet.

'Yes, we were court-martialled to rights,' said Pritchard, 'but we should have been tried for murder if Boy Niven 'adn't been unusually tough. He told us he had an uncle 'oo'd give us land to farm. 'E said he was born at the back o' Vancouver Island, and *all* the time the beggar was a balmy Barnado Orphan!'

'*But* we believed him,' said Pyecroft. 'I did – you did – Paterson did – an' 'oo was the Marine who married the cocoanut-woman afterwards – him with the mouth?'

'Oh, Jones, Spit-Kid Jones. I 'aven't thought of 'im in years,' said Pritchard. 'Yes, Spit-Kid believed it, an' George Anstey and Moon. We were very young an' very curious.'

'*But* lovin' an' trustful to a degree,' said Pyecroft.

''Remember when 'e told us to walk in single file for fear o' bears? 'Remember, Pye, when 'e 'opped about in that bog full o' ferns an' sniffed an' said 'e could smell the smoke of 'is uncle's farm? An' *all* the time it was a dirty little outlyin' uninhabited island. We walked round it in a day, an' come back to our boat lyin' on the beach. A whole day Boy Niven kept us walkin' in circles lookin' for 'is uncle's farm! He said his uncle was compelled by the law of the land to give us a farm!'

'Don't get hot, Pritch. We believed,' said Pyecroft.

'He'd been readin' books. He only did it to get a run ashore an' have himself talked of. A day an' a night – eight of us – followin' Boy Niven round an uninhabited island in the Vancouver archipelago! Then the picket came for us an' a nice pack o' idiots we looked!'

'What did you get for it?' Hooper asked.

'Heavy thunder with continuous lightning for two hours. Thereafter sleet-squalls, a confused sea, and cold, unfriendly weather till conclusion o' cruise,' said Pyecroft. 'It was only what we expected, but what we felt – an' I assure you, Mr Hooper, even a sailor-man has a heart to break – was bein' told that we able seamen an' promisin' marines 'ad misled Boy Niven. Yes, we poor back-to-the-landers was supposed to 'ave misled him! He rounded on us, o' course, an' got off easy.'

'Excep' for what we gave him in the steerin'-flat when we came out o' cells. 'Eard anything of 'im lately, Pye?'

'Signal Boatswain in the Channel Fleet, I believe – Mr L. L. Niven is.'

'An' Anstey died o' fever in Benin,' Pritchard mused. 'What come to Moon? Spit-Kid we know about.'

'Moon – Moon! Now where did I last . . .? Oh yes, when I was in the *Palladium*. I met Quigley at Buncrana Station. He told me Moon 'ad run when the *Astrild* sloop was cruising among the South Seas three years back. He always showed signs o' bein' a Mormonastic beggar. Yes, he slipped off quietly an' they 'adn't time to chase 'im round the islands even if the navigatin' officer 'ad been equal to the job.'

'Wasn't he?' said Hooper.

'Not so. Accordin' to Quigley the *Astrild* spent half her commission rompin' up the beach like a she-turtle, an' the other half hatching turtles' eggs on the top o' numerous reefs. When she was docked at Sydney her copper looked like Aunt Maria's washing on the line – an' her 'midship frames was sprung. The commander swore the dockyard 'ad done it haulin' the pore thing on to the slips. They *do* do strange things at sea, Mr Hooper.'

'Ah! I'm not a taxpayer,' said Hooper, and opened a fresh bottle. The Sergeant seemed to be one who had a difficulty in dropping subjects.

'How it all comes back, don't it?' he said. 'Why, Moon must 'ave 'ad sixteen years' service before he ran.'

'It takes 'em at all ages. Look at – you know,' said Pyecroft.

'Who?' I asked.

'A service man within eighteen months of his pension is the party you're thinkin' of,' said Pritchard. 'A warrant 'oo's name begins with a V., isn't it?'

'But, in a way o' puttin' it, we can't say that he actually did desert,' Pyecroft suggested.

'Oh no,' said Pritchard. 'It was only permanent absence up-country without leaf. That was all.'

'Up-country?' said Hooper. 'Did they circulate his description?'

'What for?' said Pritchard, most impolitely.

'Because deserters are like columns in the war. They don't

move away from the line, you see. I've known a chap caught at Salisbury that way tryin' to get to Nyassa. They tell me, but o' course I don't know, that they don't ask questions on the Nyassa Lake Flotilla up there. I've heard of a P. and O. quartermaster in full command of an armed launch there.'

'Do you think Click 'ud ha' gone up that way?' Pritchard asked.

'There's no saying. He was sent up to Bloemfontein to take over some Navy ammunition left in the fort. We know he took it over and saw it into the trucks. Then there was no more Click – then or thereafter. Four months ago it transpired, and thus the *casus belli* stands at present,' said Pyecroft.

'What were his marks?' said Hooper again.

'Does the Railway get a reward for returnin' 'em, then?' said Pritchard.

'If I did d'you suppose I'd talk about it?' Hooper retorted angrily.

'You seemed so very interested,' said Pritchard with equal crispness.

'Why was he called Click?' I asked, to tide over an uneasy little break in the conversation. The two men were staring at each other very fixedly.

'Because of an ammunition hoist carryin' away,' said Pyecroft. 'And it carried away four of 'is teeth – on the lower port side, wasn't it, Pritch? The substitutes which he bought weren't screwed home, in a manner o' sayin'. When he talked fast they used to lift a little on the bed-plate. 'Ence, "Click". They called 'im a superior man, which is what we'd call a long, black-'aired, genteelly speakin', 'alf-bred beggar on the lower deck.'

'Four false teeth in the lower left jaw,' said Hooper, his hand in his waistcoat-pocket. 'What tattoo marks?'

'Look here,' began Pritchard, half rising. 'I'm sure we're very grateful to you as a gentleman for your 'orspitality, but per'aps we may 'ave made an error in –'

I looked at Pyecroft for aid – Hooper was crimsoning rapidly.

'If the fat marine now occupying the foc'sle will kindly bring 'is *status quo* to an anchor yet once more, we may be able to talk like gentlemen – not to say friends,' said Pyecroft. 'He regards you, Mr Hooper, as a emissary of the Law.'

'I only wish to observe that when a gentleman exhibits such a peculiar, or I should rather say, such a *bloomin'* curiosity in identification marks as our friend here –'

'Mr Pritchard,' I interposed, 'I'll take all the responsibility for Mr Hooper.'

'An' *you*'ll apologize all round,' said Pyecroft. 'You're a rude little man, Pritch.'

'But how was I –' he began, wavering.

'I don't know an' I don't care. Apologize!'

The giant looked round bewildered and took our little hands into his vast grip, one by one.

'I was wrong,' he said meekly as a sheep. 'My suspicions was unfounded. Mr Hooper, I apologize.'

'You did quite right to look out for your own end o' the line,' said Hooper. 'I'd ha' done the same with a gentleman I didn't know, you see. If you don't mind I'd like to hear a little more o' your Mr Vickery. It's safe with me, you see.'

'Why did Vickery run?' I began, but Pyecroft's smile made me turn my question to 'Who was she?'

'She kep' a little hotel at Hauraki – near Auckland,' said Pyecroft.

'By Gawd!', roared Pritchard, slapping his hand on his leg. 'Not Mrs Bathurst!'

Pyecroft nodded slowly, and the Sergeant called all the powers of darkness to witness his bewilderment.

'So far as I could get at it, Mrs B. was the lady in question.'

'But Click was married,' cried Pritchard.

'An' 'ad a fifteen-year-old daugher. 'E's shown me her photograph. Settin' that aside, so to say, 'ave you ever found these little things make much difference? Because I haven't.'

'Good Lord Alive an' Watchin'! . . . Mrs Bathurst . . .' Then with another roar: 'You can say what you please, Pye, but you don't make me believe it was any of 'er fault. She wasn't *that*!'

'If I was going to say what I please, I'd begin by callin' you a silly ox an' work up to the higher pressures at leisure. I'm trying to say solely what transpired. M'rover, for once you're right. It wasn't her fault.'

'You couldn't 'aven't made me believe it if it 'ad been,' was the answer.

Such faith in a Sergeant of Marines interested me greatly. 'Never mind about that,' I cried. 'Tell me what she was like.'

'She was a widow,' said Pyecroft. 'Left so very young and never re-spliced. She kep' a little hotel for warrants and non-coms close to Auckland, an' she always wore black silk, and 'er neck –'

'You ask what she was like,' Pritchard broke in. 'Let me give you an instance. I was at Auckland first in '97, at the end o' the *Marroquin*'s commission, an' as I'd been promoted I went up with the others. She used to look after us all, an' she never lost by it – not a penny! "Pay me now," she'd say, "or settle later. I know you won't let me suffer. Send the money from home if you like." Why, gentlemen all, I tell you I've seen that lady take her own gold watch an' chain off her neck in the bar an' pass it to a bosun 'oo'd come ashore without 'is ticker an' 'ad to catch the last boat. "I don't know your name," she said, "but when you've done with it, you'll find plenty that know me on the front. Send it back by one o' them." And it was worth thirty pounds if it was worth 'arf-a-crown. The little gold watch, Pye, with the blue monogram at the back. But, as I was sayin', in those days she kep' a beer that agreed with me – Slits it was called. One way an' another I must 'ave punished a good few bottles of it while we was in the bay – comin' ashore every night or so. Chaffin' across the bar like, once when we were alone, "Mrs B.," I said, "when next I call I want you to re-member that this is my particular – just as you're my particular." (She'd let you go *that* far!) "Just as you're my particular," I said. "Oh, thank you, Sergeant Pritchard," she says, an' put 'er hand up to the curl be'ind 'er ear. Remember that way she had, Pye?'

'I think so,' said the sailor.

'Yes, "Thank you, Sergeant Pritchard," she says. "The least I can do is to mark it for you in case you change your mind. There's no great demand for it in the Fleet," she says, "but to make sure I'll put it at the back o' the shelf," an' she snipped off a piece of her hair ribbon with that old dolphin cigar-cutter on the bar – remember it, Pye? an' she tied a bow round what was left – just four bottles. That was '97 – no, '96. In '98 I was in the *Resiliant* – China station – full commission. In Nineteen One, mark you, I was in the *Carthusian*, back in Auckland Bay again. Of course I went up to Mrs B.'s with the rest of us to see how things were goin'. They were the same as ever. (Remember the big tree on the pavement by the side-bar, Pye?) I never said anythin' in special (there was too many of us talkin' to her), but she saw me at once.'

'That wasn't difficult?' I ventured.

'Ah, but wait. I was comin' up to the bar, when, "Ada," she says to her niece, "get me Sergeant Pritchard's particular," and, gentlemen all, I tell you before I could shake 'ands with the lady there were those four bottles o' Slits, with 'er 'air ribbon in a bow round each o' their necks, set down in front o' me, an' as she drew the cork she looked at me under her eyebrows in that blindish way she had o' lookin', an', "Sergeant Pritchard," she says, "I do 'ope you 'aven't changed your mind about your particulars." That's the kind o' woman she was – after five years!'

'I don't *see* her yet somehow,' said Hooper, but with sympathy.

'She – she never scrupled to feed a lame duck or set 'er foot on a scorpion at any time of 'er life,' Pritchard added valiantly.

'That don't help me either. My mother's like that for one.'

The giant heaved inside his uniform and rolled his eyes at the car-roof. Said Pyecroft suddenly:

'How many women have you been intimate with all over the world, Pritch?'

Pritchard blushed plum colour to the short hairs of his seventeen-inch neck.

''Undreds,' said Pyecroft. 'So've I. How many of 'em can you remember in your own mind, settin' aside the first – an' per'aps the last – *and one more?*'

'Few, wonderful few, now I tax myself,' said Sergeant Pritchard relievedly.

'An' how many times might you 'ave been at Auckland?'

'One – two,' he began – 'why, I can't make it more than three

276

times in ten years. But I can remember every time that I ever saw Mrs B.'

'So can I – an' I've only been to Auckland twice – how she stood an' what she was sayin' an' what she looked like. That's the secret. 'Tisn't beauty, so to speak, nor good talk necessarily. It's just It. Some women'll stay in a man's memory if they once walk down a street, but most of 'em you can live with a month on end, an' next commission you'd be put to it to certify whether they talked in their sleep or not, as one might say.'

'Ah!' said Hooper. 'That's more the idea. I've known just two women of that nature.'

'An' it was no fault o' theirs?' asked Pritchard.

'None whatever. I know *that*!'

'An' if a man gets struck with that kind of woman, Mr Hooper?' Pritchard went on.

'He goes crazy – or just saves himself,' was the slow answer.

'You've hit it,' said the Sergeant. 'You've seen an' known somethin' in the course o' your life, Mr Hooper. I'm lookin' at you!' He set down his bottle.

'And how often had Vickery seen her?' I asked.

'That's the dark an' bloody mystery,' Pyecroft answered. 'I'd never come across him till I come out in the *Hierophant* just now, an' there wasn't anyone in the ship who knew much about him. You see, he was what you call a superior man. 'E spoke to me once or twice about Auckland and Mrs B. on the voyage out I called that to mind subsequently. There must 'ave been a good deal between 'em, to my way o' thinkin'. Mind you, I'm only giving you my *résumé* of it all, because all I know is second-hand so to speak, or rather I should say more than second-'and.'

'How?' said Hooper peremptorily. 'You must have seen it or heard it.'

'Ye-es,' said Pyecroft. 'I used to think seein' and hearin' was the only regulation aids to ascertainin' facts, but as we get older we get more accommodatin'. The cylinders work easier, I suppose ... Were you in Cape Town last December when Phyllis's Circus came?'

'No – up-country,' said Hooper, a little nettled at the change of venue.

'I ask because they had a new turn of a scientific nature called "Home and Friends for a Tickey".'

'Oh, you mean the cinematograph – the pictures of prize-fights and steamers. I've seen 'em up-country.'

'Biograph or cinematograph was what I was alludin' to. London Bridge with the omnibuses – a troopship goin' to the war – marines on parade at Portsmouth, an' the Plymouth Express arrivin' at Paddin'ton.'

'Seen 'em all. Seen 'em all,' said Hooper impatiently.

'We *Hierophants* came in just before Christmas week an' leaf was easy.'

'I think a man gets fed up with Cape Town quicker than anywhere else on the station. Why, even Durban's more like Nature. We was there for Christmas,' Pritchard put in.

'Not bein' a devotee of Indian *peeris*, as our Doctor said to the Pusser, I can't exactly say. Phyllis's was good enough after musketry practice at Mozambique. I couldn't get off the first two or three nights on account of what you might call an imbroglio with our Torpedo Lieutenant in the submerged flat, where some pride of the West country had sugared up a gyroscope; but I remember Vickery went ashore with our Carpenter Rigdon – old Crocus we called him. As a general rule Crocus never left 'is ship unless an' until he was 'oisted out with a winch, but *when* 'e went 'e would return noddin' like a lily gemmed with dew. We smothered him down below that night, but the things 'e said about Vickery as a fittin' playmate for a Warrant Officer of 'is cubic capacity, before we got him quiet, was what I should call pointed.'

'I've been with Crocus – in the *Redoubtable*,' said the Sergeant. 'He's a character if there is one.'

'Next night I went into Cape Town with Dawson and Pratt; but just at the door of the Circus I came across Vickery. "Oh!" he says, "you're the man I'm looking for. Come and sit next me. This way to the shillin' places!" I went astern at once, protestin' because tickey seats better suited my so-called finances. "Come on," says Vickery, "I'm payin'." Naturally I abandoned Pratt and Dawson in anticipation o' drinks to match the seats. "No," he says, when this was 'inted – "not now. Not now. As many as you please afterwards, but I want you sober for the occasion." I caught 'is face under a lamp just then, an' the appearance of it quite cured me of my thirsts. Don't mistake. It didn't frighten me. It made me anxious. I can't tell you what it was like, but that was the effect which it 'ad on me. If you want to know, it reminded me of those things in bottles in those herbalistic shops at Plymouth – preserved in spirits of wine. White an' crumply things – previous to birth as you might say.'

'You 'ave a beastial mind, Pye,' said the Sergeant, relighting his pipe.

'Perhaps. We were in the front row, an' "Home an' Friends" came on early. Vickery touched me on the knee when the number went up. "If you see anything that strikes you," he says, "drop me a hint"; then he went on clicking. We saw London Bridge an' so forth an' so on, an' it was most interestin'. I'd never seen it before. You 'eard a little dynamo like buzzin', but the pictures were the real thing – alive an' movin'.'

'I've seen 'em,' said Hooper. 'Of course they are taken from the very thing itself – you see.'

'Then the Western Mail came in to Paddin'ton on the big magic lantern sheet. First we saw the platform empty an' the porters standin' by. Then the engine come in, head on, an' the women in the front row jumped: she headed so straight. Then the doors opened and the passengers came out and the porters got the luggage just like life. Only – only when anyone came down too far towards us that was watchin', they walked right out o' the picture, so to speak. I was 'ighly interested, I can tell you. So were all of us. I watched an old man with a rug 'oo'd dropped a book an' was tryin' to pick it up, when quite slowly, from be'ind two porters – carryin' a little reticule an' lookin' from side to side – comes out Mrs Bathurst. There was no mistakin' the walk in a hundred thousand. She came forward – right forward – she looked out straight at us with that blindish look which Pritch alluded to. She walked on and on till she melted out of the picture – like – like a shadow jumpin' over a candle, an' as she went I 'eard Dawson in the tickey seats be'ind sing out: "Christ! there's Mrs B.!"'

Hooper swallowed his spittle and leaned forward intently.

'Vickery touched me on the knee again. He was clickin' his four false teeth with his jaw down like an enteric at the last kick. "Are you sure?" says he. "Sure," I says, "didn't you 'ear Dawson give tongue? Why, it's the woman herself." "I was sure before," he says, "but I brought you to make sure. Will you come again with me tomorrow?"

'"Willingly," I says, "it's like meetin' old friends."

'"Yes," he says, openin' his watch, "very like. It will be four-and-twenty hours less four minutes before I see her again. Come and have a drink," he says. "It may amuse you, but it's no sort of earthly use to me.' He went out shaking his head an' stumblin' over people's feet as if he was drunk already. I anticipated a swift drink an' a speedy return, because I wanted to see the performin' elephants. Instead o' which Vickery began to navigate the town at the rate o' knots, lookin' at a bar every three minutes approximate Greenwich time. I'm not a drinkin' man, though there are those present' – he cocked his unforgettable eye at me – 'who may have seen me more or less imbued with the fragrant spirit. None the less when I drink I like to do it at anchor an' not at an average speed of eighteen knots on the measured mile. There's a tank as you might say at the back o' that big hotel up the hill – what do they call it?'

'The Molteno Reservoir,' I suggested, and Hooper nodded.

'That was his limit o' drift. We walked there an' we come down through the Gardens – there was a South-Easter blowin' – an' we finished up by the Docks. Then we bore up the road to Salt River, and wherever there was a pub Vickery put in sweatin'. He didn't look at what he drunk – he didn't look at the change. He walked an' he drunk an' he perspired in rivers. I understood why old Crocus 'ad come back in the condition 'e did, because Vickery an' I 'ad two an' a half hours o' this gipsy manoeuvre, an' when we got back to the station there wasn't a dry atom on or in me.'

'Did he say anything?' Pritchard asked.

'The sum total of 'is conversation from 7.45 p.m. till 11.15 p.m. was "Let's have another." Thus the mornin' and the evenin' were the first day, as Scripture says ... To abbreviate a lengthy narrative, I went into Cape Town for five consecutive

nights with Master Vickery, and in that time I must 'ave logged
about fifty knots over the ground an' taken in two gallon o' all
the worst spirits south the Equator. The evolution never varied.
Two shilling seats for us two; five minutes o' the pictures, an'
perhaps forty-five seconds o' Mrs B. walking down towards us
with that blindish look in her eyes an' the reticule in her hand.
Then out walk – and drink till train time.'

'What did you think?' said Hooper, his hand fingering his
waistcoat-pocket.

'Several things,' said Pyecroft. 'To tell you the truth, I aren't
quite done thinkin' about it yet. Mad? The man was a dumb
lunatic – must 'ave been for months – years p'raps. I know
somethin' o' maniacs, as every man in the Service must. I've
been shipmates with a mad skipper – an' a lunatic Number
One, but never both together I thank 'Eaven. I could give you
the names o' three captains now 'oo ought to be in an asylum,
but you don't find me interferin' with the mentally afflicted
till they begin to lay about 'em with rammers an' winch-handles.
Only once I crept up a little into the wind towards Master
Vickery. "I wonder what she's doin' in England," I says. "Don't
it seem to you she's lookin' for somebody?" That was in the
Gardens again, with the South-Easter blowin' as we were makin'
our desperate round. "She's lookin' for me," he says, stoppin'
dead under a lamp an' clickin'. When he wasn't drinkin', in
which case all 'is teeth clicked on the glass, 'e was clickin' 'is
four false teeth like a Marconi ticker. "Yes! lookin' for me," he
said, an' he went on very softly an' as you might say affec-
tionately. "*But*," he went on, "in future, Mr Pyecroft, I should
take it kindly of you if you'd confine your remarks to the
drinks set before you. Otherwise," he says, "with the best will
in the world towards you, I may find myself guilty of murder!
Do you understand?" he says. "Perfectly," I says, "but would it
at all soothe you to know that in such a case the chances o' your
being killed are precisely equivalent to the chances o' me being
outed." "Why, no," he says, "I'm almost afraid that 'ud be a
temptation." Then I said – we was right under the lamp by that
arch at the end o' the Gardens where the trams come round –
"Assumin' murder was done – or attempted murder – I put it

to you that you would still be left so badly crippled, as one
might say, that your subsequent capture by the police – to 'oom
you would 'ave to explain – would be largely inevitable."
"That's better," 'e says, passin' 'is hands over his forehead.
"That's much better, because," he says, "do you know, as I am
now, Pye, I'm not so sure if I could explain anything much."
Those were the only particular words I had with 'im in our
walks as I remember.'

'What walks!' said Hooper. 'Oh my soul, what walks!'

'They were chronic,' said Pyecroft gravely, 'but I didn't
anticipate any danger till the Circus left. Then I anticipated
that, bein' deprived of 'is stimulant, he might react on me, so to
say, with a hatchet. Consequently, after the final performance
an' the ensuin' wet walk, I kep' myself aloof from my superior
officer on board in the execution of 'is duty, as you might put
it. Consequently, I was interested when the sentry informs me
while I was passin' on my lawful occasions that Click had asked
to see the captain. As a general rule warrant officers don't
dissipate much of the owner's time, but Click put in an hour
and more be'ind that door. My duties kep' me within eyeshot
of it. Vickery came out first, an' 'e actually nodded at me an'
smiled. This knocked me out o' the boat, because, havin' seen
'is face for five consecutive nights, I didn't anticipate any
change there more than a condenser in hell, so to speak. The
owner emerged later. His face didn't read off at all, so I fell
back on his cox, 'oo'd been eight years with him and knew him
better than boat signals. Lamson – that was the cox's name –
crossed 'is bows once or twice at low speeds an' dropped down
to me visibly concerned. "He's shipped 'is court-martial face,"
says Lamson. "Someone's goin' to be 'ung. I've never seen that
look but once before when they chucked the gun-sights overboard in the *Fantastic*." Throwin' gun-sights overboard, Mr
Hooper, is the equivalent for mutiny in these degenerate days.
It's done to attract the notice of the authorities an' the *Western
Mornin' News* – generally by a stoker. Naturally, word went
round the lower deck an' we had a private over'aul of our little
consciences. But, barrin' a shirt which a second-class stoker
said 'ad walked into 'is bag from the marines' flat by itself,

nothin' vital transpired. The owner went about flyin' the signal for "attend public execution", so to say, but there was no corpse at the yard-arm. 'E lunched on the beach an' 'e returned with 'is regulation harbour-routine face about 3 p.m. Thus Lamson lost prestige for raising false alarms. The only person 'oo might 'ave connected the epicycloidal gears correctly was one Pyecroft, when he was told that Mr Vickery would go up-country that same evening to take over certain naval ammunition left after the war in Bloemfontein Fort. No details was ordered to accompany Master Vickery. He was told off first person singular – as a unit – by himself.'

The marine whistled penetratingly.

'That's what I thought,' said Pyecroft. 'I went ashore with him in the cutter an' 'e asked me to walk through the station. He was clickin' audibly, but otherwise seemed happy-ish.

'"You might like to know," he says, stoppin' just opposite the Admiral's front gate, "that Phyllis's Circus will be per-formin' at Worcester tomorrow night. So I shall see 'er yet once again. You've been very patient with me," he says.

'"Look here, Vickery," I said, "this thing's come to be just as much as I can stand. Consume your own smoke. I don't want to know any more."

'"You!" he said. "What have you got to complain of? – you've only 'ad to watch. I'm *it*," he says, "but that's neither here nor there," he says. "I've one thing to say before shakin' 'ands. Remember," 'e says – we were just by the Admiral's garden-gate then – "remember, that I am *not* a murderer, because my lawful wife died in childbed six weeks after I came out. That much at least I am clear of," 'e says.

'"Then what have you done that signifies?" I said. "What's the rest of it?"

'"The rest," 'e says, "is silence," an' he shook 'ands and went clickin' into Simonstown station.'

'Did he stop to see Mrs Bathurst at Worcester?' I asked.

'It's not known. He reported at Bloemfontein, saw the ammunition into the trucks, and then 'e disappeared. Went out – deserted, if you care to put it so – within eighteen months of his pension, an' if what 'e said about 'is wife was true he was a free man as 'e then stood. How do you read it off?'

'Poor devil!' said Hooper. 'To see her that way every night! I wonder what it was.'

'I've made my 'ead ache in that direction many a long night.'

'But I'll swear Mrs B. 'ad no 'and in it,' said the Sergeant, unshaken.

'No. Whatever the wrong or deceit was, he did it, I'm sure o' that. I 'ad to look at 'is face for five consecutive nights. I'm not so fond o' navigatin' about Cape Town with a South-Easter blowin' these days. I can hear those teeth click, so to say.'

'Ah, those teeth,' said Hooper, and his hand went to his waistcoat-pocket once more. 'Permanent things false teeth are. You read about 'em in all the murder trials.'

'What d'you suppose the captain knew – or did?' I asked.

'I've never turned my searchlight that way,' Pyecroft answered unblushingly.

We all reflected together, and drummed on empty beer bottles as the picnic-party, sunburned, wet, and sandy, passed our door singing 'The Honeysuckle and the Bee'.

'Pretty girl under that kapje,' said Pyecroft.

'They never circulated his description?' said Pritchard.

'I was askin' you before these gentlemen came,' said Hooper to me, 'whether you knew Wankies – on the way to the Zambesi – beyond Bulawayo?'

'Would he pass there – tryin' to get to that Lake what's 'is name?' said Pritchard.

Hooper shook his head and went on: 'There's a curious bit o' line there, you see. It runs through solid teak forest – a sort o' mahogany really – seventy-two miles without a curve. I've had a train derailed there twenty-three times in forty miles. I was up there a month ago relievin' a sick inspector, you see. He told me to look out for a couple of tramps in the teak.'

'Two?' Pyecroft said. 'I don't envy that other man if –'

'We get heaps of tramps up there since the war. The inspector told me I'd find 'em at M'Bindwe siding waiting to go North. He'd given 'em some grub and quinine, you see. I went up on a construction train. I looked out for 'em. I saw them miles ahead

along the straight, waiting in the teak. One of 'em was standin'
up by the dead-end of the siding an' the other was squattin'
down lookin' up at 'im, you see.'

'What did you do for 'em?' said Pritchard.

'There wasn't much I could do, except bury 'em. There'd
been a bit of a thunderstorm in the teak, you see, and they were
both stone dead and as black as charcoal. That's what they
really were, you see – charcoal. They fell to bits when we tried
to shift 'em. The man who was standin' up had the false teeth.
I saw 'em shinin' against the black. Fell to bits he did too, like
his mate squatting down an' watchin' him, both of 'em all wet
in the rain. Both burned to charcoal, you see. And – that's what
made me ask about marks just now – the false-toother was
tattooed on the arms and chest – a crown and foul anchor with
M.V. above.'

'I've seen that,' said Pyecroft quickly. 'It was so.'

'But if he was all charcoal-like?' said Pritchard, shuddering.

'You know how writing shows up white on a burned letter?
Well, it was like that, you see. We buried 'em in the teak and I
kept . . . But he was a friend of you two gentlemen, you see.'

Mr Hooper brought his hand away from his waistcoat-pocket
– empty.

Pritchard covered his face with his hands for a moment, like
a child shutting out an ugliness.

'And to think of her at Hauraki!' he murmured – 'with 'er
'air-ribbon on my beer. "Ada," she said to her niece .. Oh,
my Gawd!' . . .

> 'On a summer afternoon, when the honeysuckle blooms,
>   And all Nature seems at rest,
> Underneath the bower, 'mid the perfume of the flower,
>   Sat a maiden with the one she loves the best –'

sang the picnic-party waiting for their train at Glengariff.

'Well, I don't know how you feel about it,' said Pyecroft,
'but 'avin' seen 'is face for five consecutive nights on end, I'm
inclined to finish what's left of the beer an' thank Gawd he's
dead!'

ꝝ Below the Mill Dam ꝝ

'Our Fathers Also'

By – they are by with mirth and tears,
    Wit or the works of Desire
Cushioned about on the kindly years
    Between the wall and the fire.

The grapes are pressed, the corn is shocked
    Standeth no more to glean;
For the Gates of Love and Learning locked
    When they went out between.

All lore our Lady Venus bares
    Signalled it was or told
By the dear lips long given to theirs
    And longer to the mould.

All Profit, all Device, all Truth
    Written it was or said
By the mighty men of their mighty youth,
    Which is mighty being dead.

The film that floats before their eyes
    The Temple's Veil they call;
And the dust that on the Shewbread lies
    Is holy over all.

Warn them of seas that slip our yoke
    Of slow conspiring stars –
The ancient Front of Things unbroke
    But heavy with new wars?

By – they are by with mirth and tears,
    Wit or the waste of Desire –
Cushioned about on the kindly years
    Between the wall and the fire.

286

Below the Mill Dam

'Book – Book – Domesday Book!' They were letting in the water for the evening stint at Robert's Mill, and the wooden Wheel where lived the Spirit of the Mill settled to its nine-hundred-year-old song: 'Here Azor, a freeman, held one rod, but it never paid geld. *Nun-nun-nunquam geldavit*. Here Reinbert has one villein and four cottars with one plough – and wood for six hogs and two fisheries of sixpence and a mill of ten shillings – *unum molinum* – one mill. Reinbert's mill – Robert's Mill. Then and afterwards and now – *tunc et post et modo* –Robert's Mill. Book – Book – Domesday Book!'

'I confess,' said the Black Rat on the cross-beam, luxuriously trimming his whiskers – 'I confess I am not above appreciating my position and all it means.' He was a genuine old English black rat, a breed which, report says, is rapidly diminishing before the incursions of the brown variety.

'Appreciation is the surest sign of inadequacy,' said the Grey Cat, coiled up on a piece of sacking.

'But I know what you mean,' she added. 'To sit by right at the heart of things – eh?'

'Yes,' said the Black Rat, as the old mill shook and the heavy stones thuttered on the grist. 'To possess – er – all this environment as an integral part of one's daily life must insensibly of course . . . You see?'

'I feel,' said the Grey Cat. 'Indeed, if *we* are not saturated with the spirit of the Mill, who should be?'

'Book – Book – Domesday Book!' the Wheel, set to his work, was running off the tenure of the whole rape, for he knew Domesday Book backwards and forwards: '*In Ferle tenuit Abbatia de Wiltuna unam hidam et unam virgam et dimidiam. Nunquam geldavit.* And Agemond, a freeman, has half a hide and one rod. I remember Agemond well. Charmin' fellow – friend of mine. He married a Norman girl in the days when we rather looked down on the Normans as upstarts. An' Agemond's dead? So he is. Eh, dearie me! dearie me! I remember the wolves howling outside his door in the big frost of Ten Fifty-Nine ... *Essewelde hundredum nunquam geldum reddidit.* Book! Book! Domesday Book!'

'After all,' the Grey Cat continued, 'atmosphere is life. It is the influences under which we live that count in the long run. Now, outside' – she cocked one ear towards the half-opened door – 'there is an absurd convention that rats and cats are, I won't go so far as to say natural enemies, but opposed forces. Some such ruling may be crudely effective – I don't for a minute presume to set up my standards as final – among the ditches; but from the larger point of view that one gains by living at the heart of things, it seems for a rule of life a little overstrained. Why, because some of your associates have, shall I say, liberal views on the ultimate destination of a sack of – er – middlings don't they call them –'

'Something of that sort,' said the Black Rat, a most sharp and sweet-toothed judge of everything ground in the mill for the last three years.

'Thanks – middlings be it. *Why*, as I was saying, must I disarrange my fur and my digestion to chase you round the dusty arena whenever we happen to meet?'

'As little reason,' said the Black Rat, 'as there is for me, who, I trust, am a person of ordinarily decent instincts, to wait till you have gone on a round of calls, and then to assassinate your very charming children.'

'Exactly! It has its humorous side though.' The Grey Cat yawned. 'The miller seems afflicted by it. He shouted large and vague threats to my address, last night at tea, that he wasn't going to keep cats who "caught no mice". Those were his words. I remember the grammar sticking in my throat like a herring-bone.'

'And what did you do?'

'What does one do when a barbarian utters? One ceases to utter and removes. I removed – towards his pantry. It was a *riposte* he might appreciate.'

'Really those people grow absolutely insufferable,' said the

Black Rat. 'There is a local ruffian who answers to the name of Mangles – a builder – who has taken possession of the outhouses on the far side of the Wheel for the last fortnight. He has constructed cubical horrors in red brick where those deliciously picturesque pigstyes used to stand. Have you noticed?'

'There has been much misdirected activity of late among the humans. They jabber inordinately. I haven't yet been able to arrive at their reason for existence.' The Cat yawned.

'A couple of them came in here last week with wires, and fixed them all about the walls. Wires protected by some abominable composition, ending in iron brackets with glass bulbs. Utterly useless for any purpose and artistically absolutely hideous. What do they mean?'

'Aaah! I have known *four*-and-twenty leaders of revolt in Faenza,' said the Cat, who kept good company with the boarders spending a summer at the Mill Farm. 'It means nothing except that humans occasionally bring their dogs with them. I object to dogs in all forms.'

'Shouldn't object to dogs,' said the Wheel sleepily . . . 'The Abbot of Wilton kept the best pack in the county. He enclosed all the Harryngton Woods to Sturt Common. Aluric, a freeman, was dispossessed of his holding. They tried the case at Lewes, but he got no change out of William de Warrenne on the bench. William de Warrenne fined Aluric eight and fourpence for treason, and the Abbot of Wilton excommunicated him for blasphemy. Aluric was no sportsman. Then the Abbot's brother married . . . I've forgotten her name, but she was a charmin' little woman. The Lady Philippa was her daughter. That was after the barony was conferred. She rode devilish straight to hounds. They were a bit throatier than we breed now, but a good pack: one of the best. The Abbot kept 'em in splendid shape. Now, who was the woman the Abbot kept? Book – Book! I shall have to go right back to Domesday and work up the centuries: *Modo per omnia reddit burgum tunc – tunc – tunc!* Was it *burgum* or *hundredum*? I shall remember in a minute. There's no hurry.' He paused as he turned over silvered with showering drops.

'This won't do,' said the Waters in the sluice. 'Keep moving.'

The Wheel swung forward; the Waters roared on the buckets and dropped down to the darkness below.

'Noisier than usual,' said the Black Rat. 'It must have been raining up the valley.'

'Floods maybe,' said the Wheel dreamily. 'It isn't the proper season, but they can come without warning. I shall never forget the big one – when the Miller went to sleep and forgot to open the hatches. More than two hundred years ago it was, but I recall it distinctly. Most unsettling.'

'We lifted that wheel off his bearings,' cried the Waters. 'We said, "Take away that bauble!" And in the morning he was five miles down the valley – hung up in a tree.'

'Vulgar!' said the Cat. 'But I am sure he never lost his dignity.'

'We don't know. He looked like the Ace of Diamonds when we had finished with him . . . Move on there! Keep on moving. Over! Get over!'

'And why on this day more than any other,' said the Wheel statelily. 'I am not aware that my department requires the stimulus of external pressure to keep it up to its duties. I trust I have the elementary instincts of a gentleman.'

'Maybe,' the Waters answered together, leaping down on the buckets. 'We only know that you are very stiff on your bearings. Over, get over!'

The Wheel creaked and groaned. There was certainly greater pressure upon him than he had ever felt, and his revolutions had increased from six and three-quarters to eight and a third per minute. But the uproar between the narrow, weed-hung walls annoyed the Grey Cat.

'Isn't it almost time,' she said plaintively, 'that the person who is paid to understand these things shuts off those vehement drippings with that screw-thing on the top of that box-thing.'

'They'll be shut off at eight o'clock as usual,' said the Rat; 'then we can go to dinner.'

'But we shan't be shut off till ever so late,' said the Waters gaily. 'We shall keep it up all night.'

'The ineradicable offensiveness of youth is partially compensated for by its eternal hopefulness,' said the Cat. 'Our dam is not, I am glad to say, designed to furnish water for more than four hours at a time. Reserve is Life.'

'Thank goodness!' said the Black Rat. 'Then they can return to their native ditches.'

'Ditches!' cried the Waters; 'Raven's Gill Brook is no ditch. It is almost navigable, and *we* come from there away.' They slid over solid and compact till the Wheel thudded under their weight.

'Raven's Gill Brook,' said the Rat. '*I* never heard of Raven's Gill.'

'We are the waters of Harpenden Brook – down from under Callton Rise. Phew! how the race stinks compared with the heather country.' Another five foot of water flung itself against the Wheel, broke, roared, gurgled, and was gone.

'Indeed,' said the Grey Cat, 'I am sorry to tell you that Raven's Gill Brook is cut off from this valley by an absolutely impassable range of mountains, and Callton Rise is more than nine miles away. It belongs to another system entirely.'

'Ah yes,' said the Rat, grinning, 'but we forget that, for the young, water always runs uphill.'

'Oh, hopeless! hopeless! hopeless!' cried the Waters, descending open-palmed upon the Wheel. 'There is nothing between here and Raven's Gill Brook that a hundred yards of channelling and a few square feet of concrete could not remove; and hasn't removed!'

'And Harpenden Brook is north of Raven's Gill and runs into Raven's Gill at the foot of Callton Rise, where the big ilex trees are, and *we* come from there!' These were the glassy, clear waters of the high chalk.

'And Batten's Ponds, that are fed by springs, have been led through Trott's Wood, taking the spare water from the old Witches' Spring under Churt Haw, and we – we – *we* are their combined waters!' Those were the Waters from the upland bogs and moors – a porter-coloured, dusky, and foam-flecked flood.

'It's all very interesting,' purred the Cat to the sliding waters, 'and I have no doubt that Trott's Woods and Bott's Woods are tremendously important places; but if you could manage to do your work – whose value I don't in the least dispute – a little more soberly, I, for one, should be grateful.'

'Book – book – book – book – book – Domesday Book!' The urged Wheel was fairly clattering now: 'In Burgelstaltone a monk holds of Earl Godwin one hide and a half with eight villeins. There is a church – and a monk . . . I remember that monk. Blessed if he could rattle his rosary off any quicker than I am doing now . . . and wood for seven hogs. I must be running twelve to the minute . . . almost as fast as Steam. Damnable invention, Steam! . . . Surely it's time we went to dinner or prayers – or something. Can't keep up this pressure, day in and day out, and not feel it. I don't mind for myself, of course. *Noblesse oblige*, you know. I'm only thinking of the Upper and the Nether Millstones. They came out of the common rock. They can't be expected to –'

'Don't worry on our account, please,' said the Millstones huskily. 'So long as you supply the power we'll supply the weight and the bite.'

'Isn't it a trifle blasphemous, though, to work you in this way?' grunted the Wheel. 'I seem to remember something about the Mills of God grinding "slowly". *Slowly* was the word!'

'But we are not the Mills of God. We're only the Upper and the Nether Millstones. We have received no instructions to be anything else. We are actuated by power transmitted through you.'

'Ah, but let us be merciful as we are strong. Think of all the beautiful little plants that grow on my woodwork. There are five varieties of rare moss within less than one square yard – and all these delicate jewels of nature are being grievously knocked about by this excessive rush of the water.'

'Umph!' growled the Millstones. 'What with your religious scruples and your taste for botany we'd hardly know you for the Wheel that put the carter's son under last autumn. You never worried about *him*!'

'He ought to have known better.'

'So ought your jewels of nature. Tell 'em to grow where it's safe.'

'How a purely mercantile life debases and brutalizes!' said the Cat to the Rat.

'They were such beautiful little plants too,' said the Rat tenderly. 'Maiden's-tongue and hart's-hair fern trellising all over the wall just as they do on the sides of churches in the Downs. Think what a joy the sight of them must be to our sturdy peasants pulling hay!'

'Golly!' said the Millstones. 'There's nothing like coming to the heart of things for information'; and they returned to the song that all English water-mills have sung from time beyond telling:

> 'There was a jovial miller once
> Lived on the River Dee,
> And this the burden of his song
> For ever used to be.'

Then, as fresh grist poured in and dulled the note:

> 'I care for nobody – no, not I,
> And nobody cares for me.'

'Even these stones have absorbed something of our atmosphere,' said the Grey Cat. 'Nine-tenths of the trouble in this world comes from lack of detachment.'

'One of your people died from forgetting that, didn't she?' said the Rat.

'One only. The example has sufficed us for generations.'

'Ah! but what happened to Don't Care!' the Waters demanded.

'Brutal riding to death of the casual analogy is another mark of provincialism!' The Grey Cat raised her tufted chin. 'I am going to sleep. With my social obligations I must snatch rest when I can; but, as our old friend here says, *Noblesse oblige* . . . Pity me! Three functions tonight in the village, and a barn-dance across the valley!'

'There's no chance, I suppose, of your looking in on the loft about two. Some of our young people are going to amuse themselves with a new sacque-dance – best white flour only,' said the Black Rat.

'I believe I am officially supposed not to countenance that sort of thing, but youth is youth . . . By the way, the humans set my milk-bowl in the loft these days; I hope your youngsters respect it.'

'My dear lady,' said the Black Rat, bowing, 'you grieve me. You hurt me inexpressibly. After all these years, too!'

'A general crush is so mixed – highways and hedges – all that sort of thing – and no one can answer for one's best friends. *I* never try. So long as mine are amusin' and in full voice, and can hold their own at a tile-party, I'm as catholic as these mixed waters in the dam here!'

'We aren't mixed. We *have* mixed. We are one now,' said the Waters sulkily.

'Still uttering?' said the Cat. 'Never mind, here's the Miller coming to shut you off. Ye-es, I have known – *four* – or five is it? – and twenty leaders of revolt in Faenza ... A little more babble in the dam, a little more noise in the sluice, a little extra splashing on the wheel, and then –'

'They will find that nothing has occurred,' said the Black Rat. 'The old things persist and survive and are recognized – our old friend here first of all. By the way,' he turned toward the Wheel, 'I believe we have to congratulate you on your latest honour.'

'Profoundly well deserved – even if he had never – as he has – laboured strenuously through a long life for the amelioration of millkind,' said the Cat, who belonged to many tile and out-house committees. 'Doubly deserved, I may say, for the silent and dignified rebuke his existence offers to the clattering, fidgety-footed demands of – er – some people. What form did the honour take?'

'It was,' said the Wheel bashfully, 'a machine-moulded pinion.'

'Pinions! Oh, how heavenly!' the Black Rat sighed. 'I never see a bat without wishing for wings.'

'Not exactly that sort of pinion,' said the Wheel, 'but a really ornate circle of toothed iron wheels. Absurd, of course, but gratifying. Mr Mangles and an associate herald invested me with it personally – on my left rim – the side that you can't see from the mill. I hadn't meant to say anything about it – or the new steel straps round my axles – bright red, you know – to be worn on all occasions – but, without false modesty, I assure you that the recognition cheered me not a little.'

'How intensely gratifying!' said the Black Rat. 'I must really steal an hour between lights some day and see what they are doing on your left side.'

'By the way, have you any light on this recent activity of Mr Mangles?' the Grey Cat asked. 'He seems to be building small houses on the far side of the tail-race. Believe me, I don't ask from any vulgar curiosity.'

'It affects our Order,' said the Black Rat simply but firmly.

'Thank you,' said the Wheel. 'Let me see if I can tabulate it properly. Nothing like system in accounts of all kinds. Book! Book! Book! On the side of the Wheel towards the hundred of Burgelstaltone, where till now was a stye of three hogs, Mangles, a freeman, with four villeins and two carts of two thousand bricks, has a new small house of five yards and a half, and one roof of iron and a floor of cement. Then, now, and afterwards beer in large tankards. And Felden, a stranger, with three villeins and one very great cart, deposits on it one engine of iron and brass and a small iron mill of four feet, and a broad strap of leather. And Mangles, the builder, with two villeins, constructs the floor for the same, and a floor of new brick with wires for the small mill. There are there also chalices filled with iron and water, in number fifty-seven. The whole is valued at one hundred and seventy-four pounds ... I'm sorry I can't make myself clearer, but you can see for yourself.'

'Amazingly lucid,' said the Cat. She was the more to be admired because the language of Domesday Book is not, perhaps, the clearest medium wherein to describe a small but complete electric-light installation, deriving its power from a water-wheel by means of cogs and gearing.

'See for yourself – by all means, see for yourself,' said the Waters, spluttering and choking with mirth.

'Upon my word,' said the Black Rat furiously, 'I may be at fault, but I wholly fail to perceive where these offensive eavesdroppers – er – come in. We were discussing a matter that solely affected our Order.'

Suddenly they heard, as they had heard many times before,

the Miller shutting off the water. To the rattle and rumble of the labouring stones succeeded thick silence, punctuated with little drops from the stayed wheel. Then some water-bird in the dam fluttered her wings as she slid to her nest, and the plop of a water-rat sounded like the fall of a log in the water.

'It is all over – it always is all over at just this time. Listen, the Miller is going to bed – as usual. Nothing has occurred,' said the Cat.

Something creaked in the house where the pig-styes had stood, as metal engaged on metal with a clink and a burr.

'Shall I turn her on?' cried the Miller.

'Ay,' said the voice from the dynamo-house.

'A human in Mangles' new house!' the Rat squeaked.

'What of it?' said the Grey Cat. 'Even supposing Mr Mangles' cat's-meat-coloured hovel ululated with humans, can't you see for yourself – that –?'

There was a solid crash of released waters leaping upon the wheel more furiously than ever, a grinding of cogs, a hum like the hum of a hornet, and then the unvisited darkness of the old mill was scattered by intolerable white light. It threw up every cobweb, every burl and knot in the beams and the floor; till the shadows behind the flakes of rough plaster on the wall lay clear-cut as shadows of mountains on the photographed moon.

'See! See! See!' hissed the Waters in full flood. 'Yes, see for yourselves. Nothing has occurred. Can't you see?'

The Rat, amazed, had fallen from his foothold and lay half-stunned on the floor. The Cat, following her instinct, leaped nigh to the ceiling, and with flattened ears and bared teeth backed in a corner ready to fight whatever terror might be loosed on her. But nothing happened. Through the long aching minutes nothing whatever happened, and her wire-brush tail returned slowly to its proper shape.

'Whatever it is,' she said at last, 'it's overdone. They can never keep it up, you know.'

'Much you know,' said the Waters. 'Over you go, old man. You can take the full head of us now. Those new steel axle-straps of yours can stand anything. Come along, Raven's Gill,

Harpenden, Callton Rise, Batten's Ponds, Witches' Spring, all together! Let's show these gentlemen how to work!'

'But – but – I thought it was a decoration. Why – why – why – it only means more work for *me*!'

'Exactly. You're to supply about sixty eight-candle lights when required. But they won't be all in use at once –'

'Ah! I thought as much,' said the Cat. 'The reaction is bound to come.'

'*And*,' said the Waters, 'you will do the ordinary work of the mill as well.'

'Impossible!' the old Wheel quivered as it drove. 'Aluric never did it – nor Azor, nor Reinbert. Not even William de Warrenne or the Papal Legate. There's no precedent for it. I tell you there's no precedent for working a wheel like this.'

'Wait a while! We're making one as fast as we can. Aluric and Co. are dead. So's the Papal Legate. You've no notion how dead they are, but we're here – the Waters of Five Separate Systems. We're just as interesting as Domesday Book. Would you like to hear about the land-tenure in Trott's Wood? It's squat-right, chiefly.' The mocking Waters leaped one over the other, chuckling and chattering profanely.

'In that hundred Jenkins, a tinker, with one dog – *unus canis* – holds, by the Grace of God and a habit he has of working hard, *unam hidam* – a large potato patch. Charmin' fellow, Jenkins. Friend of ours. Now, who the doooo did Jenkins keep? ... In the hundred of Callton is one charcoal-burner *irreligiosissimus homo* – a bit of a rip – but a thorough sportsman. *Ibi est ecclesia. Non multum.* Not much of a church, *quia* because, *episcopus* the Vicar irritated the Nonconformists *tunc et post et modo* – then and afterwards and now – until they built a cut-stone Congregational chapel with red brick facings that did not return itself – *defendebat se* – at four thousand pounds.'

'Charcoal-burners, vicars, schismatics, and red brick facings,' groaned the Wheel. 'But this is sheer blasphemy. What waters have they let in upon me?'

'Floods from the gutters. Faugh, this light is positively sickening!' said the Cat, rearranging her fur.

'We come down from the clouds or up from the springs,

exactly like all other waters everywhere. Is that what's surprising you?' sang the Waters.

'Of course not. I know my work if you don't. What I complain of is your lack of reverence and repose. You've no instinct of deference towards your betters – your heartless parody of the Sacred volume (the Wheel meant Domesday Book) proves it.'

'Our betters?' said the Waters most solemnly. 'What is there in all this dammed race that hasn't come down from the clouds, or –'

'Spare me that talk, please,' the Wheel persisted. 'You'd *never* understand. It's the tone – your tone that we object to.'

'Yes. It's your tone,' said the Black Rat, picking himself up limb by limb.

'If you thought a trifle more about the work you're supposed to do, and a trifle less about your precious feelings, you'd render a little more duty in return for the power vested in you – we mean wasted on you,' the Waters replied.

'I have been some hundreds of years laboriously acquiring the knowledge which you see fit to challenge so light-heartedly,' the Wheel jarred.

'Challenge him! Challenge him!' clamoured the little waves riddling down through the tail-race. 'As well now as later. Take him up!'

The main mass of the Waters plunging on the Wheel shocked that well-bolted structure almost into box-lids by saying: 'Very good. Tell us what you suppose yourself to be doing at the present moment.'

'Waiving the offensive form of your question, I answer, purely as a matter of courtesy, that I am engaged in the trituration of farinaceous substances whose ultimate destination it would be a breach of the trust reposed in me to reveal.'

'Fiddle!' said the Waters. 'We knew it all along! The first direct question shows his ignorance of his own job. Listen, old thing. Thanks to us, you are now actuating a machine of whose construction you know nothing, that that machine may, over wires of whose ramifications you are, by your very position, profoundly ignorant, deliver a power which you can never realize, to localities beyond the extreme limits of your mental horizon, with the object of producing phenomena which in your wildest dreams (if you ever dream) you could never comprehend. Is that clear, or would you like it all in words of four syllables?'

'Your assumptions are deliciously sweeping, but may I point out that a decent and – the dear old Abbot of Wilton would have put it in his resonant monkish Latin much better than I can – a scholarly reserve does not necessarily connote blank vacuity of mind on all subjects.'

'Ah, the dear old Abbot of Wilton,' said the Rat sympathetically, as one nursed in that bosom. 'Charmin' fellow – thorough scholar and gentleman. Such a pity!'

'Oh, Sacred Fountains!' – the Waters were fairly boiling. 'He goes out of his way to expose his ignorance by triple bucketfuls. He creaks to high Heaven that he is hopelessly behind the common order of things! He invites the streams of Five Watersheds to witness his su-su-su-pernal incompetence, and then he talks as though there were untold reserves of knowledge behind him that he is too modest to bring forward. For a bland, circular, absolutely sincere impostor, you're a miracle, O Wheel!'

'I do not pretend to be anything more than an integral portion of an accepted and not altogether mushroom institution.'

'Quite so,' said the Waters. 'Then go round – hard –'

'To what end?' asked the Wheel.

'Till a big box of tanks in your house begins to fizz and fume – gassing is the proper word.'

'It would be,' said the Cat, sniffing.

'That will show that your accumulators are full. When the accumulators are exhausted, and the lights burn badly, you will find us whacking you round and round again.'

'The end of life as decreed by Mangles and his creatures is to go whacking round and round for ever,' said the Cat.

'In order,' the Rat said, 'that you may throw raw and unnecessary illumination upon all the unloveliness in the world. Unloveliness which we shall – er – have always with us. At the same time you will riotously neglect the so-called little but vital graces that make up Life.'

'Yes, Life,' said the Cat, 'with its dim delicious half-tones and veiled indeterminate distances. Its surprisals, escapes, encounters, and dizzying leaps − its full-throated choruses in honour of the morning star, and its melting reveries beneath the sun-warmed wall.'

'Oh, you can go on the tiles, Pussalina, just the same as usual,' said the laughing Waters. '*We* shan't interfere with you.'

'On the tiles, forsooth!' hissed the Cat.

'Well, that's what it amounts to,' persisted the Waters. 'We see a good deal of the minor graces of life on our way down to our job.'

'And − but I fear I speak to deaf ears − do they never impress you?' said the Wheel.

'Enormously,' said the Waters. 'We have already learned six refined synonyms for loafing.'

'But (here again I feel as though preaching in the wilderness) it never occurs to you that there may exist some small difference between the wholly animal − ah − rumination of bovine minds and the discerning, well-apportioned leisure of the finer type of intellect?'

'Oh, yes. The bovine mind goes to sleep under a hedge and makes no bones about it when it's shouted at. We've seen *that* − in haying-time − all along the meadows. The finer type is wide awake enough to fudge up excuses for shirking, and mean enough to get stuffy when its excuses aren't accepted. Turn over!'

'But, my good people, no gentleman gets stuffy as you call it. A certain proper pride, to put it no higher, forbids −'

'Nothing that he wants to do if he really wants to do it. Get along! What are you giving us? D'you suppose we've scoured half heaven in the clouds, and half earth in the mists, to be taken in at this time of the day by a bone-idle, old hand-quern of your type?'

'It is not for me to bandy personalities with you. I can only say that I simply decline to accept the situation.'

'Decline away. It doesn't make any odds. They'll probably put in a turbine if you decline too much.'

'What's a turbine?' said the Wheel quickly.

'A little thing you don't see, that performs surprising re-volutions. But you won't decline. You'll hang on to your two nice red-strapped axles and your new machine-moulded pinions like – a – like a leech on a lily stem! There's centuries of work in your old bones if you'd only apply yourself to it; and, mechanically, an overshot wheel with this head of water is about as efficient as a turbine.'

'So in future I am to be considered mechanically? I have been painted by at least five Royal Academicians.'

'Oh, you can be painted by five hundred when you aren't at work, of course. But while you are at work you'll work. You won't half-stop and think and talk about rare plants and dicky-birds and farinaceous fiduciary interests. You'll continue to revolve, and this new head of water will see that you do so continue.'

'It is a matter on which it would be exceedingly ill-advised to form a hasty or a premature conclusion. I will give it my most careful consideration,' said the Wheel.

'Please do,' said the Waters gravely. 'Hullo! Here's the Miller again.'

The Cat coiled herself in a picturesque attitude on the softest corner of a sack, and the Rat without haste, yet certainly without rest, slipped behind the sacking as though an appointment had just occurred to him.

In the doorway, with the young Engineer, stood the Miller grinning amazedly.

'Well – well – well! 'tis true-ly won'erful. An' what a power o' dirt! It come over me now looking at these lights, that I've never rightly seen my own mill before. She needs a lot bein' done to her.'

'Ah! I suppose one must make oneself moderately agreeable to the baser sort. They have their uses. This thing controls the dairy.' The Cat, pincing on her toes, came forward and rubbed her head against the Miller's knee.'

'Ay, you pretty puss,' he said, stopping. 'You're as big a cheat as the rest of 'em that catch no mice about me. A won'erful smooth-skinned, rough-tongued cheat you be. I've more than half a mind –'

'She does her work well,' said the Engineer, pointing to where the Rat's beady eyes showed behind the sacking. 'Cats and Rats livin' together – see?'

'Too much they do – too long they've done. I'm sick and tired of it. Go and take a swim and larn to find your own vittles honest when you come out, Pussy.'

'My word!' said the Waters, as a sprawling Cat landed all unannounced in the centre of the tail-race. 'Is that you, Mewsalina? You seem to have been quarrelling with your best friend. Get over to the left. It's shallowest there. Up on that alder-root with all four paws. Goodnight!'

'You'll never get any they rats,' said the Miller, as the young Engineer struck wrathfully with his stick at the sacking. 'They're not the common sort. They're the old black English sort.'

'Are they, by Jove? I must catch one to stuff, some day.'

Six months later, in the chill of a January afternoon, they were letting in the Waters as usual.

'Come along! It's both gears this evening,' said the Wheel, kicking joyously in the first rush of the icy stream. 'There's a heavy load of grist just in from Lamber's Wood. Eleven miles it came in an hour and a half in our new motor-lorry, and the Miller's rigged five new five-candle lights in his cow-stables. I'm feeding 'em tonight. There's a cow due to calve. Oh, while I think of it, what's the news from Callton Rise?'

'The waters are finding their level as usual – but why do you ask?' said the deep outpouring Waters.

'Because Mangles and Felden and the Miller are talking of increasing the plant here and running a saw-mill by electricity. I was wondering whether we –'

'I beg your pardon,' said the Waters, chuckling. '*What* did you say?'

'Whether *we*, of course, had power enough for the job. It will be a biggish contract. There's all Harpenden Brook to be considered and Batten's Ponds as well, and Witches' Fountain, and the Churt's Hawd system.'

'We've power enough for anything in the world,' said the

Waters. 'The only question is whether you could stand the strain if we came down on you full head.'

'Of course I can,' said the Wheel. 'Mangles is going to turn me into a set of turbines – beauties.'

'Oh – er – I suppose it's the frost that has made us a little thick-headed, but to whom are we talking?' asked the amazed Waters.

'To me – the Spirit of the Mill, of course.'

'Not to the old Wheel, then?'

'I happen to be living in the old Wheel just at present. When the turbines are installed I shall go and live in them. What earthly difference does it make?'

'Absolutely none,' said the Waters, 'in the earth or in the waters under the earth. But we thought turbines didn't appeal to you.'

'Not like turbines? Me? My dear fellows, turbines are good for fifteen hundred revolutions a minute – and with our power we can drive 'em at full speed. Why there's nothing we couldn't grind or saw or illuminate or heat with a set of turbines! That's to say if all the Five Watersheds are agreeable.'

'Oh, we've been agreeable for ever so long.'

'Then why didn't you tell me?'

'Don't know. Suppose it slipped our memory.' The Waters were holding themselves in for fear of bursting with mirth.

'How careless of you! You should keep abreast of the age, my dear fellows. We might have settled it long ago, if you'd only spoken. Yes, four good turbines and a neat brick penstock – eh? This old Wheel's absurdly out of date.'

'Well,' said the Cat, who after a little proud seclusion had returned to her place impenitent as ever. 'Praised be Pasht and the Old Gods, that whatever may have happened *I*, at least, have preserved the Spirit of the Mill!'

She looked round as expecting her faithful ally, the Black Rat; but that very week the Engineer had caught and stuffed him, and had put him in a glass case; he being a genuine old English black rat. That breed, the report says, is rapidly diminishing before the incursions of the brown variety.

Notes

Abbreviations used in the Notes

Birkenhead   Lord Birkenhead, *Rudyard Kipling*, Weidenfeld & Nicolson, 1978

Carrington   Charles Carrington, *Rudyard Kipling, His Life and Work*, Macmillan, 1955 (Pelican Books, 1970)

Cohen   Morton Cohen (ed.), *Rudyard Kipling to Rider Haggard: The Record of a Friendship*, Hutchinson, 1965

RG   R. E. Harbord (ed.), *The Reader's Guide to Rudyard Kipling's Work*, Gibbs & Son, 8 vols., 1961–72

SM   Rudyard Kipling, *Something of Myself*, Macmillan, 1937

Mason   Philip Mason, *Kipling: The Glass, the Shadow and the Fire*, Jonathan Cape, 1975

Tompkins   J. M. S. Tompkins, *The Art of Rudyard Kipling*, Methuen, 1959

Wilson   Angus Wilson, *The Strange Ride of Rudyard Kipling*, Secker & Warburg, 1977

Verse   *The Definitive Edition of Rudyard Kipling's Verse*, Hodder & Stoughton, 1940

Notes to Introduction

1. *SM*, p. 214.
2. 'The English Flag' (1891), *Verse*, p. 221.
3. 'Pharaoh and the Sergeant' (1903), *Verse*, p. 199.
4. 'India for the Indians' (31 December 1889), *RG*, vol. V, p. 2418.
5. 'Chant-Pagan' (1903), *Verse*, p. 462.
6. T. S. Eliot, Introduction to *A Choice of Kipling's Verse*, Faber and Faber, 1941, p. 28.
7. W. H. Auden, quoted by John Bayley in 'The Puzzles of Kipling', *The Uses of Division*, Chatto & Windus, 1976, p. 53.
8. Robert Buchanan, 'The Voice of the Hooligan', *Contemporary Review*, vol. LXXVI, December 1899, pp. 774–89. Quoted in

The Critical Heritage, ed. R. L. Green, Routledge & Kegan Paul, 1971, pp. 233–49.

9. Quoted in Birkenhead, p. 223.
10. 'The Islanders' (1902), *Verse*, p. 303.
11. Mason, p. 251.
12. C. S. Lewis, 'Kipling's World' (1948), in *They Asked for a Paper*, Geoffrey Bles, 1962, p. 91. (Also in *Kipling and the Critics*, ed. Elliott Gilbert, Peter Owen, 1966.)
13. John Bayley, op. cit., p. 65.
14. 'William the Conqueror' (1895), *The Day's Work*, 1898.
15. *A Fleet in Being: Notes on Two Trips with the Channel Squadron*, 1898, p. 35.
16. Quoted in Jan Morris, *Pax Britannica*, Faber and Faber, 1968 (Penguin, 1979, p. 124).
17. Joseph Conrad, 'Heart of Darkness', 1899, ch. 1.
18. Jan Morris, op. cit., p. 125.
19. George Orwell, 'Rudyard Kipling' (1942), in *Kipling's Mind and Art*, ed. Andrew Rutherford, Oliver & Boyd, 1964, p. 83.
20. T. S. Eliot, op. cit., p. 29.
21. Wilson, p. 259.
22. See Janet Montefiore, 'Day and Night in Kipling', *Essays in Criticism*, vol. XXVII, no. 4, pp. 299–314.
23. Edmund Wilson, 'The Kipling That Nobody Read' (1941), in Andrew Rutherford, op. cit., p. 57.
24. 'The Puzzler' (1906), *Actions and Reactions*, 1909.
25. T. S. Eliot, 'Burnt Norton' (1935), *Four Quartets*, Faber and Faber, 1935.
26. Wilson, p. 40.
27. See general note to 'Steam Tactics'.
28. Rayne Kruger, *Goodbye Dolly Gray: The Story of the Boer War*, 1959 (Pan, 1983, p. 148).
29. ibid., p. 507.
30. Speech to the Anglo-African Writers Club, 16 May 1898, in *RG*, vol. VII, p. 3327.
31. *SM*, p. 50.
32. Letter to Dr J. Conland, 20 February 1901, quoted in Carrington (Pelican Books, p. 379).
33. L. M. Thompson, quoted in *The South African War: The Anglo-Boer War 1899–1902*, ed. Peter Warwick, Longman, 1980, p. 376.
34. *SM*, p. 166.
35. Speech at a dinner at Bloemfontein for Kipling, Lord Roberts and Sir Alfred Milner, 28 March 1900, in *RG*, vol. III, p. 1536.

36. Birkenhead, p. 229.
37. Letter to Dr J. Conland, 24 July 1900, quoted in Carrington, p. 376.
38. 'The Islanders', *Verse*, p. 303.
39. Wilson, p. 245.
40. C. A. Bodelson, *Aspects of Kipling's Art*, Manchester University Press, 1964, ch. 8.
41. *SM*, p. 158.
42. See Carrington, pp. 482–3.
43. *SM*, p. 130.
44. See Wilson, p. 222, C. S. Lewis, op. cit., p. 73, and Kingsley Amis, *Rudyard Kipling and his World*, Thames & Hudson, 1975, p. 97.
45. See general note to 'Mrs Bathurst'.
46. John Bayley, op. cit., p. 77.
47. Wilson, p. 222.
48. Tompkins, p. 93.
49. See general note to 'Wireless'.
50. *SM*, p. 210.
51. Randall Jarrell, 'The English in England' (1963), in *Kipling, Auden & Co.*, Carcanet, 1981, p. 362.
52. John Barnard, notes to 'The Eve of St Agnes', *John Keats: The Complete Poems*, Penguin, 1973, p. 621.
53. W. W. Robson, 'Kipling's Later Stories', in Rutherford, op. cit., p. 267.

Traffics and Discoveries

Traffics and Discoveries: cf. Richard Hakluyt's *The Principal Navigations, Voyages, Traffiques and Discoveries of the English Nation* (1598–1600).

General Note on the Poems

Traffics and Discoveries was the first of Kipling's collections for adults which interspersed stories and poems. Apart from 'The Necessitarian', none of the poems accompanied the stories when they were first printed in magazines. The first publication of the poems was as follows: 'From the Masjid-al-Aqsa', 'Poseidon's Law', 'The Wet Litany', 'The Egg-shell', 'Kaspar's Song', 'The Return of the Children' and 'Our Fathers Also' in *Songs from Books*, 1912; 'The Runners', 'Song of the Old Guard' and 'From Lyden's "Irenius"' in *Verse*, Inclusive Edition, 1927; 'The King's Task' in *A History of England*, 1911; 'The Necessitarian' in the *Saturday Evening Post*, 6 December 1902, and then in *Songs from Books*.

All the poems are collected in *The Definitive Edition of Rudyard Kipling's Verse* (referred to in the Notes as *Verse*).

The Captive

First published in the U.S.A. in *Collier's Weekly*, 6 December 1902, then in England in the *Illustrated London News*, Summer Number, 1903. See Birkenhead, ch. 16; Wilson, ch. 4, esp. pp. 219–20; and Carrington, ch. 13, esp. p. 389: 'R.K.'s letters to Conland reveal (1) that Rudyard himself imported an experimental machine-gun for trial in the field, and (2) that he made friends at Cape Town with an American soldier of fortune, a sergeant "who had been at San Juan, and was a Democrat – a grey, grizzled tough old bird". This American, unlike the "captive", had volunteered to fight on the British side.' See also *SM*, pp. 209–10: 'In a South African, post-Boer War tale called "The Captive", which was built up round the phrase "a first-class dress parade for Armageddon", I could not get my lighting into key with the tone of the monologue. My Daemon said at last: "Paint the background first once for all, as hard as a public-house sign, and leave it alone." This done, the rest fell into place with the American accent and outlook of the teller.'

From the Masjid-al-Aqsa

Title 'The Captive' in *Verse*.

The Captive

He that believeth . . .: Isaiah xxviii.16.

cutter: small, lightly armed ship's boat.

Simonstown: major naval port in False Bay, south of Cape Town in Cape Colony, where p.o.w.s were kept during the Boer War.

Barracouta, Gibraltar, Penelope: cruisers and an ironclad, in service in the Boer War between 1901 and 1902.

transport: troopship.

bow and stern: front and rear ends of a ship.

Dutch Reformed Church: the Calvinist Church of the Afrikaners, and not at all 'conciliatory'.

Harper's and *M'Clure's*: American magazines, in which some of Kipling's stories were published.

The American Tyler: probably an invented Masonic journal.

automatic two-inch field-gun: in which the force of recoil is used to eject the empty cylinder and load the next round.

hopper: funnel-shaped reservoir from which explosive is discharged.

flake, cannonite, etc.: various kinds of explosives.

Bull Durham: American tobacco for rolled cigarettes.

our Filipeens: In 1898, after the Spanish–American war, Spain ceded the Philippines to the U.S.A. In 1899 Emilio Aguinaldo, a Filipino national leader, demanded Philippine independence from the U.S.A. and led a resistance movement from February 1899 to April 1902. See p. 46.

Delagoa Bay: south of Lourenço Marques, in Mozambique.

deadheads: non-paying passengers.

Pentecostal sweepings: cf. 'Et Dona Ferentes' (*Verse*, p. 287), 'I have watched them in their tantrums, all that Pentecostal crew'.

Pretoria: capital of the Transvaal Republic.

Kruger: Paul Kruger (1825–1904), the Boer leader, President of the Transvaal Republic from 1882 to 1900, when he left South Africa to seek aid in Europe.

Kaffirs: native Africans (from *caffre*, Arabic for unbeliever).

kloof: narrow, steep ravine.

Teddy Roosevelt's Western tour: Roosevelt (1858–1919), President of the U.S.A. from 1901 to 1909, and a friend of Kipling, took his 'Western' campaigning tour before the election of November 1900 when he was running for Vice-President.

Schenectady: on the Mohawk River, New York State.

veldt: open prairie land in South Africa.

Mauser: high-velocity ·311-inch repeating magazine rifle used by the Boers. The British found that the Boers were excellent marksmen and were equipped with magazine rifles, Maxims (machine-guns) and artillery.

Georgia Crackers: poor whites from the southern state of Georgia.

Pennsylvania Dutch: German-speaking settlers in eastern Pennsylvania from south-west Germany and Sweden.

Grover Cleveland: (1837–1908), Democratic President of the U.S.A., 1885 to 1889 and 1893 to 1897. This was a much-quoted phrase from his message to Congress in 1887.

Stompiesneuk, etc: invented place-names.

vedettes: mounted sentries.

cossack-picquets: mounted detachment of troops posted as early-warning look-outs.

Thirty-fourth Street ferry: crossing from Long Island to Manhattan, before the tunnel under the East River.

Tom Reed: Republican Congressman from Maine, Speaker of the House of Representatives in 1895, 1898 and 1899.

mezas: flat table-lands with steep sides (U.S.A.).

breeching: from the harnessing of gun horses, meaning to be reluctant to go forward.

Colesberg: on the border of the Cape Colony and the Orange Free State, annexed by Free State commandos in November 1899; the setting of 'The Comprehension of Private Copper'.

Nooitgedacht: (or Noitgedacht) in the western Transvaal, forty miles west of Pretoria; scene of a surprise attack on a British convoy in December 1900.

Umballa: district and town in the Punjab, where Boer p.o.w.s were sent.

man with the hoe: probably a reference to the poem 'The Man with the Hoe' by the American Edward Markham (1852–1940).

Chamberlains: Joseph Chamberlain (1836–1914), Colonial Secretary in the Conservative–Unionist governments of Salisbury and Balfour from 1895 to 1903. The Boers (and some British) thought him a liar for disclaiming any part in the Jameson Raid of 1895. He was felt to be guilty by association, and a formal clearing of his involvement by a Select Committee in 1897 was satirically referred to as 'The Lying in State at Westminster'.

Santos-Dumont: Alberto Santos-Dumont (1873–1932), Brazilian aeronaut living in France who constructed dirigibles and aircraft, including a monoplane in 1909.

Professor Langley: Samuel Pierpoint Langley (1834–1906), American physicist, astronomer and civil engineer who established the possibility of powered flight in 1896. He was Secretary of the Smithsonian Institution, the national museum and institute in Washington especially concerned with ethnology, zoology and astrophysics.

donga: steep-sided gully resulting from soil erosion.

twist of molasses: a thread of treacle.

deserter: the British soldiers were fighting the Boers in often appalling conditions, and many defected to the Dutch republics.

yeoman: member of voluntary cavalry force, the Imperial Yeomanry, founded in January 1900 and consisting mainly of keen amateurs with little training. 34,733 men were recruited during the Boer War.

captive of your bow and spear: Jeremiah vi.23.

taffy: toffee.

Männlicher rifle: a German repeating rifle loaded with a clip of five cartridges.

brainy men languishing under an effete system: see Introduction.

Ladies' Home Journal: a monthly magazine for women, in which some of Kipling's stories were published.

Lydia Pinkham: (1819–83), whose Vegetable Compound for 'female troubles' was advertised in all American newspapers.

Pisgah-sight: the mountain from which Moses first viewed Canaan, which he was not allowed to enter.

star-route: in thinly-populated districts in the U.S.A. mail was carried by private firms under contract; these routes were indicated in postal publications by a star.

Zalinski: Edmund Zalinski (1849–1909), Polish–American Captain in the U.S. Artillery who invented in 1888 a pneumatic gun which used air instead of explosive as a propellant.

ox-bows: wooden yokes for draught oxen.

Bracebridge Hall: by Washington Irving, 1822. The hero is Squire Bracebridge, a nineteenth-century version of Sir Roger de Coverley.

The Cricket on the Hearth: a Christmas book by Dickens, 1846.

a bit of a pro-Boer: cf. 'Piet' (*Verse*, p. 479), in which a British soldier praises his enemy: 'I've known a lot o' men behave a dam' sight worse than Piet'.

De Wet: Christiaan de Wet (1854–1922), Commandant General of the Orange Free State and one of the leading figures in the guerilla stage of the Boer War from 1900 to 1902.

Bloemfontein: capital of the Orange Free State. After the humiliating defeat of the Boers at Paardeberg on 27 February 1900, Bloemfontein was captured by British troops under Lord Roberts on 13 March 1900.

Free Stater: Boer living in the Orange Free State, a republic recognized as independent by Britain in 1854, governed by President Steyn.

'I'd like this war to last another five years': cf. p. 52, 'It's a first-class dress-parade for Armageddon'.

Delarey: in the western Transvaal, about 150 miles from Johannesburg.

Vierkleur: the Transvaal Republic flag of four colours.

Native Army: cf. 'A Sahibs' War'. The Indian Army, of Indian soldiers commanded by British officers, was not used in South Africa. (By tacit agreement, blacks were also excluded from the fighting on both sides, though the British did use the Africans as troops in the later stages of the war.) It is clear from this and from 'A Sahibs' War' that Kipling thinks the Indian Native Army should have been used against the Boers.

Worcester, Paarl, Stellenbosch: all towns in the Cape Colony.

Cronje: General Piet Cronjé, a Transvaal farmer, who surrendered and was captured at Paardeberg on 27 February 1900 by British forces under Kitchener.

St Helena: a British possession, where Boer p.o.w.s were sent.

Ordnance: army department dealing with military supplies.

Orange Free State: annexed by the British on 28 May 1900.

Steyn: Martin Theunis Steyn (1857–1916), President of the Orange Free State, who, with Kruger, began the hostilities against the British (hence much disliked by Adrian Van Zyl, Kipling's anti-War, pro-British Boer).

picayune: of little value.

aas vogels: vultures (Afrikaans).

Federals . . . rebels: Van Zyl comes from the Transvaal, which was made part of a 'federation' of loyal states in 1877. The Liberals abandoned the federal policy in 1881, but Salisbury and Chamberlain reiterated it in 1895. In the Cape Colony, the 'rebs' joined the Free Staters against the British (and against the 'loyalist' Afrikaners). In 1900 several hundred Cape rebels were captured or surrendered. But in the second stage of the war there was renewed guerilla activity by the 'rebs' in the Colony and in 1901 much of the north-western Cape was in rebel hands.

the Colony: the Cape Colony.

the Kimberley siege: Kimberley, on the borders of the Cape and the Orange Free State, was besieged by the Boers in November 1899, and was not relieved until 15 February 1900.

Tammany: corrupt; from the corrupt politics of Tammany Hall in New York.

bight of a lariat: looped rope of a lasso.

Monroe Doctrine: principle of U.S. policy which opposed the interference of outside powers in the U.S.A., enunciated by James Monroe, fifth President, in 1823.

long after the north is quiet: the guerilla war of the 'rebs' against the Colony is anticipated as outlasting the war in the Transvaal and the Free State.

The Bonds of Discipline

First published in the U.S.A. in *Collier's Weekly*, 15 August 1903, and in England in the *Windsor Magazine*, August 1903. It contains the account of the narrator's first meeting with Petty-Officer Emanuel Pyecroft, but was not the first Pyecroft story to appear (see 'Steam Tactics'). Four of the six Pyecroft stories are in *Traffics and Discoveries*; the others are 'A Tour of Inspection' (1904; not in the Uniform Edition, but collected in the Sussex Edition) and 'The Horse Marines' (1910; *A Diversity of Creatures*, 1917). There is also an unpublished one-act play concerning Pyecroft, *The Harbour Watch*, performed in 1913. (See *RG*, vol. IV, pp. 1836ff.) For Kipling's brief anti-French phase, and for the Pyecroft stories, see Carrington, pp. 483, 485, and Wilson, ch. 4, pp. 207–8, 209–10.

Poseidon's Law

leeward: sheltered side.

Hadria: town between the mouths of the Po and the Adige, exposed to storms.

tempt with painted cloth: see the disguise of the torpedo-boat in 'Their Lawful Occasions'.

dromond: large medieval ship.

catafract: armed Greek ship.

bireme: galley with two banks of oars.

thranite . . . and thalamite: the rowers on the upper and lower benches of an ancient trireme are compared with the high and low pressures in a steam engine.

The Bonds of Discipline

endurance: ship's radius of action.

profile plates: illustrations to a naval reference book.

dispositions: strategic allocation of warships to particular stations.

lead boards: as for official secret publications.

cruisers: high-speed, long-range warships armed with medium-calibre weapons.

Funchal: capital and chief port of the Madeira Islands.

Devonport: naval dockyard town.

cutter: see p. 307.

wardroom: officers of a warship, excepting the captain.

on the beach: on shore.

Red Marine: until 1923 the Royal Marine Light Infantry wore red tunics (unlike the other branch of the Royal Marines, the Artillery, who wore blue).

second-class petty-officer: N.C.O., comparable in rank to a sergeant in the army. Pyecroft's status is frequently queried in *RG*, where Kipling is criticized for making him a warrant-officer, since this was a *full* officer, on a par with a second lieutenant in the army, and should not have been ranked as a petty-officer. (See *RG*, vol. IV, p. 1861.)

Number One: first lieutenant.

the picket: a party on police duty, keeping law and order on shore.

Plymouth Brother: member of the Plymouth Brethren, a puritanical fundamentalist religious sect.

first cutter: one of two, hoisted on the starboard side of the ship.

our owner: the Captain.

Ascension: Ascension Island in the Atlantic, part of the British Empire.

matlow: from *matelot* (French for sailor), self-adopted nickname for all blue-jackets.

Yeoman of Signals: petty-officer, in a Second Class cruiser usually senior signals officer.

line-head: as in 'line ahead', formation adopted by naval unit for manoeuvring straight on.

ong eshlong: or *en échelon*, formation adopted by naval or military unit for manoeuvring gradually.

breech: lower part.

starboard: right-hand side of ship when facing nose or bow.

four point seven: naval gun of 4.7″ calibre.

buntin'-tosser: signalman.

Boots: forbidden in the galley.

lyin' to: being hove to, stopped.

sugared: euphemistic expletive.

after-'atch: opening in the poop or quarterdeck with ladder going down to the officers' quarters.

under forced draught: very high speed, got by increasing the supply of air to the boilers by special fans.

ram-bow: a bow with a projecting underwater spur for ramming the enemy, i.e. a protruding jaw.

piebald warrant-rank: between a commissioned officer and an N.C.O.

foot: seamen were usually barefoot on deck.

Nay, nay, Pauline: catch-phrase from *The Lady of Lyons* (1838) by Bulwer-Lytton.

post-captain: captain in the Royal Navy who has commanded an important warship; the term distinguished a real captain from a commander (who might also be referred to as 'captain').

part brass-rags: quarrel.

R.M.L.I.: Royal Marine Light Infantry. See note on p. 313.

without anythin' more: the ship's company's main meal was at midday.

Vigo: port in north-west Spain.

Dick Deadeye: a one-eyed seaman in Gilbert and Sullivan's *HMS Pinafore*.

leather-neck: Royal Marine (a seaman's term).

wardroom: here, officers' mess.

cordite mouth: used by malingerers; chewing it produced a headache and slight nausea.

wardroom joints bein' lower-deck hash (or mess-deck stew): i.e. when officers' conversation is heard aft and retailed on the mess deck.

sailing-cutter (fancy-rig) championship: sailing race in which boats could depart from the standard official rig.

squee-jee band: made up of anything to hand (e.g. combs), and called after the implement used for drying the decks.

three points off the port bow: about 34° to the left of the direction of the front of the ship.

collier: coal-ship.

broke the boom: a boom placed across the mouth of the harbour, which could be used to prevent torpedoes entering, and could be blown up by attaching explosives to it and firing them all together.

three 'undred and ninety-six revolutions: i.e. very high speed.

'olystones: holystones, slabs used for scrubbing and whitening the decks.

three-way-discharge devil: a three-way-discharge pipe attached to the ship's fire main, which allowed three hoses to be used.

eight bells: end of the second dog-watch at 8 p.m.

inverse ration: i.e. slowly.

flat-foot: seaman.

detail: personnel for specific duties.

magazines: weapons store.

ong reggle: en règle.

slave-dhowin': Arab sailing-ship carrying slaves from Africa to Arabia.

Tajurrah Bay: at the western end of the Gulf of Aden, on the Red Sea.

My sword: During the court-martial of an officer his sword is put on the table before the court. If acquitted, his sword is turned with its hilt towards him.

blue slop rig: sailor's ready-made outfit issued from paymaster's store.

thort-ships: athwart ships, at right angles to the ship's fore and aft lines.

split: half whisky, half soda.

ash-hoist: device for removing ash from the boiler-room to the upper deck, worked by a small steam-engine.

fore-an'-aft bridge: a gangway connecting the forecastle and the poop.

'*Listen to the Band*': hit song from *A Runaway Girl* (1898), musical by Seymour Hicks and Harry Nicholls.

sanakatowzer: (or sanakatowmer), a violent blow.

Gosport: naval base near Portsmouth.

spit-kid: spittoon.

cheero-party: ship's picnic party.

Chips: carpenter.

tiffies: artificers.

Pusser: ship's storekeeper (purser).

bed-plate: engine seating.

Maxim: machine-gun.

Fratton: seedy area of Portsmouth.

booms: storage for spars and bigger boats, above the weather deck.

Charley Peace: an English criminal (1832–79), hanged at Leeds and represented in the Chamber of Horrors.

makee-pigeon: conduct of business.

trysails: still used at that time on cruisers in case of engine failure and for steadying.

stun'sles: stunsails, light auxiliary sails used for speed.

calaboose: jail.

Voltaire's Habakkuk: 'Habacuc était capable de tout' (see *Notes & Queries*, clxxxi, 46).

commerce-destroyers: Before the *Entente Cordiale* of 1904, some French cruisers were threatening British merchant ships.

'*A Life on the Ocean Wave*': a song by Epes Sargent (1813–80), adopted as the march of the Royal Marines.

tohu-bohu: pandemonium.

vigias: navigational hazards which have been reported but not confirmed.

chenaler: to follow the winding of a channel, to seek a passage in shallow water.

lead: weight for plumbing depths.

bonnets in a needlecase: the French *bonnettes en étui* means studdingsails: could be mistranslated as 'bonnets in a needlecase'. (See *RG*, vol. I V, p. 1720.)

bundoop: (or bundook), rifle.

free-knowledge-ist: i.e. phrenologist.

Captain of the Head: the ship's lavatory attendant, normally excused other duties.

sno —: Pyecroft was about to say snotty, for midshipman.

cock-bill the yards: to set at a lopsided angle as a sign of mourning.

yellow jack: yellow fever.

broken firebars: to sink the corpse.

shotted: weighted.

sixteen-inch kick: 16¼″ guns were the largest in the Navy until 1917.

a change . . . came o'er: from 'The Dream' by Byron.

Elphinstone an' Bruce: Conservative Members of Parliament for Portsmouth, elected in 1874.

Amalekites: tribe hostile to the Israelites (Exodus xvii).

'Do captains talk like that . . .?': Mr Chucks, in Captain Marryat's *Peter Simple* (1834), does.

The Strict Q.T.: on the quiet.

brass-'atted: officers.

A Sahibs' War

First published in the U.S.A. in *Collier's Weekly*, 7 December 1901, and in England in the *Windsor Magazine*, December 1901. See *SM*, ch. 6, esp. pp. 158–62, for Kipling's experience of the Boer War in and around Bloemfontein, and for his involvement as a spectator in the Battle of Kari (or Karee) Siding in March 1900, which was the basis for this story. See also Carrington, ch. 13, esp. pp. 368–72.

The Runners
Subtitled 'Indian Frontier, 1904' in *Verse*.

Nimrud: Nimrod, the Hunter.

A Sahibs' War

Kroonstadt: in the Orange Free State.

Eshtellenbosch: (or Stellenbosch) in the Cape Colony, about 800 miles from Kroonstadt.

where the horses are: Stellenbosch was the Main Remount Depot in the Boer War.

Gurgaon: district and town to the south of Delhi.

Punjab: in Kipling's time, a province in the north-west of British India, where he and his parents lived, in Lahore.

Sikh: monotheistic Hindu sect; like the Gurkhas, famous fighters.

Amritzar: (or Amritsar), the holy city of the Sikhs, in the Punjab.

Attaree: between Lahore and Amritsar.

Sirdar Dyal Singh Attareewalla: i.e. a man from Attaree whose name was Dyal Singh, and who was a Sirdar, or noble.

Surtee woman: a woman from Surat, about 150 miles north of Bombay.

Jullundur: (or Jalandhar), about seventy-five miles east of Lahore, fifty miles from Attaree.

Sobraon: decisive battle on 16 February 1846, in the first Sikh war.

Lance-Duffadar: lance-corporal.

Buwwa: i.e. 'burra', great.

Pathans: Muslims from north-west India.

Boer-log: the people of the Boers.

a Sahib called Eger: In December 1898 unrest spread among the Uitlanders on the Rand following the shooting of one of them, a man called Edgar, by a Boer policeman after a brawl. (Uitlanders were the mostly British immigrants who had moved into South Africa during the gold boom years of the 1890s, and whose claim for political rights was the sparking-point for the Second Boer War.)

Tirah: border country between India (now Pakistan) and Afghanistan, where there was a winter campaign from October 1897 to April 1898.

'It is for Hind that the Sahibs are fighting this war': not only for the prestige of the Empire, but to keep the Cape sea-routes to India, one of the Empire's main life-lines.

ringstraked: having bands of colour round the body.

Tochi ... Tirah ... Buner: men from the tribes on the north-western border: often recruited into the government army.

Watson's Hotel: a famous Bombay hotel which carried on until 1919.

Khalsa: meaning 'pure'; a Sikh religious organization.

dak-bungalow: one of a series of government bungalows put up for travellers along the principal district roads. Government officials had priority for their use and often transacted business in them.

grass-cutter: a caste, with a specific occupation.

Puttiala: (or Patiala), the chief native state of the Punjab, which remained loyal to the British during the Mutiny. See 'In the Presence' (1912; *A Diversity of Creatures*, 1917).

horses: About 352,864 horses were sent to South Africa during the war, including about 3,000 from India. The avoidable wastage of mounts was huge and was due to incompetent horse-management, lack of care of the horses after disembarkation, and the remorseless treatment of the columns under Kitchener's generalship. Out of a total of 750,000 horses in use on both sides, probably 500,000 perished. (See *The Boer War*, Eversley Belfield, Cooper, 1975.)

Fingoes: Bantus, thought to be a reliable tribe and used as servants by the British.

Jehad: holy war against infidels undertaken by Muslims.

Indus: one of the great rivers in northern India.

tall, light Sahibs: Canadians. The New Zealand and Queensland colonies were the first to send volunteers to fight for the Uitlanders. The Royal Canadian Regiment was prominent at Paardeberg. The 'vine leaf' was the maple leaf emblem on the Canadian uniform.

Rajputs: Hindu military caste descended from the original warrior caste.

Ustrelyahs: Australians.

Khaibar: Khyber Pass.

Hlinedatalone in Burma: expedition against King Thebaw, last of the Burmese monarchy, who was deported to India; his kingdom was annexed by Lord Dufferin on 1 January 1886.

Kabul: where the British legation was massacred by Afghan troops on 3 September 1879. The British Resident at Kabul was Sir Pierre Cavagnari (1841–79).

Bala Hissar: the south-eastern fort of the city of Kabul.

eight wars: these would have included the Afghan War of 1878–90, the Black Mountain Expeditions of 1888 and 1891, the campaign against the Waziris in 1895, the defence and relief of Chakdara and Malakand in 1897, and the fighting in the Tirah in 1898.

Zenab valley: the Chenab Valley in the Punjab.

nullah: ravine or watercourse.

kraal: enclosure.

babul: acacia.
pom-pom: long-range Maxim automatic one-pounder quick-firing gun.
cartouches: i.e. cartridges.
Si monumentum . . .: 'If you would see his monument, look around' (epitaph to Christopher Wren in St Paul's).

'Their Lawful Occasions'

First published in two parts in the U.S.A. in *Collier's Weekly*, 3 and 10 October 1903, and then in England in the *Windsor Magazine*, December 1903 and January 1904. The second, chronologically, of the Pyecroft stories, and the third to be printed. Based on Kipling's experience of two weeks of naval manoeuvres with the Channel Fleet in July 1897, and another trip in September 1898 on H.M.S. *Pelorus*, a 20-knot, Third Class cruiser. Described in *A Fleet in Being: Notes of Two Trips with the Channel Squadron*, 1898. See also Wilson, pp. 206–7, Carrington, pp. 300–301, 307–9, and letter to Rider Haggard of 10 July 1897, quoted in Cohen, p. 33: 'I've just come off a fortnight with the Channel Squadron off the North Coast of Ireland – rather a jolly time. Now, any nation save ourselves, with such a fleet as we have at present, would go out swiftly to trample the guts out of the rest of the world; and the fact that we do not seems to show that even if we aren't very civilized, we're about the one power with a glimmering of civilization in us.'

The Wet Litany

squattering: to squatter, to plunge through water.
lettered doorways: the watertight doors, lettered for identification, which divide the ship into a series of separate compartments, closed for security.
leadsmen: taking soundings by hand from a platform forward of the bridge.
lessened count: i.e. ship moving into shallower waters.
turn: keeping the line ahead formation. The lead ship would signal its change of direction by a code signal.

'Their Lawful Occasions'

Navy Prayer: from 'Forms of Prayer to be used at Sea' in the Book of Common Prayer.

Portland: naval base in Dorset.

destroyers: heavily armed warships.

flagship: on which the commander is aboard.

15,000 tons: In 1903 the typical battleship was a steel ship of about 17,000 tons with four 12-inch guns in two turrets and up to forty smaller guns, with a speed of 18 to 19 knots.

leader of the second line: second group of forces. The phrase combines 'the lee line', used from sailing-ship days, and 'the second division'. The *Pedantic* was the flagship of the Rear-Admiral second-in-command.

tender: Fleet repair ship.

torpedo-boat: small high-speed warship for torpedo attacks.

Frobisher: fictional, but something like Sir Harry Stephenson, commander of the Channel Squadron when Kipling made his two naval cruises.

tiffy: engine-room artificer.

dynamos: cf. generators.

stick-and-string bateaus: sailing-ships.

groovin': rifling of a gun, which when worn makes the gun shoot wildly.

camber: upward curve at centre of ship's deck, meaning that they are on deck 'abaft the forecastle'.

between the first-class torpedo-boat and the full-blooded destroyer: i.e. 140 feet long, displacement 130 tons, armed with three light guns and three torpedo-tubes, with a maximum speed of 23 knots.

dragoman: Middle Eastern guide.

cutter: ship's boat used as a lifeboat.

snotty: midshipman.

casement: i.e. casemate, an armoured compartment on the main deck for a 6-inch gun.

tripes – swipes – ullage: all naval slang for garbage.

bulkhead: upright partition in a ship.

Thornycroft boat ... Yarrow mark: both famous shipbuilders of torpedo craft on the Thames.

Grecian bend: a fashionable shape in the early and late nineteenth century, produced by a narrow waist and a bustle.

wash-streak: wash-strake or washboard, a portable plank which can be fitted to the gunwale to raise the height of a boat's side.

torpedo-coxswain: helmsman, and key rating, of a torpedo-boat. For the variations in Pyecroft's rating, see note to 'The Bonds of Discipline', p. 313. Here he is a first-class petty-officer.

L.T.O., T.I., M.D.: Leading Torpedo Operator, Torpedo Instructor, Doctor of Medicine.

the Start: Start Point, at the southern tip of Devon.

executin' in anticipation: A flagship would normally signal an order, wait for the ships to acknowledge it, and then make the Executive signal for the order to be carried out. Captains trying to steal a march in competition with other ships would sometimes carry out the order before receiving the Executive signal.

Britannia: naval training ship.

steam-pinnace: (or picket boat), between forty and fifty-six feet long and of 12 to 18 tons.

jams his turrets: i.e. silences his arguments.

copper punt: light craft with a copper sheath over the wooden hull; not a fast boat.

De Rougemongs: Louis de Rougemont, alias of Louis Grin (1847–1921), famous world traveller, whose articles in the *Wide World Magazine* in 1898 described his (mostly unbelievable) adventures.

gouged 'is unprotected ends open: The central section of the ship, with the turrets, magazines and main machinery, was enclosed inside thick armour. Forward and aft of this 'citadel', the bow and stern had no vertical armour.

holdin'-down bolt: needed to keep up the pretence that they are a destroyer with a 12-pounder gun.

packet: transport-boat for goods, passengers, etc., on short journeys.

Lizard: the Lizard peninsula, the southernmost tip of Cornwall.

Torbay: inlet of the English Channel near Torquay in Devon.

economical radius: how fast a steamship can travel, starting with full bunkers (i.e. as much fuel as possible), if it is to make maximum distance.

swept bunkers: i.e. emptied of fuel.

forty-nine, forty-five, or four about, and three east: according to *RG*, vol. IV, p. 1741, this should be 3° west, not east: Kipling has applied his longitude in the wrong way and this position would put him miles inland in France.

small balls of fire: With coal-fired boilers, sudden changes of speed could produce flames from the funnels (which could give away the position of destroyers attacking by night).

lammies: duffel coats worn on torpedo-boats.

gimbals: device of interlocking rings for suspending compass, chronometer, etc.

lop: awkward movement.

full-sailed: sailing-ships were still common.

gobbies: coastguards.

yeoman o' signals: minor officer in signals.

five-flag hoists: group of five signal flags.

caulk: sleep.

war: the Spanish–American war of 1898.

stokers: cinders.

'The wind went down . . .': In *Verse* as 'The Egg-shell' with alterations and additions:

First verse, line 1, 'went down' changed to 'took off''; line 7, '*him*' to '*him*'.

Second verse added:

> The wind fell dead with the midnight –
> The fog shut down like a sheet,
> When the Witch of the North heard the Egg-shell
> Feeling by hand for a fleet.
> 'Get!' she said, 'or you're gone,' she said,
> But the little Blue Devil said 'No!
> The sights are just coming on,' he said,
> And he let the Whitehead [torpedo-boat] go.

Third verse, line 7: 'think' to '*think*'.

reformers and revolutionists: In 1905 Fisher, the First Sea Lord, carried out major reforms in the British Navy, which had been under discussion for some time.

Hat Crusade: possibly a movement against the wearing of hats in the late nineteenth century?

zoetrope: a scientific toy, also known as 'The Wheel of Life', converting a series of still pictures into a semblance of motion.

Berthon: Edward Lyon Berthon (1813–99), an Anglican clergyman who invented a folding canvas boat.

Chinaman: sailing-vessel trading to China.

purfled: with a border.

steerage-way: speed sufficient to allow the rudder to control the ship's course.

scrooped: creaked.

barks: sailing-vessels.

bowsprit: spar projecting from the bow of a vessel.

bobstay: a strong rope between a bowsprit and the stem of a vessel, for holding down the bowsprit.

fenders: cushioning protection (made of ropes, etc.) against collision, thrown over the side of a ship.

Brixham: fishing village near Torbay.

to port: on the left-hand side of the trawler when facing nose or bow.

windlass: for weighing anchor or handling a rope under strain.

trawl-beam: or trawl-line? A long line to which shorter hooked lines are attached.

bight: slack middle part of an extended rope.

condenser water: sea water used to cool and so condense the steam from the engines.

Prawle Point: fifteen miles south-west of Brixham.

gaff: spar sloping upwards from a mast, from which the ensign is flown at sea.

pouched: pocketed.

frock coat . . . and a comforter: an odd combination of a formal long coat and a woollen scarf.

compass deviations: one of the errors of the magnetic compass when it is affected by the iron of the ship. The implication is that the *Agatha* is navigated by instinct rather than science.

donkey-man: engineer.

'*M. de C.*': see 'The Bonds of Discipline'.

the forward three-pounder: one of the ship's guns.

The bar of the back-sight: the sight of the gun nearest to the stock.

foresight: the sight of the gun nearest to the muzzle.

Livermead Beach: about a mile west of Torquay.

Navy-stroke: some ships had an individual style of rowing, but there was probably less of a standard Navy style than Kipling is suggesting here.

torpedo-nets: wire nets which protected a ship at anchor from torpedo attacks.

Marconi installation: radio or wireless set; cf. 'Wireless' for Kipling's interest in Marconi. The Marconi radio was contracted by the Royal Navy in 1900.

'*Short on your anchor!*': reduce the amount of cable out, to make the ship swing with a shorter radius.

gooseneck: a connection on the inner end of a boom or derrick, allowing it to pivot freely.

casements: see note on p. 320.

stern-walk: a balcony round the stern outside the captain's cabin.

sponson: outboard support for a gun.

stem: the bow.

Patti: Adelina Patti, the famous nineteenth-century soprano.

lymph: i.e. the paint for stencilling.

bald an' unconvincin': from Gilbert's *The Mikado*.

nix mangiare: i.e. thin or starving. Naval phrase derived from the Custom House steps at Malta, known to sailors as the 'nix mangiare' steps because of the beggars there.

Casquet: the Casquets, rocky islands six miles west of Alderney.

Dodman: Dodman Point, a headland on the south coast of Cornwall.

pivot-ship: the Guide of the Fleet.

pipes: boatswain's signals.

whaler: a ship's boat.

ram: lower part of a ship's stem.

half a tide: about six hours.

breech-block: metal block in breech-loading firearms, which is withdrawn to insert the cartridge and replaced to close the breech before firing.

call-boys: who repeated the signals all over the ship, in the days before public address systems.

flash-plates: steel or iron plates fitted under the muzzle of the after gun to protect the teak quarter-deck from the flash.

Abigail: Nabal's wife, who ingratiated herself with King David and then became his wife (Samuel 1.25).

make and mend clothes: a naval holiday.

blue peter: signal flag of blue, with a white square, displayed by vessel about to leave port.

opus alexandrinum: ornate marble and mosaic work.

jargoon: colourless type of zircon.

The Comprehension of Private Copper

First published in *The Strand* and *Everybody's Magazine* in October 1902. The Boer War had been over for six months when it was published. See Wilson, pp. 217–20, and C. A. Bodelson, *Aspects of Kipling's Art*, 1964, ch. 8. Cf. the essay 'The Sin of Witchcraft', *The Times*, 15 March 1900, in *RG*, vol. V, pp. 2546–52.

The King's Task

Alternative title, 'The Saxon Foundations of England'. There is a very much longer version in *Verse*, in which the Saxons count the cost of their victory over 'a foolish people' in a speech to King Edward:

Also a vision betrayed us and a lying tale made bold,
That we looked to hold what we had not and to have what we did not hold.

The Saxons say that the battle has purged them of 'Sloth and Pride'.

The Comprehension of Private Copper

Colesberg: see note on p. 309.

helmet back-first: the helmet came straight down over the forehead and made it impossible to see properly when crawling.

Naauwport: important railway junction in the Cape Colony.

khaki: operational uniform for the British soldiers in the Second Boer War (after their red coats had made them vulnerable in 1880).

Lee-Metford: British army rifle, invented by William Ellis Metford and improved by S. P. Lee in 1888.

grey tweed: if he were a Boer he would have been wearing broadcloth, probably black.

Umballa: (or Amballa), a city in India with a large Eurasian (or Anglo-Indian, or half-caste) population.

Wilmington ... Cuckmere: in Sussex.

Ragged Schools: free elementary education for the poor.

Tommy: any private soldier.

'True Affection': see *SM*, p. 151, for Kipling's supplying 'Hignett's True Affection', cake tobacco for smoking and chewing, to the troops in South Africa.

East India Railway: largely staffed by Eurasians.

drift: ford (S.A.).

an English gentleman, who could not tell a lie: After the annexation of the Transvaal by Disraeli to the British Crown in 1877, with the aim of creating a loyal self-governing federation of South African colonies, relations with the Boers were not improved by Sir Garnet Wolseley, High Commissioner for South-East Africa from 1879 to 1880, announcing when he took up his position that 'the sun would forget to shine and the Vaal flow backwards sooner than the British flag would cease to fly over the Transvaal'. Kruger revolted in 1880, resulting in the First Boer (or Transvaal) War. As a result of the defeat at Majuba, Gladstone's Liberals abandoned the federation policy, and in August 1881 the Transvaal was granted self-government under the 'suzerainty' of Queen Victoria and renamed the South African Republic.

prisoner of war: This may be the speaker's exaggeration. His father would have been subject to the Boer government of the Transvaal after 1881, but not as a prisoner of war. He would have been treated by the Boers like the other Uitlanders, both British and foreign – treatment which gave rise to great dissatisfaction.

sjambok: heavy whip, still used by the South African police (cf. 'shambuk', p. 151).

Majuba: scene of the crushing defeat of Sir George Colley by the Boers in the First Boer War.

Ladysmith: under siege by the Boers in October–November 1899. British forces were unable to relieve it in 'Black Week' of December 1899. It was eventually relieved in February 1900.

Estcourt: south of Ladysmith, scene of a British withdrawal in November 1899 and of the derailing of an armoured train on 15 November.

loyall [sic] *people in Cape Town*: the Cape Dutch.

There isn't a nigger: Kipling anticipated very clearly the way the blacks would be treated in South Africa in the twentieth century.

cross-bandoliers: shoulder-belt for cartridges.

finger-nails: the discoloration of the cuticle in a Caucasian is supposed to indicate the persistence of Indian or negro blood.

pukka bazar chee-chee: authentic half-caste intonation as heard in the Indian bazaars. The implication is that the man was *not* a Eurasian, and that Kipling is drawing an analogy between racial debasement and disloyalty to British rule. (Wilson, p. 219, however, supposes him to be a Eurasian.)

Jerrold's Weekly: *Lloyd's Weekly News*, edited by the Jerrolds, father and son, a pro-Boer periodical banned from circulation among the British troops in South Africa.

militia subaltern: officer of inferior rank in citizen army.

givin' it you 'ot: Kipling is satirizing anti-war rhetoric, which up to 1900 had been swept under by 'Mafeking' fever – though critics such as H. M. Hyndman, leader of the Social Democratic Federation, were calling the war a conspiracy of 'Jew capitalists and Christian financiers' in 1899. After 1900 the anti-war voices were growing. J. A. Hobson, especially, writing in the *Manchester Guardian*, called the Boer war a 'war waged on behalf of capitalists'. W. K. Stead led the Stop-the-War committee in 1900.

reservists: serving in the reserve forces.

Old Barbarity: Sir Henry Campbell-Bannerman (1836–1908), Secretary of State for War in Gladstone's and Rosebery's governments of 1892–5, Liberal opposition leader at the time of the war (and Liberal Prime Minister from 1906 to 1908, when he gave self-government to the defeated Boer states), called Kitchener's methods of burning farms and lands and putting civilians into camps the 'methods of barbarism' in a speech on 14 July 1901 to the National Reform Unit. Emily Hobhouse drew attention in 1901 to the appalling conditions in the concentration-camps (where about 26,000 Boer women and children and 14,000 Africans died between September 1900 and June 1902). Kipling's comment (in *SM*, p. 162) is: 'From the business point of view the war was ridiculous. We charged ourselves step by step with the care and maintenance of all Boerdom – women and children included. Whence horrible tales of our atrocities in the concentration-camps.'

Bermuda . . . Umballa . . . Ceylon: stations to which Boer p.o.w.s were sent.

'E sent us 'is blessin': Campbell-Bannerman was defeated on a Commons vote in June 1895 that he had failed to secure an adequate supply of cordite for the army, and the government resigned.

the Times: not *The Times*, but *Lloyd's Weekly Newspaper*, which, being officially banned to the troops, could not be asked for by name by an officer.

K. o' K.: Kitchener of Khartoum, successor to Lord Roberts as Commander-in-Chief in 1900.

Steam Tactics

First published in England in the *Windsor Magazine*, December 1902, and in the U.S.A. in the *Saturday Evening Post*, 6 December 1902 (with 'The Necessitarian'). This is the first published Pyecroft story and in the *Windsor Magazine* was prefaced by a letter to Pyecroft, which reads in part:

I always thought, as you said three years ago, that it would be a sin and a shame not to make a story out of some of the things that have happened between you and Hinchcliffe and me, every time we met.

Now I have written out some of the tales. Of course, I ought to have stuck to what I knew would go down quietly; but one thing leading to another, I put it all in, and it made six Number One tales. I put in about the reply-telegram at Wool – when you and Cordery tried to help the dumb girl with the pig; I put in about the Plymouth baby – the night after the *Belligerent* paid off; and I put in about Portland Station and the Captain, and the penny-piece which we saw. Nevertheless, when it was all done, a man that I can trust in the literary line said that, to go down at all, those last three numbers would have to be translated into French; and he commended me to hand them over to a captain in the

French navy called Loti. [Pierre Loti (1859–1923), writer and French naval officer.] I did not care to accede to this, so I took them out and laid them by till happier times . . .

The other two tales ['Their Lawful Occasions' and 'The Bonds of Discipline'] you checked yourself, *viva voce*, before last Manoeuvres; but I put some more to them on my own later, and it is very likely that I have not got all the Navy *minutiae* quite right . . . You will see, as these stories come out, the care I have taken to disguise your name and rating, and everything else that might reflect upon you. Unless you care to give yourself away, which I never known you to do yet, detection is quite impossible . . .

P.S. Since writing the above there has been a hitch about the Antonio tale ['The Bonds of Discipline'] and the proceedings of No. 267 ['Their Lawful Occasions']; it being freely alleged that Antonio won't go down, because it is a bit too thick (this shows how much people know), and 267 would be subversive to discipline, as well as likely to annoy admirals. Consequently I have had to begin at the wrong end – with the motor trips – which is about the same as securing arms at the beginning of G.Q.'s [General Quarters, i.e. practice action exercises], if I am right in my technical inferences. Both you and Hinchcliff will thus suffer from being presented to the public manoeuvring upon the land, which is not your natural element, instead of the sea, which is. I, being the author, am not supposed to have any feelings.

For Kipling's enthusiasm for motoring, see *SM*, pp. 177–8; Birkenhead, pp. 236–7; Carrington, pp. 431–2; and letter from Kipling, April 1904, included in Alexander Filson Young, *The Complete Motorist*, 1904, pp. 285–8, which reads in part:

I like motoring because I have suffered for its sake. I began seven years ago in the days of tube ignition, when 6 h.p. was reckoned fair allowance for a touring car, and fifteen miles an hour was something to talk about . . . The chief end of my car, so far as I am concerned, is the discovery of England. To me it is a land full of stupefying marvels and mysteries; and a day in the car in an English county is a day in some fairy museum where all the exhibits are alive and real and yet none the less delightfully mixed up with books. For instance, in six hours, I can go from the land of the *Ingoldsby Legends* by way of the Norman Conquest and the Barons' War into Richard Jefferies' country, and so through the Regency, one of Arthur Young's less known tours, and *Celia's Arbour*, into Gilbert White's territory. Horses, after all, are only horses; but the car is a time-machine on which one can slide from one century to another at no more trouble than the pushing forward of a lever.

For other motoring stories, see 'The Vortex' (1914; *A Diversity of Creatures*, 1917), and 'The Village that Voted the Earth was Flat' (*A Diversity of Creatures*, 1917). Rider Haggard, in a letter to his wife of 22 November 1904 (Cohen, p. 53), noted that Kipling 'don't drive himself'.

Steam Tactics

Steam Tactics: term used by the Navy for manoeuvres training flag officers and captains to handle ships, after steam had superseded sail.

bell: bells preceded horns on early cars.

My engineer: The manufacturers of the Locomobile, Kipling's first car, sent an engineer and chauffeur (A. F. Kent) with the car.

kopjes: small hills (S.A.).

in derogation of good manners: official punishable offence in the Naval Discipline Act.

Twenty-five: Kipling bought a Locomobile in the summer of 1900. It was a steam car designed by the American Stanley brothers in 1899, a very light petrol-burning steam runabout, popular at the turn of the century but too troublesome and faulty for serious work. 25 m.p.h. would have been its absolute maximum, and the engineer is probably 'loyally' exaggerating here.

pinnace: ship's tender.

forced draught: means of increasing the air pressure in a boiler (so as to increase fuel consumption and hence power).

artificer: engineer in the Navy.

bulgine: engine.

The petrol will light up: In the Locomobile, vaporized petrol provided the fuel for the boiler, and could explode if the car upset.

three hoops up: full of beer.

evolution: naval drill or exercise.

mid-link: i.e. in neutral.

T.B.D.: torpedo-boat destroyer.

tiffies: engine-room artificers.

the immortal Navy doctor: possibly Smollett, one-time naval surgeon and author of *Roderick Random*.

con: steer.

wakes: track left by a ship in the water. Hinchcliffe is steering erratically.

Nay, nay, Pauline: see note on p. 314.

South-Easter at Simonstown: Until 1909, ships at the naval port south of Cape Town had to lie at anchor exposed to the strong south-east wind. An artificial harbour was built in 1909.

drag-ropes: reference to the Naval and Military Tournament field-gun competition.

three-mile limit: limit of national territorial waters.

sudorific: causing sweating.

Boxer: member of a Chinese anti-foreign secret society who attacked

329

foreign missions and legations. There was a movement to suppress it in 1900 called the Boxer War.

Out pinnace . . . an' creep for it: Objects lost overboard were recovered by a boat towing a hook with several prongs called a grapnel, along the bottom, a process known as 'creeping'.

runnin' trials: Kipling attended the speed trials of H.M.S. *Mallard* in 1897.

Twenty-three and a half miles an hour: In 1896 the law requiring a man to walk ahead of a motor vehicle carrying a red flag (with the speed limit at 4 m.p.h.) was changed, and the speed limit became 12 m.p.h. In 1899 a driver was convicted at Brighton for exceeding the limit. He was fined £3 and costs, or twenty-one days in jail. His speed was 12 m.p.h. He was told by the clerk of the court that 4 m.p.h. should be fast enough for anyone. In 1903, the Motor Car Act made it necessary for all vehicles to be registered, and the speed limit was raised to 20 m.p.h. Throughout this period there was enormous hostility to drivers from carters, carriage drivers, cyclists and the police, who frequently used police 'speed traps' (as in this story) to get their own back on the 'nobs'.

Then was seen . . .: cf., in Napier's *History of the Peninsular War*, the description of the 'Fusilier Brigade' at Albuera in 1811: 'Then was seen with what strength and majesty the British soldier fights.'

ratin': status of a man in the Navy.

concentrated Boer: Pyecroft means a Boer prisoner in a concentration-camp. See note on p. 326 (*Old Barbarity*).

traverse: zig-zag course (nautical).

jaunty: Master-at-Arms in charge of ship's police.

dhow: see note on p. 314.

Tajurrah: see note on p. 314.

Robert: any constable, after Sir Robert Peel who founded the English police.

St Leonard's Forest: in Sussex, between Horsham and Crawley.

Octopod: invented name (the car is like Kipling's second car, a Lanchester).

Saul . . . Nimshi: Saul was the son of Kish; Nimshi 'driveth furiously' (II Kings ix. 20).

Furious: a cruiser of 5,750 tons and 10,000 horsepower; the *Jaseur* was an 810-ton torpedo-boat of 2,500 horsepower.

daped: bounced.

Nellie Farren: cockney music-hall star of the 1890s, much admired by Kipling.

Vokes: a pantomime family of dancers, singers and clowns, famous in the 1870s and 1880s.

Judic: Anne Marie Louise Judic (1850–1911), famous French actress and singer.

Long Man of Hillingdon: suggested by the Long Man of Wilmington, a man's figure 240 feet long, grasping a staff in each hand, cut on the hillside above the village of Wilmington, between Pevensey and Lewes.

Captain Nemo: commander of the submarine *Nautilus* in Jules Verne's *20,000 Leagues Under the Sea* (1869).

The private zoo: Sir Edmund Loder created a garden at Leonardslee, near Horsham, in which he turned the hammer ponds into a 'miniature lake land' (*Kipling Journal*, no. 30, June 1934, p. 33) and acclimatized a large number of foreign animals, including antelopes, zebras, springboks, prairie dogs and kangaroos. The Kiplings visited Leonardslee in July 1902.

'Wireless'

First published in *Scribner's Magazine*, August 1902. See Kipling's schoolboy parody of Keats in his copy of *Longer English Poems*, ed. J. W. Hales, 1878 (reprinted in *Early Verse by Rudyard Kipling 1879–1889*, ed. Andrew Rutherford, Clarendon Press, 1986). For comment on the story see Tompkins, pp. 91–3; Carrington, p. 440. See Haggard's diary for May 1918 in Cohen, p. 100: 'He went on to show that anything which any of us did *well* was no credit to us: that it came from somewhere else: "We are only telephone wires."' Cf. D. H. Lawrence, *Studies in Classic American Literature*, 1924 (Penguin, 1971 pp. 115–16: 'The human mind beats a wireless station to nothing'; and Elizabeth Bowen, *Anthony Trollope: A New Judgement*, 1945: 'You suggest . . . that the novelist is a sort of receiving station – picking up and transmitting all sorts of things that are in the air.' Cf. 'The Finest Story in the World' (1891; *Many Inventions*, 1893).

Kaspar's Song

In *Verse*, the poem is titled 'Butterflies', the subtitle is omitted, and 'where Psyche flies' in verse 1 and 'Radiant Psyches' in verse 4 are replaced by 'the butterflies' and 'glorious butterflies'.

'Wireless'

this Marconi business: Until the discovery in 1887 by Heinrich Hertz of electric waves transmitted through space, telegraphy had been operated through wires. In 1896, the Italian Guglielmo Marconi (1874–1937) patented his invention of a wireless telegraphy, and in 1901 succeeded in transmitting signals across the Atlantic. (The use of a Marconi telegraph on the sinking *Titanic* in 1912 saved 700 lives and ensured Marconi's reputation.) Kipling had been fascinated by wireless since his cruise with the Channel Fleet in 1898, when the Navy was experimenting with it. He met Marconi in 1899: 'I got Marconi to talk about wireless, and at the end of an hour I felt that I knew as much about wireless as it was possible for a layman to learn. During the talk I consciously or unconsciously was gathering much material for my story, "Wireless", in which I carried the idea of etheric vibrations into the possibilities of thought transference' (*Kipling: Interviews and Recollections*, ed. Harold Orel, Macmillan, 1983, vol. 2). Kipling's interest in new inventions is also found in his stories 'With the Night Mail' (1905; *Actions and Reactions*, 1909), and 'As Easy as A.B.C.' (1912; *A Diversity of Creatures*, 1917).

Poole: one of Marconi's early stations. 'Here' is presumably Torquay or Brighton.

Italian warehouse: used to be the name of a grocer selling Italian products.

Pharmaceutical Formulary: book containing a list of pharmaceutical products with their formulas and means of preparation.

Nicholas Culpepper: (Culpeper) (1616–54). Puritan apothecary, author of *The English Physician Enlarged, or the Herbal*, 1653.

job-master: who kept horses and carriages for hire. (Keats's father managed a livery stable: this is the first link between Shaynor and Keats.)

Christy's New Commercial Plants: an invention?

glass jars: sign of a chemist's shop.

Rosamund: children's story of a girl who chose a chemist's jar of coloured water rather than a new pair of shoes (in *The Parent's Assistant* (1796–1800), by Maria Edgeworth).

orris: root of iris plant, used for perfume.

vulcanite: black rubber with sulphur element.

coherer: the most sensitive detector of electronic waves. In 1890, Edouard Branly noticed that Hertz waves, falling on iron filings in a tube, could conduct an electric current. If the tube with the filings was connected to the electric circuit, the coherer made it possible to trace the waves. Marconi's coherer – which paved the way for the wireless-set – contained silver nickel filings.

cubeb: fruit of several species of pepper, used for asthma, pharyngitis, etc.

benzoin: balsamic resin used in treatment of respiratory diseases.

sparklet bottles: soda syphons.

malachite: a carbonate of copper.

chypre: perfume from sandalwood.

induction: When a charged conductor of electricity is brought near an uncharged insulated conductor, this acquires a charge by induction, which disappears when the charged conductor is removed. By analogy, Kipling imagines Shaynor as a conductor in whom Keats's inspiration is 'induced'.

Keats: Keats was apprenticed to an apothecary surgeon in 1811 and completed his medical training in 1816; he was in love with Fanny Brawne, and he died of T.B. 'The Eve of St Agnes', written between 18 January and 2 February 1819, was based on the legend that on St Agnes' night (21 January) young girls can have visions of their loved ones. Kipling has been working towards the chemist as a conductor of Keats's poetry throughout the story. 'Bitter cold' (pp. 181, 183) echoes 'St Agnes 'eve – Ah! bitter chill it was!' (stanza 1). The wind blowing the fur off the dead hare next to the 'feathered birds' (p. 183) is like 'The owl, for all his feathers was a-cold/ The hare limped trembling through the frozen grass' (stanza 1). The name of the church is St Agnes (p. 184). The chemist's girlfriend is called Fanny Brand. The descriptions of the shop echo the descriptions of Madeline's room in stanzas 24 and 25. The reference to the 'tiger-moth' on p. 188 echoes the 'tiger-moth' in stanza 24. The chemist's reaction to the drink (p. 188) echoes the 'beaded bubbles winking at the brim' of the 'draught of vintage' in *Ode to a Nightingale*. Kipling has 'Madeleine' for Keats's 'Madeline'.

vile chromo: a chromo-lithograph, a popular and often badly executed process of colour-printing.

Incense in a censer: cf. stanza 1, 'Like pious incense from a censer old'.

And my weak spirit fails: cf. stanza 11, 'and his weak spirit fails/ To think how they may ache in icy hoods and mails'.

its little smoke in pallid moonlight died: Keats has 'moonshine'.

Candied apple: cf. stanza 30:

> Of candied apple, quince, and plum, and gourd,
> With jellies soother than the creamy curd,
> And lucent syrups, tinct with cinnamon;

> Manna and dates, in argosy transferred
> From Fez; and spiced dainties, every one,
> From silken Samarkand to cedared Lebanon.

The sharp rain: cf. stanza 36:

> Meantime the frost-wind blows
> Like Love's alarum pattering the sharp sleet
> Against the window-panes; St Agnes' moon hath set.

A savage spot: Coleridge's lines from 'Kubla Khan' (written under the influence of opium) read: 'A savage place! as holy and enchanted', etc.

Our magic windows: Shaynor is now trying for the lines from *Ode to a Nightingale*:

> The same that oft-times hath
> Charmed magic casements, opening on the foam
> Of perilous seas, in faery lands forlorn.

Keats made alterations in these lines; he originally had 'the wide casements' and 'keelless' or 'ruthless' seas. (See *John Keats: The Complete Poems*, ed. John Barnard, Penguin, 1973, p. 657).

The Army of a Dream

First published in the (right-wing) *Morning Post*, 15–18 July 1904. Intended as the 'keynote' of the volume (see Carrington, p. 377, and Wilson, p. 232). See the poem 'The Islanders' (4 January 1902) for Kipling's plea for national conscription. (See Carrington, pp. 375–6, for his own rifle club at Rottingdean, which Kipling started in 1900.) See also 'The Parable of Boy Jones' in *Land and Sea Tales*, 1923, where an upper-class young man realizes his military incompetence when he visits the Village Rifle Club:

'There seems to be a lot in it,' said Boy Jones, after a while, to his friend. 'But you needn't tell me,' he went on in the tone of one ill at ease with himself, 'don't tell *me* that when the hour strikes every man in England wouldn't – er – rally to the defence of his country like one man.'

'And he'd be *so* useful while he was rallying, wouldn't he?' said the Friend shortly. 'Imagine one hundred thousand chaps of your kidney introduced to the rifle for the first time, all loading and firing in your fashion! The hospitals wouldn't hold 'em!'

'Oh, there'd be time to get the general hang of the thing,' said Boy Jones cheerily.

'When that hour strikes,' the Friend replied, 'it will already have struck, if you understand. There may be a few hours – perhaps ten or twelve – there will certainly not be more than a day and a night allowed us to get ready in.'

See also Kipling's letter to the *Daily Mail*, 6 August 1904, which reads in part:

A youth interested in public life might be careful to join a Volunteer corps soon after his majority as possible; for, in my dream, the law of the land laid down that he who did not volunteer should not vote ... I dreamed that the professional and semi-professional players of games, worshipped by hundreds of thousands, had lent their influence, power, popularity and prestige to help their country in its need, by ruling that ... the professional athlete's only possible road to notoriety, money and applause should lie through the ranks of his corps.

Song of the Old Guard

Subtitled 'Army Reform – After Boer War' in *Verse*, with quotation from Exodus (xxvi. 31, 35, 36) omitted. Parody of an anti-puritan satire by Francis Quarles in *The Shepheards Oracle*, Eclogue XI (see *The Times Literary Supplement*, 25 December 1959, p. 755). The poem was inspired by the rejection, by a War-Office committee, of a critical history of the recent war by General J. M. Grierson.

The Army of a Dream

Tyneside Tail-twisters: 2nd Battalion (Royal) Northumberland Fusiliers, the 5th Foot.

Mount Nelson Hotel: in Cape Town.

Fusiliers: private infantrymen, foot soldiers.

Fontenoy: battlefield in Belgium, where on 11 May 1745 the French defeated the English.

a Rowton lodging-house: Baron Montague Rowton (1838–1903) founded his very successful 'poor man's hotels' in 1892.

Line and Militia: combatant forces and citizen soldiers.

the Stores: the Army and Navy Co-operative Society, known as 'The Stores', membership of which was confined to officers of the services. Cf. 'The Edge of the Evening' (1913; *A Diversity of Creatures*, 1917) in which the American Zigler calls it 'one of the most wonderful institutions in the world'.

Volunteer: soldier who is not a professional. In 1900 a force of 119,000 Volunteers had been created, and about a third of the whole force volunteered for service in South Africa. In 1908 Lord

Haldane would absorb the Volunteers into the Territorial Army.

Aldershot: military camp in Hampshire.

Spiers and Pond: military catering firm.

on the hoof: on the march.

Hythe: near Folkestone; chief musketry school of the army.

Athabasca: in Alberta, Canada.

Mian Mir: the Lahore military cantonment.

Bean Derig: (or Beinn Darg), mountain in Easter Ross, Scotland.

Sghurr Mhor: mountain in Ross and Cromarty.

Sappers: Royal Engineers who dig trenches, etc.

squad-drill: drill formation, usually of a dozen soldiers.

company-drill: usually of two or more platoons.

battalion-drill: of three or more companies.

Nootka Sound: in British Columbia, Canada.

Canuck: Canadian.

Cornstalk: Australian.

Maori: here meaning white New Zealander.

picquet-work: i.e. guard duty.

C. B. Fry: Charles Burgess Fry (1872–1956), a great all-round English sportsman.

Oddfellows: secret benevolent and fraternal society dating from the eighteenth century.

I.O.G.T.: The International Organization of Good Templars, founded in Utica.

Buffaloes: The Royal Antediluvian Order of Buffaloes.

Burkes: *Peerage, Baronetage and Knightage*, with the pedigree of British titled classes, first issued in 1826.

Debretts: *Peerage, Baronetage, Knightage, and Companionage*, first issued in 1802.

Facey Romford: a reference to *Mr Facey Romford's Hounds* (1865), by Surtees.

Yeomanry: see note on p. 309. They were to be absorbed into the Territorial Army, like the Volunteers.

Bisley: rifle range near Farnborough, Hampshire.

fleet-reserves: reserve warships.

Bantry: on the south-west coast of Ireland; much used by the Royal Navy for manoeuvres.

Gib: Gibraltar.

Kitchener: Lord Kitchener (1850–1916), Commander-in-Chief in South Africa from 1900 to 1902, who had to recruit for troops in the Cape Colony during the later part of the Boer War against guerilla fighters. The war led to extensive reforms in the British

Army, including the superseding of the Volunteer Army by the Territorials, and the training and organization of expeditionary forces.

dockyard-mateys: workers in a naval dockyard.

quick-firers: term used for a variety of guns, from small machine-guns with automatic loading to 4-inch and 6-inch guns loaded by hand and firing far fewer rounds per minute.

tan: oak bark used to cover the floor of a riding school.

man-ropes: a rope railing.

Ally Sloper: a reference to a weekly comic paper, *Ally Sloper's Half Holiday*. The hero had a big red nose and a huge top hat.

colour-sergeants: who carry the regimental colours.

Coolgardie: Western Australia.

en état de partir: ready to go.

Blue Peter: see note on p. 324.

storm-cone: canvas cone hoisted as a warning of high winds.

Moltke: Count Helmuth von Moltke (1800–1891), Chief-of-Staff of the Prussian Army and a great strategist.

'*Give me back my legions*': Augustus Caesar's words after his defeat in Germany.

'*A Life on the Ocean Wave*': see note on p. 315.

bolt action: i.e. not the regular bolt action rifle used in England but something more like a U.S. firearm.

the Lincolns: the Lincolnshire Regiment.

Jemmy Fawne: James Fawn, popular music-hall singer of the 1890s.

Sanna's Post: scene of the ambush of British forces by Christiaan de Wet on 31 March 1900, a display of British bravery and incompetence. See *SM*, pp. 156–7, and *A Book of Words*, 1928, p. 87.

'They'

First published in *Scribner's Magazine*, August 1904. For the death of Josephine Kipling in 1899, see Introduction. Cf. the poem 'Merrow Down' in *Just So Stories* (1902). See Carrington, pp. 436–8; Wilson, pp. 264–6; Tompkins, pp. 203–4; Mason, pp. 204–8. T. S. Eliot invokes the story in 'Burnt Norton', in *Four Quartets*.

The Return of the Children

In *Verse*, 'radiant' in stanza 1 is replaced by 'splendid'.

'They'

way-waste: Sussex dialect word for unused land by the roadside.
the Egg: the mythological Orphic egg.
dene: Sussex dialect word for a deep, narrow valley with a stream.
Ushant: westerly island off the coast of France.
In the pleasant orchard-closes: from 'The Lost Bower' by Elizabeth Barrett Browning. The missing line is 'Listen, gentle – aye, and simple! Listen, children on the knee!' Also used to preface 'The Education of Otis Yeere' (*Wee Willie Winkie*, 1888).
in hand: under cultivation.

Mrs Bathurst

First published in the U.S.A. in the *Metropolitan Magazine* and in England in the *Windsor Magazine*, September 1904. For the source of the story, see *SM*, p. 101:

> All I carried away from the magic town of Auckland was the face and voice of a woman who sold me beer at a little hotel there. They stayed at the back of my head till ten years later when, in a local train of the Cape Town suburbs, I heard a petty officer from Simons Town telling a companion about a woman in New Zealand who 'never scrupled to help a lame duck or put her foot on a scorpion'. Then – precisely as the removal of the key-log in a timber-jam starts the whole pile – those words gave me the key to the face and voice at Auckland, and a tale called 'Mrs Bathurst' slid into my mind, smoothly and orderly as floating timber on a bank-high river.

The story has been extensively commented on. See Carrington, pp. 435–6; Wilson, pp. 221–3; Mason, pp. 158–64; Tompkins, pp. 89–91; E. L. Gilbert, 'What Happens in "Mrs Bathurst"', *PMLA*, LXXVII, 1962; John Bayley, *The Uses of Division*, 1976, pp. 76–8; C. A. Bodelson, *Aspects of Kipling's Art*, 1964, ch. 7; Craig Raine, 'Double Thunder: Review of *The Strange Ride of Rudyard Kipling* by Angus Wilson', *New Statesman*, 11 November 1977, vol. 94, pp. 657–8. Cf. 'A Madonna of the Trenches' (1924; *Debits and Credits*, 1926) for a story of a soldier haunted by the woman he loves, told by a shocked, bemused narrator.

Some changes were made in the text of 'Mrs Bathurst' between the publication in the *Windsor Magazine* and in the Uniform Edition. Most of these are minor; some suggest that the magazine publication required censorship, or at least toning down. The most notable differences are as follows:

p. 272, *l.* 26: WM 'Look at Click'; UE 'Look at – you know.'

p. 274, *l.* 34: WM omits 'She wasn't *that*!'

p. 276, *l.* 28: WM 'affectionate'; UE 'intimate'.

    l. 34: WM omits '*and one more*'.

p. 277, *l.* 7: WM 'know'; UE 'live with'.

    l. 9: WM 'were black or white'; UE 'talked in their sleep or not'.

    l. 13: WM omits 'I know *that*!'

    l. 16: WM '"He's liable to go crazy," was the answer'; UE '"He goes crazy – or just saves himself," was the slow answer.'

    l. 21: WM 'I can't say.'; UE 'That's the dark an' bloody mystery.'

p. 279, *l.* 8: WM omits '– previous to birth as you might say.'

    l. 18–19: WM 'the very thing itself, when you think of it – all from nature'; UE 'taken from the very thing itself – you see.'

    l. 23: WM 'she ran so lifelike.'; UE 'she headed so straight.'

    l. 37: WM 'Look! That's Mrs B.!'; UE 'Christ! there's Mrs B.!'

p. 281, *l.* 8–9: WM omits 'his hand fingering his waistcoat-pocket.'

p. 283, *l.* 21: WM omits 'Consume your own smoke.'

    l. 27: WM 'I'm not a murderer'; UE 'I am *not* a murderer'

    l. 28: WM 'my lawful wife died in 'er bed.'; UE 'my lawful wife died in childbed.'

p. 284, *l.* 30: WM has 'It's all black, boggy soil.' after 'without a curve.'

p. 285, *l.* 16: WM omits 'It was so.'

    l. 19–20: WM 'But I kept . . . four in the lower jaw wasn't it? . . . But since you gentlemen knew him –'; UE 'and I kept . . . But he was a friend of you two gentlemen, you see.'

From Lyden's 'Irenius'

Fragments of a play called 'Gow's Watch' are used in *Kim* and in *Debits and Credits* (one attached to 'A Madonna of the Trenches') and are reprinted in *Verse*. This, though not called 'Gow's Watch', has the same characters and style; the speech on Fortune is included as part of Act II Sc. 2 of 'Gow's Watch' in *Verse*. The relevance to 'Mrs Bathurst' seems to be the killing power of 'woman's love'. See *RG, Verse*, pp. 5391–2.

Mrs Bathurst

Simon's Bay: see note on Simonstown on p. 307.

my train: from Cape Town.

the Greeks: Greek families commonly owned shops and cafés in South Africa at that time.

tickey: threepence (S.A.).

Wankies: in what was then Southern Rhodesia, on the railway, about sixty miles south-east of Victoria Falls.

Belmont: near the border of the Orange Free State, where a British Naval Brigade took part in the Boer War for the first time, on 23 November 1899.

Tristan d'Acunha: island about 1750 miles west of Cape Town.

boiler-seatings: the bed-plates of boilers, liable to erode.

Muizenburg, St James's, and Kalk Bay: on the coast of False Bay above Simonstown.

Number One rig: sailor's best uniform, worn for shore leave.

'purr Mary, on the terrace': from the Royal Marines' motto 'Per mare, per terram'.

Barnado: Dr Barnardo founded the first orphans' home in 1867.

steerin'-flat: compartment in after end of a ship where the steering gear is housed.

Benin: district on the west coast of Africa where an expedition in 1897 was heavily decimated by fever.

Buncrana: town in County Donegal often used by Navy ships.

run: deserted.

Mormonastic: polygamous.

copper: copper sheathing to protect the underwater hull from the teredo worm.

'midship frames was sprung: the ribs of the ship's hull were split or loosened.

Nyassa: Lake Nyasa in East Africa.

Flotilla: the lake was much used by slave traders serving the Arabian market.

P. and O.: Peninsular and Oriental Steamship Company. The implication is that jobs are easy to get there.

Bloemfontein: see note on p. 310.

Four months ago: the story must be being told in April 1903 of December 1902, since it is just post-war (see p. 284).

warrants and non-coms: naval warrant-officers would not usually mix with N.C.O.s, but there would be some relaxing of this rule where facilities were limited.

China station: service in China.

never scrupled: see general note, above.

Phyllis's Circus: Fillis was a well-known circus proprietor in Johannesburg.

cinematograph: the first moving pictures. The cinema was becoming a thriving industry in 1900 and few music-halls were without their 'bioscope' or 'viagraph'.

Durban: on the east coast, in Natal; it had a large Indian population.

peeris: fairies or sprites in Persian mythology.

submerged flat: a compartment containing underwater torpedo-tubes.

gyroscope: a steering device only introduced to torpedo ships in 1898.

the Western Mail: a famously fast train from Cornwall to London.

enteric: typhoid.

measured mile: marked out for a ship's speed trials.

that big hotel: the Mount Nelson.

Salt River: an eastern suburb of Cape Town.

Marconi ticker: an early wireless telegraph. The ticker was the receiving instrument which recorded the dots and dashes of the Morse code.

cox: coxswain or helmsman.

epicycloidal: a curve described by a circle as it rolls around the outside of another fixed point.

Admiral's front gate: of Admiralty House, near the Dockyard.

Worcester: sixty-five miles east of Cape Town.

'The Honeysuckle and the Bee': popular music-hall song by Albert Fitz.

kapje: lady's bonnet.

Lake what's 'is name: Nyasa.

a couple of tramps: Hooper and Pyecroft both assume that Vickery's companion is a man, but the narrative does not confirm this, and it is possible that we are supposed to think that the other 'tramp' is Mrs Bathurst. This has been much debated.

black as charcoal: not a common effect of being struck by lightning.

foul anchor: impeded or obstructed.

First published in the *Monthly Review*, September 1902. For Kipling's purchase of Bateman's (and his installation of a hydro-electric generating plant to light the house and buildings), and his growing interest in the history of Sussex, see *SM*, ch. 7; Carrington, ch. 15, esp. p. 442. See also Wilson, pp. 244, 245. Cf. 'The Ship That Found Herself' (1895; *The Day's Work*, 1898), where the separate parts of the ship talk in different voices until they learn to work together, and 'The Mother Hive' (1908; *Actions and Reactions*, 1909) for another anthropomorphic political fable about the need for interdependent loyal work in the national hive.

Our Fathers Also

In *Verse*, the poem starts with this extra verse:

> Thrones, Powers, Dominions, Peoples, Kings,
> Are changing 'neath our hand.
> Our fathers also see these things
> But they do not understand.

Below the Mill Dam

Domesday Book: 'the book of the day of the assessment', the great survey of the lands of England made by order of William the Conqueror in 1086. Contains a record of the ownership, area and value of lands, and of the numbers of tenants, livestock, etc. The object of the survey was to ascertain and record the Crown's fiscal rights.

Robert's Mill: There is a mill on the north side of the road bridge over the River Rother in Sussex.

freeman: Under the feudal system, the typical English manor consisted of the lord's demesne, and the land of the freemen (or free tenants) and villeins (or serfs), who paid the lord rents in money, kind or labour. The villein could not own property and had no legal right against the lord.

rod: unit of square measure – $30\frac{1}{4}$ square yards.

geld: land-tax.

nunquam geldavit: 'it never paid the national land tax'.

cottars: serfs occupying a cottage and land in return for labour.

fisheries: the right to fish river or pond at 6d. a family per year.

Black Rat and *Grey Cat*: The satire is against the old officer class and the 'Old Guard' of the upper-class cultured Tories like Arthur

Balfour and the 'Souls', a club whose members included Lord Curzon, the Viceroy of India, and liberals such as Wilfred Blunt and Percy Wyndham. Kipling associated these men with 'the infernal and eternal slackness of the last years of the Government [of Balfour's Conservatives]' (letter to H. A. Gwynne, 7 February 1906). Cf. 'My Son's Wife' (*A Diversity of Creatures*, 1917) for the language of the silly metropolitan intellectuals.

rape: one of the six divisions of Sussex, each consisting of a strip of country with a town or borough, a harbour and a market.

In Ferle tenuit: In Ferle the Abbey of Wilton held one hide (approx. 120 acres) and one virgate (approx. 15 acres) and one half of a virgate (approx. $7\frac{1}{2}$ acres). Firle is about three miles from Lewes.

hide: amount of land sufficient to support a family, that could be tilled with one plough and eight oxen in one year; usually between 100 and 120 acres.

Essewelde: A *hundredum* was a division of a rape or shire. At first the word meant a group of 100 families, then the district which those families occupied. The Hundred of Essewelde (Essewelle or Shoywell) rendered no land tax.

middlings: the coarser part of flour.

Faenza: a reference to 'A Soul's Tragedy' by Robert Browning, in which the Papal Legate twice says that he has seen twenty-three leaders of revolt in Faenza, but by the end alters it to twenty-four: i.e. history repeats itself.

Abbot of Wilton: The abbey of Wilton was a famous nunnery; the Mill has slipped up here.

Aluric: evidently fined because he objected to being dispossessed.

burgum: town.

'*Take away that bauble!*': the Waters are quoting Oliver Cromwell's words about the Mace, in dismissing the Long Parliament on 2 April 1653.

Raven's Gill Brook: For the landscape and history of the country around Bateman's, see also *Puck of Pook's Hill*, 1906, and *Rewards and Fairies*, 1910. From 1902 Kipling saturated himself in local history from the Sussex Records Office and the parts of the Domesday Book referring to Sussex. The local names in the story are mostly invented.

One of your people: 'Curiosity killed the cat.'

tail-race: the part of the mill race below the water wheel.

squat-right: no legal basis, but an assumption that someone who has settled on land without being its possessor, and remained there undisturbed, can claim ownership.

trituration: grinding to powder. The wheel still thinks it is being used to make flour. See *SM*, pp. 179–80, for Kipling's project 'for de-clutching the water-wheel from an ancient mill at the end of our garden, and using its microscopical mill-pond to run a turbine'.

dim delicious half-tones: very Nineties phrasing, reminiscent of Swinburne and *The Yellow Book*.

Pasht: Egyptian cat god.

FOR THE BEST IN PAPERBACKS, LOOK FOR THE

In every corner of the world, on every subject under the sun, Penguin represents quality and variety – the very best in publishing today.

For complete information about books available from Penguin – including Puffins, Penguin Classics and Arkana – and how to order them, write to us at the appropriate address below. Please note that for copyright reasons the selection of books varies from country to country.

In the United Kingdom: Please write to *Dept E.P., Penguin Books Ltd, Harmondsworth, Middlesex, UB7 0DA.*

If you have any difficulty in obtaining a title, please send your order with the correct money, plus ten per cent for postage and packaging, to *PO Box No 11, West Drayton, Middlesex*

In the United States: Please write to *Dept BA, Penguin, 299 Murray Hill Parkway, East Rutherford, New Jersey 07073*

In Canada: Please write to *Penguin Books Canada Ltd, 2801 John Street, Markham, Ontario L3R 1B4*

In Australia: Please write to the *Marketing Department, Penguin Books Australia Ltd, P.O. Box 257, Ringwood, Victoria 3134*

In New Zealand: Please write to the *Marketing Department, Penguin Books (NZ) Ltd, Private Bag, Takapuna, Auckland 9*

In India: Please write to *Penguin Overseas Ltd, 706 Eros Apartments, 56 Nehru Place, New Delhi, 110019*

In the Netherlands: Please write to *Penguin Books Netherlands B.V., Postbus 195, NL 1380AD Weesp*

In West Germany: Please write to *Penguin Books Ltd, Friedrichstrasse 10–12, D–6000 Frankfurt/Main 1*

In Spain: Please write to *Alhambra Longman S.A., Fernandez de la Hoz 9, E–28010 Madrid*

In Italy: Please write to *Penguin Italia s.r.l., Via Como 4, 1-20096 Pioltello (Milano)*

In France: Please write to *Penguin Books Ltd, 39 Rue de Montmorency, F-75003 Paris*

In Japan: Please write to *Longman Penguin Japan Co Ltd, Yamaguchi Building, 2–12–9 Kanda Jimbocho, Chiyoda-Ku, Tokyo 101*

CLASSICS OF THE TWENTIETH CENTURY

The Outsider Albert Camus

Meursault leads an apparently unremarkable bachelor life in Algiers, until his involvement in a violent incident calls into question the fundamental values of society. 'The protagonist of *The Outsider* is undoubtedly the best achieved of all the central figures of the existential novel' – *Listener*

Another Country James Baldwin

'Let our novelists read Mr Baldwin and tremble. There is a whirlwind loose in the land' – *Sunday Times*. *Another Country* draws us deep into New York's Bohemian underworld of writers and artists as they betray, love and test each other – men and women, men and men, black and white – to the limit

I'm Dying Laughing Christina Stead

A dazzling novel set in the 1930s and 1940s when fashionable Hollywood Marxism was under threat from the savage repression of McCarthyism. 'The Cassandra of the modern novel in English' – Angela Carter

Christ Stopped at Eboli Carlo Levi

Exiled to a barren corner of southern Italy for his opposition to Mussolini, Carlo Levi entered a world cut off from history, hedged in by custom and sorrow, without comfort or solace, where, eternally patient, the peasants lived in an age-old stillness, and in the presence of death – for Christ did stop at Eboli.

The Expelled and Other Novellas Samuel Beckett

Rich in verbal and situational humour, these four stories offer the reader a fascinating insight into Beckett's preoccupation with the helpless individual consciousness.

Chance Acquaintances and Julie de Carneilhan Colette

Two contrasting works in one volume. Colette's last full-length novel, *Julie de Carneilhan* was 'as close a reckoning with the elements of her second marriage as she ever allowed herself'. In *Chance Acquaintances*, Colette visits a health resort, accompanied only by her cat.

FOR THE BEST IN PAPERBACKS, LOOK FOR THE

CLASSICS OF THE TWENTIETH CENTURY

Petersburg   Andrei Bely

'The most important, most influential and most perfectly realized Russian novel written in the twentieth century' (*The New York Times Book Review*), *Petersburg* is an exhilarating search for the identity of the city, presaging Joyce's search for Dublin in *Ulysses*.

The Miracle of the Rose   Jean Genet

Within a squalid prison lies a world of total freedom, in which chains become garlands of flowers – and a condemned prisoner is discovered to have in his heart a rose of monstrous size and beauty.

Labyrinths   Jorge Luis Borges

Seven parables, ten essays and twenty-three stories, including Borges's classic 'Tlön, Uqbar; Orbis Tertius', a new world where external objects are whatever each person wants, and 'Pierre Menard', the man who rewrote *Don Quixote* word for word without ever reading the original.

The Vatican Cellars   André Gide

Admired by the Dadaists, denounced as nihilist, defended by its author as a satirical farce: five interlocking books explore a fantastic conspiracy to kidnap the Pope and place a Freemason on his throne. *The Vatican Cellars* teases and subverts as only the finest satire can.

The Rescue   Joseph Conrad

'It matters not how often Mr Conrad tells the story of the man and the brig. Out of the million stories that life offers the novelist, this one is founded upon truth. And it is only Mr Conrad who is able to tell it to us' – Virginia Woolf

Hangover Square   Patrick Hamilton

London 1939. In the grimy publands of Earls Court, George Harvey Bone is pursuing a helpless infatuation. Netta is cool, contemptuous and hopelessly desirable to George. George is adrift in hell, except in his 'dead' moments, when something goes click in his head and he realizes, without doubt, that he must kill her...

CLASSICS OF THE TWENTIETH CENTURY

Victory Joseph Conrad

Victory is both a tale of rescue and adventure and a perceptive study of a complex relationship and the power of love. Its hero Axel Heyst was described by Jocelyn Baines as 'perhaps the most interesting and certainly the most complex' of Conrad's characters.

The Apes of God Wyndham Lewis

'It is so immense, I have no words for it,' commented T. S. Eliot on this blistering satire on twenties Bohemianism. Lewis's prose is as original and exciting as Joyce's, and the verbal savagery of his lampooning reads like a head-on collision between Swift and the Machine Age.

Despair Vladimir Nabokov

With shattering immediacy, Nabokov takes us into a deranged world, yet one full of an impudent, startling humour, dominated by the egotistical and scornful figure of a murderer who thinks himself an artist.

The Rainbow D. H. Lawrence

Suppressed by outraged moralists within six weeks of publication, *The Rainbow* is today seen as a great work of the metaphysical imagination that, despite its meticulous attention to detail and local colour, is both visionary and prophetic.

Tales of the Pacific Jack London

Shattered by tropical disease, London spent the last months of his life writing in Hawaii. Springing from his desire to reconcile the dream of an unfallen world with the harsh reality of twentieth-century materialism, these stories combine the power of Hemingway with a mastery of the short story form equal to Conrad's.

Clayhanger Arnold Bennett

The first book in the Clayhanger trilogy is a vivid portrayal of English provincial life at the turn of the century, revealing Bennett's fascination with the romance of manufacturing industry and also its slovenly ugliness. 'There is ... a complete lack of contrivance on the part of the author; Bennett follows the grain of life' – Walter Allen

CLASSICS OF THE TWENTIETH CENTURY

Thirst for Love   Yukio Mishima

Before her husband's death Etsuko had already learnt that jealousy is useless unless it can be controlled. Love, hatred, and a new, secret passion – she can control them all as long as there is hope. But as that hope fades, her frustrated desire gathers a momentum that can be checked only by an unspeakable act of violence.

The Collected Dorothy Parker

Dorothy Parker, more than any of her contemporaries, captured in her writing the spirit of the Jazz Age. Here, in a single volume, is the definitive Dorothy Parker: poetry, prose, articles and reviews.

Remembrance of Things Past (3 volumes)   Marcel Proust

'What an extraordinary world it is, the universe that Proust created! Like all great novels, *À la Recherche* has changed and enlarged our vision of the "real" world in which we live' – Peter Quennell

The Sword of Honour Trilogy   Evelyn Waugh

A glorious fusion of comedy, satire and farcical despair, Waugh's magnificently funny trilogy is also a bitter attack on a world where chivalry and nobility were betrayed at every hand.

Buddenbrooks   Thomas Mann

Published in 1902, Mann's 'immortal masterpiece' was already a classic before it was banned and burned by Hitler. 'The richness and complexity ... the interplay of action and ideas ... has never been surpassed in German fiction' – J. P. Stern

A Clergyman's Daughter   George Orwell

The rector's daughter's submissive routine shatters, and Dorothy finds herself down and out in London. She is wearing silk stockings, has money in her pocket and cannot remember her name. Among unemployment, poverty and hunger, her faith is challenged by a social reality that changes her life.

CLASSICS OF THE TWENTIETH CENTURY

Memoirs of a Dutiful Daughter Simone de Beauvoir

The first of her four volumes of autobiography takes Simone de Beauvoir from her early childhood to her meeting with Jean-Paul Sartre at the Sorbonne. Her intellectual honesty leads inevitably to a rebellion that she charts with moving sincerity.

Arrival and Departure Arthur Koestler

'Koestler is one of the very few novelists who attacks the most difficult and troubling issues of private and public morality and who, having raised serious questions, never tries to satisfy us with ready-made answers or evasions' – Saul Bellow

The Heart is a Lonely Hunter Carson McCullers

Set in a small town in the American South, Carson McCullers's first novel deals with isolation, the need for human understanding and the search for love. 'A poet's sensitivity interlocks with a novelist's gifts' – Cyril Connolly

Howards End E. M. Forster

'"Only connect..." Such is the epigraph of a novel much concerned with the relationships, and the possibility of reconciliation, between certain pairs of opposites' – Oliver Stallybrass. *Howards End* expresses, more perhaps than any other of his novels, themes close to Forster's heart.

Gertrude Hermann Hesse

A sensitive young composer, the narrator is drawn to Gertrude through their mutual love of music. Gradually, he is engulfed by an enduring and hopeless passion for her. 'It would be a pity to miss this book – it has such a rare flavour of truth and simplicity' – Stevie Smith

Eva Trout Elizabeth Bowen

Monolithic, rich, unloved, and with a genius for unreality, Eva Trout has an endless 'capacity for making trouble, attracting trouble, strewing trouble around her'. In her last completed novel, Elizabeth Bowen's elegant style and intense sensibility combine with her gift for social comedy to create one of her most formidable – and moving – heroines.

RUDYARD KIPLING IN PENGUIN

'The most complete man of genius I have ever known' – Henry James

The Light That Failed	**The Jungle Books**
A Diversity of Creatures	**Life's Handicap**
The Day's Work	**Limits and Renewals**
Debits and Credits	**Something of Myself**
Wee Willie Winkie	**Plain Tales from the Hills**
Just So Stories	**Puck of Pook's Hill**
Traffics and Discoveries	**Rewards and Fairies**
Kim	**Stalky and Co.**

'For my own part I worshipped Kipling at thirteen, loathed him at seventeen, enjoyed him at twenty, despised him at twenty-five, and now again rather admire him. The one thing that was never possible, if one had read him at all, was to forget him' – George Orwell